PRAISE FOR SANDRA HILL'S VIKING ROMANCES!

THE RELUCTANT VIKING

"I really enjoyed Ruby's story. Wouldn't it be wonderful if we could all have these sorts of second chances when we are at risk of losing something as precious as love."

—*Affaire de Coeur*

"The Reluctant Viking is a wonderfully in-depth, ambitious challenge for a first time author, and Ms. Hill pulls it off with style!"

—*The Literary Times*

THE OUTLAW VIKING

"An entertaining battle-of-the-sexes romance that will keep readers laughing to the very end!"

—*Romantic Times*

"A well-told story, funny and heartwarming. Ms. Hill has created characters who will stay alive long after you close the book. This is a time-travel that shouldn't be missed."

—*The Paperback Forum*

"Ms. Hill transports not only the heroine but the reader back to the period in this fast-paced story."

—*Rendezvous*

THE LAST VIKING

"A fun, fast-paced page turner."

—*Romantic Times*

"The humor is delicious. Ms. Hill's Viking stories are always a thrill to read, and *The Last Viking* is no exception."

—*Rendezvous*

"Ms. Hill once again shows her talented, witty writing skills in narrative and character development . . . another winner for Ms. Hill!"

—*Old Book Barn Gazette*

VIKING PASSION

"For a month and more you have teased and taunted me with promises of delights we have shared in the past. What say you now?" Thork asked in a tightly controlled, low voice.

Holding her eyes, he began to undo the shoulder clasps of her outer gown. Ruby wanted to ask if he would marry her again or if he'd accepted the fact that she might have to leave, but, instead, she decided to follow Gyda's advice for patience.

Ruby licked her lips nervously. She had to have made love with this man a thousand times in the past twenty years, but it seemed all new now. He was her husband and yet a stranger at the same time.

"Do you still insist we share a past?" he asked hoarsely.

Ruby scrutinized Thork closely, trying to see the differences, not the similarities, between him and Jack. It was hard. "I think you and I may very well make our own history tonight."

THE RELUCTANT VIKING

SANDRA HILL

LOVE SPELL BOOKS NEW YORK CITY

LOVE SPELL®

February 1999

Published by

Dorchester Publishing Co., Inc.
276 Fifth Avenue
New York, NY 10001

ISBN 0-505-52297-7

*For my mother, Veronica Cluston, who taught me how
to be a strong woman long before strong women
were in vogue.*

*And for my husband, Robert, who taught me how to be a
coyote. May we always howl together.*

Author's Note

From 1976 to 1981, the York Archaeological Trust under-
took one of the most impressive historical excavations of
all time: Jorvik, the Viking Age town of York. More than
15,000 small objects taken from the site gave historians
a clear picture of everyday Viking life and allowed
specialists to re-create a replica of the Viking city that
flourished there under a series of Viking kings from 850
to 954 A.D.

Archaeological studies, like the "Coppergate" dig at
Jorvik, prove that the Northmen, who made a highway of
the seas during the Viking Age, 800–1100 A.D., weren't
always the heathen rapers and pillagers portrayed by
early historians, usually Anglo-Saxon clerics with biased
viewpoints. They were, in fact, men of incredible bravery,
daring, loyalty and talent, driven by a ruthless hunger for
new lands to settle as farms and trading centers.

The Vikings respected justice and, in fact, introduced
the word *law* into the English language. They created in

Sandra Hill

their *Things,* or local courts, the forerunner of our modern jury system. Furthermore, the Viking sagas and *skaldic* poetry show evidence of a surprising wit, sensitivity and appreciation for culture.

The Northmen began their extensive spearhead onto foreign soil at the end of the eighth century with small, hit-and-run raids that soon escalated into massive warheads, sometimes involving hundreds of ships and thousands of men. Over the next two centuries, they penetrated Europe, North Africa and Russia. They proudly served as hand-picked members of the Byzantine emperor's personal bodyguard in Constantinople. Some discovered America.

Yet, there is no Viking nation as such today. Why? It's because the Northmen blended into the local societies they conquered, adopting the language, customs and religion. Many of the noble knights of the Middle Ages were actually close descendants, even grandsons, of Vikings, such as the "outlaw" Viking Hrolf (or Rollo), first Duke of Normandy, my own grandfather *thirty-three times removed.* Hrolf also was the great-great-great grandfather of William the Conqueror.

The monk-historians also ignored in their biased records an elite group of Viking knights called Jomsvikings. The oaths of loyalty and reputed valor of these great warriors were reminiscent of the earlier King Arthur and the Knights of the Round Table.

Although the word *Viking* was not used until later years, I've chosen to use it for the sake of my modern reader. For the same reason, I use twentieth-century names for countries.

Finally, despite the barbaric reputation attributed to the Nordic invaders, even the harshest critics never disputed their incredible bravery, huge stature and remarkable good looks. No wonder women of vanquished, pre-Medieval European countries were attracted to these exceedingly handsome men who carried such fanciful names as Gudrod the Magnificent, Harald Fairhair, Thorfinn the Mighty, Halfdan of the Wide Embrace, Rolf the Marcher, Thorkel the Handsome, Sven Forkbeard and Cnut the Great.

No wonder my twentieth-century heroine, caught in a web of desertion and despair, learns to love these proud, fierce people in her travel through time to 925 A.D. Jorvik, where living was more simple, but human relationships were just as complicated.

Her brows were bright, her breast was shining,
Whiter her neck than new fallen snow . . .
Blond was his hair, and bright his cheeks,
Grim as a snake's were his glowing eyes.

Rigspula
c. 10th century

Chapter One

"This is the first lecture in the 'Mind Over Matter' series. Before we start, clear your mind of all extraneous thought. Picture yourself floating on a cloud high above the earth— floating . . . floating . . . floating . . ."

"Stupid, damn tapes!" Ruby Jordan complained aloud as she stomped into her husband's study to turn off the machine. Rhoda, her ditzy cleaning lady, had probably touched the switches on the complicated deck when she'd dusted earlier.

A killer headache pounded behind Ruby's eyes, and she knew it would get worse before Jack got home. Would there be another argument?

Ruby stopped short when she saw Jack selecting some of his business motivation tapes and putting them into a briefcase.

"I didn't know you were home. Why didn't you—"

"Don't start on me again, Rube," Jack Jordon interrupted his wife, a silken thread of warning in his deep-timbred voice. "I've had it up to here with the fighting."

He slashed his throat emphatically with a forefinger to make his point.

"Me, too," Ruby whispered on a broken sigh, then noticed his suitcases lined up next to the door. So, he really was leaving. She'd expected it for weeks, but still tears welled in her eyes.

"Jack, are you sure you want this?" How many times had she asked that question the last two weeks? What a fool to think the answer might be different this time!

Jack straightened from his bent position over the stereo, turned it off and rubbed his eyes wearily with the fingers of one hand before darting an impatient glare at her. He still wore the dark blue business suit he'd donned early that morning.

Ruby knew that the recession-hit real estate market had put him through the wringer this past year. One month they'd even had to use her salary to pay the bills—a walloping blow to his ego. Jack's wide shoulders sagged now with sadness and exhaustion. He probably hadn't eaten all day. For a moment, Ruby's heart softened and she almost asked him if she could fix his dinner. Almost.

"Rube, our marriage sucks. We've been hurting each other for a long time, and I'm tired of trying anymore. I've got to get on with my life . . . we both do. These arguments tear me apart . . . affect my work."

Ruby listened with rising dismay, and a cold foreboding sealed her lips. When she didn't respond, he continued in a harsh, pain-raw voice, "I'm thirty-eight years old, and I don't want to spend the rest of my life with a woman who gets more turned on by her job and her clients than me."

"Oh!" she gasped, stunned by his bluntness. "That's not true. It's just like you to put a sexual connotation on everything."

"Hey, that's about the only thing that works for us anymore, and even that doesn't happen all that often these days," Jack said with a wry grin and a shrug.

His smile, as intimate as a kiss, could still make Ruby's heart do cartwheels after all these years, and Ruby had to steel herself to his charm before asking tremulously, "You're not saying you're leaving because of sex problems?"

"You know better than that." His smile faded as his bleak blue eyes stabbed her accusingly. "We could go upstairs right now and screw each other's brains out, and it wouldn't solve a thing."

"You are *so* crude!"

"Yeah, well, you won't have to put up with it much longer," Jack retorted hotly. His jaw tensed visibly, but then he softened, touching her trembling lips with a fleeting, whisper-soft caress of his fingertips. "I'm sorry, babe. I didn't want things to end like this. Can't we just part amicably?"

Ruby shriveled inside a little at his words. She tried to picture a future without Jack in it. Anguish tore at her insides with steely fingers, and she had to hold her knuckles to her mouth to hold back the pain.

"Is there . . . another woman?" Ruby persisted in a soft, faint voice that broke with the emotion she couldn't hide.

Jack turned on her angrily. "No! I've told you that a dozen times." His glittering eyes challenged her. "You can be sure, though, that I *intend* to find a woman who won't consider me a male chauvinist just because I want to take care of her." Bitterness limned his voice as he took a deep breath and continued, "I'll tell you something else. Our kids need a full-time mother. Good Lord! How much time have you spent with them lately? They feel as neglected as I do."

The force of his seething reply caught Ruby off guard. She pushed back the hysteria that threatened to rise biliously to her voice and asked, more calmly than she felt, "Why do men feel threatened when women become successful? Why can't they accept professional women combining a career and a home?"

"I refuse to get involved in this women's-lib debate with you again," Jack said with cold finality, putting more tapes in his briefcase and slamming it shut.

"I suppose you'll end up with some twenty-year-old chippie in spandex who'll talk you into buying a motor-cycle or Corvette or something," Ruby mocked cynically, biting her bottom lip to hold back the tears.

A sad smile played at the corners of Jack's mouth. He countered in the quick, easy manner that came with years of living together, "Nah, I'm thinking more of a thirtyish woman with a Dolly Parton body, a Barbara Walters mind and a Joan Rivers sense of humor." Jack's grim eyes belied his light banter.

Ruby couldn't deny the pain and jealousy that surged through her. "Dolly Parton! Get real! I could see Jane Fonda, maybe, but Dolly Parton!"

Jack still grinned at her teasingly, which gave Ruby the nerve to offer, "Except for the Dolly Parton body, I could fill the other two criteria . . . I think."

The glint of humor faded from his face as Jack asked seriously, "What will you be looking for?"

Ruby cringed, momentarily deflated at his failure to respond to her offer. And did he really think she wanted another man?

Bruised pride stiffened her neck, but embarrassment soon turned to annoyance. She met Jack's eyes defiantly. "Movie-star looks would be nice but aren't the most important thing. Besides, I have to be realistic, I guess. I'm no raving beauty, and, at my age, men look at younger women."

"Oh, Rube, that's not true. You could get any man you wanted." Tenderly, his appreciative eyes traveled over her all-too-familiar body.

Any man except the one she needed, Ruby thought, but, instead of speaking her mind, she swallowed with difficulty and gently upbraided him, "Jack, take off the rose-colored glasses and be honest. Thirty-eight-year-old men don't look at thirty-eight-year-old women."

"They do when the women look like you." Jack studied her a moment, then went on, "You still haven't answered my question. What are you looking for in a man? It obviously isn't me."

Pain, stark and intense, formed a huge knot in Ruby's throat, and Jack asked her silly questions. Still, she continued with her pointless description of an ideal mate. "He should be intelligent. Yes, intelligence is essential. And successful . . . oh, not moneywise success, just good at whatever he does . . ."

Her voice trailed away and her bravado failed for a second. When she regained her composure, she steeled herself to go on. "Actually, none of those things matter at all. I'd just want a man who loves me. You know, the way you used . . ." Ruby's voice cracked and she couldn't continue.

Jack tried to touch her shoulder but Ruby shrugged his hand away angrily. "Don't feel sorry for me. I don't want your pity. Just go if you're going. You're right. We can't keep postponing the inevitable. Go!"

After a few seconds, she heard Jack moving toward the door. "I'm staying at the lake house until I can find an apartment," he said in an oddly rasping voice. "I'll call the boys tonight."

Ruby forgot her pride then in the face of this final, wrenching end to a twenty-year marriage. Lord, how many times had she sworn she wouldn't ask *the* stupid question, the one most women invariably ask at some point in their lives?

"Don't you love me anymore?"

Jack froze in the doorway and then turned woodenly.

Ruby's heart lurched. This handsome man could still make her pulse do flip flops with just a glance—even after

17

twenty years of marriage and despite the light sprinkling of gray in his dark blond hair. The past year of stress had etched cruel lines in the chiseled planes of his mature face, but years of disciplined jogging and racquetball had kept his six-foot-three body lean and well-conditioned. He'd have no trouble at all attracting a woman. Ruby closed her eyes for a moment at that painful thought before searching his face once again.

Where were the sense of humor and seductive sensuality that had knocked her for a loop in high school and lured her enticingly into a young marriage in which she had willingly, joyfully stayed home during those early years to bear his children? How had they let things deteriorate so far?

The long silence in answer to Ruby's question told her volumes before Jack sighed, then finally responded hoarsely, "I don't know. I just don't know how I feel anymore. I'm not sure it matters."

His words sliced through Ruby's heart.

"We just need time—"

"No! What we don't need is more time to drag this out. I've asked you repeatedly to cut back on hours at your lingerie company so we can work on our marriage. You've refused."

"I haven't refused. I just couldn't do it right away. Sweet Nothings has stockpiled so many orders. I would have to hire someone to take over some of my responsibilities. By next month, two months at the latest, then I might be able . . ."

Jack looked at her incredulously and threw his arms out in resignation. "I give up! I've been hearing this same story for months. Call me when you can work me in."

For a few long seconds, Jack hesitated—almost regretfully. Time stood still for them both, freezing them in a tableau of cloudy nostalgia. Jack's heartrending expression bathed her in a gentle caress, giving her hope.

But then he turned and left.

Ruby stared at the closed door through a mist of tears. Why couldn't Jack understand how hard she'd worked to build up her custom lingerie company, how hard it was to let go—even a little? She loved Jack. She *did*. Why couldn't she have both him and her career?

A hot tear trickled down her cheek. Regret squeezed her heart as she thought of Jack and all she'd lost. Memories seared her mind. Finally, she yielded to the racking sobs that shook her, rocking back and forth.

Ruby cried for a long time until tides of hollow weariness engulfed her. Then she sank down in a well-worn recliner—Jack's favorite chair since his college days—and let her gaze scan the room. She reached for her fifteen-year-old son's Walkman, needing something to fill the silence. Unable to cope right now with the overwhelming sense of loss, Ruby absently inserted the tape Jack had been listening to, adjusted the headset and leaned back wearily. Maybe one of the motivational tapes would inspire her with some miraculous message on how to get her marriage back in order.

Lord, what a mess I've made of my life!

Ruby shifted her blue-jean-clad bottom into a more comfortable position as her eyes scanned the tapes on the bookshelves of the study. She wasn't opposed to motivational tapes, but Jack had become obessed with them during the real estate slump.

The worst of them, and the funniest, had been the coyote tapes. How many mornings had he awakened her and the two boys with a coyote howl, declaring that every day should start on a positive note? She forgot the significance of the coyote—something to do with coyotes being able to survive in the wilderness and businessmen being able to do likewise in the coming bad times, or some such thing.

What she did remember was the boys hiding their heads

19

under their pillows at the sound of the howl, and refusing to ride in a car with their dad because he forced them to listen to his tapes rather than their favorite rock group. Despite her sadness, Ruby grinned.

That seemed so long ago. Eons!

She looked back to the shelves. Hundreds of the blasted cassettes lined the shelves, not to mention video tapes, books and plaques—everything from the old standby *The Power of Positive Thinking* to *You Can Do Anything!*

She knew what she'd do if she could do anything. She'd be twenty years younger, Ruby thought defiantly. She would give anything for a chance to live her life over again, knowing what she did today. She'd certainly never get involved with another male chauvinist. She wouldn't let herself love another Jack. It hurt too much.

In fact, she didn't think she'd get married. Sure, there'd been lots of good times with Jack, but men demanded too much of the women they loved. They sucked the very dreams out of them. Barefoot and pregnant, that's how they all still wanted their women!

Ruby wiped her tears with a tissue, rewound the tape, and pushed the play button on the cassette machine, trying to forget her worries and all the decisions she'd have to make. Eddie and David knew their parents had problems, but they'd be devastated to find their father gone. Ruby felt as if she were hanging from a cliff by her fingernails. Would she find the strength to climb up or should she just give in and let go?

Hot tears scalded Ruby's eyes once again as the mesmerizing voice declared, "You *can* control your own life."

Hah!

The speaker continued, "Before we start, clear your mind of all other thoughts. Picture yourself floating out of your body—floating . . . floating . . . floating . . .

"There's nothing—nothing—in the world you can't

have if you want it badly enough. The mind is a powerful tool."

"Oh, God, help me find a way out of this mess," Ruby prayed aloud. "I don't know if I can live without Jack."

"Some people consider prayer the answer to their problems," the speaker said, and Ruby's eyes shot open in surprise. Was she going crazy now, too? Geez! Mental telepathy with a tape recorder!

"Prayer is fine," the voice soothed, "but even God wants you to help yourself. I'm telling you there's nothing in the world you can't do. Where the will's strong enough, there *is* a way!"

The speaker's evangelizing voice droned on and on as Ruby allowed her mind to lift out of herself. Totally relaxed, she felt as if she were floating above her own body. A heavenly feeling! Lighter than a feather, her buoyant body drifted from cloud to cloud in a clear blue sky.

Her problems disappeared. The five extra pounds she'd gained during these past stressful months melted away. She felt twenty years younger.

Even in her sleep, Ruby smiled.

It was the odor that first pulled Ruby from her deep sleep—human body odor. "Okay, Ruby baby," she muttered to herself. "Go with the flow." Sense-dimensional dreams! That would be something to tell her therapist— if she ever got one.

Ruby opened her eyes lazily, then shut them quickly in horror. When she peeked out again, she realized she must still be asleep, awash in the most realistic dream she'd ever had. About a dozen wretched-looking people, wearing bizarre, drab clothing, like burlap sacks, crowded her in a long boat, which moved swiftly toward shore. By the smell of them, they hadn't bathed in weeks.

Ruby wrinkled her nose in distaste and edged away

from one toothless harridan, who resembled her flaky cleaning lady Rhoda. She giggled aloud. Imagine! The dream of the century and she got to take her cleaning lady along. Some women got handsome actors like Kevin Costner in their fantasies with his preference for "long, slow, deep, soft, wet kisses that last three days" in *Bull Durham;* she got Rhoda. How would Rhoda survive without her tabloids?

"M'God, be you a boy ur a girl?" the Rhoda person exclaimed.

Ruby realized then that everyone in the boat was staring at her—as if *she* were the oddball. Ruby looked down at herself. She saw nothing unusual in her Nike-clad feet, her blue jeans and her son's oversized Brass Balls Saloon T-shirt. Oh, that was probably the problem. The T-shirt logo offended some people.

She started to explain that her shirt really belonged to her fifteen-year-old son Eddie who had bought it at the shore without her permission, but stopped herself. Really! She didn't have to defend herself in a dream.

Ruby smoothed the fabric of her shirt over her slim waist and hips, then jerked alert. *Slim!* Dear Lord, she hadn't been this thin since before her first pregnancy. Not that she was ever fat, but this kind of body tone came with youth, not childbirth and thirty-eight years of easy living.

Ruby discreetly lifted the edge of her T-shirt, peeled away the loose waistband of her jeans and peeked at her skin just above her navel. *Hallelujah! No more stretch marks!* Her wish had come true. She was twenty years younger.

Smiling widely, Ruby looked back over her shoulder . . . then gasped. Three Viking-style dragonships rode at anchor on the sunny horizon of what appeared to be the confluence of two huge rivers. Hundreds of other ships stretched along the shore or headed in or out of a wider river which must lead to the sea. She hadn't seen anything so spectacular since the Tall Ships event held on the Hudson River in New York years ago. They were magnificent.

A loud thud caused her to turn forward. Their boat had hit the dock and was being tied ashore. Hundreds of people swarmed on the wharf, all dressed in strange clothing.

Some of the men wore short tunics that barely reached their knees and left their arms bare, while others wore plain, collarless, long-sleeved shirts down to their hips over tight pants. Belts, ranging from leather thongs to ornate gold chains, cinched in their waists. Short swords and scabbarded knives clanged at their sides.

Long, pinafore-type tunics, mostly open-sided, covered the women's pleated, linen chemises which trailed on the ground in the back. Ornate brooches, with dangling keys or scissors or small knives, fastened the tunics together at the shoulders.

Ruby noticed an inordinate amount of blond hair sparkling in the afternoon sunlight, from almost-white to fire-red and all the colors in-between. The older women knotted their hair at the back of the neck and covered it with scarves or cloth headdresses, while others braided their long tresses or let them lay loose down their backs. The men's hair hung shoulder-length and longer, often in braids, too, framing faces that ranged from clean-shaven to heavily bearded and mustached.

Finely wrought, heavy wrist and arm bracelets of solid gold or silver, studded with jewels, adorned the better-dressed men and women. Some appeared to be museum-quality pieces. *Wow!*

Fascinated, Ruby asked Rhoda, who still eyed her suspiciously, "*Where* are we?"

"Jorvik."

"Jorvik? Where's that?"

"To Saxons, it be *Eoforwic,* but the heathen Vikings call it Jorvik. Be you a Saxon?"

Puzzled, Ruby said, "Huh?" Then she mulled Rhoda's words. Jorvik? Something clicked in her mind. Hadn't she read recently about an archaeological dig there, something involving Vikings? Suddenly, remembrance jolted her.

"Oh, my God! You mean York, like in England? And those boats out there—are those Viking ships?"

Rhoda just stared at her, open-mouthed. Then a crazy thought entered her mind. At first, she dismissed it, but then asked tentatively, "What year is this?"

Now Rhoda really did look at her as if she'd escaped from a looney bin. "Nine hundred 'n twenty-five. You bin locked up fer a long time ur sumpin? A dungeon, mebbe? Ur a nunnery, I wager? Them nuns do be barmy sum times. I heared onct 'bout a girl who liked men too much and her mother put her in a convent an' she went stark ravin' mad jus' cuz no man touched her in a year."

Good Lord! Rhoda didn't need her tabloids, after all. Even in these primitive times she found sources for the sensational gossip she loved.

Ruby started to laugh hysterically, just corroborating Rhoda's mental-illness assumption about her. What a dream this was turning out to be! Why couldn't she dream about cowboys or knights in shining armor? Why conjure up Vikings in a pre-Medieval England? Well, what else did she expect, the way her life was going?

She couldn't wait to get back and tell Jack his "Mind Over Matter" tapes really did work. Wait. She forgot. Jack wouldn't be there when she returned. Would he?

A brutal headache began to throb behind her eyes, especially when a giant of a man, who smelled like a bear she'd once whiffed at a zoo, pulled her and her companions out of the boat and shoved them roughly into a group at one side of the wharf.

"Hey," she protested loudly. "Watch it, buster!" The rest of her motley group looked aghast at her temerity,

24

as if she were even more daft than they'd thought. The Goliath glared down at her.

"What's your name?" Ruby persisted, sputtering with indignation. "I'm going to report you to your . . . supervisor."

"Olaf," he snarled and gave her another rude shove.

"Olaf. That figures. The name matches the face."

Rhoda pulled her back and cautioned, "Shhhh! Ain'tcha afeared? Do ya wanna git kilt?"

Then Ruby saw Jack.

Oh, his brownish-blond hair had lightened and hung down to his shoulders, and his black tunic covered a younger, more powerful body—one that would put Arnold Schwarzenegger to shame—but the face was definitely that of the man she'd been sleeping next to for the past twenty years. Thank God! This dream business got stale quick. She wanted to wake up.

At the same time, Ruby's heart thudded wildly at this first glimpse of her husband's new golden, hard body. She felt like a breathless girl of eighteen again.

"Jack," Ruby called out happily, while Rhoda tried to hold her back. The dolt! He ignored her. He was mad at her, of course. Hadn't he just walked out on their marriage?

He seemed to have arrived on one of the big ships, and the attention he aroused indicated that he was a man of importance. When he stopped to talk to someone, Ruby realized that his right arm encircled the shoulders of a buxom, blond "Vikingess" in a green silk tunic with enough gold and jewels at her neck and arms to ransom a king.

Ruby's initial hurt turned quickly into jealousy and then a white-hot anger. Furious, Ruby yelled "Jack" again, but he still looked the other way. Lying pond scum! He'd said there was no other woman.

"Two-timing sonofa . . ." Ruby muttered on a sob, breaking away from Rhoda and Olaf to approach Jack.

She'd show him. She picked up a clump of mud the size of a cantaloupe, took careful aim and hurled the clod, hitting him square in the face. She smiled widely in satisfaction. She hadn't been an ace softball pitcher in high school for nothing!

The tall figure swiveled, azure eyes wide with shock, but before he could react, Ruby pointed a finger at his stunned companion and warned, "Stay away from my husband if you know what's good for you."

Looking as if she'd seen a ghost, the wide-eyed woman backed away, slipped in the mud and fell flat on her rear.

Ruby laughed at the comical picture until Olaf came up behind her, lifted her off the ground with massive arms wrapped around her like steel bars and squeezed until she thought her ribs would crack.

"Put me down, you oaf," Ruby shrieked. Then she turned to her husband, demanding, "Jack, tell this goon to put me down. He's hurting me."

"Not Oaf. *Olaf*," the giant corrected Ruby.

Ruby grimaced with impatience and looked up over her shoulder. "Put me down, *Oaf*." He reacted by lifting her higher in the air, as if she weighed no more than a feather.

Jack studied her icily, his jaw clenched with suppressed violence. He slowly wiped the mud from his face with a square of linen cloth. His girlfriend wailed loudly at his side until one of his companions reached over with a burly arm and cuffed her into silence.

A deathly quiet surrounded Ruby. The crowd stopped all activity to watch the spectacle.

Well, okay, maybe she shouldn't have hit him, especially in a public place, but he had no right to look at her so angrily. After all, he was the one in the wrong. Adultery was adultery—even in a dream.

With a commanding air, the Viking walked purposefully over to where Olaf still held her with feet dangling off the ground. His well-developed, massive body moved with an easy grace, not unlike her own modern-day husband. Standing so close she caught the familiar masculine scent of his skin, Jack extended a questioning forefinger to lift her chin in a whisper of a caress. Ruby leaned into his stroke reflexively, but then jerked back at the sensuous shock that shot hot flames through her. Jack's furrowed brows and intense, puzzled eyes told Ruby without words that he, too, had been affected by the simple touch. The very air around them seemed electrified.

But then anger transformed Jack's face. She soon found out why. Taking her chin in a painful, viselike grip, Jack snarled, "What manner of fool are you, boy, that you dare to strike Thork, son of Harald, high-king of all Norway?"

Boy? He thought she was a boy, Ruby realized. No wonder he was upset by the sexual chemistry between them. Well, compared to the way these people dressed, she supposed she might look like a young male in her pants and short Sassoon haircut. And, hey, wasn't Jack aiming high these days—son of a bloody king? Should she bow or what?

"Who are you?" Jack growled again, bruising her chin with his fingers. "Do you spy for Ivar?"

"Ivar? Who the hell is Ivar?"

"You dare much with your coarse tongue, boy."

"Jack, don't you recognize me? I'm Ruby . . . your wife."

"Nay, no wife have I," he declared in a steely voice, shifting indignantly from foot to foot. "Nor am I a sodomite," he added distastefully, looking at what he obviously considered her masculine attire. Then he released her chin and cocked his head in puzzlement.

What now? she wondered. Was it something she'd said?

Olaf let her slide down his body to her feet, but he pulled her arms behind her back and pinioned them there.

Jack stared at the inscription on her chest and his eyes widened. That stupid Brass Balls logo again!

Jack reached out a hand. His forefinger trailed sensuously over her bare arm as if asking a question, then grazed her quivering lips for affirmation. He smiled wickedly and nodded, as if answering his own question, at the same time pleased with the goose bumps he'd raised on her flesh with a mere touch.

Then her husband did the unthinkable. He reached out with lightning swiftness and outlined the tips of her breasts. He actually touched her breasts in front of all those people! She'd kill him for humiliating her. Outraged, Ruby tried to squirm out of Olaf's grasp.

"Thor's blood! 'Tis a wench," Jack exclaimed, turning with a grin to his companions for confirmation.

"No kidding! This has gone far enough, Jack. Tell this bozo to release me. This joke . . . or dream . . . or whatever it is has gone far enough. I want to go home."

"Explain this 'jack' you speak of."

"It's your name, Jack. Jack Jordan. And I'm your wife, Ruby. And I'm tired of this stupid dream."

Tears choked her. Why was Jack acting like this? Ruby squeezed her eyes shut tight. She would have pinched her own cheeks, but Olaf still held her arms behind her back; instead, she bit her bottom lip until she tasted blood, hoping to awaken herself from the nightmare.

It didn't work.

Some members of the crowd stepped closer, staring in amazement at her bloody lip as if she were truly crazy. She *was* crazy! Only a crazy person would find herself in this situation. Perhaps Jack's leaving her had pushed her over the edge.

"Nay, my name is Thork," the Jack clone said. "Heed me well. No wife have I, nor ever want one. I am a Jomsviking." Jack's deep voice rang coldly, loud and clear, through the crowd, which nodded and smiled in approval at his putting this woman in her place.

The people spoke an odd mixture of what sounded like Medieval Anglo-Saxon she'd once heard in an English Lit course and what was probably Old Norse. The languages were very similar. Strangely, she could understand both. Not so strange for a dream, she supposed.

Before Ruby could respond to Jack's astounding pronouncement, he stepped closer and his forefinger traced the letters on her shirt. He said the words aloud slowly, "Brass Balls," looked questioningly at a man standing next to him, then back at her and grinned, apparently understanding what the words symbolized. Several men chuckled behind him. However, his amusement turned to anger again.

"So . . . you carry a message to us from Ivar that his men have superior male parts made of metal?" He spoke loud enough for all the people to hear. Good Lord! She'd landed in some kind of Bedlam.

"Know you the male parts of Ivar's men from experience, wench?" he baited snidely.

"Shut up, Jack. You're embarrassing me."

He took hold of her sore chin and squeezed, looking her directly in the eye. "Thork. Mark my words well, wench. My name is Thork."

Ruby whimpered in pain, but still he didn't relent.

"Say it."

When she refused, he squeezed harder, and Ruby gasped out, "Thork, you jerk! Thork! Thork!"

" 'Jerk' best be a title of respect," he warned.

"Oh, yes, it means something like 'lord and master.' "

Jack looked unconvinced but, nevertheless, released her chin and addressed the mob. "Ivar sends the boy-woman to challenge us, methinks. Yea, he taunts us to war again. Bad enough he raids our lands whilst we are gone a-Viking or trading. Now he sends this insulting message.

Brass balls! Hah! Shall we show Ivar now and forever who the best men be?"

A roar rose like thunder through the crowd. Good grief! Who ever heard of a T-shirt causing a war? Ruby tried to express her opinion on their mistaken notions, but Olaf clamped a smelly palm over her mouth. She stomped on his soft leather shoes, and, to her chagrin, he didn't budge an inch. Looking over her shoulder, she saw his smirk as he stated with smug self-satisfaction, "Not Oaf. Olaf."

Maybe the guy wasn't as dumb as she'd thought.

"We must bring this spy to King Sigtrygg," Thork said. "Let him decide the fate of the thrall and whether or not we go to war with Ivar." Another roar of approval went through the crowd.

"Now ya done it," Rhoda whispered in her ear. "Sigtrygg One-Eye be a mean buzzard. Prob'ly lop off yer head. Or pluck out yer eyes. Or—"

"Give me a break, Rhoda. You've been reading too many tabloids again."

"Come, thrall," Jack commanded. "The other slaves stay."

"Just who do you think you're calling a thrall?" Ruby protested, finally squirming out of the giant's grasp. "I'm no more a slave than . . . than you are."

Jack had the gall to grin down at her. He was really enjoying her discomfort. Then he surprised her by putting a protective arm around her shoulder and saying, "Hold your tongue if you have a fondness for your fair head, sweetling. This crowd smells blood."

Sweetling! Ruby smiled, hopeful for the first time that day of a possible reconciliation between her and Jack. But she had only a moment to enjoy Jack's quaint endearment.

"Chop off 'er head here 'n now," one man shouted with perfect timing. "Send it to Ivar in that shirt she wears." Ruby looked over at a nodding Rhoda, whose expression said, "I told you so."

Another person yelled, "Why wait? Chop off 'er head now. She be a spy. Mebbe even Ivar's woman. What better way to send a message!" If the roar of the crowd was any indication, a lot of people liked that idea.

Instinctively, Ruby moved closer to Jack. Why wasn't he revolted at the idea of beheading her? She'd been on enough camping trips with him to know he couldn't even gut a trout without gagging. He should be her knight in shining armor. He should gallantly rescue her so they could ride off into the sunset. Wasn't that the way it was supposed to happen in dreams?

Instead, Jack asserted loudly, "Nay, the king must decide. Mayhap he will await a vote of the Althing when it meets next month." Then he turned abruptly and confided to a well-dressed man standing beside him, "Selik, we malinger overlong whilst I carry important messages for Sigtrygg from King Athelstan in Wessex—more important than a mere thrall."

Jack turned to Ruby once again and grabbed her arm, pulling her through the people who stepped back to make a path for them. "I will take this spy to my bedchamber later for a private examination," he disclosed suggestively with a wink to those companions closest to him. "Mayhap the women of Ivar's land have metal parts also."

The men laughed at his words, and someone suggested lewdly that he make his examination then and there. Jack stopped, his arm still resting possessively on her shoulder, and he actually seemed to consider the prospect of a public stripping.

Humiliated, Ruby tried to kick Thork's bare legs. She no longer thought of him as Jack. Jack would never be so cruel.

Thork laughed as Ruby hammered his immovable chest with clenched fists, then picked up her struggling, screaming body and deftly slung it over his shoulder, giving the crowd more fodder for laughter. He ordered one man to go ahead to the castle to inform King Sigtrygg of their arrival and another to ride to his grandfather's home in Northumbria and tell him he would be there late the next day. He told yet another man to supervise the unloading of his ships and to report to him that night.

When he settled her in place like a sack of flour, Ruby bit his shoulder to get his attention. With a gleeful chuckle, Thork whacked her with an open palm across her bottom which arched provocatively across his shoulder, and then he kept the widespread fingers there familiarly, rubbing her with an intimate circular motion. Ruby could feel her face flush, and not just because she hung upside down.

The jerk got another roar of approval when he commented in an aside to his friends, "Mayhap the women of Ivar's land do have metal female parts, after all. Her arse feels as bony as a winter-starved rabbit."

He would pay for this, Ruby vowed as he carried her away. Somehow, some way, she would find a way to get back at this crude excuse for a man.

Chapter Two

"Ivar is vicious, but not lackwitted. He would never send a simpleminded wench to spy," Thork stated emphatically, peering over his shoulder at Ruby whose blood-suffused head bounced against his back with each wide stride he took. "Who in the name of Odin are you?"

"Simpleminded!" Ruby protested, but the word came out garbled and unintelligible, considering her position.

A sharp object pressed against her waist, and she shifted slightly, as best she could, to relieve the pressure. Twisting her head sideways and looking up awkwardly, she saw an intricately carved brooch which held together the edges of a short shoulder mantle. The design profiled a writhing animal with limbs contorted out of recognition. Surely it wasn't a coyote. That would be too much of a coincidence. No, it was probably a wolf. And it appeared to be solid gold! Unable to see it closer, Ruby dropped her head down, laying her cheek against the small of Thork's back. Her skin prickled with delight at even that casual touch. The familiar musk of his skin comforted her jarred senses.

Olaf and two other men walked beside Thork, sharing opinions about the unlikelihood of Ruby being a spy. All agreed that Sigtrygg must be the final arbiter of her fate but wondered how he would react to even the possibility of the hated Ivar infiltrating Jorvik. In soft, guarded voices, they also updated Thork on recent events in Jorvik.

"Sigtrygg expected you a sennight past. We have all suffered his wrath," complained a young man with flowing, silver blond hair whom Thork had called Selik earlier. Even from her position, Ruby could see that the exceedingly handsome, almost beautiful, male drew the admiring attention of many of the passing women.

Thork swore aloud, using a famous Anglo-Saxon word that survived even to the twentieth century.

"Sigtrygg chomps at the bit to return to Dublin and reclaim the throne from his cousin Godfred," Selik added. "Everyone in his vipers'-nest court suffers his raging temper outbursts as he waits for you."

"So Sigtrygg still hopes for a united Northumbrian-Irish kingdom?" Thork questioned.

"Yea, and more. He cannot see that the Saxons lay waste our lands while he and his cousins bicker over power among the two countries," Selik answered.

Olaf added, "He tries to force a pagan government on Christian Danes who have lived here for generations and are no longer content with the old ways."

"I tell you, Thork, when Viking fights Viking, the bloody Saxon will be the winner," Selik asserted vehemently.

"I see now why Sigtrygg stews," Thork said pensively, "and 'twould seem our fair maid here has much to fear if our king rages so." He swatted Ruby on the behind for emphasis, calling everyone's attention back to her.

34

" 'Twill depend on Ivar's mood," Olaf stated matter-of-factly, with a shrug of unconcern. "If he be of a mean temper, as he is wont at the flip of a coin, he will likely behead her on the spot. Or mayhap flay all the skin off her body just to amuse himself."

Behead her! Flay her! To amuse himself! Ruby's stomach churned.

"Or spread her legs and skewer her on the spot if she appeals," Selik drawled with a suggestive chortle, "or bugger her like the boy she appears."

"Thor's toenails! Too much mead under his belt and 'twill not matter a whit if she be fair or barley-faced, I warrant," Thork added with unflattering frankness. His deep voice held a trace of laughter. "Sigtrygg can be a man of uncommon appetites, in all ways!"

"Comes of being a berserker, I say. Wild in battle, wild in bed, or so I've been told," Selik interjected lewdly. "But, even so, I cannot fathom Sigtrygg being attracted to this scrawny bird."

Thork laughed and pinched Ruby's bottom to halt any protest she might be contemplating. "But you forget, Selik, our king relishes the odd perversion. Didst ye hear of the night Sigtrygg . . ."

The men laughed companionably when Thork's risqué story ended. It involved a nun, ropes and a wide variety of feathers.

Ruby was not amused. Thork had probably invented the sexual tale to alarm her before meeting the king. She punched him in the back hoping to stop his laughter, to no avail. It was like pounding a brick wall.

Then Thork turned serious, stating softly in a hushed voice, "Actually, Sigtrygg's mood is sure to sweeten once he hears my news." He paused significantly to get the men's full attention. "King Athelstan would strengthen the alliance between Wessex and Northumbria by wedding his sister to our ruler."

At first, stunned silence prevailed. Then they all protested at once.

"Thor's blood!"

"The gall of the Saxon!"

"The proposal smacks of trickery! Why would the king give his own blood to mix with a heathen dog? 'Tis what the Saxons call us Vikings, and worse."

After they all vented their consternation, Selik said, "They say the Saxon king be godly handsome. Did ye find his sister pleasing . . . or skinny and horse-faced like the other Saxon bitches?"

Thork laughed at Selik's one-track mind. "What difference? Our power-hungry Sigtrygg would wed a pig if 'twould bring him more lands."

"So, think you there will be a royal wedding?"

" 'Tis uncertain, Olaf, but I trust not these Saxons—even Athelstan who has been fairer than most. Some say he walks the same line as his grandfather, the so-called 'Good Alfred.' Still, 'twould be wise of Sigtrygg to proceed slowly . . . and watch his back."

All agreed. Then Thork turned to another man, who had not spoken yet. "What think you, Cnut?"

Ruby craned her neck to see him.

The older man spoke slowly, with authority. "The Saxons teach us treachery at every turn. The greedy bastards have chopped away at the Danelaw like bloody berserkers. 'Tis little more than a score of years since I stood with Guthorm when King Alfred agreed to the Danelaw boundary between Viking and Saxon England."

A respectful silence followed his words.

"Our territory then ran up the Thames to London, along the Lea to its source, on to Bedford, then up the River Ouse to Watling Street," Cnut went on, "but what have we now? Little more than Northumbria, with Jorvik as our center! A piss ant in the midst of a beehive!"

Ruby heard him spit for emphasis, then add, "Even

that, they begrudge us. The 'Five Boroughs' we Vikings founded—Lincoln, Nottingham, Derby, Leicester and Stamford—all taken. Mayhap you forget the lies and deceit, Thork, on both sides, but mark my words, blood will spill soon—wedding or no."

Ruby interrupted then; she could wait no longer.

"Thork, put me down. I'm going to throw up."

Thork ignored her complaint and continued talking to his companions as they walked through the ancient walled city, along the bustling narrow streets. Even from her upside-down perspective, Ruby saw the Vikings they passed do double takes at the remarkable spectacle she presented. Long blond braids swirled as young girls turned quickly. Mustaches twitched on men's hugely bearded faces.

The myriad smells and sounds of the tightly congested market area assailed Ruby's senses. Church bells rang out the noon hour. Church bells? In a Viking city? How odd!

Pigs and chickens squealed and squawked from their market stalls. Wooden-wheeled carts rumbled by laden with produce. Hawkers cried out their wares. The smell of dung, crated fish, tanned leather and horseflesh mixed with the sweet river breeze. Ruby really did feel sick now. She started to gag.

"Do not dare," a suddenly alert Thork warned and immediately allowed her to slide to the ground. Ruby's shaky knees buckled, and Thork grabbed her shoulders to hold her upright.

"Holy Thor! You look peckish. Do you ail?"

Ruby wanted to say something sarcastic, but bile clogged her throat. Thork must have noticed something amiss in her face because he pulled her to the side of the road so people behind them could pass. Then he motioned for his companions to continue on to King Sigtrygg's palace without them, telling them he'd follow shortly.

"Take deep breaths," Thork suggested in a surprisingly

gentle voice, which was at odds with his earlier behavior. He took her hand and led her toward the river which ran behind the buildings lining the busy thoroughfare in an orderly fashion, so close that their eaves almost touched across the narrow alleylike streets.

Thatched roofs covered rectangular structures made of primitive wattle and daub—branches interwoven horizontally and filled with clay, straw and hair, then plaster. Long backyards stretched down to the river, distinguished from their neighbors by post and withy fences. Craftsmen worked and sold their wares on tables set up under awnings in front, like a giant flea market or street bazaar.

"Are those homes or businesses?"

Thork pulled her along beside him as they neared the river, her hand still held firmly in his much larger one.

"Both. On Coppergate, many artisans and merchants live and trade. The buildings combine homes, workshops and markets. Where you come from—is it not the same?"

Ruby noticed a slight narrowing in Thork's piercing eyes as he asked the question and knew his kindness masked a motive. He wanted information from her.

"And this?" Ruby asked, disregarding his question about her home and pointing to the river which flowed near their feet. She felt better now although her stomach still churned with nervousness.

"The Ouse. 'Tis a tidal river. It flows in from the North Sea by way of the Humber River," he explained, pointing to serpentine ships moving gracefully toward the harbor. He answered her questions with consideration, but Ruby had known this man too long not to sense the impatience underlying the even tone of his voice.

With fluid grace, he dropped down to a large boulder and indicated with a jerk of his head that she should join him. Ruby swallowed tightly as her leg brushed his warm, sinewy thigh. His nearness kindled feelings in Ruby that had been dormant much too long.

His narrowed eyes studied her in a shrewd, assessing manner. Ruby could almost see his mind working. If she was a spy, did he really think she would spew out all her secrets so easily? Probably.

"Are you not familiar with the Ouse? It flows through Ivar's land, too, does it not?" Thork probed blatantly.

Ruby decided to have fun with this overly suspicious Viking. "I don't really know. The only river near me is the Mississippi." Then she clamped her hand over her mouth as if she'd just disclosed something she shouldn't have.

"The Missi . . . the Missis . . . whatever you said!" Thork exclaimed. "God's breath! I have heard naught of it."

"Really? It's one of the largest rivers in the world. I thought everyone had heard of it." Ruby batted her eyelashes at him innocently.

Lord, he was a handsome man—even better looking than Jack had been at that age! Momentarily lost in sweet reverie, Ruby sighed. A kaleidoscope of images flitted through her mind. Jack in a white tuxedo at their senior prom. Jack in a black tuxedo on their wedding day. Jack wearing nothing on their wedding night.

Ruby's face flushed at the unbidden recollections. She couldn't think about Jack just yet and what his absence would mean to her life. Later. She would think about Jack later when she was stronger, more in control of her emotions, better able to handle the anguish.

But the resemblance between Thork and Jack disconcerted Ruby. The sharp planes of Thork's deeply tanned face mirrored her husband's, even though his long hair glistened like white gold in the sunlight, no doubt due to the bleaching effect of long, sunlit days on board ship. Even his devastating smile, displaying large, white teeth, was the same, right down to the one slightly crooked incisor. The only difference was Thork's more muscular body, probably strengthened by the necessity for battle readiness, and an ugly scar above his right eye which cut right through his eyebrow.

Her fingertips ached to touch his rock-hard body, to investigate the differences—intimately. Shivers of delight rippled through Ruby's body at the enticing prospect, and, without thinking, she blurted out on a whisper, "You take my breath away."

To Ruby's mortification, Thork raised one eyebrow questioningly, understanding perfectly what she meant. Good heavens! She'd been gawking at him like a hormone-humming teenager. With supreme conceit, he winked at her knowingly. Criminey! Women probably swooned over him all the time.

Just as Ruby started to turn away from him in embarrassment, Thork raised his left hand to brush a breeze-blown tress from his face. Ruby inhaled sharply. The pinky finger was missing.

She grabbed his hand and tenderly touched the place where the finger should have been. "What happened? How did you lose your finger?"

Thork shrugged. "My half-brother Eric chopped it off when I was five. He aimed for my . . . male part, but then he always was a poor swordsman." He grinned at the shock on her face but his eyes told a different, pain-ridden story. "Eric Bloodaxe, they call him. Appropriate, would you not say?"

"Oh, Thork, how sad!"

Caught off-guard at first by her concern, Thork darted her a curious glance, then touched the scar on his face. "He was unsuccessful in removing my eye as well. 'Twas long ago, though. 'Tis no longer important."

Ruby studied Thork, and her heart ached for the pain he must have endured. She yearned to comfort him, to hold the memory of his ugly childhood at bay. Locked in a private hell of recollection, his expression turned bleak for a moment. It occurred to Ruby then that maybe, just maybe, she'd been given a clean slate with Jack in this dream or self-hypnosis or whatever it was. What fun it would be to go back to the beginning with Jack, knowing what she did today! She could avoid all the proven mistakes. She could capitalize on all the good things that had worked with them.

A second chance! Wasn't that just what she'd prayed for before being hurtled back in time?

Scanning Thork speculatively, Ruby considered flirting mischievously with the fierce Viking to lighten his mood, the way she used to do with Jack. Actually, she hadn't flirted with Jack in a long, long time. Maybe that was one of their problems. She inspected Thork through lowered lashes and grinned impishly. This dream business might prove interesting, after all.

"Have you ever heard of Kevin Costner?" she asked abruptly in a husky voice, hoping she wouldn't lose her nerve.

"Who?"

"Never mind. It doesn't matter. I was just wondering . . . how do you feel about long, slow, deep, soft, wet kisses that last three days?" she asked brazenly.

That got his attention!

Ruby recognized the bright flame of desire in Thork's sapphire eyes before he deliberately shuttered them, but he couldn't conceal their quick blink of surprise. He opened his mouth as if to speak, closed it, swallowed, then stood abruptly. She and Jack had seen the Kevin Costner movie together. The screen words had aroused them both. At a glance, Ruby saw that Thork was no different.

Their eyes locked. Acutely aware of Thork's scrutiny, Ruby parted her lips unconsciously in unspoken invitation.

But Thork ignored the temptation of her lips as he regained his composure and swore explicitly. "Fine words for a whore, mayhap. Be that what you are? If so, name

41

your price and be done." He stood and paced, deep in thought, before confronting her again. "Mayhap, though, you really do spy, after all," he concluded with narrowed eyes. "For a certainty, methinks you treat your situation much too lightly and hope to divert my attention. Your life hangs in the balance, wench, and you speak of . . . of . . ."

"Kisses?" Ruby offered impudently. "Don't Vikings kiss?"

Thork blushed. He actually blushed. Ruby loved it.

"We like kisses fine," he rasped thickly. Suddenly realizing her game, Thork twitched his lips sensuously as he offered, "Mayhap you'd like a demonstration?"

He obviously expected her to demur. Instead, Ruby decided to play along. "Perhaps. Of course, there wouldn't be much attraction for you in kissing such a *bony-arsed* female as me. That is what you called me, isn't it?"

Thork grinned provocatively, then watched with fascination as Ruby slowly wet her suddenly dry lips with the tip of her tongue. He moved enticingly close. Ruby thought he was about to kiss her, and she parted her lips reflexively. Instead, he placed his lips a hairsbreadth from hers and blew softly until the dewy wetness evaporated.

Ruby's senses reeled. Thork's tantalizing sensuality ignited a flame in Ruby's midsection which hopscotched to all the sweet spots in her body that only Jack had ever touched before. Held prisoner by the magnetic pull of his drugging almost-kiss and the compelling masculine scent that was Jack's alone, Ruby leaned forward, her heartbeat playing a rapid counterpoint to the hammering pulse in Thork's neck. Ruby recognized the white-hot sexual desire she hadn't felt for months with Jack.

But Thork soon jolted her from her carnal reverie as he brushed her cheek with his warm lips, then whispered into her ear an answer to her earlier comment, " 'Twas not your bony arse I was of a mind to kiss."

At first, the insulting words didn't register on Ruby's muddled senses. She pulled away abruptly when sanity returned to jar her from her seductive trance.

Thork followed his outrageous comment with a suggestive wink. *The cad!*

The only salve to Ruby's wounded pride was the fact that Thork couldn't hide his obvious male reaction to her.

"Oh! You always were crude."

Thork cocked his head quizzically. "Your manner of speaking—'tis strange. Not Saxon. Nor Norman." A look of determination altered the thoughtful expression on his face, and he warned her, "Before this day ends, by Thor's blood, I'll know your whole story or else . . ."

He pulled her to her feet and put an end to their conversation. "Enough foolery! Too much time I have already wasted on such as you. Important business do I bring to my king. Tell me your tale . . . or tell Sigtrygg. Little difference it makes to me."

"I'll tell you, but I don't know if you'll believe me."

His face showed wary interest but nothing more.

"Thork, this is a dream," Ruby explained tentatively.

Thork stared at her, expecting more. When she remained silent, he snarled in disgust and turned to go. "That is all? 'Tis your explanation? Enough! We are off to Sigtrygg where I will be well rid of you."

"Thork, listen to me," Ruby pleaded, pulling on his arm as she realized how important his understanding might be when they got to the palace. He held himself stiffly, unyielding, but Ruby plunged ahead anyway. "Thork, I come from the future, the year nineteen hundred and ninety-four. I know, I know. It sounds unbelievable. It *is* unbelievable. But it's only a dream."

Thork's eyes widened in surprise at her pathetic story. When she didn't elaborate, he exclaimed in disgust, " 'Tis outrageous that you would try to dupe me thus. Can you be so addlewitted that a dream is the best excuse you conjure up for your presence in our land? A dream! The future!" He shot her a haughty look of disdain and laughed snidely. "Fortunate for you that you did not mention this to the harbor mob. 'Twould be food for the vultures you would be by now."

"You must believe me, Thork," Ruby urged, speaking rapidly to forestall him and make sure she got a chance to explain everything. "In the future, your name is Jack and you're my husband. In fact, we've been happily married for twenty years—that is, we *were* happily married until lately. You left me today. And that's why this all happened. At least, I think that's why it happened."

At first, Thork looked incredulous that she'd spout such an outrageous story; then a slow-burning rage flushed his cheeks.

Ruby rushed to complete her rambling explanation. "I was really upset when you left . . . to think our twenty-year marriage was over. I was crying and I wished that I was twenty years younger and could start all over again." She raised her palms in a helpless shrug. "And . . . and I guess my wish came true, except—did I already tell you?—I'm twenty years younger. Anyhow, I made my wish, but I certainly didn't expect to travel back in time more than a thousand years.

"The strange thing, though, is this seems so real; yet I know it must be a dream . . . or something." She looked up at Thork hopefully when she finished.

"Twen . . . twenty years of wedlock!" Thork sputtered. Ruby could see his impatience growing to explosive proportions. "Only twenty-nine winters have I seen my entire life. You may dream, but, I assure you, I do not. I swear by Thor's hammer Mjollnir that I am alive and standing here, not in a damned dream. Explain that. And what would make you think I would believe such a story? Do I strike you as simple?"

"Jack . . . Thork, it's the truth. We're married. We have two beautiful children. Can't you feel the bond between us?"

"Bond? Hah! Not even a thread!"

He grabbed her by the upper arms and lifted her off the ground and toward him so that her face was level with his. "You dare much, woman, to try such lies on me," he informed her through clenched teeth. "I told you an hour past and will repeat it one last time. No wife have I. Never have I seen you afore today, nor care aught if I ever see you again. Willingly, nay, joyfully, do I place your fate in another's hands afore this day fades. Fair warning, though, wench: try this tale on Sigtrygg and 'tis certain few will be able to stomach the results." The contempt in his harsh voice forbade further argument.

Thork laced the fingers of her left hand with his and pulled her along the still bustling streets, presumably toward the Norse castle. He practically smoked with anger. She knew she'd botched her story but wasn't sure how she could have done better, considering her extraordinary circumstances. But still she had to try again.

"What if I can prove it?"

He ignored her and dragged her behind him with his wide strides.

"What if I can prove it?" Ruby repeated shrilly.

Thork stopped dead in his tracks and Ruby tripped. His right hand still held her left in a rigid clasp.

"Odin, forgive me," Thork said, looking up to the sky, then back to Ruby. "I hate myself for asking, but what canst thou prove?"

"Well . . . well . . . ," Ruby stammered, not having thought that far. Then she brightened and offered, " . . . prove that you're my husband."

"Pray tell!" Thork exhaled disgustedly, then released her and put both hands on his hips.

She held her breath and asked hopefully, "Do you still

have that mole on your upper thigh?" Thork lowered his eyes but not before she saw the surprise in their blue depths.

"Moles be not uncommon. Your statement proves naught."

"No? Well, I think yours should be right about here," she said, touching his inner thigh, almost at the groin.

He looked shaken at her bold gesture and glanced from his thigh to her face questioningly. His baffled expression bespoke the accuracy of her aim. The mole was exactly where she'd said.

She continued quickly, more sure of herself now, "And you grind your teeth in your sleep. And you like honey on your bread. And peaches, in season. You're left-handed but can throw equally well with your right hand. And . . . and those long kisses I told you about earlier . . . well, you *do* like them. A lot."

Ruby put both hands on her hips and glared up at Thork, daring him to contradict her.

His eyes widened in disbelief before he exclaimed, "A sorceress! I should have known. Wait till Sigtrygg hears this. There is nothing he likes better than a witch-burning. He blames the curse of a sorceress for his muti-lated eye. Too bad I leave on the morrow for Ravenshire, my grandsire's home in Northumbria. 'Tis likely Sigtrygg will declare a holiday to celebrate your slow demise. 'Twould be a pleasure, I am thinking, to throw a twig or two on the fire myself."

"You're scaring me. I'm not a sorceress," Ruby moaned.

"What then?" Thork asked stonily. "A witch, or a spy? 'Tis one or the other, I wager. But, if you do spy, someone, most likely Ivar, has gone to much trouble to feed you information about me. For what purpose, I wonder?" He looked at her questioningly. "Either way—sorceress or spy—the deed be done. Your fate is sealed."

She started to speak, but he shook his head with a

finality that Ruby sensed wouldn't be brooked this time.

"Enough! We go to Sigtrygg."

Thork's coldness quickly extinguished any spark of hope Ruby may have been entertaining. She soon developed a stitch in her side, trying to keep up with Thork's rapid pace. She barely noticed her strange surroundings as they proceeded through the large Viking city.

Stone-cold fear chilled Ruby's blood. A numbness crept through her veins to her fingertips, down to her toes and up to her brain, which could no longer register coherent thought. This dream-turned-nightmare frightened Ruby to death, but the most worrying thing of all, Ruby began to realize, was a nagging suspicion that it might not be a dream, after all.

What if she really had traveled back in time? What if she never returned to the future—to Jack, or her sons Eddie and David, to the custom lingerie business she'd painstakingly built from a sewing hobby to a thriving mail-order catalog business?

Worst of all, if she were lost in time for good, she would never have a second chance to make things right with Jack. Desolation overwhelmed Ruby.

She and Thork climbed a slight incline to a fortified area and passed through a well-guarded gate. All around the courtyard, nobly dressed Viking men and women stepped aside to make way for them. Thork nodded to those who greeted him. Curious stares fell on Ruby.

They climbed steps to a massive timber and stone building, its wooden eaves carved with intricate Nordic symbols. King Sigtrygg's castle! At the top of the steps, Olaf stood, holding open a heavy oak door for her and his master. When she passed, Ruby glanced up at the giant and saw a gentle compassion there. For her! The terrifying realization numbed her.

The cold fear which had flowed forebodingly through her blood earlier turned into daggers of ice.

Chapter Three

Like Alice in Wonderland falling through the garden hole, Ruby felt as if she'd plunged into another world. Indeed, she had.

Olaf held Ruby back with a raised arm as they entered the great hall of the Norse palace, an enormous room whose stone walls were adorned with magnificent tapestries and primitive weaponry. Selik and Cnut joined a group of well-dressed Viking men who saluted them with hearty shouts and comradely slaps on their backs. She and Olaf followed several yards behind Thork, crushing fragrant rushes in their path. Thork strode toward a raised dais.

"Good tidings, Thork! Welcome to Jorvik."

"Well met, Sigtrygg. 'Tis good to be home."

An immense, hairy man stood and lumbered toward Thork, dwarfing his six-foot-three frame by at least a head. A wide chain belt dangled noisily at the waist of his knee-length purple tunic, which was embroidered exquisitely with gold thread and accented by three jewel-encrusted brooches at one shoulder. Soft leather cross-gartered shoes and tight black leggings covered limbs as big as tree trunks.

Despite the fine attire, the bearlike Viking was ugly as sin. Puckered and scarred skin, devoid of eyebrows and eyelashes, surrounded the one mutilated eye, which stared straight ahead endlessly. Other battle scars marred his face and neck and every area of exposed flesh. God pity Athelstan's sister, Ruby thought.

Thick gold bracelets encircling the bulging muscles of Sigtrygg's upper arms sparkled in the lamplight as he embraced Thork and drew him to an empty chair beside him, where Thork nodded to the men and women already seated there.

" 'Tis overlong we have waited for you, Thork," the king complained accusingly. "What news bring you?"

"Thank Thor for my delay and mayhap the mischievous Loki," Thork responded quickly, unbending under the king's cool question, refusing to apologize.

"More likely wenches from here to Hedeby and beyond still lay with widespread legs," the king remarked snidely with an unpleasant snort of disbelief.

Thork's face stiffened, but he wisely chose not to rise to Sigtrygg's bait.

"I bring you greetings from my father Harald, as well as an important message from King Athelstan in Wessex."

Sigtrygg and the others leaned forward with interest.

" 'Tis naught of importance the Saxon bastard could say to me," Sigtrygg bragged, taking a deep swallow from his goblet, then holding it out to a servant for a refill.

"He offers you his sister in marriage to strengthen the alliance between Wessex and Northumbria," Thork blurted out.

Stunned, the king just gaped at Thork dumbly. Then he hooted gleefully and began to laugh loud enough to raise the roof, joined by the other Vikings. When he finally stopped, tears glistened in the giant king's one good eye and he held his side.

"By Freya's tits, the Saxon cub oversteps himself! Thinks he we Vikings are so starved for females in our beds that we drool over the maidenheads of their skinny bitches?" His crude remark drew guffaws from the men and blushes from the women before he continued, "Three wives I cover now. What need have I for another?"

"Nay, Sigtrygg. Think on it. 'Twould be folly to toss this offer in the midden without further thought," Thork cautioned. "Much there is to be gained in this marriage for you."

Sigtrygg appeared ready to argue but then demanded of Thork, "Explain yourself. What profit be there for me in the bedding of an English whelp?"

"Even as the Saxons grasp our hands in treaty, they plot our downfall," Thork lashed out. "Alfred agreed to the Danelaw some fifty years ago, but, at the same time, he launched a plan to fortify towns so that no part of Wessex would be more than twenty miles from a military center."

"We know all that." Sigtrygg disregarded Thork's information with a wave of his hand.

"Know you that Alfred's son, King Edward, and now his son Athelstan continue that fortification plan? Know you that more than thirty walled military *burhs* dot the Wessex countryside and more are planned?" Thork's angry voice echoed loudly across the silent hall. He boldly looked Sigtrygg in his one good eye and informed him bravely, "I mislike being the butt of any man's joke, least of all the bloody Saxons. A favorite saying amongst them these days is, 'Edward broke the back of the Norsemen. Athelstan will cut off their balls.' "

At those words, Thork looked directly at Ruby's shirt logo and frowned, as if wondering for the first time if the

Saxons, not Ivar, had sent her. Pensively, he studied her.

"Thor's lips! You go too far!" Sigtrygg bellowed, standing to his full height like an outraged grizzly. Spittle flecked his thick, reddish beard.

"Nay, 'tis not far enough." Thork stood, facing off his outraged leader. " 'Tis time someone bespoke the truth about the weakness of your position and—"

Sigtrygg let out a bull-like yell that echoed through the hall, and his face turned purple with rage. To Thork's credit, he didn't cower.

"Dare you call me weak? You upstart get of a jackal! Be you Jomsviking or the son of King Harald matters naught to me. 'Tis tempted I am to cut out your wayward tongue."

Ruby couldn't believe her eyes and ears. King Sigtrygg with his volatile moods was clearly a dangerous man, but suddenly the king started to laugh loudly and clapped Thork so hard on the shoulder he almost fell forward.

"My friend, you do well to warn me. 'Tis certain you think only of my best interests and those of Jorvik. Come. Tell me more."

It happened so fast Ruby blinked disbelievingly. How could Sigtrygg's temper swing so rapidly back and forth? God help the man who suffered his wrath before his mood switched back. Or woman? she thought, and cringed.

As Thork and the king discussed the pros and cons of the marriage agreement, Ruby noticed the servants pulling out heavy trestles and large boards to serve as table tops. The wide wooden benches lining the walls would be used now as dining seats and later as beds for the lower classes.

The servants, probably thralls, wore undyed wool garments poncho-style with leather thongs tied at the waist—the men's and boys' were knee-length, while the women's and girls' hung down to their ankles. These contrasted sharply with the fine fabrics of the high-born Viking nobles and noblewomen. Ruby, with her sewing background, recognized the richness of the bright-colored cloth and the excellent workmanship.

The Vikings were unusually tall, even the women, and surprisingly clean, with sparkling white teeth and well-cared-for hair. Some of the males even sported intricately braided beards, an incongruous, almost feminine vanity at odds with the huge muscles knotting their arms and legs. A few of the women looked as if they could wield battle-axes themselves.

An endless stream of servants placed platter after platter of enticing food on the tables as the men and women seated themselves alternately in some type of predetermined order. The servers put enormous salt cellars midway down each of the long tables; from this came the expression of being seated "below the salt," Ruby presumed. The better the dress, the closer to the dais, Ruby observed. Olaf, apparently a favorite in this court, sat at the first table near the platform, and, to Ruby's chagrin, told her to stand behind him. When would she get to sit and eat?

Rhoda sidled up to her then, along with the other thralls who'd been with them in the boat.

"Still gotcher head, I see," Rhoda quipped.

"Yes, but I don't know for how long. That Sigtrygg is a mean man."

"I toldja, din't I?"

"When do we get to eat?"

Rhoda shrugged disinterestedly. "I be more worried if I wuz you 'bout where I sleep tonight—if you still be alive by then—'stead of whether you sup or not."

Ruby was about to answer when Olaf turned with a black look and told her to shush. Thork and Sigtrygg were ending their discussion.

"The deed be done then," Sigtrygg agreed, raising his goblet in a toast before the crowd. "We will discuss the details at the Althing to be held one month hence, but word goes out today to Athelstan. I will wed his bitch sister." With a lusty laugh and a vulgar gesture at his genitals, he added, "Mayhap this old body can still father more sons for Odin." The Viking men offered lewd rejoinders to his toast.

Ruby noticed an odd thing. Not once did Sigtrygg ask the name of the woman he would wed, whether she was young or old, how she looked, if she was willing or being coerced into this marriage. Just as Thork had predicted earlier, Sigtrygg would wed a pig if it was to his advantage.

The king and all assembled turned to the feast being laid before them. The massive serving platters held every type of fish conceivable—cod, haddock, herring, even something that looked like a snake in cream sauce. Probably eel. Ruby recognized chicken and duck but couldn't identify the other types of poultry, never having eaten pigeon or pheasant or whatever these pre-Medieval people hunted. Of course, the requisite massive haunch of beef held center stage, with its bloody juices dripping over the sides of a gigantic tray.

At the lower tables, couples shared wood trenchers using spoons or personal knives, but at the upper tables big, round slices of manchet bread were distributed, thick enough to sop up the gravy and be eaten. Rhoda whispered that the soggy, leftover manchets were given to beggars at the castle gate. Ruby felt like begging for one herself.

Innumerable side dishes accompanied the main courses, such as onions, cabbage, beets and peas, not to mention a warm, flat bread and butter, custards, pastries, honey, cheeses, nuts and a variety of fresh fruits. They drank a type of beer or ale in vast quantities from animal horns, as well as carved wood or silver goblets.

No wonder these Vikings grew so big if they ate like this everyday, Ruby thought. She wondered what they would think of the dangers of cholesterol, then decided they probably didn't live long enough to be worried about natural causes of death.

Ruby prodded Olaf in the back. "Give me something to eat, you selfish lout."

Olaf looked at her as if he couldn't believe his ears, then shook his head from side to side. "Methinks Thork has more of a handful than he realizes." He turned back to the table but not before handing her an apple and a chunk of cheese, both of which she shared with Rhoda.

As she munched, she looked up to the dais where Thork ate heartily. The pig! She caught his eye just as he held a piece of bread in his right hand and was about to put a dollop of honey on it with his left hand.

Honey! His left hand!

Ruby smiled knowingly, and Thork dropped the honey ladle like a hot iron. He turned away sullenly, not wanting to be reminded of her strange knowledge of his body and tastes.

After the servants cleared away the food and tables, the people moved closer to the dais, wanting to hear the rest of Thork's news. They cleaned their teeth with little slivers of wood. The ale and the wine flowed freely.

"So, I hear you go to Dublin, Sigtrygg," Thork said.

"Yea. My grandfather, Ivar the Boneless, may he rest now in Valhalla, bred too many children and grandchildren. My cousins and I mistrust each other sorely. I left my Dublin throne in the hands of my cousin Godfred when I came to Northumbria four years ago on my cousin King Rognvald's death, but I worry now that the power-hungry Godfred may be overfond of my domain."

Thork nodded in understanding.

"And your father?" Sigtrygg asked companionably. " 'Twas ever a man who knew the meaning of power-hungry, 'tis Harald Fairhair. No offense meant."

"None taken. My father is as he ever was. Vikings flee

Norway right and left to escape his leaden thumb. Many even settle in Iceland."

"Do you still refuse to be jarl of one of his holdings?"

"Yea. I much prefer the rigors of Jomsvikings to the pincers of his heavy-handed rule. I give him credit, though. He has united all Norway, and 'twas no mean feat."

Sigtrygg concurred. "I understand you just delivered your half-brother Haakon to Athelstan's court for fostering." He shook his head in wonder. "Your father breeds sons like a rabbit, even in his old age, and well he knows the rewards of developing good relations with the Saxons when 'tis to his benefit, even if it means using his youngest child."

"To be sure. Didst thou know of the tribute he sent to Athelstan?"

"Nay."

"My father sent a great warship with golden prow and purple sail, replete with row upon row of gilded shields."

People around the king gasped, recognizing the vast wealth betokened by the grand tribute.

Then Sigtrygg spoke the words Ruby had been dreading. "The thralls out there—are they captives you mean to keep for yourself or will you sell them?"

Uh oh!

Thork looked at Ruby and the other slaves. The closed expression on his face told her nothing of his feelings.

"They will be sold . . . except one. Methinks you must talk with her. The slave may be a spy for Ivar."

"What!" Sigtrygg roared and jumped from his seat. "You do not mean that snake Ivar sends a spy into Jorvik! Bring the man forward so I may torture his secrets from him."

"Well, 'tis not exactly a man," Thork admitted reluctantly, motioning Olaf to bring Ruby forward. "Actually, 'tis a woman."

Sigtrygg glared stonily at Thork. "Do you try to make the fool of me?"

"Nay. You must see her to believe it," Thork commented dryly.

Olaf led Ruby to the bottom of the steps where she waited until Thork and the king came down. The other Vikings in the hall moved closer, even those on the dais, all expecting to be entertained in some way. Then Olaf stepped away.

Ruby felt strangely unprotected without the giant by her side.

Sigtrygg gawked at her, astounded by her unusual appearance. " 'Tis a woman, you say?" he asked Thork skeptically.

"Yea."

The king looked her up and down, walked around her, then stood in front of her. First, he touched her short hair, fingered the fabric of her T-shirt, then reached a big paw out and grasped her breast.

Ruby started to protest but saw Olaf signal her to be still. Actually, she was too scared to move.

Sigtrygg grinned lewdly. Up close, he was even more ugly than Ruby had thought. When he smiled, she saw that one front tooth was missing. Then Sigtrygg noticed the words on Ruby's shirt and said them aloud: "Brass Balls."

"Think you Ivar sends me this message? Tell me what you think it means," Sigtrygg imperiously demanded of Thork, no longer amused by Ruby's appearance.

Ruby pinched her arm, hoping one last time that she could end this nightmare and return to the present. Not so! All she got was a sore forearm and a dark look from Thork.

" 'Tis unknown how she got here," Thork said slowly, weighing each word carefully. "Mayhap on my ship. 'Tis hard to believe, but not impossible, I wager, that Ivar would send a woman to spy."

Sigtrygg started to vent his outrage at Thork's words, but Thork held up his hand and went on, "And the message, well, methinks it implies that the men of Ivar's land have superior male parts made of metal. You know Ivar resents your wordfame and ever looks for ways to goad you into battle. What else could it mean?"

Ruby snorted and spoke for the first time, addressing Thork. "Don't be ridiculous. It was *your* son who bought this stupid T-shirt in Ocean City."

Both men pivoted to look at Ruby incredulously.

"My son! I have no sons," Thork scoffed furiously. "Missay your lies elsewhere, wench."

"*Your* son Eddie bought it last year at the shore. And forget about this Ivar stuff. I never heard of the guy."

Thork and the king exchanged puzzled looks, as if they didn't understand her words. Then Thork said heatedly, "I have no son, and most definitely none named Ed-die who spies for Ivar."

"Yes, you do. We have two sons—fifteen-year-old Eddie and twelve-year-old David."

"Says she that you have children with her?" Sigtrygg questioned Thork. "Dares she say such and—"

"He's my husband, and we have two children," Ruby interrupted the king and heard some people gasp behind her.

Sigtrygg looked at Thork questioningly. "You would jeopardize your Jomsviking to marry this . . . this man-woman?"

"*Nay!*" Thork denied vehemently. "She lies. No wife have I."

The king locked furious eyes with Ruby and challenged her: "Who are you?"

"My name is Ruby Jordan. I live in America. I come from the future, not Ivar, and—"

Sigtrygg backhanded Ruby so hard across the face her knees buckled and she dropped to the floor. Tears welled in her eyes and spilled down her cheeks at the pain. Her cheekbone felt as if it were broken. She looked to Thork for help but he just stared back at her unsympathetically.

"Stand," Sigtrygg ordered.

After she awkwardly groped her way to her feet by holding on to one of the steps, Sigtrygg warned her, "Do not ever, *ever* lie to me with tales of the future or mythical sons or marriages. Now, take it off."

"What? Take what off?"

"The shirt. Take it off."

"Do you chop off her head and send it to Ivar in the shirt?" one man shouted out from the back of the hall, and others muttered in agreement.

At first, Sigtrygg frowned at the unasked-for advice but then pouted his lips thoughtfully. "Mayhap. Mayhap." Turning back to Ruby, he repeated icily, "Take it off."

Ruby realized, with horror, that the Viking king expected her to remove her T-shirt in front of everyone. She glanced at Olaf who nodded his head up and down vigorously. It appeared she had no choice.

With a burning face, Ruby lifted the shirt over her head and slapped it into Sigtrygg's extended hand, ignoring his growl of annoyance over her lack of respect. Despite her mortification, she held her head proudly high, not bothering to hide her bra-covered breasts with her hands. She somehow knew she wouldn't be allowed to do that.

Muted murmuring and shuffling rippled through the crowd behind her while Thork and the king gaped at her black lace bra. Sigtrygg's one good eye almost bugged out, and Thork seemed to have trouble swallowing. *Humph!* Ruby thought. He'd seen her custom lingerie often enough in the past!

Reluctantly, Thork's puzzled blue eyes locked with hers. Despite her dangerous predicament, the smoldering flame in their depths ignited a tenuous fuse connecting them in some odd way and caught fire in her most secret places.

Without touching, Thork caressed her body with his eyes. Without speaking, he told her all her heart wanted to know. Ruby yearned to touch this man who was her husband and yet was not. She needed to connect with him in the most basic, intimate way known to men and women throughout the ages. Perhaps then she could satisfy this raging hunger he stirred in her. Perhaps then she could save her marriage. Perhaps then she would understand this crazy free-fall through the time warp.

Their seductive trance was broken by Olaf loudly clearing his throat. At their dazed expressions, Olaf threw back his head and hooted with laughter. "Odin's staff! You two have raised the heat in this room to a fiery pitch. Best you find a private corner soon afore you drop your braies afore one and all."

Clearly embarrassed by his intense reaction to her, Thork shook his head to clear his mind, then glared angrily at her as if she had cast a spell on him. One dark look at Olaf ended his ridicule immediately.

Then Ruby's jeans drew Sigtrygg's attention. "Take them off, too."

"Whoa! Wait a minute. Enough is enough. I don't do public stripteases." At the questioning tilt of the king's head, Ruby explained, "Public disrobing. No way!"

"Do you dare say me nay?" the king asked through gritted teeth in a voice that forbade further argument from her. He raised his hand in warning, about to strike her again.

Olaf coughed slightly, signaling her to do as the king asked.

Ruby closed her eyes wearily, wishing desperately that this sleepwalk through time would end but sensing it wouldn't—at least, not yet. She wondered if this were one of those nightmares people have where they stand naked in a roomful of clothed, laughing people. Anyway, her safest route seemed to be compliance.

"Oh, all right. But that's all."

She bent over to remove her shoes, then thought better of presenting her backside to the Viking men behind her. Instead, she sat on the bottom step and took them off.

Oh, Lord, she prayed, *please let me wake up before they kill me.* Did it hurt to be decapitated in a dream? Ruby wondered with macabre humor.

After removing the shoes, Ruby stood and defiantly faced Thork and Sigtrygg again, refusing to cower. Really, it wasn't the worst thing in the world. After all, her models paraded around in underwear at fashion shows before even larger crowds. Why should she be ashamed?

With reluctant resignation, Ruby unbuttoned her jeans and pulled the zipper down. But Sigtrygg reached out a hand and stopped her.

Was she being given a reprieve?

No such luck!

"Do that again," he demanded, awestruck.

"Do what again?"

"Open your braies again. With that *thing.*"

Ruby looked down, not understanding.

Thork pointed to her zipper, his lips twitching with suppressed laughter. "He means *that.*"

The zipper must intrigue him, Ruby surmised, realizing that, of course, zippers hadn't been invented yet. She pulled the zipper back up, then down, then up, over and over as the fascinated Sigtrygg ordered, even though she tried to tell him it was just a simple fastener.

Thork grinned in amusement at Ruby's discomfort and the king's childlike glee.

The jerk!

Finally, Ruby removed her jeans and handed them to Sigtrygg so he could play with the damn zipper ad infinitum at his leisure.

Thork's eyes traveled over Ruby's body with a familiar gleam only she would recognize, spending several long seconds on her black lace panties. Not quite a bikini style, the fairly conservative, far from transparent briefs rode below the waist to the hip line, while the sides were cut provocatively high.

Thork liked her lingerie. No question about it. He always had. And black was his favorite. Despite the danger she knew she faced, Ruby relished the moment, loving the fact that Thork shifted uncomfortably. He refused to make eye contact, however, probably fearing a recurrence of their earlier spectacle.

Ruby liked the hard body she saw when she looked down. She was still tall, about five-feet-nine, but small-boned and lean, with firm breasts, small waist, slightly rounded hips and very long legs. Definitely twentyish!

The crowd murmuring behind her and the lewd remarks from the men told her the other Vikings noticed her unusual underwear, too, even if Sigtrygg still fooled with the damn zipper. He'd probably break it with his clumsy hands, then blame her for its not working.

When Sigtrygg finally turned back to her, his one good eye narrowed suspiciously. He looked from the zipper to her and said, "What manner person are you? Mayhap you are a sorceress."

"No!" Ruby exclaimed immediately, remembering Thork's warning about Sigtrygg's aversion to witches.

"Methinks a witch-burning could be called for here," Sigtrygg said with relish.

The crowd murmured louder behind her and not in disagreement, Ruby noted ruefully. They liked the idea.

Good grief! These Vikings were as bloodthirsty as her research had shown her a few years ago when she'd done a family genealogy tracing her roots back to pre-Medieval times. She'd thought then that they were biased accounts of the heathen invaders by the cleric recorders of history. Now she wasn't so sure.

When Thork said nothing on her behalf at Sigtrygg's

question of sorcery and her possible execution, Ruby knew she was on her own. Her mind worked desperately on a plan to save herself.

Hey! That just might work.

In a final gasp for self-preservation, Ruby proclaimed audaciously, "You know, I'm a Viking, too."

"Huh?" Thork and Sigtrygg both exclaimed. And the blasted crowd started its murmuring again. But Ruby saw Olaf give her a mock salute, then smile at her with a wink of encouragement. *Geez!* She was starting to like the brute.

"Explain yourself, wench, and no more lies," Sigtrygg said, taking hold of her chin which still ached from Thork's manhandling.

"My grandfather about fifty times removed is the Viking Hrolf, first Duke of Normandy." She frowned in thought before adding, "I believe the Saxons call him Rollo."

A loud gasp at her outrageous declaration went through the hall. Thork's face reddened, and he looked as if he'd like to strangle her.

A stunned Sigtrygg questioned, "Claim you to be the granddaughter of our ally, Hrolf?"

Obviously, he hadn't heard the "fifty times removed" part. Ruby started to correct him, then remembered his admonition not to tell him she came from the future. Instead, she said, with fingers crossed for luck, "Yes, I'm a direct descendant of Gongu-hrolfr," using his full Nordic name, "The Marcher."

Ruby looked at Olaf and he nodded his approval. So far, so good.

"Know you that Hrolf and my father are allies?" a doubting Thork inquired.

Sensing that he sought to trick her, Ruby replied, "No, that's not true. Hrolf's father, Earl Rognvald of More, was Harald's best friend, but King Harald declared Hrolf an outlaw and exiled him from Norway."

Ruby's hopes soared at the uncertainty in Sigtrygg's eye, but plummeted when Thork declared vehemently, " 'Tis ridiculous! She is no more a Viking than . . . than I am a Saxon. She bloody well lies."

"Mayhap," Sigtrygg answered hesitantly, biting his bottom lip thoughtfully. Then he suddenly seemed bored with the whole subject. "What say you, Thork? You decide. Do you torture her secrets from her? Or will you decapitate her and send the head to Ivar in the garment as a warning?"

"Me?" Thork swore a blue streak and told Sigtrygg, " 'Tis my first night back in Jorvik in two years. The bloody wench is not *my* responsibility."

"Oh," Sigtrygg said smoothly, "methought she arrived on one of your ships."

" 'Tis not proven."

" 'Tis not disproven." Displeasure edged the king's voice. Sigtrygg's mood had swung again—to the down side.

Olaf stepped forward to address the king. "What if she really is kin to Hrolf? Should we not be sure? Have we not enough trouble with the Saxons without calling such a powerful man down on us? Can we afford to offend our friends?"

Right! Ruby raised thankful eyes to Olaf. Then she turned to Thork, whose thin lips reflected his irritation over Olaf's interference. She mouthed silently, "Traitor."

His jaw tightened but he said nothing. Apparently her earlier comment about his sons still rankled, as well as his unwelcome attraction to her.

Ruby vowed that Thork would pay for deserting her like this. Deserting her! Hah! Just like Jack, Ruby thought. She had no time to pursue this line of logic, though, because Sigtrygg was roaring like an angry mountain lion again.

"Quiet!" he shouted over the loud hum of dissenting voices in the hall. *"Enough!"*

When absolute silence overtook the cavernous room, he proclaimed, "The thrall's fate will be decided at the Althing next month. In the meantime, I place her in the able care of Thork Haraldsson."

Sigtrygg stared stonily at Thork, daring him to disagree.

"Guard her carefully, Thork," Sigtrygg continued, "but treat her with the respect due Hrolf's granddaughter—just in case her story be true."

Granddaughter! She'd never said "granddaughter." Oh, well! A moot point, really. Hopefully, she'd wake up before she ever had to prove her case.

She would wake up soon, wouldn't she?

People dispersed into milling groups throughout the hall, and the Viking men chugged down huge draughts of ale, Thork included. Thork's eyes pierced her over the rim of his drinking horn, warning her of a future reckoning. Then he motioned to Olaf, who handed Ruby her clothes and shoes.

"We will take the wench to your home where I yearn to see my . . ." Thork's words to Olaf trailed off as the two men exchanged guarded looks. "I will give you an hour or two to show your wife how much you have missed her," Thork continued with a lascivious grin. "Then we must return to the harbor to oversee the ships' unloading."

"Yea, if I know Selik, even now he lays betwixt a woman's thighs, 'stead of at the wharf where he should be."

Thork and Olaf both laughed.

"I must go to my grandfather's home in Northumbria on the morrow. Dar expected me weeks ago. I know you will guard the wench well until my return."

"Will you sleep at my home tonight?"

Thork hesitated. "Nay, 'twould be unwise." Again, he and Olaf shared a secret understanding with knowing nods.

"When do you return?" Olaf's face betrayed none of

his feelings about having Ruby dumped in his lap.

"Two . . . three days."

Three days! Ruby cringed at the prospect of a life without Thork, even for only a few days. "Thork, you can't abandon me like this. We must talk. You're my husband. You *really* are. Take me with you."

"In a pig's eye!"

Tears welled in Ruby's eyes at his cruel treatment. She swiped at them with the back of her hand. "Don't you care at all what happens to me?"

"Not a whit!"

The slimebucket! How could she be so attracted and repulsed by this man at the same time? Ruby wondered. "You're not at all like Jack."

"Good."

"Come to think of it, you're not even as good-looking," Ruby lied in childish petulance.

"Think you I care if I appeal to a homely chit like you? Methinks you are the runt of a low-breed litter and should have been drowned at birth like the scrawny cat you are."

"Why, you . . . you . . ."

"Lost for words, sweetling?" Thork asked as he tweaked her bottom impudently in passing. "Thor's toenails! Your silent tongue has got to be the best thing that has happened to me all day." He opened the door and called over his shoulder to Olaf with a laugh, "Good fortune, my friend. I will meet you in the courtyard after I say my farewells to Sigtrygg. Methinks I do you no favor putting her in your care."

"Friend?" Olaf grumbled. "There's naught of friendship in this chore you lay on me. More like punishment."

Thork's chuckle echoed after him as he departed, abandoning both Ruby and Olaf.

Ruby's heart ached as she watched Thork walk away. He was going to desert her. Oddly, despite the insufferable

Sandra Hill

nature of this Viking version of her husband, it felt just like Jack leaving her all over again. The pain didn't get any better the second time around.

Thork probably wasn't her husband. He *couldn't* be her husband, but Ruby felt bereft, nonetheless, when it appeared that her only link with reality would splinter with Thork's departure from Jorvik.

Seeing the disappointment on Ruby's face, Olaf warned, "Your eyes reveal your heart's leaning, little one. Best you guard your emotions better with such as Thork. Women mean little to him beyond the bed linens."

Ruby looked up at Olaf, in whose hands her fate seemed to lay now, and asked hopefully, "Did I tell you I come from the future?"

Olaf literally snarled, grabbed her forearm and pulled her toward the door.

"Tell it to my wife Gyda. She will likely bang you on the head with her cooking ladle. Perchance then we will all get some blessed relief."

Chapter Four

Ruby practically ran to keep up with Olaf's and Thork's long strides as they walked along the streets to Olaf's home. Apparently it was on the edge of the town.

She tried to ask them questions about the intriguing things she saw—the crude, thatch-covered buildings with exquisitely carved wood eaves, the pan pipes and board games being played by fair-haired children in open doorways, the craftsmen turning out fine furniture and jewelry, and everywhere a busy, industrious populace—but they either answered in monosyllables or not at all.

A sharp object rubbed the bottom of Ruby's aching foot, and she stopped. Stubbornly plopping down on a bench at the shaded side of a woodworker's shop, Ruby waited for Thork and Olaf to notice she lagged behind. It didn't take long.

"What mischief do you brew now?" Thork asked menacingly.

"No mischief. Just a stone in my shoe, a sore side and

two men who think we're in the Boston Marathon."

"Marathon?"

"Never mind."

Ruby replaced her running shoe with a sinking feeling she'd be saying that phrase a lot before this dream ended.

Thork stood with legs splayed, shifting impatiently from foot to foot. "Put on the damn shoe and stop dawdling."

"Don't be so darned cranky," Ruby muttered.

Olaf watched them both with amusement.

"Those shoes—naught would they be worth in a storm or in the midst of battle," Thork commented, disdain ringing his voice. "A sword could slice right through the fabric."

Ruby couldn't help but smile. "You're right. They wouldn't be worth much in battle, but they're great for jogging."

"Jigging? What the hell is that?"

"No, silly. I said jogging. I'll show you. Come on." Ruby took off onto the street in the direction they had been heading. It took Thork and Olaf several stunned moments before they realized she was running away from them. A few seconds later, they caught up with her. Grabbing her forearm tightly, Thork pulled her to a halt.

"Think you to escape from me? Wouldst you leave me to answer to Sigtrygg?"

"No," Ruby protested. "I was just demonstrating jogging to you. It's what people—men *and* women—do for exercise in my country." Aware of his annoyance, she goaded him by pulling her arm out of his grip and jogging around him in a circle to demonstrate.

"Thor's blood!" Thork exclaimed. "Why would people do such? Do your men not use their bodies each day in hard work or military drills? And women! 'Tis unseemly that women would run so!"

68

Ruby started to answer but knew it would be impossible. How could she explain that men in her time often worked in offices where they sat all day, that service in the military was voluntary and that the most exercise some men got was to hit a small ball with a stick on a field of grass? Or that modern women did a lot of things that would appear *unseemly* to Viking men? She shrugged.

Thork looked her over with disgust.

His cool appraisal hurt Ruby. "You don't believe we're married, do you?"

Thork made a rude, snorting sound. "Humph! Best you forget that lie. Granddaughter to Hrolf, some might believe, but marriage to me? Never!" He flashed a mocking smile at her. "Mayhap you lust after me. Verily, many women do. Perchance your hot blood caused you to follow me from your land to ours. But I never married any women, least of all the likes of you."

"Why, you egotistical chauvinist! What's wrong with me?"

Thork gave her a disdainful once-over from head to foot. "Thor's toenails, girl! You be mannish, with your short hair and bold manner. And little flesh have you on your bones—nothing to cushion a man when he sinks into your sheath. A man likes softer, more feminine women."

"I saw the look in your eyes when I stood in the hall," Ruby argued, despite her embarrassment. "You weren't immune."

"Hah! Didst thou expect anything less? Thor's blood! You raised the staffs on *every* man in Sigtrygg's hall when you removed your clothing and flaunted those scandalous undergarments." His glittering eyes assessed her frankly, reminding her he knew exactly what lay beneath her shirt and pants.

"Staffs! Flaunted!" Ruby sputtered. Then she grinned and gave him the same once-over. She knew this man inside and out. She'd learned his sexual tastes from years of practice. Who was he kidding? "You're wrong if you think I can't attract you," she challenged with her chin raised haughtily. "Or that you'd never marry me. I know more about your sexual libido, buster, than any woman alive. Would you like to make a little bet?"

"A wager?" Olaf hooted, laughing at the two of them. "Do you not see what Thork means, wench? Men make wagers, not women."

"By all the gods, I must admit, never have I met the likes of you afore." Thork shook his head in wonderment.

"Well, is it a bet?"

"Nay, I do not wager with women, especially when it is a sure win for me."

Ruby was pleased to see a speck of uncertainty in his eyes, despite his cocky words.

"Come," Olaf urged impatiently. "'Tis two years I have been gone from Jorvik and sore anxious I am to see my wife again." He jiggled his eyebrows suggestively.

After walking about a mile through the narrow city streets, they came to a less-populated area where the buildings were larger and set farther apart. They stopped before the biggest of these—wattle and daub sides with a thatch roof like the rest, but distinguished from the others by a carved oak door and eaves and immaculately cared for outbuildings. A long, clipped grassy plot led down to the river.

Suddenly the door swung open and a horde of shrilly squealing young people swarmed out—all girls—ranging in age from about five to fifteen, with every shade of red hair in the spectrum.

"Father! Father!"

"At last! At last! You came home!"

"What did you bring me?"

"How long will you stay?"

"Pick me up. Pick me up."

"Will you take me for a boat ride like you did afore?"

With one girl in each arm and the others clustered around him, hugging tightly, Olaf smiled widely, trying to answer each of their questions in turn with fatherly patience. Finally, as he put the two youngest girls on the ground gently, he said, "Girls, I would introduce you to our guest."

He motioned Ruby forward and said proudly, "Ruby, these are my daughters." One by one he pointed them out in order of size, starting with the youngest. "Tyra, Freydis, Thyri, Hild, Sigrun, Gunnha, Astrid."

Seven! He had seven daughters!

A woman standing quietly in the doorway, watching the joyous reunion of father and children, motioned to Thork and whispered something to him. He walked to the side of the building and disappeared out of sight. Then Gyda turned to her husband with a warm smile.

Olaf's pretty wife had blond braided hair wound into a coronet atop her head. About the same age as Olaf, who seemed to be in his late thirties, Gyda was short, slightly plump and feminine—definitely the womanly ideal Thork and Olaf had spoken of earlier.

"Welcome home, husband," Gyda said softly as she stepped forward.

"Good it is to be home again," Olaf responded with a wide grin and a gleam in his eye.

With a whoop, Olaf scooped Gyda into his arms and swung her in a circle, hugging her warmly. Gyda buried her face in his neck, holding on to his shoulders tightly as her skirts swung high off the ground. When she raised her misty eyes, Olaf kissed her soundly, put an arm under her knees and carried her resolutely into the house, leaving them all alone outside.

Ruby turned embarrassed eyes to the children who stood near her, hoping they hadn't heard Olaf ask his wife meaningfully, before the door closed, "Would you

71

like to see the present I have for you?"

But the girls weren't self-conscious at all. The oldest girl, Astrid, told Ruby unabashedly, "They like to welcome each other in private." There was no question the girl knew exactly what her parents were doing.

"Do you wanna see the ducks in the river?" the littlest girl, Tyra, who was about five years old, asked hopefully. When Ruby nodded, the child smiled enchantingly, showing two missing front teeth. She put a small hand in Ruby's and pulled her to the side of the house.

Ruby's heart lurched. She'd always wanted a little girl of her own, one just like the gap-toothed Tyra who innocently offered Ruby her first real welcome to this foreign land—a daughter she could pamper with frilly dresses and flowery bubble baths, a daughter who would weep with her at sad movies, share her love of sewing.

She and Jack should have had another child. That sudden thought jolted Ruby. They'd always planned to have more children, but once she'd started her lingerie business and the recession had hit the real estate market, there never seemed to be enough time. Ruby couldn't remember the last time they'd even talked about it.

Was it too late now? Was she too old? Did Jack still want more children? It was a moot point, really, unless Jack came back to her. Or if she never returned to the future.

Ruby's headache slammed back in full force. She shook her head to halt her straying thoughts.

They circled the house and walked past a well and a covered garbage cesspit, then down the cushiony slope to the river. Tyra's curious sisters followed closely behind them, like ducks themselves in their long, vividly colored dresses covered by crisp white pinafore-style aprons.

Ruby sat on a sturdy wood bench at the riverbank as Tyra reached deep in her apron pocket and pulled out a heaping handful of bread crumbs.

"Do you wanna feed the ducks?"

"Oh, yes," Ruby answered enthusiastically, noting idly how such little things made children happy. What happened to people when they became adults, that they lost this ability to savor the little gifts of life—a beautiful sunset, a laughing child, ducks waddling on a summer afternoon, the love of a good man?

Dozens of ducks soon converged on the scene. The girls laughed delightedly at the antics of the gluttonous animals who shoved each other aside in their efforts to get the food.

The girls slowly inched closer to the bench, and finally Astrid, the oldest girl, perched at the other end from Ruby and asked, "Did Father say your name was Ruby?"

Ruby smiled. "Yes. Ruby Jordan."

"Like the jewel?"

"Yes."

"Oh. Never have I heard that used as a name afore."

"Lots of girls are named after jewels in my country," Ruby explained, "like Emerald, Opal, Pearl, Garnet and Jade. But actually, I wasn't named after the jewel. My mother named me and my sister—" She never got to finish her explanation because a wild squawking commenced and Tyra came clambering quickly up the riverbank, complaining that a duck had almost bitten her, just because she held the last crust out of its reach.

"You know, Tyra, your bread crumbs remind me of a story my children used to love about a boy and girl who got lost in the forest even though they had a plan involving—can you believe it!—bread crumbs. Would you like to hear the story?"

"Yea! Yea! Yea! I love stories ever so much! Almost as much as ducks! Or puppies! Or strawberry tarts!"

"Shush, Tyra," one of her sisters said. They'd all moved closer, and it seemed Tyra wasn't the only one who loved storytelling. Some slid onto the bench beside her and others sat on the grass in front.

"The name of my story is *Hansel and Gretel*," Ruby began. "Once upon a time . . ." When she finished the beloved children's story, the girls begged her to tell it again.

"Will you be staying with us long?" Tyra asked.

"I don't know. King Sigtrygg has a foolish notion that I might be a spy for some enemy called Ivar."

"Ivar the Vicious!" several of the girls gasped simultaneously and moved away from her in horror. "A spy!"

"Actually, the king is more interested in investigating my claim of kinship with the Viking Hrolf in Normandy."

"You're related to Hrolf?" a once-again fascinated Astrid asked. "I saw him years ago in Hordaland. Massive built he was. Even taller than my father. And handsome as all the gods." She blushed then at her overexuberance.

"Girls, your mother needs your help," Olaf called from the back of the house. His daughters turned and ran up the yard to hug him once again. Ruby laughed to hear certain names mixed in their excited chatter, like Hansel, Gretel, Ivar, Hrolf and Ruby.

Olaf raised questioning eyes to Ruby after the girls went into the house by a back door. He sauntered down the yard, looking very pleased with himself, and sank down onto the bench beside her, legs outstretched, totally relaxed.

Men! They were the same throughout the ages. Give them a little love and they became putty. Out of the blue, a niggling idea crept into Ruby's mind. Maybe she should have done a lot more of that with Jack during the past year. In fact, there was no question about it.

Shelving that guilty thought to the back of her mind, Ruby turned to Olaf and said, "So, it's *that* good to be home again?"

"Better," he countered and smirked. Then he added,

"In my excitement over being home, I neglected to take precautions over you. 'Tis my good fortune you did not escape. In the future, one of my servants will guard you at all times."

"Humph! That's not necessary. Where would I go? Down to the harbor? I can see it now, me trying to stowaway on a ship bound for America. It probably isn't even discovered yet, for heaven's sake!"

Olaf shook his head at her strange words. "Ever do you persist with these far-fetched stories. Did Sigtrygg not warn you about it?"

"Yes, but I didn't think you would mind."

"That I do and especially with my children."

Olaf stood to return to the house when Ruby's attention was caught by Thork, who approached from downriver, accompanied by two small boys with fishing lines over their shoulders.

When the boys, about eight and ten years old, saw Olaf, they dashed forward, calling out his name. As the dark-haired boys got closer, Ruby's heart started beating wildly. It couldn't be possible! Oh, my God! They looked just like her sons did at that age.

Ruby jumped from the bench and ran toward them. "Eddie! David! How did you get here? I'm so happy to see you!"

Before they could react, she hugged each of them, causing their fishing catches to drop to the ground. She felt them pull away from her embrace and saw their eyes roll pleadingly toward Olaf and Thork for assistance.

She turned in bewilderment to Thork, while Olaf told the boys to come to the house with him and wash up before dinner. Both boys looked back over their shoulders at her as they walked up the hill, the older one with some hostility at her familiar embrace, the younger one with a curious longing.

"Woman, you must stop this nonsense," Thork exploded

as soon as the boys were out of sight. "You walk a fine line now between life and death. Risk alienating any more people and someone will give you a push, I wager."

"But, Thork, they're my sons . . . our sons," Ruby protested hoarsely, swiping at her eyes.

"Nay, no sons are they to you. They are orphans who live here with Olaf's family. Stop these tales at once or I will be the one to slit your lying tongue," Thork stated furiously.

Ruby glared at him defiantly. "Threaten me all you want, but I know my own sons when I see them."

His eyes burned her with their blue fire. "Wench, you have not seen enough winters to bear a ten-year-old child. And I will not have you alarming the boys or Olaf's family with such foolishness."

"Thork, I'm thirty-eight years old in my other life. I tried to explain before that—"

"I swear, on Odin's head, if you continue, I will lop your head off myself."

"There's no way in the world you can convince me that those boys aren't your sons."

"Argh!" Thork put both hands to his head and pulled his hair in frustration. Then he grabbed her by the shoulder. "Listen to me and listen well, wench. You are not to repeat those words to anyone. If you value the lives of those boys, you will accept that they are mere orphans and naught else."

Puzzled, Ruby stared at him for a moment. Then she asserted vehemently, "I don't understand, but I give my word not to betray their paternity."

He considered her pledge, then nodded. They continued walking toward the house. When they were almost there, Ruby couldn't stop herself from asking, "You claim to be unmarried. Who's the mother of the boys?"

Thork shook his head with disgust at her persistence, but, surprisingly, he answered her. "Thea, a Saxon thrall, was Eirik's mother. She died in the birthing. Asbol, a Viking princess, abandoned Tykir when he was two months old. Mayhap she still lives. I know not." He shrugged disinterestedly. "She sought a nobler marriage than I could offer, not that I had been willing."

"Why don't the boys live with you?"

Thork stopped abruptly, with his hand on the leather door strap, and stabbed her with ice-cold eyes. "Because I do not want them."

Ruby held a hand to her mouth in horror and wanted to ask more, but Thork spit out coldly, "Tell Olaf I am in the barn saddling our horses. I will wait for him out front." Then he shoved her through the door roughly.

Thork had two illegitimate sons! And he didn't want them! What kind of man was he? Jack loved his sons to distraction. This proved to Ruby, as nothing had before, that Jack and Thork must be two different people.

Ruby gave Olaf the message. He introduced her quickly to his wife before giving Gyda a quick kiss on the cheek and rushing out.

Olaf's great hall, about one hundred feet in length, had a freestanding, rectangular-shaped hearth in its center, about ten by four feet and four feet off the ground, open on all sides. It obviously served as both the heat source and the cooking fire for the household. Smoke escaped through a hole in the high ceiling.

Gyda kept an immaculate home, including the clean and fragrant rushes that covered the hard-packed dirt floor. Not a bit of clutter could be seen anywhere. The Viking household efficiently stored kitchen utensils and wooden dishes on pegs and shelves built near the fireplace, as well as hanging from the roof beams. Wooden vats and barrels holding butter, cheese, curds and milk lay open near the cooking area.

Woven cloth drapes stretched across the walls to hold out the drafts that would inevitably gust into the room during the winter. Built-in benches lined the two longer sides.

Spacious sleeping lofts were located on the second floor at either end of the room. Underneath, on the first floor, at one end there were smaller sleeping chambers, presumably for the two female and three male thralls Ruby saw working around the hall, setting up trestle tables and laying out plates and soapstone oil lamps. At the other end, a loom and spinning wheel dominated a cozy sitting area, which contained a half-dozen armed chairs, covered with soft cushions.

Eirik and Tykir played some kind of board game off to one side of the room. Although they wore the same loose trousers and handwoven cloth shirts, they'd scrubbed their faces and slicked back their too-long, wet hair. Ruby yearned to go to them, but halted at Gyda's warning look.

When Gyda finished giving directions to two female servants in the meal preparation, she told Ruby, "I bid you welcome to my home, Ruby. Tyra will show you to a guest chamber where you can refresh yourself afore dinner."

Tyra led Ruby upstairs to the small chamber which was to be her home for the time being. The plain, cell-like room had only a small pallet, a chest for storing clothing and a wood table holding a pottery pitcher and bowl filled with water, as well as a soapstone oil lamp. Two linen towels lay over a chair.

"Mother says I am not to pester you," Tyra commented, lingering in the doorway, obviously hoping Ruby would invite her to stay.

"Oh, I don't think a sugarplum like you could ever be a nuisance," Ruby stated truthfully. "You're too sweet."

Tyra flashed another of her engaging, gap-toothed smiles and asked, "How many children do you have?"

"Two boys," Ruby answered without hesitation. "Eddie and David."

"Do you miss them?"

"Very much." Ruby hadn't had much time to dwell on her sons. Her heart ached at the prospect of never seeing them again. How would they manage without her? Of course, Jack would come home, but did they think she was dead? Or what?

No! Ruby refused to think about all that now. Survival was the number one priority. After that, she'd find a way to return to the future. If that failed, then and only then would she somehow deal with her loss.

Just like she would have had to deal with her separation from Jack. Oh, Lord, was it only today that he'd left her? Or a lifetime ago?

"Will you tell me the saga of *Hansel and Gretel* again?" Tyra begged sweetly. "After dinner?"

"Of course, sweetheart . . . if it's all right with your parents. But they might not like me telling you stories."

"Nay!" Tyra said quickly. "They *love* tales ever so much. We all do."

After Tyra left, Ruby removed her clothes and washed herself all over with the linen towel and a white, unscented soap, like the kind her great-grandmother made out of wood ashes for laundry. After she dressed, Ruby went downstairs where the meal was being placed on the tables.

Olaf, who'd just returned, sat at the head of the table, with Gyda on his right and Ruby on the left. The girls sat on either side of the trestle table, and Thork's sons sat beyond them.

Olaf explained awkwardly, exchanging quick looks of embarrassment with his wife, that Thork had stayed in the city and would stop at the house in the morning before going on to his grandfather's estate. Ruby felt heartsick at the look of disappointment on Eirik and Tykir's faces. And she couldn't deny how much she missed him already herself.

Before they ate, Ruby was surprised to see everyone bow their heads.

"Thank you, Lord, for this good food . . . and for bringing husband and father home to us safely," Gyda said.

"And thank Odin and Thor, too, for our good fortune," Olaf added wryly.

Ruby's amazement at their mention of both Christian and Norse gods must have shown on her face.

"We practice both religions here," Olaf explained. "Baptism to the Christian faith is the price most Vikings pay for settling in foreign lands. Most often 'tis a political expedient, nothing more."

"Nay, husband, some of us are true converts," Gyda argued.

Informal conversation flowed throughout the dinner, plain, delicious fare including an unleavened flat bread called bannock which Ruby learned was baked daily by the Vikings. Even the children talked freely as the family caught up on all the news that had happened while Olaf was gone.

Gyda told of unexpected deaths, new babies born, marriages made and growth in the city. " 'Tis claimed there are now more than thirty thousand adults living in Jorvik. Could that be true?" Gyda asked her husband.

"Mayhap an exaggeration, but 'tis a fact the city grows like wild weeds. At least, there is still some order to the growth. I noticed as we walked from the palace that the *gate* pattern is being followed in an orderly fashion."

"Yea. We now have Coppersgate, Petergate, Andrewgate, Skeldergate, Bishopgate—"

Ruby interrupted, "What does *gate* mean? In my land, a gate is a door in a fence."

"*Gate* is a Norse word for street," Olaf explained, "'Tis how we name our roadways."

The children gave Olaf all their important news. Tyra showed off her missing teeth and told of five kittens born just last week to an aging cat which had apparently been

80

around before Olaf left on his voyage. Astrid asked shyly about the handsome Selik, which seemed to disconcert Olaf. The other girls told of talents learned, minor injuries, gossip and trifles they wanted to purchase.

Thork's sons remained silent, except to whisper among themselves. They seemed a part of, but separate from, this warm family. Lonely, Ruby thought. They were neglected, lonely children.

How could Thork be gone for two years and not spend his first night with his sons? Why did they live with Olaf's family? If Thork could not care for them himself, why not the grandfather Dar that Thork had mentioned? Something was wrong here. Ruby shook her head in confusion, determined to get to the bottom of the mystery. She yearned to help the boys but remembered Thork's warning. Later! she vowed. Later she would go to them, Ruby promised herself. She couldn't wait until Thork's return, though. She had a few choice words to deliver to him.

"Thork!" Olaf exclaimed suddenly, and everyone turned with a start to the doorway where Ruby's wayward Viking stood with wide shoulders propped against the doorjamb and arms folded across his chest, listening with amusement to the domestic conversation. "You said you would be staying at the palace tonight," Olaf accused.

In truth, Thork couldn't believe that he had returned to Olaf's house, against his better judgment. For years, he had followed a wise policy of avoiding his sons in public or in front of strangers, like Ruby. He could not let his enemies know these were the fruit of his loins. Holy Freya! His brother Eric would kill the boys in a trice to protect his accession. Or if he thought he could hurt Thork in the process.

It was Ruby's fault. She had woven her magnetic siren's web about him, and for some inexplicable reason he had felt compelled to return to Olaf's house. He made eye contact with the mysterious wench and felt an intense rush of warmth surge through him. He inhaled sharply.

Why did the man-woman affect him so? It could not be her questionable beauty. She was not uncomely, but, in truth, he knew many women more pleasing to behold, though not half so enticing. Mayhap it was the manner in which she sometimes gazed at him with her heart in her eyes, thinking he was her husband.

More likely I have been too long without a woman and must needs get my mind out of my braies, Thork berated himself. Or hers!

Involvement with this woman spelled peril, pure and simple—to her, to him, to his sons, to Olaf's family. And yet, knowing this, he had defied the warning bells in his head and come back anyway.

"Thork, what do you here?" Olaf asked. "You said I would not see you until the morn."

Thork shot a cryptic, warning glance at Olaf. He deliberately avoided looking at his sons, even as he realized sadly that the boys could not hide their joy at his unexpected return.

Gyda stood to get another plate, and Thork took her seat opposite Ruby. Everyone at the table watched him with open mouths, clearly surprised by his out-of-character behavior. Odin's ears! He should jump up right now and return to the castle where he could relieve all this pressure boiling inside him in Esle's arms.

Instead, Thork studied Ruby intensely and said in a more husky voice than he intended, "I changed my mind." Ruby's open delight at his presence disarmed him, and his fingertips drummed a tension-filled melody on the tabletop.

"Humph!" Olaf muttered under his breath, recognizing the carnal flush on Ruby's cheeks and the smoky sensuality on his friend's loosely parted lips. " 'Tis not your mind, but another part of your body, lower down, that has taken over, I wager." Olaf threw back his head and hooted with laughter at Thork's discomfort over his all-too-correct insight.

Thork flashed him a forbidding glare, and Olaf finally managed to get his mirth under control as Gyda placed goblets of ale in front of them both and a plate heaping with food at Thork's place. Thork ate ravenously as conversation resumed once again around the table.

When the others looked away, Ruby whispered, loud enough for only him to hear, "I thought you would be back at the palace screwing the Viking bimbo from the harbor."

"Screwing? Bimbo?" At first, Thork didn't understand her words. When comprehension dawned, an easy smile tipped the edges of his lips. "You mean Esle?" he asked innocently. His smile widened at the hot color that flooded the face of the sharp-tongued wench who was shifting uncomfortably now.

"Not that I care who you sleep with!" she added defiantly, and Thork felt a deep pull inside at the sure knowledge that she lied.

"Thor's balls! You have a blunt manner of speaking."

"No more blunt than those coarse Viking swear words of yours."

Thork found himself relishing this strange word sparring with Ruby. He frowned in concentration. In truth, he could not remember the last time he had cared what words came from a woman's mouth, only what she did with it. How odd!

He leaned forward across the table and told her in a warm, silky voice, "If I had more time for dalliance, wench, methinks I would enjoy you."

Ruby turned her head to the side, trying unsuccessfully to hide her ragged breaths and parted lips at his frankness. Finally, she calmed herself, but obviously couldn't control her curiosity.

"Enjoy? How?"

Sandra Hill

Thork took a deep draught of ale and set the goblet on the table with careful deliberation before speaking. "In all ways, wench." He closed his eyes for a second at the overwhelming emotion that prospect evoked. Then he opened his eyes and held hers captive, almost drowning in the greenish pools, before repeating in a husky voice, "In every way you ever imagined, and then some."

After the meal, the family moved to the sewing area to continue their conversations. They settled in comfortable chairs or sat upon the large Oriental carpet laid over the rushes. Thork surprised himself by staying.

Olaf told of their journey. They'd expected to be gone for only nine months when they'd left on a trading voyage for Thork's grandfather Dar, but weather and complications at some of the Eastern trading villages extended their trip. Olaf mentioned trading in the Danish market towns of Hedeby and Birka in Sweden, getting furs and ivory from Russia, silks and fine carpets from Turkey and spices from the Orient. He also spoke disgustedly of a long stay in Jomsborg while Thork joined his Jomsvikings on a six-month foray into enemy lands.

Thork nodded occasionally but added little to the conversation. He stared into his goblet and occasionally glanced surreptitiously over to Ruby. He forced himself not to look toward his sons who sat at the edge of the circle, painfully aware of their isolation even when he was present. It was the only way, he told himself. He had learned that lesson the hard way.

"What is this *Jomsviking?*" Ruby asked.

Olaf looked at Thork questioningly. Thork pondered how much to tell the wench. After all, there was still the possibility she spied for Ivar, or Athelstan. Finally, he replied carefully, "I have been a Jomsviking since I was fourteen. I lied and said I was eighteen. Jomsvikings are select warriors who swear oaths of loyalty to a brother-hood of Viking comrades. We vow always to think of victory, to never speak words of fear—"

"Oh, my goodness!" Ruby interrupted. "That sounds just like Jack and his positive-thinking philosophies." She told them about some ungodly things called "Coyote tapes," and, at the looks of confusion on their faces, she explained, "At one time in parts of my country, the coyotes—"

"Coyotes?" Thork interrupted.

"Wolflike animals. They posed a menace to farmers and ranchers, so the government put a bounty on them, encouraging people to kill them. Well, not only didn't they kill them off, but the stupid beasts reproduced by the thousands. Coyotes were found alive in the wild with metal traps hanging on their bodies. Some still lived minus paws or ears or despite serious wounds. The whole point was that coyotes survived, no matter what adversity."

"Sort of like Vikings," Olaf quipped, and Thork nodded.

"Are you a Jomsviking?" Ruby asked Olaf.

"Nay. They live in fortified towns where no women and only men between the ages of eighteen and fifty may dwell."

"So that's why Sigtrygg said Thork would jeopardize his Jomsviking oath by marrying." Ruby looked at Thork with new understanding.

"If I were not married, 'twould be an honor to be a Jomsviking," Olaf added. "Much revered are they by Norsemen for their bravery and ideals."

Ruby weighed the words, then commented with a little laugh, "Jomsvikings seem like a cross between mercenaries and the noble knights of King Arthur's round table."

Thork laughed spontaneously at her analogy. "Perchance you are right. I have heard tales of that Welsh lord and his men who fought the Saxons. Now you call my attention to it, mayhap there are similarities, but one big difference— Jomsvikings are mainly unmarried men, with no families." He put special emphasis on those last words, wanting her to see why her words of marriage had outraged him so.

Ruby silently pondered all he had said, looking over to Eirik and Tykir for their reactions. The stories about him engrossed the boys. Thork somehow knew that Ruby noticed the same yearning in their eyes as he did. They obviously wanted, nay, *needed,* a father. But that could not be.

When everyone seemed talked out, Olaf asked Astrid, "Will you play the lute for us?" But Tyra interrupted, "Nay, Father, we want Ruby to tell us her tale of *Hansel and Gretel* again." Olaf looked indulgently at his daughter and over to Astrid to see if her feelings were hurt, but she appeared as eager for a repeat of the saga as her sister.

The excited girls urged Ruby to tell the silly story several times. Soon they would be able to relate it themselves and undoubtedly would, Thork mused, as he watched the wench weave her strange magic around them all.

When encouraged to tell yet another story, Ruby said, "Eirik and Tykir, this story is dedicated to you two because you look just like my sons and this was their favorite story." Both boys jumped in surprise. They apparently weren't singled out for attention very often, Thork realized miserably. Ruby defiantly faced Thork, challenging him to stop her. A muscle jumped angrily in his jaw, but Thork said nothing, allowing Ruby to begin: "Once upon a time there was a boy named Pinocchio . . ."

Afterward Tyra delighted them by holding short fingers to her nose, testing. She must have told a fib recently.

"Humph!" Thork said testily to Ruby. " 'Tis a wonder *your* nose does not stretch out to here." He held a forefinger about two feet from his face. "With all the missaying you do, if noses truly grew with every lie, yours would need a sling to hold it up."

In truth, Thork marveled at her storytelling talent, surely a harmless activity. And Thork's heart tugged at Ruby's delight in the smiles she saw spreading on his sons' faces.

The Reluctant Viking

Thork knew Ruby thought of them as her own sons, impossible as that was. The boys sat spellbound, forgetful of their loneliness and other concerns. Leastways, Thork had Ruby to thank for that.

But then Thork's eyes narrowed as he saw a mischievous light glitter in the wench's eyes. What now?

"There's one more story I forgot," Ruby said, looking directly at Thork. He tried to give her silent warning that she pushed too far, but she barged ahead heedlessly, as usual.

"Once upon a time, there was a big, ugly giant named Thork and a boy named Jack who planted a magic beanstalk . . ."

Thork frowned at her teasing but let her go on as he sipped from his goblet. Later, he would get back at the wily wench for her audacious behavior.

As Ruby portrayed the giant as a bumbling, stupid oaf, his tolerance level lowered, but he couldn't protest because of the children. When Ruby lowered her voice to a deep growl, mimicking his voice exactly, and chanted, "Fee, fie, fo, fum. I smell the blood of an Englishman," the children squealed madly, repeating the refrain three times, and Thork couldn't help but smile indulgently.

She told the infuriating story three times. At the end, Ruby glanced at him hesitantly. They shared a smile that made Thork's heart thud wildly. What was the witch doing to him?

Enough was enough! Thork stood abruptly to leave for the palace but pulled Ruby aside first. He whispered in her ear, "I concede this one small battle to you, wench, but do not mistake it for aught but a skirmish. You will pay, and pay well, in the end." With that, he gave her a quick pinch on her deliciously rounded bottom and left, much pleased with her squeaky yelp of indignation.

Chapter Five

Ruby awakened to dawn light streaming through the unshuttered window in her room. Surprisingly, she'd slept soundly through the night. No dreams. No return to the future, either, she realized grimly.

Ruby used the chamber pot under her bed, next to which was stacked a neat pile of worn linen squares—the Viking equivalent of toilet paper. She'd always wondered about *that*.

Then she washed briskly with the cold water left in the pitcher on the table and dressed in the same clothes, hoping to slip out of the house for her usual early morning run. She might not be able to return to her normal life, but she hoped that adhering to some of her regular routines would put some stability in this shaky world she'd entered, keep her from going totally, over-the-edge crazy.

She tiptoed down the stairs without attracting the notice of the two thralls who already worked at the fireplace preparing the morning meal. The one named Lise ground grain into flour on a stone quern. Bodhil, the other female thrall, kneaded dough in an enormous trough and, without allowing time for leavening, rolled the batter into small loaves and placed them in long-handled, circular metal pans in the hot ashes of the fire.

Ruby slipped out the back door and did some leg bends to warm up. Then she saw Tyra walking out of the barn.

"My goodness, Tyra, what are you doing up so early? And all by yourself!"

"Nay, I am not alone. Helping Gudrod with the horses I am. And the new kittens. Mayhap you would like to see them?" she asked hopefully.

"Later, honey. Right now I'm going jogging."

"Jogging? What is that?"

"Running. It is . . ." Ruby searched for a substitute word for exercise that Tyra would understand. Failing that, she said, "Running makes me feel good."

"Oh. I like to run, too, but Mother says 'tis not comely for a girl to gallop around like a colt." Tyra giggled and added, "But sometimes I cannot help myself."

"Sweetheart, all little girls like to run. It's natural. But where I come from women do it, too."

"Really?" She gaped at Ruby in wonder. "Can I come with you?"

"Well . . . I suppose," Ruby agreed hesitantly. Since they would only be gone a short time, Ruby assumed it would be all right. They'd probably be back before the family awakened.

Ruby jogged at a slow pace so that Tyra could keep up. She tried to follow the river as much as possible and steered away from the business district.

Even this early, the industrious inhabitants of Jorvik moved about the day's business. Thralls and house-wives had already done their laundry and were laying the garments out to dry on bushes and lower tree limbs. Ruby wondered what Gyda would think of a suggestion to put up a clothesline. She didn't want to overwhelm the Vikings with her modern ideas, although a clothesline hardly counted as an amazing invention.

When they had gone as far as some farms on the outskirts of town, Tyra showed Ruby a plot of land where Olaf kept farm animals. A beautifully maintained vegetable garden occupied a large part of the site, surrounded by an orchid of apple, peach, pear and plum trees. Heavy clusters of purple grapes weighed down a grape arbor.

Olaf's family—in fact, most of the Vikings she'd seen thus far—were apparently very self-sufficient. Ruby found that domestic image hard to reconcile with her picture of Vikings as bloodthirsty villains riding the seas. Thinking of King Sigtrygg, though, Ruby concluded they were probably both.

Take Thork, for instance. No matter how noble the profession of Jomsvikings, when you got right down to it, he was a professional soldier. He killed for a living. Ruby's stomach knotted at the thought.

Ruby and Tyra sat on the grass resting as they ate an apple and a peach each and watched the cows grazing contentedly nearby. Ruby spotted a small boy peeping from behind one of the trees. She smiled. Tykir had followed them from Olaf's house.

"Tykir, come and join us," Ruby invited warmly.

At first, Tykir hesitated; then he walked forward shyly. Ruby offered him some fruit. He took the peach without hesitation and bit into it hungrily.

Like father, like son, Ruby thought.

When he finished and boyishly wiped his mouth with the sleeve of his shirt, he complimented Ruby, "You tell good stories."

"I'm glad you liked them."

"Do I really look like your little boy?"

Ruby nodded.

"Are you my mother?"

Ruby's heart lurched and almost broke at his revealing words.

"He asks everybody that question," Tyra interrupted with a disgusted snort. "The answer is ever the same. He has no mother."

Ruby knew that Tyra didn't intend to be mean, but her childish cruelty hurt Tykir, nonetheless, as evidenced by the tears that welled in his eyes. Ruby put a gentle hand on Tyra's shoulder and chastised her softly, "That's not true, Tyra. Everybody has a mother."

"I know, but—"

"No buts."

Ruby couldn't help herself then. She folded Tykir into her arms and pressed his head against her breast in comfort. Thork definitely had a lot to answer for in the neglect of this child—both children, actually.

"Perhaps we better start back now," Ruby advised. "We've been gone longer than I expected."

The three of them jogged back slowly, with the children answering all of Ruby's questions about the intriguing sights they passed. When they neared the house, Ruby saw Gudrod and an obviously furious Thork and Olaf approaching while Gyda and the girls stood outside the front door wringing their hands in worry.

"Tyra, Tykir, go into the house—immediately," Olaf ordered coldly. They both obeyed without question, although Tykir looked back over his shoulder at Ruby fearfully.

Grabbing Ruby's forearm roughly, Thork pulled Ruby toward the house. Neighbors stood outside on the street watching the spectacle.

"You don't have to drag me. I can walk."

"Yea, but will you be able to when I am done with you?" Thork's voice shook with anger.

"You wouldn't dare touch me."

"Would you like to make another wager, wench?" Thork jeered icily.

Ruby sensed he was dead serious. His fingers held her arm in a pincerlike, painful grip. She tried to shrug away unsuccessfully. Ruby tried to fathom the stormy emotions raging behind Thork's piercing eyes. What happened to the man who'd looked at her so warmly last night at the dinner table, who'd smiled at her children's stories, who'd pinched her playfully before he left? Was he as unpredictable in his moods as the volatile King Sigtrygg?

"Warned were you repeatedly about attempting to run away. And you dared involve Olaf's daughter and my son, besides!" he hissed low enough so no one could overhear.

"Don't be ridiculous. We were jogging."

"Ridiculous am I? We shall see who laughs when the whip blisters your back from head to toe."

Ruby lifted her head defiantly, but her hands shook in fear. Surely this man who resembled her gentle husband could never hurt her. She glanced sideways at his rigid profile, seeing no softening of his anger, only a tightening of his clenched jaw.

When they entered the yard, Olaf ordered Gyda to take all the children inside. "Punish Tyra and Tykir, or I will do it for you and the two will be the worse for it," he told his wife.

Gyda didn't even flinch.

"No!" Ruby protested to Olaf. "Don't harm them. They didn't do anything wrong. We just went as far as your farm. It was *my* fault."

"Nay, they know the rules. Neither is to leave this house without permission—ever!"

Then her other words seemed to sink in for Olaf and Thork.

"*The farm!* Do you know how unsafe it is for children to wander so far?" Thork exclaimed. "Our enemies abound. The Saxons, or Ivar, would love to get the hated King Harald's grandson for ransom, bastards or naught." Thork lowered his voice so that no one could overhear his acknowledgment of his sons. He raked her scornfully with his glittering blue eyes, then added, "But then, mayhap this was all part of your plan."

Thork continued to pull Ruby around the house and toward the barn, with Gudrod and Olaf trailing behind them. When they entered the dark, steamy barn, Olaf told Gudrod in a clipped voice, "Gather your belongings."

"But, master—"

"Do not dare to beg for mercy, or offer useless explanations," Olaf said icily.

Not understanding, Ruby watched as the thrall walked fearfully, but with dim resignation on his face, over to the small cubicle where he apparently slept. Just once, he looked up and cast her a look of utter hatred, obviously blaming her for his fate. Then he put his pitifully small supply of clothing and personal items in a large square cloth and pulled the four corners into a knot.

Motioning Gudrod toward the doorway, Olaf addressed Thork, "I will take the wretch to the harbor and sell him to the first slave trader I see."

Thork nodded grimly.

"No!" Ruby screamed when she realized their intent. She moved in front of the slave and held her arms out protectively. "You can't penalize Gudrod for my mistake."

"'Twas his mistake as well. Ordered he was to guard you at all times. No man shirks his duty without punishment. No man! Step back."

When Ruby refused, Thork pushed her aside roughly.

"Before I come back," Olaf called over his shoulder to Thork, "I will go to the farm and find out why Tostig was remiss in his duties. Freeman he may be, but I want to know where he was when the children idled there unsupervised."

"Unsupervised!" Ruby objected. "I was with them."

The looks of cold disdain Thork and Olaf gave her told what they thought of her supervision.

Ruby watched dolefully as Gudrod shuffled out of the barn with downcast eyes, following after Olaf.

She turned furiously on Thork. "Beast!"

"Not as beastly as I soon shall be." He shoved her toward the cubicle formerly occupied by Gudrod. Coming right behind her, he ordered, "Take off your garments. All of them."

"Wha . . . what?"

"Do not force me to repeat myself. You will not like the consequence." His blue eyes, so like her gentle husband's and yet so different, flashed fiercely with anger.

"Why?"

"Do you say me nay?" He began to advance on her into the small room which was barely big enough for one person, containing only a pallet and a chamber pot.

She backed away. "What are you going to do to me?"

Thork suddenly seemed to understand her fear of undressing before him, and his upper lip curled with disgust. "I intend to do naught to your traitorous body. You revolt me."

Ruby flinched at the scathing contempt in his voice. "Then why do you want me to take off my clothes?"

"So you do not escape, you witless wench. I will ensure that you stay in this room till I am well rid of you."

"Escape! Where would I—"

"Nay! I have listened to more than enough of your lying words. Either remove your garments, or I will return you to the palace. And, believe me, you will not relish our king's manner of treating bothersome slaves when he gets you naked."

Refusing to show Thork her terror, Ruby took off every item of clothing, even her socks and shoes, which Thork gathered in his arms, preparing to leave. Her face hot with embarrassment, she refused to cower. She wanted to cover her breasts and lower body with her hands, but, instead, raised her chin defiantly.

Thork stared at her—all of her. Unsmiling, he showed no regret or sympathy for his abominable actions. Only a muscle twitching next to his thinned lips showed any emotion on his blank face.

Through a screen of tears, Ruby looked at Thork and declared vehemently, "I hate you." Then, with a barely stifled whimper, she added in a raspy, broken voice, "I thought you were my husband. I thought you loved me."

She saw his fists clench before he spun on his heels and left, barring the door after him.

Ruby sat down on the pallet and cried endlessly for all she had lost. Jack. Her old life. Thork. All mixed together in her mind and became one.

Hours later, Ruby awakened to find herself lying face down on the bed in the dreary, windowless room. Ruby turned over and saw Gyda entering the doorway flanked by all her daughters who watched her in fascination.

She drew her knees up to her chest to cover her nakedness.

"Astrid, did you bring the bed linens?" Gyda asked.

"Yea," Astrid said and handed her mother a pile of linen cloths and a fur bed cover. She put them on the bed beside Ruby. Another daughter carried in a wooden tray with a jug of water and a piece of flat bread. Still another put a clean chamber pot in the room and took out the old one.

With a flick of her hand, Gyda motioned all the girls to leave. Gyda's voice and stern face spoke of broken trust and disappointment. Ruby couldn't let her think the worst.

"Gyda, I would never deliberately hurt Tyra . . . or Tykir. To me, Tykir is my son. And Tyra, well, she's just like the daughter I never had. I couldn't love her more if she were my own."

95

"Humph! Good intentions mean naught. Whether you are truly a spy and would kidnap our own, I cannot say. At the least, your carelessness put my child, and Thork's, in jeopardy, and that we cannot tolerate. Trusted you no longer are."

Every day after that, Gyda returned, no longer with her daughters. With silent condemnation, she would hand her a new tray of bread and water, and exchange her chamber pot for a clean one, refusing to answer her questions.

By the end of the fifth day, Ruby admitted to herself that she'd been careless, but not just in taking the children jogging without permission. She'd miscalculated the fierceness of the Vikings and the dangerous time period in which she'd landed. Because she'd seen a softer side of Thork in the panorama of Olaf's family, she'd made the mistake of thinking of him and the other Vikings as being the same as modern man.

They were not.

Later that day, Thork stood leaning against Ruby's doorjamb. He had been waiting for nigh on an hour for the sorry wench to awaken from her deep sleep. She lay sprawled on her stomach, the bed fur having fallen to the floor.

Thork could not believe he had delayed his trip to Ravenshire for five days, sending one missive after another to his grandfather making excuses for his absence. All he could think about was the maid he had imprisoned in this dismal room. Truly, she had bewitched him with her tearful words, "I thought you loved me."

Thor's blood! He loved no one, least of all a pitiful wench like her.

Still, he could no longer resist coming back to see for himself that she was well. To understand why he was so attracted to her.

He scanned her naked body. How could he have thought

her a boy? Her slender waist and rounded buttocks, her deliciously long legs were *definitely* feminine. His fingers ached to trace the flare of her hips, the hidden shadow between her legs. Holy Freya! He had to get a grip on his reckless emotions—and the hardening evidence of his arousal.

Sensing a presence in the room, Ruby glanced up to see him leaning against the doorway, watching her intently.

"How long have you been there?" she asked sleepily before the memory of his ordering her imprisonment jolted her wide awake. Suddenly aware of her nakedness, Ruby jumped, reaching for the bed linen at the foot of the bed. She pulled the linen sheet up over her bare breasts before turning angrily back to him.

Thork couldn't help but grin at her embarrassment. And, Odin's eyeballs, covering herself now was a wasted exercise. He had already got an eyeful.

"What do you want?"

"I have come to release you, to take you back to Olaf's house."

"Why? Did you decide you were wrong?"

Thork's face heated with chagrin. The wench should have been grateful for her release. "Nay. You deserved all you got and more. I was lenient with you."

"Hah! And how about Gudrod?"

Thork could have told her that he had relented and sent the slave to work in his grandfather's fields, but he refused to explain himself. Especially when he was right.

He straightened to his full height and rolled his cramped shoulders wearily. "If 'twere not for the king's uncertainty about your ties with Hrolf, you would have been sold, as well," he lied testily.

Ruby made a small wounded sound of dismay, then modestly pulled the sheet even higher over her body, slanting a condemning look at his appreciative eyes.

Ah, well! he shrugged. He had seen enough—for now.

Still, he could not reconcile his conflicting emotions concerning the odd wench. Something about the sorry female pulled at him. Some strange, unwelcome bond tied his stomach in knots and set his blood racing. He shook his head in disgust at his lackwit behavior. Bloody hell! He was dawdling like a moonstruck calf in the maid's room. Mystified, Thork studied her face and shroud-wrapped body, looking for answers she refused to give.

I thought you loved me, Ruby had cried, thinking he was her husband. Somewhere deep inside, Thork envied the man.

Thinking to soften her anger, Thork commented in a light, bantering tone, "Mayhap when your hair grows a bit and your body fattens on good Viking food, you will not be as uncomely as I first thought."

Immediately, Thork saw his mistake in teasing her. Her wide, greenish-gray eyes flickered with umbrage.

"I don't think you're funny," Ruby spit out.

"Don't get your hackles up, little cat." He stepped closer to the bed and ran a gentle finger along the edge of the sheet near the bottom of her neck where a pulse beat frantically. "Leastways, your feeble attempts at modesty are ill-timed," he said thickly. "You didst not do as much to cover yourself when you stood near bare-arsed afore the entire court."

"I was not naked," Ruby said indignantly. "I wore the lingerie I designed for my own company. My models wear it in fashion shows all the time. I was *not* naked."

"Fashion shows? Lingerie? Be that what you call those flimsy undergarments you wear? And your own business! By the saints and all the Norse gods, your stories get more and more far-fetched."

Ruby raised her head proudly and informed Thork, "My company is called Sweet Nothings. We sell custom lingerie in seventeen countries. *USA Tomorrow* magazine listed me among the top twenty up-and-coming business-women last year."

"I give you this, wench, you tell a fine tale. I could almost believe you. Almost!"

"I don't care what you believe anymore. All I want to do is go home."

"Nay! That you will not!" Thork barked. The thought of Ruby leaving caused him sudden inexplicable pain. At first he could not speak over the lump in his throat. Finally he ground out, "Never are you to leave this house without guard again. You are to do nothing without permission, not so much as a walk to the river at the end of Olaf's property. Is that understood?"

He grabbed her by the upper arms and shook her for emphasis, stopping only when the sheet slipped perilously close to the tips of her breasts. He jerked his hands back as if scalded and turned away to get his harsh breathing under control while Ruby adjusted herself once again.

"I understand, all right, but let me tell you something," Ruby asserted, rubbing her arms peevishly. "In my country, and in my time, we don't punish people unjustly. The only thing Gudrod and I were guilty of was carelessness. The crime didn't warrant the punishment."

Thork stiffened and his face flushed.

Suddenly weary of the whole sorry mess, Thork sat on the bed next to Ruby. She scuttled clumsily away from him toward the wall, clutching her sheet awkwardly. He took her right hand in his and would not let her pull it away. He twined her fingers with his, and closed his eyes briefly at the rightness and perfect fit of her small hand in his. When he opened his eyes, he gazed at her pale, apprehensive face. She no longer tried to pull her hand from his grasp. Could she feel their two pulses beating a perfect counterpoint in their embracing palms?

"I did not want to hurt you, sweetling," Thork explained

softly, "but I will not apologize for my anger where my son's endangerment is concerned. Know this, though, I take no pleasure in the punishment of women, especially not you, even though your treatment was not cruel."

Thork felt her pulse jump at the words *especially not you,* but instead of treading the dangerous waters of questioning his warm phrasing, she chose to jump on his other words. "Not cruel? Why, you bastard! You can't even apologize without being arrogant."

Thork released her fingers before he stood, but not before giving the inside of her wrist a light kiss, which caused her to inhale sharply. "'Twas not an apology I was giving you, but an explanation. If you had obeyed orders, there would have been no problem."

"Well, I'll tell you one thing, buddy, when the time is right, I *will* be returning to my home—and gladly."

The prospect of Ruby leaving—before he'd had a chance to unravel her mystery and the seductive web she'd woven around him—was untenable. But enough of attempting to placate her! "Try you to escape and ropes will bind you till my return. And keep this in mind, as well—questionable guest you may consider yourself, but 'tis more my prisoner you are. You would do best not to rile me further."

He took her back to Gyda's house then and determined to leave the city immediately and put the foolish wench from his mind.

Ruby slept that night in her own bedchamber in Gyda's house, where she was treated coolly, but with the respect due an unwelcome guest. When she woke the next morning, everyone was up, busily performing their assigned chores when Ruby walked down the steps.

"Help yourself," Gyda offered, indicating cold food laid out on a side table. Ruby put a thick slice of rare roast beef on a hunk of unleavened white bread and sipped a cup of watered mead handed her by the servant, Adeleve.

Ruby pulled a stool over to watch as Gyda and Adeleve, worked over the bubbling cauldrons on the cooking fires. Sweet aromas of peaches and strawberries and elderberries permeated the room. They would fill the flaky pastry dough being rolled by Bodhil, the other servant, on a nearby board.

Ruby commented dryly, "Knowing Thork's sweet tooth, it's too bad you couldn't put a bunch of these peach things on board ship when he goes a-Viking."

"How did you know he likes peaches?" Gyda asked in surprise.

Ruby shrugged. "He's my husband."

Gyda and Adeleve stopped working and gaped at her.

"Nay," Gyda finally said. "How could it be so?"

"No one believes me. I won't even try with you, but, I assure you, in my time we are married, and we have two sons who look identical to Eirik and Tykir."

"Your time?" a wide-eyed Gyda inquired.

"The king and Thork warned me not to talk about it anymore."

Gyda laid her wood ladle down and looked Ruby directly in the eye. "What did they tell you not to discuss?" It seemed Gyda was not quite the obedient wife she would have everyone believe.

"That I come from the future, the year nineteen hundred and ninety-four."

"Sweet Jesus!" Gyda exclaimed and made the sign of the cross three times.

Ruby smiled. "I know it's hard to believe. It's hard for me to accept. Even harder to believe is the fact that I'm twenty years older in my other life, and Jack—that's Thork's other name—and I have been married for twenty years. Well, until he left me yesterday."

Ruby blinked away the pain that that thought caused.

Gyda placed a hand on her arm and drew her to a

private spot on the other side of the room. "Tell me," Gyda encouraged.

When Ruby was done, Gyda pulled back. Of course, she didn't believe her. How could she? But she loved a good gossip, and the story Ruby told her must have beat them all.

"Where is everyone anyhow?" Ruby asked, noticing the unusual quiet in the hall.

"Tyra and Tykir muck the horse and cow stalls in the barn. Astrid and Gunnha went with their father to the harbor where he takes care of Thork's business. The others are picking vegetables and fruit with Tostig at the farm. Thork left last night." She tilted her head quizzically. "Thork stayed until he was sure you were settled in." Gyda was obviously surprised by his concern.

"Gyda, I don't think I will ever be able to forgive Thork for locking me up the way he did."

"'Twas deserved."

"What? How can you, a woman, say such cruelty is fair?"

Gyda shook her head sadly. "You still do not understand, do you? Being man or woman has naught to do with Viking law. Or with a father protecting his own. 'Tis the way of things."

"Humph! Well, how about the way Olaf and Thork sold Gudrod?"

Gyda slanted a look of surprise at her. "Sold? Nay, the stupid thrall was given a second chance. He was sent to Ravenshire, though he deserved to be sold, if you ask me."

"He wasn't sold?" Ruby asked with amazement. "I wonder why Thork didn't tell me." Ruby thought of something else then. "Gyda, you didn't beat Tyra and Tykir for going with me, did you?" Ruby asked with concern.

"Nay. At least not with a whip. But their bottoms I

warmed with the palm of my hand, and I can wield a heavy arm when need be. They did not sit comfortably for a day."

Gyda raised her chin defiantly, daring Ruby to challenge her punishment, then added, "Viking children do not misbehave without suffering the consequences. Surrounded we are by enemies. We cannot watch our young constantly. They must learn at a young age to obey all orders without question."

Ruby bit her bottom lip guiltily, realizing that her carelessness had somehow endangered the children. How would she have felt if some stranger had taken her children off without permission when they were only five and eight years old? Ruby decided that she had much to ponder.

"Can I help you?" Ruby asked then, and spent the rest of the morning in pleasant domestic duties, finally ending in the cold cellar under the house which they entered by a slanted wood door outside. Gyda displayed well-earned pride as she showed Ruby her neatly arranged shelves fairly creaking with crocks and covered wooden vats filled with pickles, vegetables, jams, honey, mead and wine. Onions and apples filled several of the bins. Salted and dried meats and vegetables hung from hooks in the ceiling.

Gyda told of her busy schedule coming up when the remainder of the summer vegetable garden and the orchard would be harvested and preserved for the coming winter.

"I get great gratification from performing these homely tasks," Gyda confided shyly, checking one of the vats of cheese for mold. "I like knowing the things I do help my family to survive, just as Olaf provides for our other needs."

Ruby smiled, trying to remember when she'd last felt like that. She was proud of her career, but this was a different kind of immediate self-satisfaction that Gyda referred to.

"It must be something like I felt when my boys were young and dependent on me to fulfill all their needs—like the way Jack and I worked *together* in the early years when we struggled just to make ends meet."

Gyda nodded, although she probably didn't understand half of what Ruby said.

Ruby paced her little room restlessly that night, unable to fall asleep in the chamber's claustrophobic heat. If only she could walk along the river until her energy burned out, she would fall into bed exhausted, too tired to dream, or worry, or think about all her problems.

Ruby felt more lonely and depressed than she had since this whole escapade started. There was no one—no one at all—she could turn to for help. And she couldn't run away from the problem, either, as she'd been escaping in her work the last two years.

Where did that thought come from? Ruby wondered.

It was true, Ruby admitted suddenly, dropping once again onto her bed. Jack may have just left her days before, but it should have been no surprise. If she were truly honest with herself, she would have to admit that she'd known for more than a year that they had serious problems. And she'd done nothing about it, except bury herself in her new company.

Ruby's sudden insight troubled her. She grimaced. How could she have been so dense? Why hadn't she done something earlier to prevent the breakup of her marriage?

The answer was all too clear. She'd wanted it all—marriage, children, a career—without conceding anything. The unrealistic ideal that women of her time raced to achieve was a myth, Ruby realized. Modern women were running in place. It was impossible for a woman—or man, for that matter—to give one hundred percent to career, marriage and family without one of them suffering.

In her selfishness, she hadn't wanted to give up any of

it. She'd pretended the problems didn't exist. Then look what happened. She'd lost it all.

Ruby put her face in her hands, but the thoughts wouldn't go away. Was Jack having these same self-recriminations? Was he sitting on the back-porch swing at the lake house missing her, remembering how good their marriage had been before it started splintering apart, bit by precious bit?

"Is something troubling you?" Gyda asked from the doorway, interrupting Ruby's painful reminiscence. "Olaf and I heard you moving around."

"Do Vikings allow divorce?" Ruby asked suddenly.

Gyda looked surprised at her question but answered, "Certainly. 'Tis not a common occurrence, but, yea, 'tis permitted."

Ruby motioned her to sit on the chair. In the dim candlelight, Gyda looked much younger with her unplaited hair hanging thick and straight down to the waist of her loose nightdress. Gyda sat silently, apparently sensing Ruby's troubled mind, waiting patiently for her to speak.

"My husband has left me. He wants a divorce," Ruby confided miserably.

Gyda's shoulders sagged wearily, and she put a hand to her forehead. "Which husband? Thork? Or the other one?"

"Jack. After twenty years of marriage, Jack left me. Well, actually, Thork left, too, in a way, when he locked me up, and now again in abandoning me here to go to his grandfather's."

"Do you really believe all these things you say?"

"Of course. Do you doubt that Jack wants a divorce?"

"No-o-o," Gyda drawled out hesitantly. "Why did this Jack leave you?"

"He said I neglected him and my sons, that I loved my career more than I loved him."

"Was he right?"

Ruby sat looking at Gyda dolefully before she whispered, "Yes. Yes, I think he was right."

Gyda took Ruby into her arms then. Ruby cried out her pain on the Viking woman's shoulder.

Chapter Six

Three days later Thork and his companions rode their horses into the side yard of Olaf's home.

Thork's brows shot up at the sight of Ruby sitting like a bloody queen in the shade of a tree near the river. A dozen giggling children surrounded her adoringly, like loyal subjects pleading for "just one more story." Ulf stood watchfully off to the side.

After dismounting, Thork handed his reins to Selik, who annoyed him with a pointed smirk in Ruby's direction before riding toward the barn. He'd already warned the hot-blooded youth to stay away from Astrid if he valued his neck. Cnut followed close behind, barely stifling a laugh.

His friends knew that Thork chafed at the abrupt interruption of a pleasant visit at his grandfather's manor and had been rubbing it in at every turn on the way back to Jorvik. The forced celibacy of his lengthy sea voyage had fueled his appreciation for the insatiable appetite of a Viking widow, Linette, who lived there, but, more than that, she'd helped him forget the troublesome wench awaiting him in Jorvik. Little did he relish being summoned back to attend a feast at Sigtrygg's court, especially when he hadn't yet tired of Linette's charms.

Hell and Valhalla! It wasn't so much the absence of Linette that rankled. There were plenty of women in Jorvik. One was much the same as the other to him and ever had been. It was the fawning atmosphere of the Norse court he abhorred.

As he approached the group of children in Olaf's yard, unnoticed thus far, Thork observed Ruby arranging the children in a line with two of the children standing in front, facing each other with linked, upraised hands. Thork's heart ached when he saw Tykir at the end of the line, watching him longingly, unable to rush to him in normal childish greeting. He followed his father's instructions well.

"I know you children will love this game because it's based on a famous Viking battle . . ."

What Viking battle? Thork wondered, furrowing his forehead.

"Anyhow, in this battle," Ruby went on with her amazing tale, "these fierce Vikings not only captured the city of London but they tore down the London Bridge to keep the Saxons from recapturing the city. Wasn't that clever?"

London Bridge? A Viking occupation of London? What mischief did the witch brew? Thork's eyebrows drew together in puzzlement. The woman truly was an enigma. To Thork's mind, women were ever simple creatures, like cats. Selfish. Little intellect. Definitely lacking in honor and loyalty. This mysterious woman did not fit the mold, and that bothered him sorely.

And she certainly looked different than she had that day he'd first seen her at the harbor. Her hair was still abysmally short and boyish, but it shone like burnished mahogany in the summer sun, accenting a flawless, creamy complexion, high cheekbones, a straight, slightly upturned nose and full, sensual lips.

Gone were the offensive shirt and braies, replaced by a soft, clinging green tunic, probably Astrid's if he was any judge of women's sizes. Every time she moved to straighten a child's arm or to position the youngsters in line, a different part of her tall, slim body was outlined—long, nay, extremely long legs, a waist his two hands itched to span, high, firm breasts, and a round bottom that invited the palm of a man's hand.

She was not beautiful—nay, far from it—but her attractive, sensual aura drew him involuntarily. Thork frowned at his gut reaction to the wench he sensed could be dangerous to his future. Thor's blood! He should have stayed in Northumbria longer—until Linette had appeased his hunger.

"London Bridge is falling down, falling down, falling down," Ruby sang while the children filed under the "bridge." She chanted merrily along until her gray-green eyes lifted and connected with his in surprise—at first with welcome, then switching to cool reserve. This woman hid much. He must be careful.

Ruby told Tyra to supervise the game and walked a short distance to where Thork stood. Tyra protested at first, wanting to go to Thork, but obeyed when Thork promised her a surprise later. He nodded imperceptibly to Tykir that he had something for him, too.

"It's about time you got back," Ruby accused him.

"What trouble do you stir now, witch?"

She assessed his figure with deliberate disdain, but Thork could see in her clear eyes, now more green than gray, that she reluctantly liked what she saw.

He grinned.

She glared.

Embarrassed, Ruby took the offensive. "I have a few

things I would like to tell you about your neglect of our sons. I can't believe—"

Thork raised a hand to halt her shrewish words.

"Do you never yield? Your refusal to heed Sigtrygg's warning, and mine, as well, about lying and the future bodes ill for your fate. We are not wed, and my sons are no one's business but mine."

"And so you take no one's advice about their suffering?"

"Suffering!" Thork slitted his eyes cynically. "Who harms them?"

"You do."

Thork threw up his hands in resignation. "Say one more word and by the sacred sword of Thor, I swear, I will—"

"What? Imprison me?" Her eyes flashed a feisty challenge.

Thork gritted his teeth, willing himself not to rise to her baiting. Finally he said stiffly, "You deserved the punishment and will get that and more if you do not change your ways. Go play your children's games now and think not of trying to escape again . . . or goading me into rage."

As Ruby turned to go, she tossed back at him over her shoulder that famous Anglo-Saxon vulgarity that even Thork in all his travels had rarely heard used by a woman.

The woman was beyond belief!

Thork grinned and shook his head. He would show the saucy tart! Reaching out a long arm, he did what he'd been dying to do ever since he had seen her bending over with the young children by the river.

He tweaked her enticing behind.

Ruby yelped and practically shot off the ground, shooting daggers at him with her fuming eyes. "How dare you?"

"I dare much, wench. And remember it well afore you try me farther."

110

"That's the second time you've done that to me," she raged. "The next time I just might do the same to you, and it won't be your backside I'll pinch. You would do well to remember *that*."

Thork threw back his head and laughed heartily at the wench's quick retort.

Ruby continued her games and stories with the children, all the while rehearsing in her mind the tirade she intended to unload on Thork once she got inside. She was disappointed, however, to learn that Thork and Olaf had gone to the harbor and that Thork would be staying at the palace while in Jorvik.

"Ruby, come quickly. We must find garments to wear tonight. We go to the palace for a feast," Astrid told her excitedly. This was the first warmth she'd shown Ruby since her punishment.

"Me?"

"Yea, the king asked specifically that you come. Father could not refuse. And I am permitted to go, too."

"Why does Sigtrygg want to see me again?" Ruby asked nervously. Even though Thork would probably be there and she might find an opportunity to discuss his sons with him, Ruby preferred to stay home. "I would rather not go."

Gyda overheard and advised sternly, "'Tis not for you to decide. We go."

The male servants brought wooden tubs for bathing while caldrons of water bubbled over the hot fires, stoked up for the occasion. When the three women had bathed, the men dumped the tubs and poured fresh water for Olaf's bath.

Upstairs in the master chamber, Gyda clucked over the several gowns she'd laid on the bed for Astrid and Ruby, first selecting, then discarding each in turn as inappropriate—too bright, too dull, too long, too worn, too tight, too loose. Ruby's expert sewing eye saw that these Viking tunic dresses were little more than two rectangles of fabric held together at the shoulder with brooch-clasped straps.

Finally Astrid selected a bright scarlet tunic, embroidered with gold thread and cinched at the waist with a belt of gold links, along with two exquisite shoulder brooches studded with blood-red stones.

Could the thread and belt be solid gold, as they appeared? And the stones! Surely not rubies!

When Astrid left the room to find Adeleve, who had a gift for fixing hair, Gyda turned to Ruby. "The green, I think," she said, holding a jade silk tunic up to Ruby. "The color brightens your eyes and calls attention away from that . . . that . . ." She pointed disgustedly at Ruby's short hair. "Let us try it on and see."

Ruby pulled on off-white, thigh-high hose, then donned a cream-colored, full-length, pleated underdress with a circular neck and long, tight sleeves to the wrist.

No underwear! Boy, could these people use some of her creations, Ruby thought. Her lips turned up in amusement. A good underdraft and a Viking woman could get a mighty chill in some private places.

Gyda helped her slip the green silk dress over her head. As in Astrid's gown, gold embroidery embellished the hem and sleeves and neck. Chunky gold, animal-shaped brooches fastened the shoulders of the open-sided garment. The twisted dragons had amber eyes. Probably worth a fortune, Ruby speculated.

"I couldn't possibly wear anything so expensive. I'd be afraid of losing them."

"Nay, be not afeard. Leastways, they belong to Thork." Gyda pointed to a small wooden chest which lay open in the corner. Ruby examined the runic letters on the box, "*Thokkr a Kistu Thasa.*" On questioning, Gyda told her the words meant "Thork owns this casket."

"Thork keeps some of his treasures here since he maintains no home of his own. He stores many others at his grandfather's, as well."

"Well, then, if they belong to Thork, I don't mind. After all, he is my husband—sort of. Besides, he owes me, after treating me so badly."

Pursing her lips, Gyda frowned at her reference to Thork as her husband. "They are only for loan, you understand."

Sure.

Next, Gyda pulled a delicate gold belt from Thork's box, which could be adjusted to size. In the center of the waist a matching dragon brooch was placed, similar to the shoulder ones, except this animal had larger amber eyes.

Elizabeth Taylor, eat your heart out, Ruby gloated. This Viking life-style might not be so bad, after all.

Meanwhile, Gyda clucked with dismay over the sorry state of Ruby's figure. "Tsk, tsk! Do you come from poor folks that could not feed you? Fair skin and bones you are." Gyda nipped and tucked quickly with thread and the precious needle she kept in a tiny cylindrical box which hung from her brooch at all times.

Ruby looked down at herself. Skin and bones? Not by a twentieth-century longshot! This slender body she now had was the modern feminine ideal, not Gyda's slightly plump, definitely curvaceous frame.

"Give you a month of good, solid Viking fare and, to be sure, we will put more padding on those bones."

Would she be here another month, for heaven's sake? And if she were, Ruby determined, she wouldn't allow these Vikings to tamper with this Raquel Welch figure she'd been fortunate enough to land in, and turn it into a Rubensesque caricature.

They rode horses to the palace, even though it was a short distance, to protect their soft leather shoes and the hems of their gowns, which trailed fashionably on the ground in back. The three females rode sideways, as was the custom—not an easy feat for Ruby, who held on to her horse's mane for dear life.

The overwhelming din of conversation and laughter from the hundreds of finely dressed men and women greeted them on entering the Norse palace. Olaf pointed out to her the parts of the building that remained of the ancient Roman city Eboracum, and those architectural touches which were clearly Nordic additions, such as the intricate carvings and runic messages on the eaves and woodwork.

"Is this feast being held for any special occasion?" Ruby asked Gyda.

"Yea. A man arrived from Athelstan with the formal marriage documents. We celebrate the official betrothal."

Ruby followed Olaf's family to a table close to the dais where Thork sat with the king and a dozen or more privileged guests. Unlike in the lower area, fine linen cloths and heavy silver graced the tables.

Resplendent in a midnight-blue tunic with silver braiding over coal-black leggings, Thork epitomized the noble Viking knight. He sipped his drink languidly, looking totally bored. Each time he raised his cup to drink, thick silver bracelets on his upper arms flashed in the reflection of oil lamps and torches scattered around the hall. A round, jewel-encrusted disc hung down to his chest from a heavy silver neck chain.

His blond hair still hung past his shoulders, but he'd pushed it behind one ear where an . . . Oh, my God! . . . an earring hung in the shape of a thunderbolt. Her husband Jack would never in a million years have worn an earring, but on Thork it fit, enhancing his masculinity, accentuating the pirate, rebel image he exuded.

Ruby wondered if she'd ever be able to talk Jack into an earring. She delighted in picturing Jack in a conservative pin-striped suit and a thunderbolt earring. She loved it!

When Thork turned his clear blue eyes on her, surprise at her appearance flickered over his face. He nodded almost imperceptibly as his steady gaze held hers for several long moments. Like his thunderbolt, a wave of warm feeling seemed to crack from him to her, nurturing the slender thread of affinity that somehow linked them.

Then Ruby noticed the woman at his side. The same bimbo from the harbor! Ruby clenched her fists at her sides and forced herself to turn away.

The banquet lasted more than three hours, with course after course of fine foods, excellent wine and hearty ale. While servants cleared the tables, people moved into clusters, waiting for the entertainment to begin. Astrid talked shyly with Selik under Olaf's watchful frown. The king and his party moved down off the dais, including the buxom blonde who hung on to Thork's arm possessively.

Jealousy ate like acid through Ruby's bloodstream, and she hated herself for it. Why should she be jealous over this Viking? He wasn't *really* her husband. Was he?

The woman reminded Ruby of someone. Oh, no! Not Dolly Parton! It would be too much of a coincidence if Thork and Jack preferred the same type of woman. Not that Jack had been serious when he spoke of looking for a woman with a Dolly Parton body. He was only teasing, Ruby told herself.

Servants arranged dozens of chairs at the bottom of the steps for the most elite. Olaf pulled her and Gyda to the edge of the crowd and lifted them both by the waist so they sat on the edge of the platform. Many people dropped onto the wide, low benches built into the sides of the hall. Other Vikings talked softly in small groups.

The entertainment began with a young Viking woman who sang a beautiful ballad, accompanied by her brother on a lute. Then a *skald,* or poet, related stories of Viking bravery in battle. His sagas told of a brave people driven from their homeland by bloody politics and overpopulation, forced to seek new lands for their families—certainly a different motivation than the bloodlust that historians claimed drove the Norsemen to go a-Viking.

One of the sagas told an interesting story about Thork's father, King Harald of Norway, and how he got the name Harald Fairhair. The *skald* started by telling of Harald's feats, the greatest of which was the unification of all Norway.

"'Tis said that his greatest success resulted from the taunt of Gyda, daughter of the King of Hordaland." Ruby looked over to Gyda to ask if she was named after this woman, but Olaf's wife was totally engrossed in the tale and didn't notice her. Ruby also cast quick peeks at Thork who sprawled, legs outstretched, in an armchair near the king, his lips curled cynically. Perhaps the story wasn't entirely true.

The *skald* claimed that Gyda refused to marry the young Harald until he united all Norway, as Gorm had done in Denmark. Harald swore never to cut or comb his hair until he achieved his purpose. It took him ten years to become high-king. After he bathed and trimmed his hair and beard, his name changed from *Harald lufa*—Harald Mop-Hair—to *Harald harfagri*—Harald Fairhair. Gyda then went willingly to his bed, joining what the *skald* described as a royal harem of wives and concubines.

"Dragon shit!" Thork's rude expletive echoed loudly through the hall, where the crowd had been following the *skald's* saga with silent appreciation.

Sigtrygg turned to Thork and asked, "Do you scoff at the *skald's* saga?"

"Yea, that I do. The end results wax true, but think you, who know my father's cunning, that the whim of a mere maid steered him ever?"

Sigtrygg thought a moment, then agreed. "'Tis right you are, Thork, but it makes for a good telling." Then he turned to the embarrassed *skald* and asked, "Know you more?"

"Yea, but naught do I know of the sagas' truth," he whined. "I only relate what has been passed on to me." The *skald* looked at Thork, wondering if he would find fault with this story, too. When Thork ignored him, staring disinterestedly into his cup, he went on.

In fine poetic detail, the man told of Ruby's ancestor Hrolf, whom Harald had declared an outlaw in Norway, despite his friendship with Hrolf's father, Rognvald, the Earl of More. The *skald* traced Hrolf's descent for eleven generations from a king called Fornjot in Finland. He droned on with his story, finally concluding, " . . . and the Frankish king, Charles the Simple, gave him the province of Normandy."

Ruby found the tale absorbing, but wished it hadn't been told. It called Sigtrygg's attention to her.

"Where's the wench that claims kinship to Hrolf?" the king demanded to know, scanning the crowd for her. "Has she been beheaded yet?"

Geez! This guy had a decapitation fixation.

Ruby tried to slide over on the platform so she'd be hidden by Olaf's massive frame. No such luck! Olaf turned and lifted her down, telling her to go forward.

Oh, great! Here we go again!

Ruby walked forward with chin high, trying to keep her knees from knocking.

"Your attire improves since last we met," the king commented snidely, seeming to forget that the last he'd seen her she hadn't been wearing much at all. Ruby wasn't about to remind him.

"Why have we not seen you at court?"

He'd apparently forgotten that he'd ordered Thork to take her away.

"I stay with Olaf's family."

Sigtrygg nodded his shaggy head, remembering now,

and looked shrewdly at Thork. "How fast did you rid yourself of the troublesome wench?" He didn't wait for an answer before turning back to Ruby. "What name do you answer to?"

"Ruby. Ruby Jordan."

"Like the gem?"

"Actually, my mother was a country music buff. She thought Ruby and Lucille . . . that's my sister . . . sounded like good country-sounding names. Of course, she was proven right when songs with those two titles later became country music legends."

The king's good eye lit up with interest. He probably didn't understand most of what she's said, except for the music part.

"You will sing for us," he declared imperiously.

"I don't sing *that* well."

Thork choked on the wine he'd been drinking, and a friend pounded him on the back to stop the fit of laughing that followed. Ruby shot him a look of disgust.

"'Tis of no importance," Sigtrygg said. "Sing."

Embarrassment flushed Ruby's face. At home she could accompany herself with chords on her son's guitar to cover her mistakes. She picked up the lute sitting on a table near the king, wondering if it would work. She strummed it a few times. Definitely not the same, but better than nothing.

"I'll try," Ruby told the king, "but don't expect much."

He said nothing but looked as if he did, in fact, expect much. What could he do? Chop off her head? Ruby quipped morbidly to herself.

"Before I start, I have to explain a few things about words you might not understand in this song. There was a famous war in my country that's referred to in this song as the Asian War. It's about a man, a brave warrior, who was injured in that war so severely that his legs are paralyzed

118

and he's lost his"—Ruby sought for the right word—"manhood."

She saw several men in the audience nod knowingly and went on, "His injuries are so severe that he expects to die soon, but still he's hurt by a young wife who wants more out of life than marriage to a handicapped man."

The room was deathly quiet. She had the Vikings' full attention.

Ruby strummed on the lute, singing hesitantly and softly at first of this poor man seeing his wife leaving him to be with another man. Whenever she sang the refrain, in a lower husky octave, where the ex-soldier begs his wife Ruby not to take her love to town, she saw smiles of appeciation dimple some of the fierce Vikings' faces and tears mist the eyes of others. Inadvertently, Ruby had chosen a song that struck a chord in the hearts of these sensitive warlords. They understood too well the price of battle, knowing it could happen to any one of them and already had to some of their comrades.

The room was totally silent when Ruby finished.

Uh oh! Did this mean head chopping time?

Ruby looked at Thork who had set his drink down and watched her intently, clearly mesmerized by her musical story. Ruby smiled at him, and a spot deep inside her moved when he smiled back. His steady, riveting gaze carried a warmth through that thin thread of magnetism that connected them, setting her blood asimmer and her heart racing. With each tension-coiled second their eyes held fast, the bond between them expanded and grew stronger.

Then the whole room burst into excited sounds of approval, and Ruby and Thork were rudely jolted from their seductive trances. King Sigtrygg stood and clapped Ruby on the back so enthusiastically she almost dropped the lute.

"Well met! Well met!" he declared. "Tomorrow you

Sandra Hill

will teach that saga to my *skald*." The storyteller didn't
look too happy at that prospect. "Now tell us the other
song-story about your sister. What is her name?"

"Lucille."

The Vikings loved this song, as well, about an adulterous wife whose husband confronts her in a barroom over
her leaving him and their four hungry children. By the
time she ended the song, the Vikings sang the refrain
along with her in deep, deep voices, chastising the flighty
Lucille for picking a fine time to leave her husband.

Ruby was a hit. The feet-stomping, beer-drinking
Vikings were country music lovers. They demanded
she sing both songs again, then asked if she knew
any others.

Only Thork didn't seem to appreciate her songs. His
mood had changed from the warm exchange of only a
few minutes ago. He grumbled coldly, "'Tis fair odd to
me that you sing such songs. I see naught to amuse in a
tale which eulogizes the ever-constant lack of loyalty in
women."

The king and a number of men howled gleefully at
Thork's words. They knew of Thork's bitter attitude
encompassing all women. In fact, they probably shared
that view.

"No, you miss the point, Thork," Ruby corrected. "The
songs speak scornfully of those *few* women who don't
appreciate a good man of honor."

What was the use of trying to defend herself with
Thork? Ruby began to think she could use a beer herself
but knew her fate might depend on keeping to the king's
good side. She racked her brain for another song and came
up with nothing.

But then she remembered two catchy songs she'd heard
playing over and over on her car radio. The Vikings
might like them because of the funny words and the
deep, deep notes required in parts. When she was done

singing Garth Brooks's "I've Got Friends in Low Places" and Hank Williams, Jr.'s "All My Rowdy Friends Are Coming Over Tonight," the roof practically lifted off the high ceiling with the raucous laughter and shouts for more. She concluded with the old Mac Davis song "Lord, It's Hard to Be Humble" and watched the burly Viking men roar with laughter, even knowing she aimed the song at them.

Thork riveted her with a strange, questioning expression. She intrigued him, as she did the other Vikings, no question of that, but there was something more on his devastatingly handsome face that Ruby couldn't quite identify. His piercing blue eyes held hers, and Ruby tried to understand what it was he was trying to tell her, to no avail. Somewhere deep inside she knew the answer, but it eluded her now. Ruby put a hand to her forehead in weary confusion.

"The wench is fair dropping with fatigue," Thork told the king, having understood her gesture immediately. "Let her go for now." Thork called the lutist and his sister back to entertain again, not waiting for Sigtrygg's answer.

Taking Ruby's arm, Thork pulled her to the side, away from the crowd, where he handed her his glass of wine. She put her lips on the rim where his had been, and drank deeply, watching him all the while, wondering at the searching look in his fathomless blue eyes.

She felt dizzy with the wave of sudden wanting that washed over her, realizing what the strange look had been on Thork's face earlier, as it was now. Jack wore that same look when he was aroused and wanted to make love. What had she said or done to touch that nerve in Thork?

"Who are you?" he whispered thickly. His eyes raked her hungrily.

"Your wife."

He shook his head negatively but asked in a hoarse, desire-ridden voice, "Would you bed with me?"

121

Ruby smiled at his blunt words. Always to the point! "Would you wed with me?"

He smiled at her quick rejoinder and shook his head, probably thinking she wasn't serious. *"I want you."* He put emphasis on each of the three words, trying to make himself clear. As if his ragged breathing and glazed eyes didn't bring the point home—loud and clear!

"I know," she whispered, laying an understanding hand on his arm. She jumped back at the jolt of sexual heat that hit her square in her womanly center with just that light touch.

A sensual smile spread on Thork's parted lips. He sensed what had happened to her, had probably felt it himself.

"You have been teasing me for days, since you first landed at the harbor, sweetling," Thork rasped out huskily. "'Tis strange this attraction I have for you. I could almost believe we have known each other afore, as you claim. Truly, you seem to know which spots to prick my desire."

A vast, inordinate pleasure swept over Ruby at his words.

"Are you a sorceress, Ruby? Have you put a spell on me?" Thork asked softly as he took her cup from her and laid it on a nearby window well. With his thumb he wiped a drop of wine from her chin. When he started to withdraw his hand to wipe it on his tunic, Ruby took hold of his thumb. The tip of her tongue peeked out, deliberately enticing him, then licked the wine off the sensitive pad, then licked again.

Thork's eyes turned dark blue as he shuddered before grabbing her by the waist, turning her back to the wall with toes barely touching the floor. He pinioned her there with his clearly aroused lower body. Expertly he moved his hips from side to side until their bodies fit together— breast to chest, womanhood to manhood.

"O-o-o-h!" Ruby sighed softly, and a low, appreciative

growl rose involuntarily from deep in Thork's throat.

Ruby shut her eyes briefly to savor the exquisite sensation. All the fine hairs on her body stood to attention, attuned to this man whose body was as familiar to her as her own.

When Thork moved back slightly, then ground himself against her—in just the right spot—Ruby gasped.

"I have shown you what I want," Thork groaned, panting through parted lips. "What do you want?"

"I think . . ." Ruby tried to speak but her voice broke with emotion. " . . . I think I'd love one of those kisses I told you about the other day."

Thork grinned wolfishly, understanding her words immediately. He lowered his lips until they almost touched hers. "How did it go? Long, slow, . . ."

When his lips finally touched hers, he moved his mouth back and forth until he shaped the kiss to his satisfaction. The kiss was as electrifying as Jack's had ever been, and more so. They kissed endlessly, never coming up for air. Ruby savored the feel of lips that matched perfectly, knowing instinctively through twenty years of practice what this man liked and needed. Her lips clung to Thork's eagerly. Ravenous, she could not seem to get enough of their sweet torture.

Finally Thork pulled back slightly and whispered, biting the edge of her bottom lip playfully, "What were the other things that man Kevin liked in his kisses? Was it . . . yes . . . deep, I think you said."

When Thork's tongue plunged through Ruby's parted lips and began a slow, rhythmic, in-and-out cadence, Ruby put her arms around Thork's neck and parted her legs slightly so she could feel him better. His manhood touched the bud of her femininity, and a shock of pleasure hit Ruby, so intense that she went limp in his arms. Thork's body spasmed in reaction. He pulled his mouth away roughly, holding her face firmly between his two hands.

So hoarsely that Ruby could barely hear him, Thork asked, his self-control obviously near the exploding point, "And the last thing this man liked in his kisses?"

"I can't think," Ruby admitted, watching smile lines crinkle Thork's eyes. But then she murmured, "I remember now. I think it was 'long, slow, deep, soft, wet kisses that last three days.' "

Thork grinned and Ruby's heart lurched, as it always did when Jack looked at her like that. There she went again, thinking of the two of them—Jack and Thork—as one.

"I don't know about the three days, but I think we can manage the next to the last one," Ruby promised shakily. "Don't you?" Playing the aggressor, she pulled his head down to hers, then wet his lips with the tip of her tongue before plunging into his mouth as he'd done to hers moments before.

Thork's low, throaty moan gave proof positive that he liked what she was doing, not to mention the increasing, delicious pressure Ruby felt below the waist.

Thork pulled away from her, passion glazing his eyes. "Truly, are you a sorceress?"

"No, just a woman."

"Will you be *my* woman this night?"

Ruby whimpered as he seduced her with a slight movement of his hips. "Oh, Thork, a part of me wants to, but—"

"Which part?" he asked with a lopsided grin, arching an eyebrow as he moved against her again.

"That's not fair," she gasped with a short laugh. "Thork, I want you, too, but I'm too old for one-night stands. I've lived with you, I mean Jack, for too many years to be satisfied with so little."

"One-night stand?"

"It means that I won't be just another notch on your bedpost, to be forgotten the next day. Unless, of course, you mean your invitation for more than one night." She looked up at him hopefully.

Thork bared his white teeth in a devastating smile. "Oh, sweetling, 'twould be more than one night, I wager, afore our appetites were sated."

No doubt about that, Ruby thought. Every inch of her skin pulsed with want of him.

Impatient, Thork asked once again, "Will you share my bed tonight?"

"Will you admit to being my husband?"

Thork tilted his head questioningly. Then his eyes stormed over as realization hit him that she wanted more from him than he was willing to give.

"Never!" Thork said vehemently, pulling back from her. Suddenly his passion turned cold. He slammed a fist into his palm angrily. "I should have known. Ever do women want something from a man. Never do they give their love unconditionally."

"That's not fair."

"'Tis the fool I am for thinking you showed honest emotion when, in fact, you sought payment for favors given. Marriage vows in exchange for your body! Hah!" His blazing eyes raked her body scornfully. "It appears you were well named after the harlot in your bloody name-song, after all."

"Thork, that's not true," Ruby cried, but he'd already turned and left. She touched her fingertips to kiss-swollen lips to stop her sobs.

Would this man ever stop hurting her?

Chapter Seven

For the next few days, thoughts of Thork tormented Ruby.
No matter what she was doing—helping Gyda to put away
summer produce, marketing with Astrid under Ulf's ever-
present surveillance, playing with the children, singing
and telling stories at Sigtrygg's court each night where
she'd gained an unwanted popularity—Ruby couldn't stop
thinking about this Viking prototype of her husband.

She should have felt guilty, having such adulterous
feelings for another man. She didn't.

The rational side of Ruby's brain told her Thork was
not her husband. The other side of her brain, however, the
one with a pipeline directly to her heart, saw no difference
between Jack and Thork.

Ruby needed to talk to Thork, but he avoided her like
the plague—rarely coming to Olaf's house and leaving
whenever she saw him in Sigtrygg's hall, usually with the
blonde she likened to Dolly Parton.

Somehow she had to convince him she came from the

future and that, for some reason known only to God, she'd
been sent to him. Then, too, Thork's sons demanded her
attention. She must convince Thork that his neglectful
behavior hurt the boys. They needed him almost as desperately as she did.

And what about Jack and her own two boys? Was Jack
sorry now that he'd left her? Did he think she'd died? She
couldn't bear to picture Eddie and David at her funeral,
having to live without a mother. But then, Jack planned
to look for another woman. He'd already told her so. As
painful as the thought of Jack with another woman was,
Ruby hoped his second wife would be a good mother for
her sons—if she didn't return.

Ruby swiped at her eyes and glanced at Gyda who'd
been chattering away while Ruby's mind wandered. A
guard, Ulf, followed close behind as they walked toward
the Norse castle.

" 'Tis a puzzle to me yet why Sigtrygg's latest mistress,
Byrnhil, would summon us. And midday, at that! 'Tis the
busiest time of the day. Leastways 'tis for honest folk."

"I don't know any more than you do. Believe me, I
would as soon stay far away from your king and his
volatile moods. I'm afraid he may behead me yet."

When they got to the palace, the empty great hall
echoed with silence. A servant escorted them to an upper
chamber where a dozen well-dressed women of Sigtrygg's
court eagerly awaited their arrival.

After the preliminary greetings, Byrnhil, a big-boned,
Amazon-like woman, whose size probably suited Sigtrygg
well, got directly to the point.

"I sat in the hall the first night you arrived and saw
those scanty underthings you wear. Could you show them
to us again, here in private?"

Ruby and Gyda exchanged looks of surprise.

"Why?" Ruby asked.

"I like nice things," the obviously vain mistress said,

127

pointing around the room where luxurious garments lay haphazardly across chairs and chests. Fine tapestries adorned the stone walls and a Persian carpet hid a portion of the rush-covered floor. "Also, I saw the look in some of our men's eyes when you disrobed. Mayhap such garb would suit me, as well."

"I guess it would be all right," Ruby said hesitantly. "I own a business that makes fine lingerie, you know."

Byrnhil and her ladies clapped their hands in delight.

"Wonderful," Brynhil declared. "You can make some for me. We will raid Sigtrygg's treasure room for fabrics."

When Ruby modeled her black silk and lace panties and bra for the ladies, they oohed and aahed, touching the fine lace, asking what other fabrics could be used and whether different styles would suit.

"Why are your legs so prickly?" one lady asked with distaste.

"I haven't shaved in two weeks." Ruby grimaced.

"You shave your legs? Why? What is your meaning?"

"In my country, most women shave their legs up to the top of their thighs. Some even shave a bikini line," Ruby explained, demonstrating with a slash of her hands.

"Oh!" several of them gasped. "Does it not hurt?"

"Not at all—when you use soap lather and a sharp blade. And the legs feel as smooth as silk."

The skeptical women questioned the wisdom of such a habit, especially when Ruby told them it had to be repeated every other day.

The treasure room overflowed with bolts of fabrics, laces, braiding and threads from all over the world, in every color imaginable. She'd known the Vikings' reputation as traders but never had she imagined such fine taste.

Realizing that paper was at a premium, Ruby pulled aside a bolt of stiff white fabric to use for patterns. She restrained the women from being too greedy and selected only a half-dozen silk fabrics—black, bright red, green, white and two shades of blue—along with matching trims. She had an especially hard time convincing Byrnhil that wool would not be a good choice for underwear, even for winter.

"I can only work on one set today," Ruby asserted. "Perhaps if the others watch carefully, they'll be able to make their own patterns."

Without hesitation or modesty, Byrnhil stripped to the buff and stepped forward to the middle of the room. The woman's magnificent body rivaled the finest female athletes Ruby ever seen, and she told her so. "What do you do for exercise? Do you ever jog?" Ruby had to explain jogging then and was pleased at Byrnhil's unfeigned interest.

"In Dublin, I practiced for battle with my brothers. Twice have I gone a-Viking with them." She beamed proudly. " 'Tis harder here. Sigtrygg forbids my joining his men on the practice field. Afeard he is that I will best his men with the short sword, I wager."

She added slyly, "Little does he know I take my servant Hedin to the outskirts of the city where I make him train with me." Then she advised Ruby, "A woman must protect her own interests."

Tell me about it!

"Mayhap I will join you in this jogging one day."

"Not if Olaf has anything to say about it! He's forbidden my jogging."

Ruby wasn't about to risk more punishment, even to satisfy the whim of Sigtrygg's mistress. She told Byrnhil about the jogging episode.

"Many times have I been locked in my chamber," Byrnhil boasted. "Sigtrygg even takes a hand to me occasionally. 'Tis naught, imprisonment or a beating, unless a bone be broken or the face marred. That I will never abide."

Sandra Hill

Ruby used ribbons to take the place of hooks and eyes on the bra and of elastic at the gathered waistband and legs of the panties. After three hours of measuring, cutting and sewing, Byrnhil stood resplendent in flame-red bikini pants trimmed with black lace. The bra, also of red silk, teased the eye with peek-a-boo black lace in strategic places.

Byrnhil pirouetted in front of a large sheet of framed polished metal, proclaiming Ruby's creation a huge success. "You will make me a dozen more of these garments tomorrow," Byrnhil directed two seamstresses at the edge of the room.

Byrnhil walked over to a lacquered Oriental chest in the corner and dug deep, tossing aside one object after another before she found what she wanted. Returning to Ruby, she handed her an emerald the size of an almond, hanging from a fine gold chain. "With my thanks."

"Oh, my goodness! I couldn't accept this. It . . . it was my pleasure to make the lingerie for you." But Gyda nodded her approval, and Ruby accepted the priceless gem. On the way home, Gyda and Ruby giggled like young girls over their strange afternoon.

"I must thank you for this, Ruby—never have I been invited to the palace by any of the royal misses or mistresses."

"It seems a dubious honor to me."

Gyda smiled, their earlier difficulties forgotten for the moment. Then she sheepishly asked, "Do you think you could show me how to make such garments for myself?"

Ruby broke into a fit of laughter, and Gyda reddened.

" 'Twould be foolish I would look in such garb, is that not so?" Gyda peeked up at her shyly.

"Of course not, Gyda. I know just the design that would be perfect for you. I laughed because of my ludicrous situation. Here I am in a strange country, worried about keeping my head on my shoulders, and still I'm drumming up business for myself. My husband Jack would say my priorities are out of kilter, as usual."

" 'Tis hard for you, is it not," Gyda asked kindly, "being away from your family? I know you have your own business and could probably start another one here with no trouble, but family—well, that is everything, is it not?"

Ruby thought about Gyda's words, then offered hesitatingly, "In my country, women are liberated. They believe that no woman should be defined by a man—or by the children she bears. She should have her own identity."

"I don't understand."

"Women used to feel that their goal in life was to get married and have children. Now they're free from that bondage. Many women *choose* not to have a man in their lives, and some married couples *choose* not to have children—ever."

"Well, ne'er have I heard such ridiculous nonsense in all my life! Of course, each woman has her own identity. When Olaf goes a-Viking or trading with Thork, I handle all his business affairs. I can supervise the unloading of a ship, keep accurate accounts, run the farm and home, but when my husband returns, I gladly defer to him the role of head of our household."

"Haven't you ever resented giving up that authority?"

"Nay. A man needs to feel he is taking care of his wife and children. If a woman wants to pursue some talent or even own a business, that would be acceptable, as long as it did naught to interfere in his role as provider and head of the family unit. Surely it is so in every country. I cannot imagine otherwise."

Ruby thought about her words before admitting, "We've made tremendous gains for women's rights in my country, but perhaps we've made some mistakes in our haste."

"Forsooth! What glory could there ever be in a woman acting the man, of carrying that burdensome job all the time? What woman could live with herself if she makes her man feels less than a man?"

What woman, indeed!

"She may as well cut off his male parts, like that song you sing about the man wounded in the Asian War." Gyda pondered a moment and then turned abruptly to Ruby, her forehead creased in concentration. "Is that why your husband left you? Did you make him feel less the man?"

Ruby closed her eyes wearily. When she opened them, she looked at Gyda bleakly. "I think so. Honest to God, without thinking, that's just what I did."

With a heavy heart, Ruby entered the front door of Olaf's home. She stopped suddenly. Thork sat at the table with his two sons playing the Viking board game Hnefatafl, similar to checkers. They laughed and joked and acted like any normal father and sons.

What was going on here?

When Thork looked up and saw Ruby standing in the doorway, his heart skipped a beat. For the love of Freya! After dozens of battles, endless women, so many he had lost count years ago, his stupid damn heart jumped at the sight of a lackwitted, skinny woman with boy-hair and the attitude of a shrew.

It was that kiss! Thork couldn't forget the delicious, bone-melting, soul-shattering kiss. Nor his anger over Ruby's refusal to follow through on the promise inherent in such a kiss. But he blamed himself, as well. He never should have allowed the kiss to happen. He had been lax. Just like today. He should not be here. Thork could not let anyone know that Eirik and Tykir were his sons. It was too dangerous. It would be so easy for his enemies to use the information against him.

Thork stood and signaled silently to the boys. They understood that he could not stay when a stranger was about. At least, he thought they understood. Sometimes when he caught a hurt look in their eyes, he wondered if he should not follow his only other alternative—to take his sons on a ship and disappear to some faraway country, mayhap even that Godforsaken Iceland where so many Vikings fled of late.

"Don't you even think it!" Ruby told Thork as she stomped up to him, placed a palm on his chest and pushed him back down into the chair. "You're not leaving here until we've had a chance to talk."

"Do you give me orders, wench?" A smile twitched the corners of Thork's lips, despite his apparent disbelief over her nerve in pushing him around.

"You bet I do! I'm so mad I could spit nickels."

"Nickels?"

"It's not important. Suffice it to say, I've had enough of your avoiding me."

Eirik and Tykir giggled at the sight of their fierce father being bullied by a woman.

"Do you seek my company, sweetling? Wouldst you try my charms, after all? I had not thought my wordfame had spread so far."

"Wordfame? Charms?" When understanding dawned, Ruby spurted out, "Why, you insufferable slime-sucking frog!"

"Frog?" Thork croaked out on a choked laugh.

"Yes, frog! Leave it to me to land in the dream of a lifetime where I get the frog instead of the prince."

Thork grinned insufferably, probably not even understanding what she meant.

Ruby clenched her fists tightly to get her emotions under control. Then she turned back to him, calmly. "I want to talk to you about our sons."

They both glanced immediately to Eirik and Tykir who stared at them, wide-eyed and wide-eared.

"Leave," Thork ordered his sons. "We will talk afore I depart."

"Will you stay for dinner, Father, now that Ruby knows?" Tykir pleaded.

Thork scrutinized Ruby speculatively.

She understood little—only that she wasn't supposed to be aware that a relationship existed between the father and sons. Why?

"Mayhap."

"Don't be ridiculous. Stay. I'm not going to spoil your little charade."

When the boys left, Thork motioned Ruby toward Gyda's private solar. Everyone else had conveniently disappeared.

"Afore you think of chastising me again," Thork warned, "not that you have any right to do so, let me assure you this is not a charade. 'Tis important no one knows I cherish my sons."

Cherish? Ruby's heart warmed suddenly toward her Viking "husband." Perhaps she'd misjudged him.

Thork continued brusquely, "Much trouble have Olaf and I gone to in the past ten years to create an image that one word from you could ruin."

"Why? Why must people think they aren't your sons?"

" 'Tis not for you to know," Thork replied stubbornly.

"Really! I think you're being overly dramatic."

"Dramatic, am I?" Thork leaned his handsome face close to her, almost nose to nose, and jabbed her pointedly in the chest for emphasis. "My enemies murdered Eirik's mother, Thea, shortly after his birth. He only escaped death himself because an old midwife in attendance switched babes. The poor bonder's son was not so fortunate."

"I thought Eirik's mother died in childbirth," Ruby gasped.

Thork dismissed that explanation as nonsense with a wave of his hand. " 'Tis the story we passed about."

"I don't understand any of this. Why can't you live as a family with your sons?"

" 'Tis not for you to understand. Just stop your bloody interfering." He held her eyes stonily until he was sure he'd made himself clear.

Finally, Ruby's confused mind accepted all that Thork had told her. "I want to help."

"Naught do we need of you except silence. Think you that is a possibility?"

Affronted, Ruby stated, "I would never do anything to hurt those boys." *Nor you, for that matter, not that you deserve it.* "They remind me of my own sons. Eirik and Tykir probably satisfy some maternal need in me."

"Satisfy your needs elsewhere, wench," Thork ordered flatly. Then he stepped away and sat down, directing puzzled blue eyes at her. "When first we met, you said your husband left you. Why? Did he take your sons with him?"

Ruby sat down, as well. "No, he would never take Eddie and David away from me." How could she explain the complicated mess their marriage had become? She couldn't. Not in a few words. And so she didn't try. Instead, she tried to change the subject by teasing, "Perhaps I was too much for him," and jiggled her eyebrows provocatively.

Thork leaned back in Olaf's comfortable chair and smiled languorously. "If you kissed him the way you did me, I doubt you not. Do not think I have forgotten that kiss of yours. You have a knack for turning a man's bones to honey."

A compliment from Thork? That was a first. Ruby felt an annoying blush spread across her cheeks and down her neck. That's probably why he said it, just to fluster her.

"Unlike your husband, though," Thork went on, "I doubt you would be too much for me. Well-matched I suspect we would be." An infuriating smile of supreme self-confidence spread across his face, and his blue eyes glittered with amusement.

"Your arrogance knows no bounds," Ruby sputtered, rising from Gyda's chair to exit the room before she embarrassed herself by hopping into his arms, as she wanted to do. To her chagrin, he pinched her behind as she turned her back on him.

"Will you stop doing that?" she snapped, rubbing her bottom.

"Just checking to see if it still fit in the palm of my hand," Thork replied in mock innocence.

Ruby glared at him.

"It does." Laughing, he left the room before she could say more, but he did get in a final jab. "I wonder if other body parts fit as well."

Thork stayed for the evening meal, at which Gyda regaled the family with an account of the afternoon's activities in Byrnhil's boudoir. They howled with laughter, even the children, when Gyda described a stark-naked Byrnhil demanding that Ruby make her a set of flame-red underwear.

"Seems likely Sigtrygg will be in a good mood tonight," Olaf said dryly. Then, tongue-in-cheek, he teased, "Methinks my Gyda might look good in one of those outfits, too."

Gyda lifted her chin defiantly and told him, "We have already made plans to do just that."

Olaf's mouth dropped open in surprise, then he laughed heartily. "For me, you would do that, Gyda? 'Tis not necessary. I like you well enough in the raiment your God gave you."

Gyda blushed attractively and stood up to her husband's ribald teasing, " 'Tis for myself I do this. A woman likes to wear nice things for herself, as well." Then she looked at Ruby meaningfully and added, "After all, a woman has her own identity."

Thork and Olaf hooted with laughter at Gyda's defiant speech, causing her to blush.

"Shut up, you male chauvinist pigs," Ruby said.

"I agree. Shut up, you male chauvinist hogs," Gyda mimicked.

Thork and Olaf howled even louder. Ruby couldn't help herself from giggling.

After the pleasant meal, they all adjourned to Gyda's solar. Surprisingly, Thork joined them. Ruby held back from the others slightly and said to Thork, "I thought you'd be off to seduce young Dolly Parton."

"Who?"

"The lady with the big . . ." Ruby held her two hands about a foot in front of her chest to demonstrate.

Thork grinned and shook his head at the unbelievable things Ruby came out with. She surprised herself sometimes. She'd never been this bold in her other life.

"You mean Esle? She visits her family. Mayhap later." His eyes twinkled at Ruby's apparent jealousy.

Ruby sniffed contemptuously.

"Lest you care to take her place. Seems I made that offer once afore." Thork teased her, she knew that. And yet his expression held a questioning, almost hopeful, lilt.

"No, thank you. Unless, of course, you've reconsidered my counter offer."

"Persistent, you are!" He shook his head in exasperation. "Nay, methinks the bedding would not be worth the price of a wedding."

"Methinks you'll never know," Ruby retorted with a quick toss of her head. But, oh, how tempted she was to take this man to her bed and make love to him until his arrogance oozed out his ears. She could do it, too, she told herself.

Thork stayed through Astrid's playing of the lute,

Gunnhild's exquisite singing and finally Ruby's story-telling. Oddly silent, he sipped his mulled wine, with Eirik and Tykir at either shoulder. He smiled faintly with amusement at Ruby's children's stories but snorted disgustedly at her caricatural retelling of "Thork and the Beanstalk."

"I think that might make great entertainment for the Althing," Ruby said with a straight face.

"By Thor's hammer! Dare you such," Thork warned Ruby, "and you will spend the rest of your life locked in the barn."

All turned suddenly quiet then, remembering Ruby's and Gudrod's irresponsible actions. Sometimes, in moments like this, Ruby forgot that these sometimes violent people were not really her friends. Even Thork.

She and the boys walked Thork to the barn for his horse. Eirik and Tykir went inside to help Ulf saddle the mare while Ruby and Thork waited, leaning against the side of the building.

"Are you sure you will not reconsider and come back with me?" He ran a finger seductively up her bare arm and left a trail of sensitized goosebumps in its wake.

She shook her head regretfully. "I can't."

Thork touched the ends of her hair with his fingertips. "Does your husband like your hair thus?" His tone of voice betrayed his lack of appreciation for the short hair style.

"He doesn't mind it. It's much easier to care for, especially since I have to get up so early for work each morning." Suddenly she remembered something she hadn't thought of for years and, without thinking, blurted it out, "Actually, when we were first married, I had long hair, down past my shoulders. Jack loved it. He used to tell me to never cut it."

That was so long ago. How could she have forgotten?

Thork cocked his head quizzically. "And you cut it anyway?" He clearly did not understand. "Did you not love him? Did you not want to please him?" Meanwhile, he held both of her hands in his, with his thumbs making sensuous circles on her wrists. Her heart beat so wildly, and her blood pounded so hard, she could barely think.

"It was such a little thing," she whispered, moving closer to his warm chest. "I'm sure it didn't matter much to Jack."

Thork said nothing, but he obviously didn't believe her. She wasn't so sure herself.

His roving hands had moved to her waist and were slowly inching up to the undersides of her breasts. Ruby held her breath, her body tingling everywhere he touched. When he stopped just short of his goal, Ruby exhaled slowly before asking shakily, "Thork, do you trust me now, or do you still think I might be a spy—that I have some ulterior motive for being in Jorvik?"

"Never have I truly thought you a spy, but I cannot trust you completely, either. There are too many unanswered questions, and leastways I have learned the hard way to trust no man—or woman—completely. Too much risk weighs in the balance to allow you free rein."

Ruby's shoulders slumped in weary resignation, and Thork put a forefinger under her chin, lifting her face so she would have to look at him.

"My opinion matters naught," he continued. "Besides, I will be gone to Jomsborg once the Althing completes its business next month."

"And how long will you be gone?"

Thork shrugged uncertainly. "Two years."

"Two years!" Ruby's heart felt like a lead weight in her chest, and her next words could barely pass the huge lump in her throat. "Why so long?"

"Two years have I devoted to my grandfather's affairs, but I took a Jomsviking oath long ago. Honor demands my immediate return."

"What honor is there in killing?"

139

Thork's shoulders stiffened. "A man does what he must to protect his people."

"Have you killed many people?"

"Yea, that I have. More than I can count."

"And you choose this life-style?" Ruby shook her head, unable to understand Thork's harsh attitude.

"Sometimes men have no choices." A tense muscle twitched in the hard plane of Thork's cheek.

They could hear the children getting closer, and Thork quickly bent down to her. "Will you favor me with a kiss to comfort me on the long ride back to the castle?"

"Not so long," Ruby countered with a smile, putting aside her concerns over Thork's ruthless nature. She could no more stop herself from leaning into his kiss than halt the wild beating of her heart.

With a hand looped round her neck, Thork pulled her closer. His lips were a hairsbreadth from hers when he hesitated, looking into her eyes in an all-too-familiar way, then kissed her deeply, turning slightly from side to side to mold their lips just right.

With a sigh of resignation, Ruby relished Thork's kiss. It felt so right to be in his arms. Somehow, some way, she knew this was where she was meant to be. She put her arms around Thork's neck and moved closer.

Thork jolted away slightly and studied Ruby's face, trying to understand this innate chemistry between them. He touched her lips lightly with the tip of his tongue, and Ruby moaned, parting her lips for more. The children's voices grew louder, and Thork forced himself to pull away, holding her firmly by the shoulders until both of their shuddering breaths slowed down. Then he gave her another slight peck on the lips and whispered, "Sleep well, heartling," before mounting his horse and riding away.

Ruby tossed and turned throughout the night. Daybreak finally crept through her bedchamber before sleep finally came. She hoped Thork suffered, as well.

Chapter Eight

Three weeks had passed since Ruby's arrival in Jorvik. Ruby had felt at peace since she started attending first-light services at St. Mary's minster with Gyda each morning. She was surprised to learn that the Viking city hosted eleven Christian churches.

No longer did she continually question when she would return to the future. Ruby believed this time-travel experience had been ordained by some force greater than man. She wasn't resigned to the fact that she might not ever go back, but she decided to take one day at a time.

When she and Gyda returned home from church one day, Ruby ate a piece of bannock and a slice of hard cheese before Byrnhil showed up at her doorstep in a Viking-version jogging suit. Between Ruby's Brass Balls T-shirt, jeans and Nikes and Byrnhil's specially made purple silk pants and tunic-style shirt, the two women were a sight to behold as they jogged the two miles that had become their morning routine.

Sandra Hill

Byrnhil had convinced Olaf to allow Ruby to jog with her. Ulf, of course, followed after them, his face burning with humiliation. Several of Byrnhil's ladies had jogged with them the first two days but refused to come anymore.

"My women are weak," Byrnhil jeered. "Too much soft living. But mayhap 'twas the butcher's remark on the size of their rumps. Methinks, though, that the blacksmith's remark about their jiggling breasts was the last straw."

"Poor Ulf! His face looks like a bloody beet."

Both women giggled.

After their return, Ruby strolled through Coppergate with Astrid and the ever-present guard. The craftsmen who plied their trades in the open air in front of their city homes fascinated Ruby, especially the instrument makers who drew sweet, haunting music from the pan pipes they carved so lovingly.

With their long, flowing manes of hair and belted tunics, the Viking artists—wood and leather workers, jewelers, gold and silversmiths, glass blowers and weavers—resembled the hippies of the 1960s. Unlike those gentle flower children, however, when winter winds blew, these swaggering males turned fierce and rode the North Seas a-Viking in their longships. Finding the difference hard to reconcile, Ruby asked Gyda about it.

"You have come to us in a rare peaceable period," Gyda explained. "Just six years ago, when Rognvald captured and became king of Jorvik, the city fair flowed with blood. Every family lost sons, brothers, husbands and fathers." She shook her head sadly before confiding, "Our oldest child Thorvald died in the battle." Gyda's voice cracked as she wept silently.

"Oh, Gyda, how inconsiderate of me! I never knew you had a son. Please forgive me."

When Gyda calmed down, she continued, "The saddest part is the fighting does not end yet. Mark my words, blood will flow again here. The Saxons will ne'er allow us to live here in peace."

"Don't the Vikings have their own lands?"

"Our homelands are small and overpopulated. The Viking leaders there wield their power as viciously as our enemies here."

"Like Thork's father, King Harald?"

"Just like. Hordes of our brethren have broken away from the yoke of tyranny and seek to settle in new lands as farmers and traders—like here in Jorvik—but 'tis ever a struggle to survive, even when we agree to give up our own culture to blend in the new lands."

"Gyda, you may find this hard to believe, but in my country people consider Vikings heathen barbarians who killed for the joy of it. And what is *a-Viking* anyway, if not raping and plundering other lands?"

"Some are driven so," Gyda admitted. "Overcome by the bloodlust they are, like the berserkers, or by the plunder, but mostly they go to seek better lives for their families. Mayhap they conquer unwilling lands in the process, but survival drives them. Nothing more."

That was one of the more serious conversations she and Gyda engaged in recently. Mostly, they laughed and enjoyed themselves as women gathered in Gyda's home each afternoon to get Ruby's expert help in making the frivolous lingerie.

Today a group of Gyda's friends from nearby homes arrived once again for a "sewing bee." Ruby had shown them once before how to make a pattern, but some had run into problems and wanted hands-on assistance.

She suspected they were more interested in seeing the washboard she'd designed with the blacksmith's help for Gyda, not to mention the hand-carved clothespins a woodworker in the market area had made to her specifications. Gyda beamed with pride when she looked at her clean laundry hung on the newly strung clothesline between two trees behind the house. She displayed the washboard, when it wasn't being used, on a special, highly visible wall peg, its rolled metal surface polished to a high sheen. And Ruby suspected that Gyda let her laundry hang out longer than necessary to impress her neighbors with her modern gadgets.

The lively, outspoken women in Gyda's solar that afternoon chattered and gossiped as their nimble fingers plied precious needles and rainbow-colored threads.

"Did you hear that Gunvor is with child again?" one woman confided. The others rolled their eyes meaningfully. Tsk-tsk's clicked through the women's teeth as they sympathized with the "poor girl."

"Ten babes and her not yet seeing twenty-five winters!" Gyda exclaimed. " 'Tis dead she will be by her thirtieth year. She near bled to death in the last birthing, I was told."

"Then what will Siegfried do for the care of all those children?" Gyda's next-door-neighbor Freydis, a rotund, jolly woman, clucked.

"Probably wed some young, unknowing bonder's daughter whose father wants one less mouth to feed," another lady snorted with disgust.

Was that sort of like a thirty-eight-year-old man looking for a sweet young bimbo after dumping his wife of twenty years? *Oh, hell!* Ruby thought. *I do not need this!*

" 'Tis ever a woman's lot and ever will be. Men lust. Women suffer," Gyda sighed, with a woman's eternal resignation to fate.

"Well," Ruby volunteered, "why don't you women do something about it? It's just as much your responsibility."

All the women turned on Ruby, wide-eyed, open-mouthed and very, very interested. Even Gyda.

Oops! Had she blundered again? Perhaps this was a subject she shouldn't have broached. But, heck, women

144

needed to stick together, to share information, to bond for their own self-interest.

The women still gaped at her, expecting her to elaborate.

"Haven't you ever heard of birth control, of taking precautions so you won't have any more children, *if* that is what you choose to do?"

Freydis pooh-poohed her suggestion with a wave of the hand. "You speak of those useless powders that promise to prevent conception but never do. Just a waste of coins!" The others nodded in agreement.

"Actually, there are powders in my country that do work," Ruby said, knowing they wouldn't understand birth control pills. "Haven't you heard of condoms or sponges or douches?" Of course they hadn't. How silly of her to ask!

"Condoms? What are they?" Gyda asked. "Do you truly say women have methods to prevent having babes?"

"Yes, they do."

Ruby had the rapt attention of every woman in the room.

"Condoms are thin sheaths that fit over a man's male part—so thin the pleasurable sensations aren't diminished, but so water-tight the male sperm, or fluid, cannot enter the woman's vagina and join with her egg."

A storm of questions followed then, and Ruby gave the standard high school health class lecture on menstruation and reproduction.

"But these condoms," one young woman asked, "where might they be purchased? And of what fabric are they made?"

"I'm not sure," Ruby admitted, "although I do think they are already being made in the Orient at this time. I think the early ones were made of a soft leather that was rinsed and used over and over, but the ones I've seen are thin, transparent membranes, disposed of after every use."

Ruby racked her brain to remember more about a subject on which she was not particularly knowledgeable.

"And the women can make love and not get pregnant?" an amazed Gyda asked.

Ruby smiled and nodded.

"What is a membrane?" another asked. "Is it like the thinnest silk?"

"No, because that isn't water-tight. It's more like the thin skin over some women's breasts, or the skin of an animal that's been scraped and scraped until it's almost transparent and used for window coverings." Ruby tried to think of a better explanation. "I know, it resembles the intestines of animals when they're thoroughly cleaned out."

Now the women understood.

"Does this birth control not anger the men in your country?" Freydis asked.

"No-o-o, I don't think so. If a man loves a woman, he wants to protect her, to keep her from having a child when it's dangerous for her health, or when there are too many for them to feed or she's past the prime child-bearing years."

After the women left, Gyda looked at Ruby oddly. "Who are you?" Gyda asked with a puzzled frown. " 'Tis strange you know so much that we do not, even though our men trade 'round the world."

"I come from the future, Gyda," Ruby tried to explain once again.

"Nay, that I cannot accept. You must come from some strange land we have not yet discovered. That must be it."

The next morning, after her jogging routine with Byrnhil, the king's mistress demanded that Ruby return to the palace with her for a private conversation. Ruby soon learned that the Viking grapevine worked almost as fast as those in modern America. Word had spread already of Ruby's birth control lecture.

At least twenty women crowded Byrnhil's solar demanding that she repeat the words she'd spoken yesterday. When she finished, they asked even more questions than Gyda's friends.

"I will tell Sigtrygg to search for some of those condoms when next his ships travel to the Orient," Byrnhil declared confidently.

"Do women in your country care naught that those strange objects are inside them?" one young maid asked shyly.

"Humph! No stranger than some male parts I have seen!" Byrnhil joked. And that led to a discussion of lovemaking, sexual prowess and good lovers these women had known. Ruby blushed at some of the graphic descriptions the Viking women gave.

Sensing Ruby's embarrassment, Byrnhil asked, "Do women care naught for lovemaking in your country? 'Tis said the Saxon women consider it a distasteful duty."

"Oh, women enjoy lovemaking almost as much as men," Ruby laughed, "especially since we've learned so much these past few decades about woman's anatomy and what brings her pleasure. Females in my country expect to have orgasms, as well as men. In fact, many have discovered multiple orgasms."

The stunned silence that greeted those words stopped Ruby short. Oh, my God! Had she really said all that?

"I think I better go home now," Ruby murmured weakly.

But no way would she be permitted to escape so easily. The set look on Byrnhil's face told Ruby loud and clear that she'd opened a can of worms the size of a snake pit.

"What is an orgasm?" Byrnhil demanded to know.

When she described *that* as briefly and succinctly as she could, Byrnhil asked, "And multiple orgasms?" Ruby's explanation drew surprised gasps from some women and snorts of disbelief from others.

"I knew that," Byrnhil claimed arrogantly. "I just did not know *your* words." Then she bragged, "Always I come at least three times."

Holy cow! No wonder Byrnhil held the fierce Sigtrygg in her spell.

Two days later the same group of neighbor ladies showed up at Gyda's door with flushed cheeks and a conspiratorial manner. When they were seated in Gyda's sewing chamber, Freydis stood up as spokeswoman. "We have something to show you."

Was it another pattern for underwear? Some of these buxom Viking women insisted there should be a way to design a push-up bra that fit them without making them look like the masthead of a ship.

Freydis pulled an object out of her bag and shoved it into Ruby's hands. The wrinkled, grayish-colored stuff looked like the pig's intestines used for sausage casings she'd seen on her grandfather's farm as a child.

"What is it?" Ruby asked, raising questioning eyes to Freydis.

"A condom," Freydis said proudly. "I made it myself."

Ruby tried not to smile as she examined the ugly object more closely. Freydis had sewn the end of the clean casing with tiny stitches to hold the sperm inside.

Before Ruby had time to react, the other women brought forth their creations. One woman had embroidered Norse symbols in red and gold thread down the length of hers. Another had used a pig's bladder and made it so long and big the husband would have to be immense to fill it. She looked sheepishly at Ruby and said, "My Gorm is fair like a tree trunk when the lust comes, but mayhap I did make it a mite too big." The women hooted teasingly at her words.

When Ruby finally had time to register what the women showed her, she started to laugh. She couldn't help herself. She laughed so hard the tears came and her side hurt, but still she couldn't stop. Finally, Gyda clapped her hard across the back and forced her to drink a cup of water. Wiping the tears from her face, Ruby looked at the curious women, who couldn't understand her reaction.

"Homemade condoms just won't work," Ruby said gently. "They're bound to leak or break. I'm sorry if I led you to believe you could make them yourselves."

"Well, I see them not as useless," Freydis argued. "Aught is better than naught. I will check each of mine to make sure they are perfect, unbroken. The finest, tightest stitches I will use." The other women concurred, ignoring Ruby's criticisms.

"You know, you could follow the rhythm method," she offered. "It's not perfect, but I think it would be more effective than your homemade condoms."

She explained the rhythm method to them, telling them how to keep a calendar and which days of the months they were most fertile. They listened attentively, but one woman summed up most of their feelings when she said, "Think you a husband in the mood will turn away when his wife says 'tis the wrong time?" Only one young lady disagreed: "Some husbands would. If the wife's life was in danger, some would wait."

Ruby resolved after that to keep her mouth shut, not to volunteer any more information. What she didn't need was to call attention to herself, and that's just what she'd been doing by creating a stir with her lingerie and birth control. No more!

Thork and Olaf had been gone the past week. They had sold most of the goods carried on Thork's ships, a percentage of which belonged to Olaf, and had stored the rest on Dar's estate where they'd been the past week. The Althing would be held in three short weeks. Thork was making a concerted effort to take care of business before he left Jorvik—and her—for a long, long time. She might not ever see him again.

149

Ruby could not think beyond the present. Her future fluttered dark and shadowy in front of her. Not only was she terrified of her "trial" at the Althing, but the prospect of being alone in the Viking land, without Thork, traumatized her with its uncertainties.

She tried to keep the fearful images at bay with busy work, but she and Gyda both froze with surprise in the midst of drying mushrooms two days later to see Thork and Olaf and a strangely familiar gray-haired man come stomping into the house.

A gamut of emotions rippled through Ruby as she faced her husband, who was not her husband—mostly just plain happiness to see him again. Her spirits were out of sync, however, with the tense drama being played out on Thork's stormy face.

"What in the name of Loki have you been up to now?" Thork demanded of Ruby, without any greeting.

His riveting gaze accused her coldly, so different from the last time she'd seen him outside Olaf's barn, where they'd shared a sweet kiss. Under his steady scrutiny, Ruby's confidence faltered uneasily.

"Less than a sennight I have been gone and already you create a furor!"

"Me?" Ruby's blood ran cold. Her mind worked overtime to understand his accusation. She had a sneaking suspicion about what prompted Thork's irritation, but hoped it wasn't true. "I don't know what you're talking about," she fabricated.

"Sigtrygg sent an urgent message demanding I return to Jorvik at once—to remove the troublesome wench from his city afore she created a rebellion among the woman. Could he perchance refer to you?" Thork asked smoothly.

Fear rose biliously to her throat, but Ruby opted for a brave front.

"Really! What could one woman do? He's just on the down side of one of his mood swings." Ruby's heart sank at the sure knowledge the king had heard about her birth control lectures. *Oh, boy!*

Ruby peered up at Thork through lowered lashes, trying to gauge just how upset he was. Thork stood in an angry, widespread stance, glowering down at her with hands on his hips. As if she were a naughty child! Should she warn him ahead of time what to expect from the king? Nah! she decided. Let him find out for himself.

"Thork, do you not introduce me?" the gray-haired gentleman asked petulantly.

Thork turned away reluctantly, not having got the needed answers from her. Before he did, he shot her a loaded look that said he would deal with her later. "Ruby, this is my grandfather Dar," Thork said grudgingly.

"Ah! The wench who claims to be your wife from the future." The old codger chuckled with relish.

"Who told you that?" Thork scoffed, taking the ale Gyda offered him and quaffing it down, then wiping his mouth with the back of a dusty sleeve. His day-old beard and his rumpled, dirty clothing bespoke the urgency of Sigtrygg's recall, Ruby realized with new foreboding.

"Word travels fast, even to our remote area." Dar winked conspiratorially at Ruby.

Ruby blinked dazedly over the fast pace of all the innuendos flying over her head. Ruby should have known the man was related to Thork. Dar was about the same height, though his shoulders stooped slightly with age and his build was not so muscular. His face mirrored a craggy, older version of Thork's, both arrogant and handsome as hell.

"Aud and her ladies ask that I bring back samples of the strange garments they hear so much about," Dar told Ruby. Amusement flickered in his rheumy eyes. "By the blood of Christ, I know not why women need waste good cloth to cover a bare arse, nor the tit that is better left uncovered to suckle the babe or succor the man."

Thork's eyes twinkled with reluctant amusement at his grandfather's vulgar words, probably because he knew how much they irritated Ruby.

"Have you no tongue in your head, thrall?" the wretched old man continued. " 'Tis certain I was told you do nothing but spout words the day long." He chortled heartily at his own words. Thork's tight expression relaxed into a faint smile at Ruby's expense.

Ruby bristled with indignation over Dar's words. She'd had it up to here with rude, crude, arrogant Vikings. Holding her arms stiffly at her sides, afraid she might slap the old fart, Ruby confronted Dar with barely suppressed fury. "The day I choose to lash you with my tongue, *old man,* you will know it. But even I, *thrall* that I am, know how to show some manners. Mayhap," she said, emphasizing the archaic word, "I could teach you some proper etiquette—if you are not too ignorant to learn."

Thork rolled his eyes, biting his bottom lip to stifle an outright laugh. Gyda made the sign of the cross. Olaf glared at her in outrage. But Dar smiled from ear to ear and put his hands on both her shoulders, squeezing hard. "Well met, wench, you will suit. Yea, methinks you will suit very well." Then he turned to Thork, who eyed him suspiciously, and snapped, "Do we dawdle here all day, boy? I thought you were summoned to Sigtrygg's castle."

Thork grumbled something incoherent about old men and sucking eggs. Dar ignored him pointedly and, before leaving, commanded Ruby, "Have some of those garments ready for my departure tomorrow. My wife, Aud, is about the same size as Gyda, do you not think so, Thork?"

"You cannot be serious!" Thork exclaimed, slamming his goblet on the table.

"That I am!" A flash of humor softened his wrinkled face.

"My grandmother would never wear such . . . things,"

Thork sputtered, turning indignant eyes on Ruby, as if this were all her idea.

"Do not wager on it," Dar countered with a wry, knowing grin. Thork's face reddened with embarrassment.

Before they were out the door, Thork warned Ruby in a loud stage whisper, "You and I have much to discuss. I mislike my life being dictated by a wench. Be here when I return."

"I'll think about it," Ruby asserted foolishly. As if she had anyplace else to go!

Gyda worked quietly, ominously, as they continued with their tasks. When Astrid asked Ruby if she wanted to go to market, Gyda advised her to stay at home that day, in case the men should return soon. Ruby was tidying her sleeping chamber when she heard the door slam below and angry voices arguing back and forth, including Gyda's.

"Nay! I will not do it. She is not my responsibility. Sigtrygg has no right to interfere with my Jomsviking commitments." Thork swore loudly and eloquently. Then Ruby heard Olaf chastise him for using coarse language in Gyda's presence, to which Thork apologized curtly and added, "Can you imagine what she would do to the men on my ship if I took her aboard? She would probably have them putting laces on the sails or designing see-through codpieces for themselves."

Laughter filtered up to Ruby at his last words. Then Gyda, the wonderful woman, defended Ruby. "Ruby only tried to help, Thork. She meant no harm."

"May all the gods spare us from her help in the future!" Thork snorted with disgust.

"There is another solution," Dar offered in a cunning voice.

"What might that be?" Thork asked dubiously.

"We could bring her back to Ravenshire till the Althing meets. After all, 'tis only three sennights from now. What more harm could the wench do?"

"What harm, indeed!" Thork scoffed, but he sounded more amenable to her being in Dar's home than on his ship. "Bring the wench down, Gyda, but warn her to keep her bloody mouth shut or, I swear, I will strip the flesh from her back this time, as Sigtrygg has suggested I do."

When Ruby came downstairs, trying to appear as meek and innocent as possible, the men sat at the table watching her somberly, like three blasted judges. Tempted to turn and run back upstairs, Ruby chose, instead, to move forward stoically.

Exasperated to the breaking edge, Thork pointed a censuring finger at Ruby and informed her without preamble, "You have now convinced Sigtrygg that you must be a spy from Ivar. His exact words were 'Not only does Ivar wish to kill off all my men, now he sends this woman to ensure that we have no young to replace our dead.'"

"That's ridiculous! All I—"

Thork raised a hand angrily to halt her speech and ordered through thinned lips, "In the future you will speak only when given permission to do so."

We'll see about that. But Ruby knew enough to remain silent for now.

"The mischievous Loki had to have sent you into my life as an enormous joke. He and all the other devils, Christian and Viking alike, are laughing heartily by now."

"Who is Loki?"

"I told you not to speak unless given permission," Thork snapped.

"What could you be thinking of, wench," Olaf intervened quizzically, "to preach the killing of babes to our women?"

Ruby didn't care what Thork ordered. She couldn't remain silent at such horrendous accusations. "I *never* discussed the killing of children—in or out of the womb. I only talked about methods of *preventing* conception."

Thork stood abruptly, overturning a goblet of ale. Her

defiance of his command of silence incensed him. Nostrils flaring, he moved toward her. Ruby momentarily panicked and jumped behind Dar's chair for protection. She cowered there for several seconds before becoming disgusted with herself. Straightening herself on wobbly knees, she said with as much dignity as she could muster, "Oh, go ahead and punish me, Thork. I can't keep quiet when I'm falsely accused."

"Falsely accused!" Thork sputtered, as Olaf reached out a hand and pulled him back to his chair. Meanwhile, Gyda refilled their cups of ale, probably hoping that would mellow them a bit. Gyda's eyes registered with Ruby's for a moment in sympathy.

"I refuse to hear your lame excuses. 'Tis not at issue here, leastways. Sigtrygg bellows madder than a wounded bear and would have you punished to the death, whether you be kin to Hrolf or not."

"Mayhap we women could go to him and explain how harmless the talks were," Gyda offered placatingly.

"Yea, and wear a black eye like the good Byrnhil does," Dar commented dryly.

"Get you from this company, Gyda," Olaf roared like a wild bull at his wife's breaking into men's talk. "Where did you learn to act the man, interrupting in such an uncomely manner? Probably from this meddlesome lackwit." He looked pointedly at Ruby, then back to Gyda. "In truth, I have been too lax with you, wife."

Weeping loudly, Gyda fled the room with her apron thrown over her face. So, this is what her interference had brought to one of the few friends she'd made here! Ruby chastised herself.

"That was unnecessary and cruel," Ruby chided Olaf, and before he could respond, she turned to Thork coldly, "What do you want me to do?"

Ruby saw the angry emotions warring inside him and

155

knew he struggled to contain them. Finally he told her in a flat voice, "We travel to my grandfather's home tomorrow. Gyda and her family accompany us—not for your company, but because my grandmother Aud requests it. There you will remain silent and biddable, causing no more trouble, until the Althing releases me from my responsibilty. Do you understand?"

Ruby nodded.

"Because, if you do not, you will be bound and gagged in his keep till you cannot move or speak."

Thoroughly subdued, at least on the surface, Ruby went back to her chamber to contemplate the fine mess she'd made of things—once again. Lying on her pallet, staring at the ceiling, Ruby eventually fell asleep. She was surprised several hours later to look up and see Thork leaning against the door jamb, watching her curiously.

"What? What have I done now?" Ruby jumped up, alarmed.

"I thought I told you not to speak," Thork said in a surprisingly soft voice, tinged with humor.

Ruby sniffed contemptuously and walked over to her small window. Dusk settled lazily over the clear sky. It would be a nice day tomorrow for traveling. Then she turned to study Thork's blank face, unable to read his emotions, or know whether there was some new crime of which she was to be accused.

Drops of moisture from a recent bath beaded in his hair and dripped down his clean-shaven face. The silky blond hairs on his bare arms and calves glistened in the afternoon sun streaming through her small window. The rich outlines of his strong shoulders strained the fabric of his crisp, buttery brown leather tunic, and the dragon belt accented his deliciously narrow waist and hips.

He was a devilishly handsome man, no doubt about it. The sheer masculinity he exuded filled the air and made Ruby blush with unbidden, secret thoughts.

Thork returned her bold gaze with hooded, hawklike intensity, as if trying to solve some great puzzle. "Tempted I am to offer you freedom in exchange for information about who you really are," he said huskily.

Ruby's traitorous heart skipped a beat at his softly spoken words. She sighed, trying to get her emotions under control, and answered him, "I've told you repeatedly who I am, but you won't believe me. I have many faults, Thork, but I'm not a liar. I despise lies."

"And I hate mysteries." He held her gaze steadily, then shook his head in wonder and a hint of humor. "What could possess you to teach the women birth control, of all things, and where would you have gleaned such information?"

Ruby bridled under his criticism. "Perhaps, if the women you and the other Viking men bed so indiscriminately knew more about birth control, there wouldn't be so many bastards around."

"Do you call my sons bastards?" Thork challenged, then softened. "Would you begrudge them life?"

"Of course not. That's not what I meant." Then Ruby thought of something. "Thork, do you have other children?" Good heavens! He probably had dozens of children in as many countries.

Tiny laugh lines crinkled at the edges of his eyes and mouth. He knew exactly what she imagined. "Nay, Eirik and Tykir are the only children I have."

"How do you know for sure?"

"I was young and careless when they were born."

He seemed so certain, and yet, if these people didn't practice birth control, how could he be so sure?

Sensing her thoughts, Thork continued with a cryptic grin, "Your Christian Bible tells it all." At Ruby's puzzled look, he explained, "Was there not a biblical man . . . Onan . . . who spilled his seed upon the ground?"

Oh, my goodness! He meant that he ejaculated outside

a woman's body. Ruby felt her face flame hotly.

Thork grinned at her discomfort and sat down on her little bed, then—oh, my God!—lay down on her pallet with his magnificent bare legs crossed and arms folded behind his head. He looked up at her innocently through the shadows of his sinfully long lashes—dark contrasts to his pale hair. Ruby licked her dry lips and had trouble swallowing. He looked so damned irresistible. Would she ever be able to sleep in that bed again without imagining him in it?

"Have you any inkling how strange 'tis to have such an intimate conversation with a woman?" Thork said nonchalantly.

Oh, great! He was back on the outside-ejaculation business again. "It's just as strange to me. Believe me, everything I've said and done since I've come to this blasted land has been out of character."

"Did you practice birth control with your husband?" Thork studied her intently.

Ruby felt herself blush once again.

His right eyebrow lifted slightly. "Do you find my question too personal? How odd! After all you have asked me! Especially since you say I am your husband—*of sorts.*"

"Yes, we did," Ruby admitted candidly.

"Why? Did you only want two children?" Thork persisted. Meanwhile, his clear blue eyes raked her sensuously.

"No. We always intended to have more, but it never seemed to be the right time," Ruby answered nervously, hardly able to think when his eyes caressed her so openly.

"The right time? How curious!"

Ruby plopped down on the chair near the bed. She peered at him curiously. Actually, she couldn't keep her eyes off him. "Are you still angry with me?" she asked, trying to maintain some semblance of dignity when what she really wanted to do was, as Jack would say, "jump his bones."

"Yea, but not because of what you told those stupid women. Your actions disrupt my life, and I cannot allow that to continue." Propping himself on his elbows, Thork turned serious. "Ruby, my life is set. There is no place in it for you, leastways not the place you would accept. I am a Jomsviking. Ever I intend to be. Can you not accept that I will never marry? That my sons must stay with Olaf and Gyda?"

Ruby knew that Thork was trying to be honest with her, not cruel, but tears welled in her eyes nonetheless. Sensing her dismay, Thork went on softly, "Honor demands I leave here as soon as possible, and you keep throwing stones in my path. Still . . ."

Ruby waited but he remained silent, his eyes deep pools of blue heat reaching out to her. Finally she could contain her curiosity no longer. "Still what?"

In one deft motion, so quick she had no time to react, Thork reached over, grabbed her by her waist and had her on her back under him on the groaning pallet. He adjusted his body on top of hers, and Ruby knew gloriously, without a doubt, what his "Still . . ." had meant.

"Thork, don't," she whispered, but, at the same time, her traitorous body betrayed her by shifting seductively under him. Her eyes froze on his sensuously parted lips, basked in the smoldering heat of his gaze.

"Shush," he rasped in a husky whisper. "Don't talk. Just lie still and . . . feel." Thork's wildly beating heart telegraphed erotic messages to her. Without moving, like a master puppeteer, he used just the pressure of his body to pull her sensuous strings to a vibrating pitch.

Thork's lips brushed her eyes shut and swept like a whisper across her cheek, to the edge of her lips, then teasingly away toward her ear. The wet tip of his tongue traced its narrow whorls, then delved inside. In and out it plunged until Ruby arched against him, unable to stand the intense pleasure he had set throbbing in her center.

"A-a-ah!" Ruby inhaled sharply, arching her neck, and Thork countered with a husky moan deep in his throat.

"Kiss me, Thork. Please . . . ," Ruby begged. Then, "Oh!" as his warm lips brushed hers, back and forth, back and forth, like a butterfly's wings, teasing the petals of her lips open, then tasting her nectar. "Sweet, sweet," he rasped out against the softness, then kissed her hungrily, demanding more and more as he shaped and reshaped her lips. Softly persuasive, then fiercely devouring, he pressed, sucked, nipped, devoured until Ruby accepted his plundering tongue. "That's it, dearling. Oh, yes, open for me," Thork murmured silkily, filling her mouth, and slowly, seductively, set a cadence with his smooth, wet strokes, a fierce counterpoint to the movement of his lower body against her sensitized womanhood.

But Tyra's loud shriek somewhere in the house recalled them both from their mindless passion. Thork groaned his frustration against her neck. Willing their breathing and aroused bodies back to normal, they lay still. Finally Thork pulled back slightly. Desire illuminated his eyes, and his warm breath fluttered against her lips.

"Still . . . ," he whispered hoarsely, " . . . still I am tempted to take the risk of making love to you, knowing I would be doomed to your siren's spell."

Ruby's body hummed at his words as he buried his face in her hair. She pondered his softly spoken words while her breathing stabilized. She, too, would take the risk—if given the chance. Ruby was about to pull his face up to tell him just that, but she was appalled to discover that his body shook—not with spasms of hot passion, but laughter.

Laughter! The jerk was laughing at her!

Ruby gave a mighty shove and Thork rolled off her. He laughed aloud by now as he sat up on the bed, trying to tell her what was so funny but unable to get the words past his mirth. Finally, when he'd laughed himself out, while she fumed, he told her disjointedly, stopping every few words to chuckle infuriatingly, "You should have seen the look on Olaf and Dar's faces when Sigtrygg told me why I had been summoned back—not because you had been doing that silly running thing again or sewing up frivolous garments, but teaching his woman how to prevent the bearing of his child."

Then a hearty laugh rippled up out of his throat, and Ruby poked him in the ribs with an elbow, threatening, "If you don't stop, I'm going to dump that pitcher of water on you."

That sobered him a bit but not for long. "The funniest part was when he told us about the . . . the orgasms, I think he called them, and Dar asked him to explain what they were. And then . . . and then"—he went off on another fit of laughter—"Sigtrygg said something about multiple orgasms. I thought Olaf would have a fit on the spot. I think Dar swallowed his tongue."

"Oh, no!" Ruby groaned. She hid her face in her hands. Could a person die of humiliation? She wished she could drop through a hole in the ground and disappear. To think that everyone, including Thork, had heard all those outrageous things she'd said.

Thork finally wiped his eyes and stood, preparing to leave. He reached down to her on the bed and ran a forefinger gently, regretfully along her lips. Then steeling himself back to his former cool composure, he told her of the time they would leave in the morning and warned her once again that, despite his lapse of laughter, she walked thin ice and must behave.

Stopping in the doorway, he gazed at her fondly, as if memorizing her features, but then he spoiled it all by getting in one last parting shot. "Fair warning, maid, I may decide afore these three sennights pass to discover for myself just how many of those multiple things you can have."

Ruby threw a cake of soap at him, but he ducked and it flew out the door into the hall. She heard the echo of his laughter long after he walked down the steps and out of the house.

Chapter Nine

Thork didn't laugh for long.

When Esle came to his sleeping chamber at the palace that night, he turned her away. Too many thoughts plagued him.

He'd been careless. Tonight, for the first time ever, he'd passed over that fine line he'd drawn long ago for his relationships with women.

Risks! He'd talked about taking risks with Ruby. By the blood of all the gods, what had he been thinking of? His own danger concerned him little. Death rode ever at his side, a constant companion, but he cared too much for Eirik and Tykir to jeopardize their well-being.

And Ruby? He knew that involvement with him would endanger her, as well. Did he care? Thor's blood! Of course, he did. The seductive witch had wedged her way into his heart like a jagged splinter. He closed his eyes in self-loathing and weary recriminations. It had to stop immediately. Surely it was not too late.

If nothing else, his more than ten years of Jomsviking had taught Thork self-discipline. By morning, he had himself under control, firmly determined to keep his distance from the tempting wench. Women abounded to warm a man's bed. He needed nothing more.

But the sight of Ruby's attractive bottom bouncing up and down on her pony in front of him as they began the first leg of their journey caused his throat to dry. Even the dark tunic she wore for traveling could not hide her graceful neck, nor the slimness of her waist and hips. Freya's bloody flux! he swore silently, then dug his heels into the sides of his mare and rode to the head of the small entourage. He refused to look at Ruby as he passed.

It was for the best—the only course of action a man of honor could follow. *Still . . .*

Thork's cold demeanor had cut Ruby deeply that morning as the horses had been saddled and panniers had been placed over the small ponies' backs, overflowing with clothing and accessories for Olaf's family and the others in their traveling caravan.

At first she'd been unable to fathom the abrupt change in Thork's mood from his laughing exit the night before, but then had rationalized it as reaction to the chaos that had overtaken Olaf's barnyard.

Olaf had roared out an order to his seven daughters, including Tyra, who'd been running off to chase a wayward duck. "If any of you moves a hair's width from the spot on which you now stand or speaks one more word, that person will be left behind with Ulf. Heed me well, for I have had enough of screeching, giggling, wandering, waspish children for one day, and it not yet begun." He'd sworn at Selik then when he'd defied him by making cross-eyes at Tyra.

Ruby had almost doubled over with laughter as they'd ridden only a short distance to the edge of Jorvik and Tyra had asked her mother, "Are we almost there?" and soon after had whined, "I have to use the garderobe."

But Ruby's laughter died now as Thork rode by her and gave no greeting. Encased in leggings, his muscular thighs guided his large horse expertly. He held his head high, with supreme self-confidence, but a tense muscle jumped in his stubbornly jutting jaw as he deliberately snubbed her.

Ruby wouldn't have been surprised at his coldness after his tirade in Olaf's hall yesterday if he hadn't come to her room later and laughed about the scene at Sigtrygg's palace. His hot, then cold, changes of emotion were driving her crazy.

Putting aside her hurt feelings, Ruby turned to Gyda. "I'm sorry for all the misery I've brought you, especially the way Olaf spoke to you."

Gyda clucked her tongue at Ruby's words. "I want naught of your apologies, girl. Leastways, I have not laughed so much in years, nor has Olaf or Thork, though ne'er would they admit it. Did Olaf and I mishear Thork in your room yestereve?"

Ruby told her about Thork's account of the events at Sigtrygg's court. When she ended, Gyda giggled with delight, then embellished the story with more from Olaf's version of the court activities. "The funniest part was when they first arrived at the court, and Sigtrygg raged at them all, shoving this gray wrinkled thing into Thork's hand, asking if he knew what the thing was."

"Oh, no!"

Gyda laughed out loud now. "You will never guess what happened next. The thing Sigtrygg handed him—'twas Freydis's condom, the one with red and gold embroidery, and, Ruby . . . ," Gyda sputtered, having to stop to control her giggles, "oh, 'twas so funny. You see, Freydis had added tassels to the end."

"No-o-o-o!" Ruby exclaimed.

Ruby rode back to help with the children. She couldn't help but notice the dozen armed men flanking their traveling party at the sides and rear, with Thork, Dar and Olaf at the front. She tied her horse to the back of the cart and crawled into the straw with the children. For the next few hours, until they stopped to eat at midday and water the horses, Ruby had amused them with stories and catchy songs. The only children's songs she could think of were Christmas carols, so the children's voices on this sunny, late summer day rang out incongruously with "Jingle Bells" and "Deck the Hall with Boughs of Holly."

Thork glanced her way several times as she, Gyda and the children sat on a large boulder eating their cold fare. Did he feel the bond between them? Even if he didn't believe her stories of the future, of a life they shared together, surely he didn't deny this instant chemistry that ignited every time they touched. But Thork's blank face betrayed nothing of his feelings, and Ruby felt sadly forsaken—again.

They expected to be at Dar's manor before nightfall, but the long, tiring journey had turned the travelers weary and listless by midafternoon. The fortunate Tyra slept soundly in one corner of the cart after hearing Ruby repeat the nursery rhyme about the old woman who lived in a shoe six times.

Everyone jolted out of their complacent lethargy with surprise when a group of six horsemen thundered out of the woods and headed off Dar, who rode with Selik near the end of the human train. The horsemen had to have been trailing them for a long time to have caught Dar at just that vulnerable moment when he'd left his grandson's side at the head of the caravan.

"Move the women and children off the road," Thork shouted anxiously to the tune of some vicious swear words directed at the hesirs who'd failed to see the enemy

166

approaching. "Selik, stay here with Eirik and Tykir and guard the women."

Grim-faced, Thork and Olaf galloped off with six of the men. For more than two hours, which seemed like days, Ruby wept and prayed and worried over Dar's fate, as well as the safety of Thork and his men.

When the somber-countenanced party rode back into the hastily made camp, Ruby quickly counted. They'd all returned, including Dar—thank God!—who appeared unharmed, except for a grimy face, torn tunic and baggy hose.

In addition, two bloodied strangers rode in their midst, arms tied behind their backs, wearing pants and nothing more. Deep whip welts covered their bare backs and chests. A sword wound in one man's shoulder bled profusely, and an enormous bruise swelled on the other man's forehead. They had obviously been beaten after their capture to obtain information.

When their horses came to a halt and they dismounted, Thork addressed Selik. "Two dead, two escaped."

"Any information?"

"Not yet. They will talk afore morning, though, that I promise." Thork's steel-blue eyes blazed with a cold-blooded fury that frightened Ruby. These enemies of Thork's would get no compassion.

"Will they die?" Ruby asked Gyda fearfully.

"That they will and not too soon, I wager. Mayhap they will torture them with the blood-eagle."

Oddly, Ruby saw no womanly distaste on Gyda's face for this barbaric behavior. True, the men had done a horrendous thing by kidnapping Dar and might have harmed him, but the threat of death did not fit the crime.

"What is a blood-eagle?"

"Have you heard naught of it?" a surprised Gyda asked. "Well, 'tis not practiced so much anymore. 'Tis what the three great Danish brothers, Halfdan of the Wide Embrace,

Ubbi and Ivar the Boneless, did to King Aella some fifty years back to avenge their father Ragnar's death. 'Twas Aella who threw Ragnar into a snake pit and watched gleefully while the vipers stung him to death.

" 'Tis said Aella bragged thus, 'The piglings would be grunting if they knew the plight of the boar.' Well, Ragnar's sons proved Aella right, because the piglings did truly avenge their father boar's death with the blood-eagle on him."

"What exactly is a blood-eagle?" Ruby choked out.

" 'Tis the slowest and most tortuous death of all. The Vikings tie the enemy to a tree and split his backbone so the ribs spring apart like wings, exposing the heart. The breathing air bags are pulled out to lay across his back, also like eagle wings," Gyda explained in gruesome detail. " 'Tis considered a noble sacrifice to Odin."

"And you think Thork would do that?" Ruby asked, gagging at the image.

Gyda's forehead creased in confusion over Ruby's question. "Why would you doubt it? He is a Jomsviking, but any man would do as much or more to protect his family."

Ruby tried not to dwell on the grotesque images called up by Gyda. She noticed that Thork ignored her still. In fact, Dar's near-fatal experience seemed to have reinforced some determination in Thork, which Ruby didn't understand but sensed had implications for her.

Because of the delays, dusk already shadowed the land when they rode onto Dar's huge estate which lay in the midst of the fields and fells famous for its Yorkshire wool. Shepherds with crooks in hand and yapping border collies at their feet worked efficiently to herd bands of sheep into a distant pasture. It was still light enough to see bonders and freedmen who seemed well fed and happy as they came in from carefully tended fields, waving to their jarl.

Gyda had explained to Ruby earlier the Viking class system: high-kings; petty kings or noblemen; rural aristocracy of jarls or earls; lesser nobles called *hesirs;* bonders or farmers; freedmen or cottagers; and finally, at the bottom, thralls. At first, Ruby had trouble sorting it all out until she learned to connect names with titles. King Harald, was, of course, high-king; Dar and Thork were jarls, even though Thork disdained the title; Olaf and Selik were hesirs.

The houses in the village they passed through were of the Viking style—long, rectangular buildings of neatly interwoven wattle and daub from forty to one hundred feet long, topped with thatch roofs. The dwellings lay in an orderly street pattern near a small river. Barns and other outbuildings stood outside the village perimeter.

Leaving the village, they approached the manor on a flat-topped hill Gyda referred to as a motte and entered the gates of a high, stockade-style, wood fence where many Viking hesirs stood guard, watching diligently over the countryside. It resembled a palisaded western fort, rather than the castle-and-moat-style, stone castle Ruby had envisioned.

Inside the bailey or courtyard were scattered stables, fowlhouses, kennels, smithy, armorer's shed, bakehouse, a separate kitchen, storerooms, open hearths and other assorted buildings, while the two-story manor house held stately prominence, resembling a small castle. The newer sections of the manor were stone, attached stylelessly to the older wood parts.

A number of well-dressed men and women stood on the steps of the keep awaiting the arrival of the weary group. The gray-haired Aud stepped forward first to greet her husband, Dar, with a warm clasp of the shoulders and a quick hug. Then she turned to Thork and embraced him as well.

Dar dispatched the two prisoners to one of the small,

separate buildings made of solid stone. Aud looked at them and back to Dar questioningly but held her queries for later.

"Well met, Thork!" A young, dark-haired woman sprang forward and leaped into Thork's arms, greeting him with a sound kiss on the lips, before pulling back and smiling invitingly up at him. With dimples indenting her wide smile, she cocked her head and said loud enough for those closest to hear, "Have you missed me near as much as I have you?"

"Tsk-tsk!" Gyda said disapprovingly of the young woman's forward behavior.

" 'Tis wanton of Linette to behave so in company," Aud told Gyda. " 'Tis more like a lowly thrall she acts than the well-born Viking widow."

But then Gyda traitorously conceded, " 'Twould be nice to see Thork settle down and leave off the wanderlust. Even if it be with such as Linette."

And Thork—the two-timing pond scum—didn't seem to mind the widow's attention a bit. In fact, he kissed her back—with relish! The brute!

Ruby blinked to hold back the tears of hurt and jealousy. She couldn't let Thork see how much his infidelity bruised her heart.

In answer to Linette's question about missing him, Thork squeezed her shoulders and replied, "More! More than you can know, dearling!" Then he looked directly at Ruby to make sure she'd heard his words.

Dearling!

So this was why Thork had ignored her all day. He'd known what awaited him here, and she was apparently no longer of any interest, if she had ever been. Ruby jumped out of the cart with the children in as dignified a manner as possible under the circumstances. Her weary muscles screamed from the long ride, and she walked like an aged cripple when she attempted to move. With a heavy heart, she dusted the bits of straw that clung to her dark dress, knowing she looked a sight.

Eventually, in the confusion of dismounting horses, greetings, unloading of baggage and orders being given to servants, Dar introduced Ruby to Aud.

"Welcome to my home. I have many questions to ask you later about the interesting undergarments I hear so much about." Aud's eyes, so like Thork's, twinkled merrily. Ruby had brought a set of lingerie to give Aud later as a gift.

Because of the large number of guests to be housed in the manor, Ruby would sleep with three of Gyda's oldest girls on temporary pallets in one small chamber. As they walked into the building, headed at Aud's direction toward that upper room, Ruby noticed that Thork and Linette were absent.

It was going to be a long three weeks!

Ruby fell asleep the minute her head hit the uncomfortable bed, heedless that it was little more than a board covered with a straw-filled sacking. Emotionally and physically exhausted, Ruby needed the restorative powers sleep would give her.

The girls awakened her with their chattering early the next morning. Olaf had already warned her not to leave the manor without permission. She presumed jogging would be out of the question—for at least the time being.

After refreshing themselves with soap and water, they visited the garderobe at the back of the manor, then went down to the great hall, where only servants moved about, and helped themselves to bannock and cold meats.

Dar's enormous great hall combined elements of both Norse and Saxon decorations. Fierce-looking battle helmets, shields and swords covered one whole wall, reminding visitors that Vikings welcomed guests but would brook no insult to their homes or families. On the other long wall, tapestries depicting the Norse gods Thor and Odin contrasted sharply with one of the Christian St. George slaying a dragon.

At one end of the hall, a massive stone fireplace in the Saxon manner dominated the entire wall, sharply different from the usual Viking household with its large open hearth in the center of the room. Many armchairs, now empty, were situated in clusters near it, for heat and conversation. Cooking was done in the separate kitchen she'd seen when they'd arrived yesterday.

The girls went off to find their mother, and Ruby was about to explore the manor when she stopped in surprise. "Rhoda! I didn't know you were here! This is wonderful!" Ruby exclaimed.

The stunned Rhoda-person looked behind her to see whom Ruby addressed, then stepped backward in fright as she realized it was the strange woman from the docks talking to her. "My name . . . my name be Ella," she sputtered out. "Why do you address me by that other name?"

Ruby hugged the shocked thrall, who backed farther away, and said, "You look like my cleaning lady Rhoda. I'm sorry if I've frightened you. It's just so good to see someone from home . . . well, someone I thought was from my home."

"Cleaning lady?" Ella whimpered weakly.

"The woman who cleaned my house two days a week."

" 'Twould seem a poor household, indeed, what only has one thrall to keep it clean," Ella muttered. "Do you not have a cook and stableboy, as well, and bonders to till yer fields?"

Ruby smiled.

"No, I mostly do my own cooking, and we have no horses that would require a stableboy."

Ella eyed her dubiously, obviously thinking her not the high-born lady she'd been led to believe from Ruby's claims of ties to the Duke of Normandy.

Ruby saw Aud, with a huge ring of keys hanging from

a circular brooch at her shoulder, enter a door which led to what seemed to be a weaving room. She gave Ella another quick hug and told her, "We'll talk later."

She followed Aud into the room where an eight-foot-high loom with soapstone weights took up most of one wall. Huge baskets held shorn wool, and spinning wheels stood ready with their spindles for making the celebrated Yorkshire yarn.

"Good morn," Aud greeted her. "Have you broken fast?"

"Yes, and was about to explore your home a little if you don't mind."

"Not at all. Chores I have pressing me now, or I would accompany you, but mayhap if you would seek out Linette she would give you the tour. Her chamber is the last on the right, at the end of the main hall on the second floor."

"Perhaps I will." *Not bloody likely!* "Where is everyone?"

"The women are still abed. The men have been up since dawn, out with the two prisoners, I warrant."

Ruby departed, going upstairs first to get a shoulder mantle for her dress. The crisp morning air chilled her, as much as Aud's reference to the prisoners and Ruby's too-vivid image of their probable fate.

After emerging from her room, Ruby's curiosity drew her to the end of the hall where Linette's door stood slightly ajar. She would just peek in a little, Ruby told herself, but when she saw it was empty, she stepped boldly inside. Apparently the manor was not so crowed that the fair Linette could not have a chamber to herself, one four times as big as the cubicle she and the three girls shared.

And opulent! A soft Oriental carpet covered the cold rushes, and lightly colored embroidered tapestries brightened the stark walls. A canopied bed held center stage on a short raised platform, with rich handwoven hangings ready to enclose her when she slept. Beautiful dresses, mantles and hose lay about in disarray.

Ruby decided she'd better make a quick exit before she was caught snooping. But then she chanced to look out the small, glassless window that overlooked the courtyard.

Her mouth opened to scream, but no sound emerged.

Ruby saw the two prisoners lying in the courtyard near the gatehouse, blood pouring in streams from the gaping sword wounds in their backs.

Slapping a palm in horror over her mouth to stifle her screams, she noticed Thork and Olaf standing dispassionately with short swords in their hands, while one of the prisoners was still screaming out his death throes.

Ruby couldn't bear to watch this cruelty and fled blindly from the room. Heading toward her sleeping chamber, Ruby staggered, losing her way in the misty shroud of her tears.

Thork had killed a man with his own hands! His sword dripped another human being's blood—not in the heat of self-defense, but cold, emotionless rage.

She didn't know this man! How could she have thought she did?

Ruby pushed open the next door, thinking it was hers, and immediately saw her mistake. A naked Linette lay sleeping in the middle of a massive bed. The room was as large as Linette's but starkly masculine with heavy carved bedstead, chests and chairs before a cold fireplace.

The hairs on the back of Ruby's neck prickled, and, like falling dominoes, the ominous sensation flickered down her spine to her toes, up to the top of her head and out to her fingertips. Ruby's eyes flew desperately around the room, and her heart lurched in recognition of the dark tunic and mantle Thork had worn the day before.

It was Thork's sleeping chamber. And Linette had slept here with him last night.

Ruby felt as if someone had kicked her in the stomach.

She shouldn't have been surprised, but somehow in her subconscious she must have hoped that Thork had put on the spectacle with Linette yesterday for her benefit. What a fool she was! Ruby sobbed miserably and turned to flee.

"Who goes there? What do you in Thork's bedchamber?" Linette screeched as she sat up groggily, pulling a sheet over her naked breasts. "Are you the bothersome thrall Thork brought from Jorvik? Do you spy here, too?" Her sultry eyes narrowed viciously. "Or mayhap you sneak into Thork's private chamber to poison his wine."

This was all too much for Ruby.

"Why, you ignorant bimbo . . . ," Ruby started to berate Linette, then waved her hands in disgust. What was the use! She swiveled and ran from the shrieking Linette.

"Come back here, you ugly wench, or I will have you beaten," Linette threatened to Ruby's retreating back. "Disobey me, will you? Just wait, thrall, you will learn to heed your betters."

Ruby didn't care what they did to her. Her eyes had been opened that morning, and she didn't think she could be hurt any more than she already was.

In her chamber, Ruby's body shook with wild weeping. She wept for the brutality she'd witnessed in the bailey. She wept for Thork's "adultery" with another woman. Then a long-delayed reaction to Jack's desertion set in. The pain of her upcoming divorce racked her, as well as the loss of her old life and exile to this cruel, foreign land.

Ruby finally cried herself out and realized that her binge of self-pity had jump-started another reaction. She was angry. Who did these people think they were—Thork, or Jack, or Linette, or the whole bunch of stupid Vikings— to trod over her roughshod?

I am Ruby Jordan. I am not going to sit down and die. I am a survivor. I will get through this nightmare.

Ruby couldn't believe her sojourn in this time warp

was a permanent one. All she had to do was stop making
waves and wait out her time here, she reasoned. She had
no one—absolutely no one—on whom she could depend.
She knew that for certain now.

Kinship with the Duke of Normandy was her strongest
protection. She must convince these people that he was,
in fact, her "grandfather" so they wouldn't dare harm
her. It would be impossible, though, if she kept letting
her emotions get in the way.

*Face it, girl, you were starting to fall in love with the
damn Viking.*

Ruby curled up in a ball on her little bed and slept
away her weariness from the trip and the mental anguish
she'd suffered that morning. She awakened several hours
later, thankful that no one had disturbed her. They were
probably too busy killing people, Ruby thought, her lips
curling in disgust.

Pouring the entire pitcher of water into the bowl, Ruby
gave herself an all-over wash with a square of linen and
soft soap. Then she searched her new Viking wardrobe
for something presentable to wear down to the great hall
for dinner. She chose a cream-colored velvet tunic with
dark green braiding to be worn over a jade, long-sleeved
chemise. Gyda had been generous in allowing her to
alter clothes that no longer suited Astrid. Over her neck,
she slid the magnificent emerald Byrnhil had given her,
then realized she had forgotten to return Thork's dragon
brooches. With absolutely no guilt, she pinned them on the
shoulders of her garment, vowing to keep them until asked
for their return. Maybe she would never give them back.

The three girls came in, talking excitedly until they saw
Ruby, and then they turned strangely silent. Ruby helped
them find more water and to dress, all the while puzzled
by their aloof attitudes.

"What has happened? What have I done now?"

The girls looked at each other sheepishly but wouldn't

answer. The only thing Ruby could think of was that Linette was causing trouble.

Well, so be it, Ruby thought. It was her against the Vikings, it seemed. All of them! Actually, it fit in with her new plan to form no attachments with these people.

They went down to the crowded hall together, then parted. Ruby went to the end of the table, well below the salt, hoping to be as inconspicuous as possible, while the girls joined their parents closer to the dais where Dar, Aud, Thork and Linette sat with several hesirs and their wives whom Ruby hadn't met.

Ruby knew immediately that some new trouble had landed at her door. Everyone turned from her coldly.

Ruby ate in peace, ignored by the lowly hesir at her side. She hadn't eaten since her meager breakfast and was famished. But a clock ticked in her head the whole time. She knew it was only a matter of time before she would be informed of her latest crime.

Ella, her Rhoda-like acquaintance, gave her the first clue, whispering in Ruby's ear, "The prisoner confessed," as she filled cups of ale along the table. Ruby looked up sharply, then realized that Ella didn't want to be seen speaking to her. Ella fussed, stacking some empty wooden bowls in front of her, then murmured hastily, "They came from Ivar. Some traitor in our midst informed Ivar of the traveling route." With those words, Ella left, carrying a load of empty trenchers to the kitchen.

Ruby glanced quickly to Thork, wounded once again, even though she'd vowed not to care about him or his people. How could he think she would hurt Dar? When Thork stared down at her in stony censure, Ruby's heart dropped. He thought just that.

Thork had watched Ruby enter the great hall before the meal, shaken by the day's information and renewed in his determination to keep his distance from the mysterious wench.

All clues pointed to her as the informant, but he could not believe she would deliberately harm his father or the boys she likened to her own sons. Mayhap the plan had gone beyond her control. Mayhap Ivar's men had been directed to kidnap Thork but had been unable to do so. Then they had chosen Dar instead, without Ruby knowing of the change of plans. But that would mean that Ruby plotted his own downfall. Thork's spirits plummeted. Could Ruby care so little for him? Truly, he upbraided himself, why was he surprised by the ever-constant duplicity of women?

Dar and Olaf wanted her tortured for information, goaded on by Linette's claim that Ruby had entered his chamber that morn, intent on murdering him. She told a convincing story.

Then Thork and Dar had gone up to Ruby's chamber to confront her with their suspicions and found her rolling back and forth on the pallet in a troubled sleep. The words that had spewed from her mouth in sleep condemned her even more, "Dead! They killed those poor men! Oh, my God! The cruel barbarians! So much blood! So unnecessary! Forgive them, God. Please . . . please . . . make them stop!" In truth, the wench had condemned herself.

Thork and Dar had let her sleep, exiting the room silently to discuss this new information in private.

"I mislike this whole affair," Dar had said. "All clues point to the wench, and yet I am not convinced."

"Nor I."

"It seems so reasonable, and yet I still doubt she is a spy."

A part of Thork wanted to believe Ruby innocent. Had she flummoxed them all? His head pounded with all the conflicting information it had been fed that day.

During the evening meal, Thork's eyes shifted to Ruby

often, taking in her fine attire, highlighted by his own jewelry. He smiled wryly. The bold wench waded neck-deep in the most serious danger, and she brazenly flaunted his borrowed ornaments, like a bloody queen. Sitting at the bottom of the table, she waxed more regal than the proudest royalty.

"Will you torture her?" Linette whined, hanging on his arm. "Will you, Thork? Will you?"

Thork shrugged her clinging hands off distastefully. He'd slept with Linette the night before and made good use of her body, but something rankled. Already he'd lost interest, as he did with all women. Her irritating mewling hastened the process.

" 'Tis my decision to make, not yours," Thork snapped. "Halt thy waspish tongue! No more do I wish to hear." Linette turned peevishly to the hesir on her other side.

When the tables were dismantled and folded neatly away into their wall enclosures, Ruby stood alone, ignored by those around her who made rude remarks loud enough for all to overhear. Thork ground his teeth at his fellow Vikings' ill treatment of Ruby. A part of him wanted to jump to her side so she would not be so defenseless. He restrained himself with a reminder of the maid's hypocrisy.

"Shall we call her forth and interrogate?" Dar asked.

"Nay, I will handle this myself," Thork answered with resigned foreboding.

All eyes followed Thork as he walked purposely toward Ruby. He held her haughty eyes the entire time, challenging her to bolt in fright or crumble in fear. To her credit, she did neither.

"Come," he ordered when he stood in front of her. His heart slammed miserably against his chest at the wide, hopeful eyes she turned on him like a damned doe. Bloody hell! What did she expect of him? Forgiveness? Angrily, he took her arm and led her toward the courtyard door,

179

turning once to those who would follow, commanding, "Alone. We go alone."

Outside, Thork drew Ruby toward the two dead prisoners who still lay on the ground, their lifeblood already soaked into the ground. Ruby scuffed her feet in reluctance.

"We are surely watched from the windows. Do naught to shame me or yourself," Thork advised through gritted teeth.

He dragged her toward the bodies and told her to look at the men. When she refused, he took her chin in pincerlike fingers and made her look down. The eyes of the two men bulged wide open in horrified agony, even in death.

Ruby gagged and vomited at his feet, spattering both of their leather shoes. Still Thork would not let her go.

"Do you know these men?" he grilled her, forcing her to look down again.

Ruby pulled her face out of his grip and glared at him coldly, her green eyes glazed with contempt. She refused to answer his question. Instead, she asked softly, as if afraid of what he might answer, "Did you do this, Thork?"

"What? Kill them?" he asked in surprise. "Yea, I did. They were trying to escape."

She blanched at his words and retched again.

"Do you sicken over the fate of your friends? Or were they your lovers?" Thork tasted bile in his throat. Somehow he could not stomach the thought of Ruby with another man. Holy Freya! he chastised himself. The woman was making him weak.

"No, I'm just revolted that you would do such a barbaric thing," Ruby replied, regarding him sadly as she wiped spittle from her lips with the back of her hand.

"Barbaric?" Thork exclaimed. "These are my enemies. They tried to kidnap my grandfather. They would have, no doubt, killed him."

"They are human beings first, Thork. For you to do this"—she indicated with a wave of her hand the two corpses—"makes you less human."

Coldly, defensively, Thork told her, "No man threatens my family and goes unpunished. It is the Viking way. I would be less the man to do otherwise."

Ruby's icy eyes stabbed him accusingly.

"These men came from Ivar," he said defensively.

"I know?"

"You know?" Thork roared. He grabbed her by the shoulders and shook her. "You know! Your words condemn you, wench. Know you that?"

Ruby's upper lip curled contemptuously. "Your Viking justice stinks, Thork. I know they came from Ivar because Ella told me so."

"Ella?"

Ruby sighed. What difference did her explanations make? They wouldn't believe her anyway. "A servant in the hall."

Thork blinked. She had an answer for everything, the cunning wench did. "If you know they came from Ivar and you are already accused of being a spy, then you must be aware that all in Dar's hall think you guilty and would have you killed, as well."

Fear flickered in Ruby's eyes for a moment, but she quickly masked it with lowered lashes. "Would you kill me, too?" she asked softly with strangely saddened eyes.

Thork's heart hammered loudly in his chest. Could she hear it? He searched her face for answers she hid too well. Ruby was the accused, and yet he felt oddly guilty.

"Mayhap," he finally admitted wearily. "Mayhap you would force me to do so."

Ruby's eyes filled with tears. She opened them wider to stem the flow. Devastation wracked the weepy wench, and tore at Thork as her fragile heart seemed to splinter at his cruel words. Like his own, damn her soul! What had she expected of him? Protection? Betrayal of his people? *Bloody hell!*

"I don't know you, Thork," she whispered bleakly.

" 'Twould seem you never did."

Chapter Ten

"Defend yourself, damn you," Thork demanded, raising his voice in exasperation when Ruby stubbornly refused to answer questions hurled at her by Dar and Olaf. She stood defiantly before her accusers in the privacy of a small chamber off the great hall.

Ruby glared at him obstinately. "Why should I? Would any of you believe my innocence?"

The deep greenish-gray pools of her eyes clouded with tears, and Thork felt he could drown in their murky depths. Thor's blood! He could not be so foolish as to allow himself to surrender to the sea witch's seeming innocence!

"Never have I condemned a man—or woman—unjustly," Dar fumed indignantly.

"And yet you would believe the lies that black-haired spider spins in her web—despite a lack of evidence?" Ruby jeered. "What proof has she that I carried poison?"

"Do you claim Linette missays the events of this morn?" Dar asked with narrowed eyes. He drummed his fingertips pensively on the arm of his chair.

"I say she is a bald-faced liar. I'm surprised she doesn't have to pin her nose to her forehead with one of those infernal brooches you Vikings favor."

"What is your meaning, wench?" Dar demanded to know.

Thork explained tonelessly, with no humor, Ruby's story of Pinocchio.

Dar reddened and stood abruptly. In a fit of temper, he slapped her hard across the face, causing Ruby's neck to snap back. She faltered and almost fell. Thork had to willfully restrain himself from going forward to help her.

"Your insolent remarks bode ill for your fate, wench," Dar warned. "Lest you convince us otherwise, I see naught we can do but torture the information from you, then confine you bodily till the Althing meets."

The unexpectedness of Dar's slap after his earlier kindness seemed to have caught Ruby off-guard. She gazed at Thork's grandfather with hurt confusion—those miserable, piercing doe eyes again!—probably trying to understand why her light remark about liars would provoke such strong reaction.

After witnessing her sympathy for the two men in the courtyard, however, Thork had to share his grandfather's condemnation of Ruby. All facts pointed to her guilt.

Truly, he should not be surprised. Most women Thork had ever encountered proved deceitful, self-serving bitches in the end. 'Twas the nature of the female breed. He had not really expected more from Ruby. Thork combed the splayed fingers of his right hand through his hair in self-disgust. In truth, though, he admitted with a sickening lurch in his stomach, he *had* expected more of Ruby.

Finally, unable to take any more self-recriminations, Thork lashed out, "Lies! All lies! Lay not your lying tongue on Linette again. Much has she suffered since her

184

husband's death. Naught does she have to gain in your disfavor, I assure you."

"Perhaps that part of your body you cherish so well blinds you to Linette's true character." Ruby's upper lip curled in contempt as she turned on him.

Thork lurched forward and almost backhanded Ruby across the other cheek for her insult. He halted abruptly at the sight of white fingermarks from Dar's blow still highlighted against the flushed skin of her cheek. She'd expected his blow, as well, indeed had provoked it, but, instead of cowering, she held on to the back of a chair and glared back at him in challenge. Thork grabbed her by the upper arms and lifted her off the floor, shaking her until he heard her teeth chattering.

"Thork," Ruby whimpered imploringly, and he dropped her like a hot coal. Holy Freya! The wench drove him to madness.

"Stupid bitch!" Thork snarled as he turned away, raking his fingers through his unruly hair once again. He forced himself to sit back down, flexing his fists tightly to bring his emotions under control. What was it about this wench that sparked his emotions afire so quickly?

"Were you in my sleeping chamber this morn?" he asked stiffly, once he had his temper banked.

"Yes."

"Why?"

"I didn't know it was your room. I was running . . . looking for my room . . . and got lost."

"Why would Linette missay you carried poison?"

"She fears I will replace her."

"How so?"

Before Ruby could answer, Dar interrupted, clearly disturbed by the direction their interrogation had taken them. "Linette is a guest in my home, much as you were. She is the widow of my faithful hesir, Godir. Why would having another guest in my keep threaten her?"

185

"Perhaps she fears I'll bump her from your bed," Ruby sneered, looking directly at Thork.

The eyes of all three men widened in understanding at the same time before they burst into laughter.

The gall of the brazen wench! Thork thought, not unimpressed by her arrogance.

"Nigh every man who enters this keep asks to wed or bed the fair Linette, whether they have five wives or none already," Dar said, explaining their laughter. "Her charms be known far and wide." He chuckled aloud and added, looking Ruby over from head to toe and obviously finding her wanting, "Nay, Linette fears naught from your competition."

Thork also scrutinized her boldly, not quite so sure that Ruby would come out on the short end in a comparison with Linette. He would not let her know that, though. Instead, he mocked her: "Think you I would choose you— bony arse and all—over Linette? I am not yet in my dotage!"

Dar and Olaf snickered, nodding in agreement.

"Men! You're all the same." Ruby lifted her chin contemptuously, putting her hands on her hips. "Put a pair of bosoms in your faces and that's as far as you can see!"

Her earthy language disconcerted them all.

" 'Twould not take much to see past yours," Thork choked out insultingly with a quick sweep of his hand toward her small, pert breasts.

"You were anxious enough back in Jorvik." Her flashing eyes challenged him.

"I must have been desperate."

"Hah! If I wanted you, I could have you just like that," Ruby boasted with a sharp snap of her fingers.

"Why, you arrogant little baggage!" Secretly amused by the wench's overconfidence, Thork wondered if she truly thought she could seduce him if she chose. Probably! He'd behaved like a horny goat thus far. 'Twould be amusing,

186

though, to see what tricks she would employ. His eyes narrowed speculatively.

Leaning her face closer, Ruby taunted him, "You Vikings are great ones for sagas and riddles. I have a good one for you, Thork. Would you like to hear it?"

A muscle twitched in his jaw, but he refused to rise to her bait; so, she continued, "What happens when a Viking man drops his braies?" Like a master *skald,* she waited in the silence, choosing just the right moment to answer her own question: "His brains fall out."

It took a moment for her words to register. When they did, Thork reached for her angrily, but Dar and Olaf held him back.

"Enough! Leave off, you two," Dar ordered. "We have dawdled enough on silly prattle betwixt you two. Thork, I cannot believe a grandson of mine would allow a chit of a woman to goad him so. And you, Ruby, truly you seek the henchman's axe with your foolhardy words." When they both looked properly chastened, Dar went on, "What do we with the wench?"

"I trust her not." Thork glowered sullenly.

"Nor do I," Olaf added. "And I do not want her in the same sleeping room with my daughters."

"The tower room then," Dar decided finally, "with a guard present at all times."

"Should she be bound?" Olaf asked.

Dar thought a moment, then replied, "Nay, not unless she tries to escape or causes further trouble."

"She must also be guarded against those who might try to rescue her," Thork cautioned. "Ivar may make a move. Then, too, some of our own villeins would have her head in a trice on the suspicion alone."

"And what of Hrolf?" Ruby asked, realizing the dangerous predicament she was in, looking for a last out. "Will you risk his anger to satisfy a suspicion, without evidence?"

Sandra Hill

Thork had forgotten Ruby's claim of kinship with the Norman Viking and Sigtrygg's fear of reprisal. "Do you still make those ridiculous assertions?"

"Of course, I do. I never lie. Why don't you take me to him for proof?"

Ruby's cunning surprised Thork. Surely she knew her lies would be proven false on Norman soil. What game did she play now? 'Twas probably just a ploy for time.

"You could always pay Hrolf *wergild* for her if he protested her death," Olaf suggested.

"*Wergild!* A man's worth, not a woman's!" Thork snorted. "Never have I heard of paying for a woman's loss!"

"And the torture?" Olaf prodded. "Shall I order her torture? If so, how far should we go? To the death?"

"Let us talk on this more," Dar offered judiciously. He leaned back in his heavy chair, feet outstretched, fingers steepled thoughtfully in front of his face. "Olaf, take her to the tower room and make sure you post a guard at the door."

After they left, Dar and Thork shared a glass of rare Frisian wine he kept for special guests. Thork rubbed his eyes wearily with the fingertips of both hands.

"What think you?" Dar asked as Thork stared solemnly into the finely wrought silver cup he held between his two palms.

"In truth, I know not what to make of the wench," Thork answered, shaking his head. "She vexes me sorely with brazen statements and her tales of the future, but still I cannot be certain of her guilt. All signs implicate her, and yet something is amiss in this puzzle."

"Perchance you just want to believe her."

"Mayhap, but I swear on Thor's hammer, as well as the Christian cross, Sigtrygg knew exactly what he was doing when he placed the waspish wench in my hands."

"Yea, that he did," Dar agreed, then burst out laughing.

188

"Did you hear what she said about bosoms? And men's brains?" He slapped his palm on his knee appreciatively and said, "God's blood! I swear she would be a fair match for you if things were different."

" 'Tis easy for you to find amusement in my discomfort," Thork grumbled. "Do you know, she asked if I would kill her?" Thork tilted his head back and drained his cup in one long swallow.

"And what said you to that?"

"I said I knew not, but, in truth, I misdoubt I could— unless I saw with my own eyes her raise the knife to my sons."

For two days, Ruby brooded alone in her tower room— a damp, stark cubicle with a pallet and table, not even a chair. The two small slits of windows were too high for her to see out.

The only person she'd seen since her interrogation was the guard who handed her food, drinking water and a clean chamber pot each morning.

Aside from feeling dirty and frightened for her future, Ruby was bored. What she wouldn't give for a good book!

When her guard, Vigi, opened her door that morning, Ruby sensed something different in his shifting eyes, but she knew from experience that he wouldn't answer her questions.

She lay daydreaming on her pallet several hours later, smelling the crisp coolness of the air coming through the little windows. Autumn would be coming soon. Ruby wondered sadly if she would be home for Christmas.

Autumn was Ruby's favorite time of the year. It reminded her of a special time in her life with Jack. She closed her eyes tightly to shut out the pain of those memories.

Twenty years! How had the time passed so quickly?

* * *

She and Jack had dated all through their senior year in high school, wildly in love. As much as she had loved him, though, Ruby had held off his heated advances, wanting to be sure, even hoping, perhaps unrealistically, that she could wait until marriage. When she told women friends about that today, they laughed at her unbelievingly, not understanding the different times and mores of twenty years ago when an eighteen-year-old virgin hadn't been an aberration.

Each night, though, they'd tempted fate, as youth always does, finding it harder and harder to halt the petting which step by hot step had approached a point of no return.

After graduation, Jack had gotten a football scholarship to a university more than a thousand miles away, while she'd enrolled at a local state college. By the end of September, Ruby had lost weight, and Jack's telephone bill had increased astronomically. The two months until Jack's Thanksgiving vacation had stretched ahead endlessly for them. Neither had been able to afford visits.

So Ruby had been surprised to open her dorm door one autumn day to find Jack standing there solemnly in his tight jeans and varsity jacket. The smell of the spicy cologne she'd bought him last Christmas hung enticingly in the air.

Jack's blue eyes had held hers in an imploring caress. He traced the sharp plane of her cheekbone lightly with a finger but did not lean down with his usual kiss of greeting.

"Let's go for a ride, Rube," he'd said in an oddly raw voice, drawing her outside toward his old MG.

She'd been frightened, wondering if he'd come to break up with her. Maybe he'd met someone else. Jack had said little, despite her nervous questions, as he'd driven to the outskirts of town. Strangely distracted, he'd parked on a little out-of-the-way road leading into a secluded, wooded area.

"How's football?"

"Okay."

"Do your parents know you're back in Pennsylvania?"

"No."

"Did something happen? Are you hurt? Did you fail a course?"

"No. No. No."

Jack had folded his arms over the steering wheel and had pressed his forehead down on them. Truly concerned now, Ruby had moved closer, but the gear shift on the floor had impeded her. She'd put her left hand on his wide shoulder and had felt corded muscles tense reflexively.

"Jack? Jack, honey, what's wrong?"

"Rube, I love you. I love you so much," Jack had groaned, pulling her into his arms.

Ruby had smiled broadly then, in relief and reaction to his loving words. He hadn't planned a breakup, after all. She'd kissed him quickly on the lips.

"I love you, too, Jack. I was so scared—"

Jack had never let her finish. He'd put hands on either side of her face and pulled her toward him in a hungry kiss that had conveyed all the loneliness and unfulfilled wanting of the last month. "I . . . love . . . you," he'd repeated huskily, and between each word, his breath had feathered her parted lips. His tongue ravaged all the secret, familiar recesses of her mouth, willing her to open all her intimate places for him.

Like a starving man, he'd passed his hands frantically over her body, grasping, caressing, never seeming to get enough. In his ravaging need, he'd jerkily unbuttoned her coat and lifted the hem of her sweater. When his fingertips had found the lace-capped tips of her breasts, she gasped, "Oh, Jack! A-a-h!" Instantly, he'd brought them to hard points of aching fruition with a mere grazing of the backs

191

of his knuckles. Jack had moaned throatily then with his own intense pleasure.

This had been too fast for Ruby. In the past, it had taken them hours to reach this point of sexual frenzy. She'd started to get frightened, and excited, at the same time. Jack had tried to pull her onto his lap in front of the steering wheel, but Ruby had cried out in pain. The stupid gearshift had scraped her thigh.

They'd both started laughing then.

"Come on. Let's go for a walk," Jack had suggested in a hoarse, raw voice. His kiss-swollen lips and passion-glazed eyes had lured Ruby onto the multicolored carpet of crisp autumn leaves which had crunched under their feet. They'd walked, arm-in-arm, into the heavily canopied forest while industrious nut-gathering squirrels scurried out of their path, squealing in outrage at being disturbed.

Jack had stopped abruptly and twirled her round and round in his arms, happily. Like young, carefree children, they'd fallen laughing to the luxuriant bed of leaves. He'd leaned over her and brushed some of the errant leaves from her hair, then held her eyes seriously, "Let's get married, Rube."

The abrupt, unexpected words had startled Ruby. "What did you say?" Then she'd whispered, "Say it again."

"Let's get married."

"Is this a proposal, Jack?" she'd gasped, tears of happiness filling her eyes.

"Yes." His breath had fluttered against her parted lips, soft as a butterfly's kiss. "Oh, yes!" Then Jack had smiled for the first time that day and begun a sweet assault of kisses. His lips had been white-hot with blistering heat as they'd seared a path from lips to throat and back to lips to pursue deep drugging kisses that had turned Ruby mindless and incoherent in her cries. Over and over, he had marked her with his stalking mouth.

Impatient, Jack had torn off his jacket and removed Ruby's as well. Her sweater and his T-shirt had followed quickly after. For a moment, Jack had pulled back to look at her exposed body appreciatively. "Oh, Rube!" he'd exclaimed before lowering himself. "Oh, sweet, sweet, Rube!" By the time his lips touched the tips of her breasts, Ruby had already arched up to meet him, yearning, aching to be suckled. He'd used his tongue to circle and flick, his teeth to rasp softly, his lips to draw her into his mouth rhythmically.

Ruby had been feverish with wanting by the time Jack had stood to remove the rest of his clothing. She could no more have halted him then than stopped her wildly careening heart. All their petting in the past had taken place in his car or on the living-room sofa, with parents nearby. This had been the first time she'd seen Jack naked. Like an ancient Viking, he'd stood proudly, his tall, muscular body perfectly in tune with the autumn background, his blond hair fluttering in the air. His erect penis had grown rock hard and huge under her flattering perusual. Jack's sheer masculinity took her breath away.

By the time Ruby had lain naked, as well, they'd both been panting. His long fingers had moved expertly in the delta between her thighs to prepare her wetly. She'd budded, then flowered under his fluttering fingertips. When he'd poised between her legs finally, he'd repeated his earlier question, "Will you marry me, Rube?" At the moment she'd whispered, "Yes," he'd buried himself in her sheath in one smooth stroke. There'd been slight pain, but mostly the overwhelming, wonderful feeling of being filled by the man she loved. After that, she'd been unable to think at all as he'd driven her to the edge of eternity and then over with catapulting waves of pleasure.

When they'd lain in each other's arms afterwards, Jack had nuzzled her neck. "Let's get married—now! We can drive out of state, get married by a justice of the peace and be back at my apartment by Sunday night. I have three hundred dollars in my checking account."

"Now? Today?" Ruby's brain had still felt muddled from their lovemaking. He couldn't be serious, she'd thought.

"Yes. I want you to come back to school with me. I don't want to be there if you're not with me. Please, Rube, marry me."

"This is just lust speaking, Jack," Ruby had commented, with a shaky laugh.

"Yeah! Ain't it great?" he'd responded with the drop-dead grin she'd always found irresistible, and Ruby had felt a deep throbbing begin in her center once again. Then he'd begun a new assault on her already weakened senses. "I love you, Rube. I'll never love any other woman," Jack had whispered as they sank to the soft autumn bed. "We can make it work. We can . . ."

Words hadn't been necessary after that as they made sweet, sweet love for the second time in the most gorgeous setting any bride could ever want.

They hadn't eloped that weekend, but they'd convinced both their parents of their seriousness. The formal wedding had taken place over Christmas vacation, and Ruby had returned to Jack's university with him. Thanks to the financial help of both sets of parents, part-time jobs, Jack's scholarship and some extremely frugal living conditions, including postage-stamp-size apartments, both had managed to graduate from college four years later.

As the fog of memories began to dim, Ruby realized she still lay on the Viking pallet with eyes squeezed shut, her body shuddering with silent sobs she didn't want her wretched guard to overhear. Jack's words lingered in her mind: "We can make it work."

What a fool she'd been!

"Do you weep for want of me or for your sorry fate?"

Huh? Jack hadn't said *that*.

Ruby's eyes shot open to the sight of Jack—no, Thork—leaning against the open doorway of her tower room, arms and legs crossed. She hadn't even heard the door open.

Standing up, she asked him huffily, "How long have you been standing there ogling me? Why aren't you off sucking up to the tarantula?"

"Sucking up?" Thork questioned on a laugh. "Can I assume 'tarantula' is a spider?"

"You got it!"

"Your manner of speaking—'tis ever a puzzle." Thork shook his head quizzically.

"You think my language is odd. I've heard enough 'twas-es and 'tis-es and 'twoulds to last me a lifetime."

Thork laughed easily.

Ruby narrowed her eyes. What was up now? A short time ago the brute had shook her and almost slapped her face. Now he stood here laughing as if nothing were wrong. He was just like Jack in that regard. A short fuse, quick outburst, and then an equally rapid recovery.

"So, is the torture going to begin now? Will you do it here, or should we move out into the bailey so everyone can watch? If we had more time, we could serve popcorn and slurpees. Hey, why not give the whip to your spider friend? I'll bet she could do a good job of skinning me alive."

Thork looked appalled at her words.

"Halt thy wicked tongue, woman. Linette is not as you think."

"Hah!"

Thork still hadn't moved from his nonchalant stance near the door. He gazed at her intently, seeming to look for answers to some great mystery.

"Why are you watching me so strangely? What am I being accused of now?"

Thork shrugged uncomfortably. "Naught do I accuse

195

you of," he started to explain, then seemed to shift course, "but I wonder what you dreamt of before you started weeping. You were making love in your dreams, were you not? Was it your husband, Jack?"

Ruby felt her face flush and pressed her fingertips to her cheek, wondering if the finger welts from Dar's slap were still there.

"The tips of your breasts swelled with passion even as you slept," Thork continued relentlessly. "You arched your womanhood and spread your thighs wantonly. You even moaned."

Involuntarily, Ruby looked down, then crossed her arms across her chest in embarrassment. The tips of her swollen breasts were, indeed, clearly outlined under her thin T-shirt.

"By the faith! Surely you do not turn shy on me now—after all the outrageous things you have said and done."

An insufferable grin spread across Thork's lips.

"All right, what's going on here?" Ruby demanded to know. "Something has definitely happened. First you run hot, then cold. One day, angry. The next, teasing. Tell me. Do I die or do I go free?"

Thork studied her, as if weighing his words carefully. "Neither. We have discovered the traitor in our midst. One of the hesirs who traveled with us from Jorvik was Ivar's man. 'Twould seem was him, not you, who sought to entrap Dar."

It took several moments for Thork's words to sink in.

Then, shrieking loudly, Ruby sprang at him, pounding his chest, trying to scrape her nails across his face, biting his shoulder when he lifted her by the upper arms off the floor. When she hit his groin with her kicking legs, Thork twisted his body and lost his footing. They both fell to the pallet, which broke with a loud crash under the impact of his weight and the force of their combined fall.

"You bastard! You son-of-a-bitch! You bucket of slime! Let me up. I'm going to cut out your stinking heart. Ouch!"

"Leave off, wench. Your voice—'tis shrill as a sea gull. Oh! Your nails are sharp."

Thork pinned her down with his hard body, her arms above her head, her legs encased in his thighs. They lay in the midst of the broken bed on the floor, straw floating in the air above them from the torn mattress cover. Ruby tried to heave him off her and realized her mistake immediately.

"Oh!" she exclaimed on a whisper as the juncture of her thighs pushed against Thork's manhood, arousing him instantly. She tried to correct her error by dropping back and turning her face away.

He wouldn't allow it.

Wolfishly his lips stalked hers, forcing a response she didn't want to give. When she fought him, Thork nipped her lower lip gently with his teeth. Ruby parted her lips to scream, and he slipped his tongue into her mouth, filling her with a pleasure she could not deny.

She could feel the smile on Thork's self-satisfied lips. *The boor!*

Palm to palm, he held her hands pressed to the bed above her head, then levered himself up slightly. He moved his body from side to side across her, back and forth, the coarse wool of his tunic-covered chest brushing her T-shirt-clad breasts, the hardness of his manhood caressing the dream-sensitized vee of her thighs. She arched involuntarily, and Thork gasped out, "Oh, yea, sweetling! You do that *so* nice."

He deftly maneuvered his thighs between hers, then shifted so he lay firmly against her jean-clad center. In an age-old dance of lift, then touch, lift, then touch, Thork undulated against her mercilessly. Meanwhile, his tongue set a matching pattern in her mouth. She tried to moan her protest, but only managed to open her mouth wider for his plundering kiss.

Unable to utter her protests aloud, Ruby soon gave up, a soaring passion overtaking her. Lost between two worlds, Ruby wasn't sure if the crackling noise under her was straw or autumn leaves. Or whether it was Jack or Thork. Perhaps they were one and the same. She couldn't think anymore. She didn't want to think.

Lost in a time warp, Ruby keened her anguish and fevered wanting into his open mouth. "Oh, Jack! I love you so much!"

Thork pulled back abruptly and stared at her in disbelief—a hurt, questioning expression shadowing his passion-glazed eyes. Then he muttered an obscenity. Ruby couldn't stop looking at his lips, which she'd bruised deliciously with her kisses.

Oh, my God! She wanted him *so* badly! Thork, Jack, whoever he was—it didn't matter.

"Jack! You called me Jack," Thork accused, stabbing her murderously with blue eyes still hazy with desire. "Do you think of another man when you yield to me?"

Ruby licked her lips nervously, trying to think of a way to explain once again that he and Jack were the same man to her. She never got a chance to answer as Dar rushed breathlessly into the room.

"What goes here? It sounded like the whole bloody keep was falling down."

Following him were Aud, Olaf, Gyda, the girls and a dozen others, including Linette.

Embarrassed, Ruby tried to shift from under Thork, but the stubborn Viking refused. Ruby smiled involuntarily, though, in a pure, unadulterated gloat at the sight of the Black Widow glaring at her in Thork's arms.

Thork rolled to his side, still holding her in his arms, his arousal pressing disconcertingly into her thigh.

"What happened? Did she attack you?" an outraged

Linette asked, pushing her way to the front of the group.

"Nay, I tripped and fell onto the pallet," Thork explained dryly, pulling a sheet discreetly over his middle.

"On top of the wench?" Olaf scoffed.

"Shush, Olaf," Gyda whispered loudly, elbowing him to behave.

Dar snickered as he shooed everyone back downstairs to the hall where the loud noises had been heard. He shook his head in disgust at the sight of the two of them on the broken bed before extending a hand to Ruby, then Thork.

"Methinks the mischievous Loki is having a grand laugh over you," Dar commented dryly, looking pointedly at Thork's crotch. "Mayhap you two deserve each other, after all." He pulled at his lower lip thoughtfully and his eyes narrowed slyly at Ruby. "Is there any chance you truly are related to Hrolf, or that mayhap he would dower you in marriage?"

"*No!*" Thork bellowed. "Do not think it! Never will I marry, and leastways not to this sorry wench!" Obviously, he'd managed to overcome his bout of passion for her.

"Hold it here," Ruby intervened. To Dar she said, "Yes, I am truly related to Hrolf, and, no, I am not, nor ever will be, an heiress. Forget any ambitious plans you may be concocting in that direction."

Dar pretended mock offense.

To Thork Ruby snapped haughtily, "As for this 'sorry wench,' she doesn't want you any more than you want her. You and that oversexed spider can live happily ever after, for all I care."

So why did the thought bother her so much? Why did her eyes linger on the well-developed muscles in his forearms and thighs as he brushed away pieces of the clinging straw?

And buns! He had the cutest backside she'd seen outside of a magazine centerfold, Ruby thought irrelevantly

199

as she watched him stride out of the room. Boy, could she picture him in a pair of tight jeans!

Ruby realized then that Dar watched her closely and seemed to know just what part of Thork's anatomy she'd been ogling. With a knowing grin, he raised a hand to halt her next words.

"Do not think to deny what I just witnessed. An old man I may be, but not yet in my dotage when it comes to recognizing that certain look in a woman's eye." Chuckling, he bid her follow him downstairs, where the servant Ella had been given permission by Thork to take her to a nearby pond for a bath—under guard, of course. Wonderful! How did Thork know she craved a bath? Probably because she stank like a pig after three days without soap and water.

"Dar, am I no longer under suspicion now that the hesir confessed to spying for Ivar?"

"Nay. We still trust you not. 'Tis even possible that the spy worked with you, though I misdoubt it. 'Twill be for the Althing to decide."

"Do you really believe I could be a spy?"

"A stranger in our lands who cannot account for her background is suspicious enough in times when danger lurks in every corner. Not only must Thork worry about the danger from his half-brother Eric or from enemies who would kidnap those he cherishes for ransom, but the Saxons merely bide their time until the right moment for attack.

"Then you made matters even worse with that birth-control nonsense you introduced to the women. Thor's blood! 'Twas a stupid move on your part if you are, in truth, a spy."

"I've tried to tell the truth, but no one believes me."

"Tell me naught of the future again, lass. I will hear naught of it. Take care, though. I tell you true—the only thing that will save you at the Althing is protection by a powerful Viking man. Since that appears nigh impossible at this point, you best pray to that Christian God of yours that they believe you are kin to Hrolf."

Dar's words of warning remained with Ruby as she and Ella walked to the pond just beyond the manor keep, followed by Vigi who looked left and right for possible intruders.

"By the saints, I ne'er thought to see you alive after you went to the tower," Ella exclaimed as soon as they were out the manor doors. "I heard once that a sorceress can put a spell on people so they gotta do her will. That mus' be it. A sorceress you are. How else could you have escaped bein' kilt so many a time?"

"Oh, good heavens, Rhoda . . . I mean, Ella, don't even think to mention the name sorceress in connection with me, or they really will kill me, especially that Sigtrygg."

Chapter Eleven

The spring-fed pond nestled in a secluded little oasis, hidden from the keep by a strand of trees. The bossy Ella ordered Vigi to go to the edge of the clearing and make sure he kept his back turned. Then she perched on a flat boulder, refusing to enter the water with Ruby.

"Are you daft? There was a girl onct who took too many baths and her skin shriveled up so bad it never got smooth agin. 'Tis not good to be so clean, poisons the blood, it does. Why, I even . . ."

Ruby let Ella ramble on as she lingered almost an hour in the soothing water. She scrubbed her hair and body over and over to remove the grime.

The servants were setting up the evening meal when Ruby returned to the manor. Aud told her that the tower room had been cleaned for her continued use but that she would be expected downstairs in the hall for dinner.

"Where are Eirik and Tykir?" Ruby asked, suddenly realizing she hadn't seen them since their arrival here several days ago, not even in the hall at mealtimes.

"In the stables," Aud replied. "They sleep there and eat in the kitchen with the servants."

"But how can you stand to see your own grandsons live such a life?"

For a split second, Aud's composure weakened, but then she straightened. "Do not think to question what is naught of your affair." She walked straight-backed to the kitchen area, summoning Ella to follow her.

Ruby decided to seek out the boys before the evening meal. Vigi followed but didn't try to stop her. Cold, suspicious eyes followed Ruby wherever she walked. The hesirs, bonders, freedmen and even thralls, who worked diligently at assigned tasks, would clearly kill her on the spot if given the choice. The spy's confession had done nothing to lessen her guilt in their eyes.

Ruby entered the stable, where she eventually found Tykir grooming a gray pony.

"Hello, Tykir."

"Ruby!" At first, Tykir's eyes lighted up with welcome, but then he shadowed them carefully. Even he must have been told to distrust the strange woman who might be the enemy.

"What is your horse's name?"

"He has none." Tykir looked surprised. "Should he have?"

"Well, not everybody names their horse, but I thought since this one seems so special to you it ought to have a name."

"Could we name him?" he asked shyly.

"Of course. Can you think of any names that you like?"

He shook his head sadly, as if he must be lacking in some important way.

"Well, my boys never had a horse—"

"They never had a horse? Ever?" To Tykir, that appeared to be the ultimate loss in the world.

"Never, but they had pet dogs. Let me think. Over the years, there were Rover, Morris, Nellie and Elvis."

"Elvis," Tykir whispered in awe. "'Tis a wondrously fine name, think you not?"

Oh, no! This was one place Elvis followers would never expect a sighting, Ruby thought, stifling a laugh. Tykir's emotions were so open and vulnerable. The little stinker looked as if he hadn't bathed in days. His blond hair, so like his father's, stuck out in greasy spikes as he gazed hopefully up at her. Ruby felt her heart expand and fill with warmth. How could Thork and Dar and Aud bear to neglect such a dear little soul?

"I think Elvis would be a wonderful name," she declared, and was rewarded with a grateful smile.

"Why is your hair wet?" Tykir asked.

"I was swimming in the pond. Have you been there?"

He nodded. "But I cannot swim. Father . . . I mean, Thork . . . is gonna teach me someday, but he mus' go Jomsviking soon." He raised his chin defiantly, his voice quivering with unshed tears "Someday I will be a Jomsviking, too. Then I kin be with my . . . with Thork . . . as much as I want."

One more bone Ruby had to pick with Thork, she thought. "Does Eirik want to be a Jomsviking also?"

"Nay, he dreams of being a fosterling at the Saxon court, like Uncle Haakon, who is of the same age," Tykir said with distaste, scrunching up his nose. "He sez we Vikings mus' learn the Saxon way to survive in their lands." Tykir blushed and looked down sheepishly then, as if he knew he'd said too much.

"Does his father know of this wish?"

"Nay, Eirik could ne'er tell him *that*."

This whole situation of separating parent and child was ridiculous, in Ruby's opinion. No, more than that, it was destructive, and she vowed to do something about it. Ruby knew she would have to employ tact in persuading Thork to act the true father to his sons—even if it meant giving up his precious Jomsviking oath, even if it meant moving to a new land. Even if it meant Thork's taking her with him—if that's what it would take to escape this dangerous nightmare, Ruby vowed.

But Ruby became increasingly alarmed the next few days as the Althing approached and Thork accelerated his activities related to his departure for Jomsborg. What would happen to her at the Viking-style court? If the venomous looks she got from Dar's knights and workers were any indication, her fate loomed bleak. All free males in Northumbria, including these very men, could vote at the open-air assembly.

Well, if no one else was going to help her, she would have to take matters in hand herself, but first she needed a plan. Not just any plan. It had to be the ultimate, sure-fire master plan—the mother of all plans.

Thork will have to marry me.

It was the only way. If he married her, none of the Vikings would dare harm her, and she could make a home for Eirik and Tykir. She had no other choice. So, finally, she settled on a three-part strategy: persuasion, seduction and/or force, in that order. She hoped the last would not be necessary. Actually, she hadn't even thought that far.

Ruby decided to enlist Ella in her plot.

"'Tis barmy ya are! I told ya that the first day I saw ya at the docks," Ella exclaimed, trying to slink away. "Mebbe ya got worms in yer head. That be it, I wager! Most folks has worms in their guts from eating maggoty food, but they unleashes them from their nether ends in the garderobe. The barmy ones, like you, well, the worms crawl up inta their heads and make 'em go mad. Onct I even heard 'bout a man whose worms crawled out his ears and—"

"No, no, no! I'm not crazy. Can't you see that marriage with Thork would protect me from these vicious Vikings who'd just as soon have my head on a pike?"

Ella shook her head dubiously.

"Eirik and Tykir need a family. Maybe we could all move to another country where there would be no danger. Perhaps you could even come with us."

A spark of interest showed in Ella's eyes. "Where? What country?"

Ruby hesitated. "Well, how about Iceland? I've heard some of the Vikings talk about emigrating to that new land."

"Iceland!" Ella exclaimed, preparing to walk off in a huff. "You *are* barmy! Freeze my arse off in some land of rebels and outlaws! When frogs fly, mebbe!"

Ruby shrugged hopelessly. "Actually, I was hoping such a drastic move might jolt me back to the future."

"Oh, that be just wunnerful! You get us all to that Godforsaken country and then you just skip off to yer own pleasures. What do I do then? Chip icicles off the boys' noses fer fun? Or play hidey-hole with the whales and seals?"

"Ella, this really isn't a bad plan," Ruby asserted, trying hard not to laugh.

"Seems ta me yer fergettin sumpin important here," Ella offered sagely. "Thork avoids ya like the bloody flux these three days past, eber since that day you two rolled aroun' in the straw in yer tower room."

"We were not . . . oh, what's the use. Can't you see that he's afraid of commitment to me? And he fears—"

"Hah!" Ella interrupted with a snort. "He does not seem too concerned 'bout committin' wid Linette. She be all over him like honey on a hot rock, and the thrall Eda what cleans his chamber sez they go at *it* all night long. Linette's moanin' and groanin' kin be heard all the way down to the hall."

"Really, Ella, must you always repeat gossip? I don't want to hear this." No, she *really* did not want to know intimate details about Thork, Ruby thought jealously.

"Mebbe ya better hear it. Mebbe ya better realize that ta make yer plan work ya gotta step over Linette first." Ella looked Ruby over critically, obviously doubting her ability to entice Thork away from the Viking widow. Turning to leave, Ella offered a tantalizing teaser over her shoulder, "Ya do know 'bout the 'sickness' Linette has, dontja?"

"What sickness?" Ruby had never seen a healthier-looking woman in her life.

"She cannot get enough of . . . *you know.*"

"What?"

"*You know*, the man's parts betwixt her legs."

"Oh, Ella! How can you say such things?" Despite herself, Ruby giggled.

"'Tis the truth, I swear. Everyone in the keep knows of it, most from having been there, I wager. Many's the time the master and mistress speak on it of late and how they best hurry and marry her off afore no respectable-like Viking will have her."

A nymphomaniac! Could it be true? No way! Ruby shook her head in doubt on the way back to the keep as the ditzy servant sashayed in front of her, self-satisfied with her latest imparting of rumors.

Ruby soon found her master plan easier to formulate than to enact. The only time she got to see Thork was at the evening meal, where Linette wrapped herself around him like cotton candy. And just as sickeningly sweet! Thork must be back in his "Avoid Ruby" mode. Hadn't he said earlier that she put stumbling blocks in his Jomsviking activities.

Hah! Hold on, Thork, I've got a few boulders coming your way.

It rankled Ruby, however, to think she'd have to deliberately seduce Thork into marriage, especially when his arrogance and cold-blooded killings repelled her. She refused to think about that other side of him that drew her enticingly, that reminded her of Jack and all the good things they'd shared. Worst of all, Ruby wasn't exactly sure how to seduce a man. Jack was the only man she'd ever been with—literally—and he'd always been the pursuer.

Late the next afternoon, she enlisted Ella's aid. "Try to lure Vigi away from me for a little while so I can slip into Thork's room. Do you think you could do that?"

"'Twill never work," Ella grumbled as she went off to do as Ruby bid. "Bloody flux! I must be as barmy as she is. Prob'ly get my head chopped off, too."

Ruby stealthily opened Thork's door, first looking right and left to make sure no one saw her. Luckily, Thork was alone.

He stood with knees bent to bring his face level with a sheet of metal on the wall above a small table. Barefoot and bare-chested, he was shaving the lather off his face with a sharp knife. Ruby took one look at his pants riding low on his slim hips, and her mouth suddenly went dry.

"Thork, I have to talk to you," she croaked out.

Caught off guard, Thork jumped and the knife cut his face. Blood immediately oozed out against the white lather. "Holy Valhalla! What do you here, jumping out of corners?" His eyes narrowed. "And where the hell's Vigi?"

"Now, Thork, don't get mad at Vigi. I needed to talk to you, and you keep avoiding me." Ruby wrung her hands nervously, not certain how to launch her mission.

Thork turned his back on her to resume his shaving. "Go away, wench," he growled through lips pressed together to accommodate his shaving. "We have naught to discuss."

Ruby moved to the side so she could see him better. Entranced, she watched as he puffed out his cheek and slid the razor in a smooth furrow through the lather. Lord! The urge to touch his skin was overpowering. "Do you want me to do that for you?" she offered weakly.

Thork arched his eyebrows at her, feigning horror. "You

with a knife at my throat? Hah! The image makes my skin crawl." He slanted an amused glance her way and shook his head despairingly. "Do I look like a lackwit?" Then quickly, without waiting for a reply, "Do not answer that!"

He didn't look like a lackwit at all, Ruby thought, mesmerized by the motions of his long fingers as they wielded neat furrows through the foam. His knee-bent stance outlined the corded muscles in his thighs and tight buttocks. Ruby was acutely aware of golden hairs that dusted the planes of his rock-hard chest, trailed down the ridges of his washboard-firm abdomen and disappeared invitingly below his exposed navel. Her eyes shot back upward from that forbidden territory to land on the flat brown nipples. She had to restrain herself from reaching out and touching them, to feel their texture in her fingertips, to test their sensitivity.

Almost done shaving, Thork winked at her devilishly, aware of her too-obvious scrutiny. With a warm chuckle, he said, "Spit it out. What did you want to say to me?"

Ruby dropped her eyes before his perceptive gaze, but then blurted out the first thought that came into her head, "You have a marvelous chest."

Laughter gurgled up out of Thork's throat at her spontaneous remark. He couldn't help but see the flush of embarrassment on her flaming cheeks. How could she have said something so stupid?

"Yours is also . . . marvelous," he offered graciously, his blue eyes twinkling. Then he scrutinized her chest in mock seriousness. "Leastways, I think it is. Of course, I have only seen it *totally* uncovered once. Would you care to remove your tunic and show me?"

"No!" Ruby retorted, irritated by his apparent humor at her expense. But then she immediately questioned her overly quick response. Why had she answered negatively when her purpose was supposed to be persuading him to marry her? Some seductress she was turning out to be!

"Oh, all right," she muttered, hot-faced with self-consciousness, as she reached for the hem of her loose tunic and pulled it up over her head.

Thork had just finished wiping his face with a square of linen when he realized what she was doing. "Odin's eyeballs! What are you about now?" he sputtered, then ordered, "Put your garment back on."

"You told me to take it off. You said you wanted to look at my chest," Ruby argued, then finally gave in to her innate modesty and covered her breasts girlishly with her hands.

"I was not serious," he choked out, unable to pull his eyes away from the sight of her standing in her black lace bra and panties. His smoldering eyes took in every inch of her exposed body.

Ruby shifted nervously from foot to foot, uncomfortable with his silent scrutiny, but before he had a chance to kick her out, she forced herself to follow through on her plan of persuasion. Reaching behind, she unsnapped her wispy bra, letting it drop to the floor.

"What do you think?" she squeaked.

Well, that certainly wiped the smile off his face!

Thork dropped his towel and gazed at her in amazement. "I cannot be sure," he said huskily. "Come closer."

The fire in his glittering eyes awakened slumbering embers deep inside Ruby that had been banked for such a long time. One part of Ruby wanted to rebel, to run like crazy from the room and the humiliation of her wanton behavior. The other part, the stronger one, pushed her feet—step by reluctant step—closer to Thork. The odor of his skin intoxicated her—sun, soap and man. Oh, yes, man! When she stopped a mere foot away, he took both breasts in his hands, weighing them, reshaping them. Cupping the undersides, he ran the pads of his thumbs over the already erect tips, and Ruby's knees turned to Jell–o.

Trembling, she reached up to his shoulders for balance.

Thork's eyes collided with hers, questioning. His lips parted and he ran his tongue over their dryness.

"Truly, they are a . . . marvel," he rasped out, "but then one cannot know for sure till the tasting." Lifting her off the floor so her breasts were level with his face, he prolonged the moment agonizingly as his breath fluttered warmly against first one and then the other of the firm mounds. Finally he took a good portion of her breast in his wide mouth, drawing deeply, pulling slowly outward until his lips closed on the nipple.

"'Tis sweet as honey," Thork whispered against her skin.

Ruby moaned and arched her back, begging softly, "That . . . feels . . . so . . . good! Oh, please, don't stop."

"As if I could!" Thork murmured in a raw voice, using his tongue expertly to lave the aureole, then circle the nipple wetly before flicking the tip in rapid vibrating motions.

Ruby cried out.

He moved to the other breast and repeated all the same motions, growling with satisfaction when she mewled softly. "Oh, yes, little cat, purr for me just so," he coaxed.

By the time he lowered her to her tiptoes, brushing her nipples against the silky hairs on his chest in the process, Ruby's mouth was level with his, and she could feel his steely erection pressing against her stomach. When his lips closed in on hers, Thork murmured in a thick, unsteady voice, "Is this what you came to talk to me about, little witch? Didst change your mind about bedding with me?"

His lips were already sealed with hers, devouring, pressing, when Ruby's bemuddled mind registered his words. No, that wasn't what she wanted to talk about, she reminded herself dazedly. What was it? Oh, yes! Now she remembered fuzzily.

"Thork," she whispered. She pulled away from his lips, but he followed her and kissed her once again. This time she spoke louder when she broke the kiss with a gasp, "Thork, this isn't what I wanted to talk about," she said and drew in her breath sharply as his tongue assaulted the sensitive recesses of her ear. "At least, not exactly."

Laughing, he backed up and took her with him, then sat down on the bed. He turned her so she sat on his lap. Ruby could feel the force of his arousal under her legs.

"What is it that's so important?" he whispered in a distracted fashion, obviously as affected by this love play as she was. He kissed the nape of her neck and ran his fingers feather lightly over the inside of her thighs.

"Oh!" she gasped, and something wonderful twisted deep within her body.

"Oh, indeed," Thork chuckled.

"Stop it, Thork. I can't think when you do that."

"'Tis the idea." Then he pulled his hand away teasingly and nuzzled her neck again. "I'm listening."

"Thork, I've decided . . . ," Ruby started, finding it hard to speak after his sensual attack, " . . . I've decided we should . . . we should . . . get . . . married."

"*You've* decided," Thork hooted derisively, dropping backward to the bed and shifting so that she lay at his side in the crook of his arm. He put his mouth to her breast again, and she could feel his smile. When his infolded lips and grazing teeth brought her to a mindless pitch once again, he looked up with passion-glazed eyes and told her, "*I've* decided we should make love, *without* the marriage."

Obviously, he didn't think she was serious.

"No," Ruby protested, trying to pull away, but he held her firmly in his arms. When she stopped struggling, Ruby implored him, "You *have* to marry me, Thork."

"I do?" he asked seductively, rolling on his back and pulling her up on top of him, chest to breast, straining manhood to throbbing womanhood. He was not making this easy, at all.

"Sweetling, how many times do I have to tell you. I will not marry—*ever*." Then he laughed and gave her a quick hug. "Leastways, in my country, the woman waits for the man to ask."

"It's pretty much the same in my country, even with women's lib," Ruby confessed, "but I don't have time to wait for you to do the asking."

"Let's talk about this later," he cajoled smoothly and pulled her knees apart and forward so that she straddled him. They both gasped simultaneously at the shock of swirling pleasure, almost too intense to be borne.

Trying to slow down the careening pace of their sexual game, Thork asked, "What is this urgent need to talk of marriage?"

Inhaling deeply to stabilize her heightened senses, Ruby said, bracing her straightened arms on his chest, "I now realize I need your protection when I go before the Althing."

"A wise conclusion."

"Thork, let me move. I can't concentrate."

"Nay," he laughed. "You are just where I have wanted you for a long time."

She laid her right hand gently on his cheek. "Thork, I'm very concerned about Eirik and Tykir. They need a family unit—a mother and father, living together."

Only the flickering muscle near his mouth betrayed his reaction to her mentioning his sons. "Do you try to cool my ardor by bringing up those subjects I forbade you to address?"

"Oh, Thork! I came to your room to try to make you see . . . oh, what's the use!" She lay her face on his chest for a moment, then looked up, determined to try once more. "Did you know that Tykir plans to become a Jomsviking like you just so he can spend some time in your company?

213

And Eirik wants to be fostered at King Athelstan's court with his Uncle Haakon. The atmosphere there couldn't be any colder than the one he lives in now."

The surprise on Thork's face showed Ruby he hadn't been aware of his sons' wishes.

"I have already told you why I cannot be with them," he said through gritted teeth.

"I know. I know. That brings me to my third point," she said, nervously drawing circles around his flat brown nipples, barely noticing his small gasp of pleasure.

"Pray tell," he laughed, probably expecting her to pop another of her surprises on him.

"You don't have to be sarcastic. I'm just trying to help."

"Odin save me!" he prayed, raising his eyes dramatically upward. "The wench would save *me* by having me give up Jomsviking to wed *her*." He wrapped his arms around her tightly, though, amused with her arguments.

"Do you want to hear the rest?"

"Do I have a choice?"

"No, but I wish you'd keep an open mind."

"Oh, I am more than open," Thork countered, moving his thighs apart slightly and spreading her straddled legs in the process, making her sensitized cleft more exposed to his hardness.

She groaned and closed her eyes a moment. When she opened them, she went on doggedly, "I think . . . I think you could solve all your problems by marrying me and then taking me and Eirik and Tykir to some other country where we would all be safe and not have to worry about any danger." She exhaled after her long-winded plea and looked at him hopefully.

"Like where?" Thork asked distractedly as her navel caught the attention of his exploring fingertips.

"Well, how about Iceland?"

"Are you daft?" he asked, then burst out laughing,

214

hugging her warmly as he rolled her over onto her back. "Oh, Ruby, I love the way you make me laugh," he said with a delighted chuckle as he playfully bit her neck. When his laughter finally stopped, Thork leaned over her, tracing the line of her jaw lazily with his thumb, then the outlines of her lips. A pulse beat wildly at the base of his throat.

"'Tis time for honesty betwixt us, sweetling. Are you ready to be my bedmate or not?"

Bedmate? Ruby hesitated, hampered by the lump in her throat. "I hoped for more."

"I cannot give more," he said, looking her directly in the eye. "I want you, more than I can ever remember wanting a woman." He, too, seemed to have trouble swallowing.

Ruby closed her eyes for a second to savor his softly spoken words. Lord, she was falling in love with this man—all over again. This heady, overwhelming, dizzy euphoria could only be likened to the way she had felt in the beginning with Jack, when everything was new, and hope made anything possible.

But Thork was not Jack, Ruby had to forcefully remind herself, as he continued, "I can only pledge my protection until the Althing, Ruby. You need to know that. But know this as well—I do not take this powerful attraction we share lightly. In different times, mayhap there could have been more betwixt us, but leastways I can promise you the best loving you have had in your life—for as long as we can be together." He kissed her lips lightly to seal his words.

"For how long?" Ruby asked weakly.

"Until I leave."

Ruby winced. She didn't like Thork's offer, enticing as the prospect of sleeping with him would be, but she knew she had no other choice. And, besides, once she'd slept with him, she might be able to convince him otherwise. "All right. I agree," she finally said and put her hands on both sides of his face, intending to pull him down for her kiss.

But Thork sensed Ruby's hesitancy. "Nay, we must first be clear on this arrangement. You will be satisfied being my bedmate? You will not be hoping for more, trying to change my mind? 'Tis no dishonor in being mistress, but 'tis dishonorable of me to bed you if you are hoping for more."

"Thork, I couldn't stop hoping, but that doesn't mean you would have to change your mind. If I'm willing to take the risk, why can't you?"

Ruby watched various emotions flicker across Thork's face as he fought to make a rational decision. Then he asked thoughtfully, "You would ask much of me, Ruby, to give up my oath of Jomsviking, to stay in the Saxon lands, to enter an institution whose bindings I abhor, but what about you? Would you promise to never leave me? To never return to your own country?"

Oh, my God! How could she have failed to consider that question? What if she returned to the future? There was no way she could ever make such a binding promise to Thork, not knowing when or if the time-travel might be reversed.

Thork scrutinized her face and read her answer. Before she could say anything, he pulled away and moved off the bed, breathing heavily.

"Thork, please let me explain. It's not what you think. It might not be my decision to make."

"And who might be making that decision for you? Ivar? Athelstan?" he snapped icily. He threw up his hands in resignation. "Holy Thor! Why am I ever surprised by women and their machinations? You tried to trap me. And fool that I am, I almost fell for your ploy."

Ruby wept silently, unable to offer Thork an explanation he could accept.

Finally he ordered, "Leave my chamber and do not dare

to tempt me again, or I swear I will kill you with my bare hands." Furious swear words spouted from Thork's mouth as he threw her tunic at her and pulled her off the bed, shoving her toward the door.

"Vigi!" he yelled out the open doorway into the hall, "Get your bloody arse here, or I will skin you alive."

"Thork, you're making a mistake. Please. You don't understand. Please. It's not what you think."

Thork would not even look at her as she donned her tunic, despite her pleas.

Soon a red-faced Vigi came running from a room down the hall, struggling to lace a hastily donned pair of pants. He cowered under Thork's stormy vindictives, which ended with an order, "Tell Linette I want her—*now!*"

"Oh, no! Oh, Thork, don't do this. Don't destroy the beauty of this thing between us. How can you be with Linette and not me?" she asked with tears choking her voice.

"Because she expects naught of me," he ground out, "and because she is honest, and you are not."

"Linette, honest? Hah! If you weren't so blind—"

Thork grabbed her by the upper arm and pushed her out into the hallway. "You have teased and tormented me for the last time, wench. Never doubt that the fire you ignited in my belly can just as easily be quenched in another sheath." He looked pointedly at Linette, who was scurrying toward him expectantly with Vigi close behind.

He pulled Linette into his arms and kissed her hungrily, uncaring of Ruby's hurt, watchful eyes. The door slammed soon behind them both, but not before Thork ordered Vigi, "Keep the wench out of my sight, or you will suffer the bloody consequences."

Stunned, Ruby stared at the closed door, knowing what was about to take place. She pounded on the locked door and screamed, "This isn't the end, you bastard. Just you wait and see. Just you wait and see."

217

Realizing the foolishness of her position, Ruby stopped. How could he? she cried with inner torment. How could he? She rocked back and forth on her heels in pain at his cruelty until Ella put a comforting hand on her shoulder and led her back to her tower room, under Vigi's guard. She stayed with her, holding her hand until the harsh sobs stopped racking her body.

"Your plan did not work, did it?" Ella asked gently when Ruby finally dried her eyes and blew her nose on a linen cloth.

"Yes and no," Ruby snuffled.

"What does that mean?"

"It means I tried to seduce Thork and ended up the seducee."

"Huh?"

Ruby suffered miserably that evening when neither Thork nor Linette showed up in the great hall for dinner. The next morning Ella informed her that Thork had gone off for several days to Jorvik where he would ready his ship for sailing.

"Linette went along fer the company," she added, rolling her eyes dramatically. "And Gyda be spittin' mad that Linette travels with her husband, sez she does not trust the witch with her man. Aud and the master bin' arguing sumpin' fierce all day and she sez she will not speak to him till he gets the wench a husbin. And the master Dar sez all the trouble began when you came to the manor."

"Me?" Ruby exclaimed after Ella's long-winded ramble. "What have I to do with Linette's alley-cat morality?"

"'Twould seem Linette hid her doin's better till this past few days when you arrived."

Ruby realized as she looked up to the dais that evening that this time Ella had her facts straight. Aud deliberately turned her face away from Dar throughout the meal and talked only to her other eating companions. Dar's face reddened as he downed one horn of ale after another, refusing food. Once he looked directly at Ruby and glared. It seemed Ruby had one more vote against her at the Althing.

The next morning, after breaking her fast on bannock and cheese, Ruby sought out Aud. She found her in the large, separate outside kitchen where she was removing several baskets from their pegs on the walls.

"I go now to gather mushrooms. Tomorrow we will dry them," Aud told the cook.

"Can I come with you?" Ruby asked.

Aud jumped in surprise, clasping her chest. "Why?"

"I used to pick mushrooms with my grandmother. I was pretty good at selecting the nonpoisonous ones, but you may have different varieties here. You could show me."

Aud looked suspicious and not too excited about her company, but she didn't deny Ruby's request.

"Would you object if I asked Eirik and Tykir to come with us? Perhaps we could bring a basket of food with us and eat our midday meal outdoors by the pond."

A brief look of something akin to pain flickered on Aud's face before she deliberately masked her face with blankness. "Eirik went with Thork and Olaf to help load the ships."

"How about Tykir?"

After a long pause, Aud replied, "If you wish."

When their baskets overflowed with the succulent fungi, they returned to the pond and spread their food over a flat boulder. Tykir played merrily at the edge of the water, trying to catch a frog which kept eluding his slippery grasp. Ruby saw Aud gazing at him with sad, yearning eyes.

Now that she had Aud alone, Ruby broached the subject that bothered her most. "Aud, I'm worried about Eirik and Tykir, especially since Thork will be leaving soon."

Aud got up and started to clear away the food items, not wanting to engage in this forbidden subject.

"Aud, I wouldn't bring this up if I didn't truly care about your great-grandsons. If Thork insists on leaving them in someone else's care, why can't they stay with you?"

"'Tis Thork's decision. Whether I agree or not is unimportant. 'Tis for their own safety."

The look on Ruby's face must have lacked understanding because Aud continued, "You have ne'er met Harald and his vicious family. Pray God, you ne'er do." Tears misted Aud's eyes and her voice cracked as she went on, "Our only child, Enid, a beautiful, gentle soul, went to him, despite our wishes. 'Tis not unusual for a Viking to have more than one wife, especially the high-kings. Two there were in Harald's household afore Enid. She loved him so much it mattered naught, but when he put her and eight other wives aside for his new wife Ragnhild, in addition to numerous mistresses, the shame killed her. They say she took her own life, but, to my mind, 'twas the evil Harald who killed her."

Aud wiped her eyes angrily. "We tried to get Thork after Enid's death, to have him live here with us, but Harald would not allow it. Ne'er mind that he has bred twenty sons or more, not that many of them lived to manhood. The brothers kill each other right and left in their ambition to succeed their father as high-king."

"That's why Thork decided to become a Jomsviking, isn't it?"

"Yea. How he lived to age fourteen in that bloody household, I will ne'er know. He will not talk of it. I do know his half-brother Eric . . . Eric Bloodaxe, they name him . . . vowed long ago to see Thork dead and all that he holds dear."

"Oh, my God!"

"Yea, and so you should pray for him. Eric fears Thork mightily, even though he renounced rights to succession. The people hate Eric and well he knows it. The least hint that Thork would fight for the kingship on his father's death, and Vikings would clamor to his call."

Ruby nodded her head. "I can understand now why Thork feels he must pretend he has no sons, even why he thinks marriage would be impossible. Still, I have to believe there's a better solution." She thought about all that Aud had told her, then asked ruefully, with a laugh, "Did Thork tell you I proposed?"

"Proposed?"

"I asked him to marry me."

"No-o-o," Aud replied in amazement, and then giggled.

"He declined, but I'm going to ask again. I have to. That's probably why he scooted off to Jorvik." Inside, Ruby quivered at the prospect of approaching Thork again, but she knew she had no choice, and not just because of her safety. She couldn't let this man she was beginning to love believe she lied to him.

"I think you will not succeed," Aud said gently, placing a comforting hand on Ruby's shoulder. "In some ways, 'tis too bad. We need him here to help fight off the Saxons when they eventually come. We have ridden the fence here, adopting Saxon ways, trying to be peaceable neighbors, but 'tis foolish to think they will allow us to keep such valuable land without a fight."

"Then why doesn't Thork stay?"

Aud shrugged. "'Tis the Jomsviking. An honorable man does not break oath lightly."

Disheartened, Ruby sighed. "I've set myself an impossible task, haven't I?"

"Child, even if Thork agreed to give up Jomsviking and stay here, he could not wed you. He would need a wife with lands and the strong hands of her family—fathers and brothers—to join us in alliance."

Ruby asked hesitantly, "Would kinship with Hrolf bring a strong enough alliance?" What was she saying? How in hell could she get to this ancient ancestor of hers, convince him she truly was his granddaughter "fifty times removed" and then talk him into sending armies from Normandy? Maybe she was becoming as daft as everyone thought.

"Do you tell me true? Are you Hrolf's kin?" Aud's face brightened and she clasped Ruby's hands hopefully.

Ruby put her right hand over her heart. "I swear to you, Aud, on the body of the Christ we both hold dear, I am kin to Hrolf." She held her left hand behind her back with fingers crossed for her half-truth of omission.

"Mayhap there will be a way out of this, after all," Aud declared.

Ruby wondered if she'd put her foot in her mouth once again.

Chapter Twelve

"By your leave, my fine lady, I would speak with you in my private chamber," Dar said several days later with exaggerated politeness.

Ruby looked behind her to make sure he'd been addressing her.

"Yea, I mean you, wench, and make haste."

He and Thork and Olaf had returned the day before, but Thork parried her overtures to speak with him like a bloody gladiator, while Linette practically purred, ignoring the gossip she'd created by going off with the men.

Ruby followed Dar into the small chamber off the great hall, where he conducted estate business. Seating her in a chair next to his by the small fireplace, Dar spoke his mind bluntly. "Aud would convince me that you are, in truth, kin to Hrolf." He leaned back in the huge, carved chair, with legs outstretched casually, but his half-veiled eyes twitched nervously as he watched her every move speculatively.

"Hrolf is a direct blood relative of mine."

"Do you swear it on the holy book of your church?"

"I swear on the Holy Bible that I am kin to Hrolf."

Dar nodded, seeming to accept her word and weighing the implications. "Have you ever met the Marcher? Would he recognize you?"

Ruby's shoulders sagged and she shook her head.

Dar gave a short wave of dismissal with the fingers of his right hand, which had been propping up his chin in a thoughtful pose. "Mayhap 'tis of no importance. To be sure, King Harald has more than fifty grandchildren and not met half by far, although only Odin knows how many still live. 'Tis not unusual that you have not met Hrolf."

"Why are you asking these questions?"

"Mayhap I would be willing to intercede on your behalf at the Althing if 'twould help to keep my grandson here in Northumbria."

"You would help me get Thork to marry me?" Ruby smiled eagerly at the craggy old man.

"Nay, I would not," Dar snorted. "Thork must needs marry for lands and military might to aid our defense against the Saxons. I have a well-born maid in mind, Elise—half Viking, half Saxon she be—with lands and fighting brothers to dower and protect her in marriage."

Ruby's heart dropped at Dar's pragmatic words. "Then why would you help me?"

"Methinks you would make a fine bedmate for my grandson. I see the attraction you hold for him, though I cannot fathom it myself. Perchance you could entice him to stay."

"*Me?* You give me too much credit," Ruby exclaimed. "Have you seen how he avoids me and allows himself to be ensnared in Linette's web?"

Dar laughed. "Yea, he avoids you with a most peculiar vengeance and makes much ado in public over Linette. These old eyes see more than that, though. Methought

Thrill to the most sensual, adventure-filled Romances on the market today...

FROM 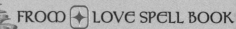 LOVE SPELL BOOK

As a home subscriber to the Love Spell Romance Book Club, you'll enjoy the best in today's BRAND-NEW Time Travel, Futuristic, Legendary Lovers, Perfect Heroes and other genre romance fiction. For five years, Love Spell has brought you the award-winning, high-quality authors you know and love to read. Each Love Spell romance will sweep you away to a world of high adventure...and intimate romance. Discover for yourself all the passion and excitement millions of readers thrill to each and every month.

Save $5.00 Each Time You Buy!

Every other month, the Love Spell Romance Book Club brings you four brand-new titles from Love Spell Books. EACH PACKAGE WILL SAVE YOU AT LEAST $5.00 FROM THE BOOK-STORE PRICE! And you'll never miss a new title with our convenient home delivery service.

Here's how we do it: Each package will carry a FREE 10-DAY EXAMINATION privilege. At the end of that time, if you decide to keep your books, simply pay the low invoice price of $17.96, no shipping or handling charges added. HOME DELIVERY IS ALWAYS FREE. With today's top romance novels selling for $5.99 and higher, our price SAVES YOU AT LEAST $5.00 with each shipment.

AND YOUR FIRST TWO-BOOK SHIP-MENT IS TOTALLY FREE!

IT'S A BARGAIN YOU CAN'T BEAT! A SUPER $11.48 Value!

Love Spell ✦ A Division of Dorchester Publishing Co., Inc.

GET YOUR 2 FREE BOOKS NOW—AN $11.48 VALUE!

Mail the Free Book Certificate Today!

Free Books Certificate

YES! I want to subscribe to the Love Spell Romance Book Club. Please send me my 2 FREE BOOKS. Then every other month I'll receive the four newest Love Spell selections to Preview FREE for 10 days. If I decide to keep them, I will pay the Special Member's Only discounted price of just $4.49 each, a total of $17.96. This is a SAVINGS of at least $5.00 off the bookstore price. There are no shipping, handling, or other charges. There is no minimum number of books I must buy and I may cancel the program at any time. In any case, the 2 FREE BOOKS are mine to keep—A BIG $11.48 Value!

Offer valid only in the U.S.A.

Name_____

Address_____

City_____

State _____ Zip _____

Telephone_____

Signature_____

If under 18, Parent or Guardian must sign. Terms, prices and conditions subject to change. Subscription subject to acceptance. Leisure Books reserves the right to reject any order or cancel any subscription.

Get Two Books Totally
FREE —
An $11.48 Value!

▼ Tear Here and Mail Your FREE Book Card Today! ▼

PLEASE RUSH
MY TWO FREE
BOOKS TO ME
RIGHT AWAY!

Love Spell Romance Book Club
P.O. Box 6613
Edison, NJ 08818-6613

you were clever enough to sense it, too." His eyes raked her over scornfully, as if he were having second thoughts about her usefulness in whatever plot he was hatching. "Mayhap I do give you more credit than you warrant."

"I know Thork wants me in his bed—for now, at least—but I need more than that, and I certainly wouldn't share him with that spider. It must be marriage or nothing, Dar."

"For a thrall, you make demands above yourself," Dar seethed, slamming his wine goblet on a small table near his chair. "Mayhap you should consider which is more important to you, your head or your affronted virtue?"

Ruby raised her chin in silent defiance. "I have to tell you one thing. I can't be sure that I won't have to . . . return to my country some day."

Dar scowled. "Keep my grandson in Northumbria, and I would not care if you went to the moon." Then he seemed disgusted with himself. "Begone! 'Twas foolish to think I could reason with a simple wench."

Later, Ruby tried to discuss the conversation with Aud.

"Mayhap you should consider taking one step at a time," Aud advised. "Many a mistress has become a second or third wife, oft the more favored of them all for her patience."

"Aud! How can you say that? I thought you were a Christian. Can you possibly sanction a man having more than one wife?"

"Yea, I am Christian, but Viking, as well. We are forced to settle in foreign lands; yet we are the ones who must give up our religion and culture," she said bitterly. "To keep the peace, little by little we become more Saxon than Viking, and that saddens my heart mightily. Still, 'tis hard to give up the old ways totally."

"But more than one wife! It's outrageous! Are women permitted to have more than one husband?"

Aud smiled at Ruby's vehemence. "Of course, not. 'Twould be foolish. At one time, though, 'twas a wise practice for men to have many wives. *More danico,* the custom was called. When the men traveled a-Viking or trading and were often gone for years at a time, babes were needed to replace the many lost in battle and the struggle to survive."

"Hogwash! I think it was a practice devised by men for men's pleasure," Ruby scoffed, "and the men got away with it for so long because women are so downtrodden they're happy just to have the jerks look at them."

Aud's lips twitched at Ruby's fiery words. "That word 'jerk,' methinks I like the sound of it," Aud commented, deliberately changing the subject. "Does it mean something like a stupid, unfeeling, crude man?"

"Exactly!" Ruby nodded, with a smile.

"Good! I will practice using the word." Aud turned and ordered, "Ella, tell that jerk Vigi to bring more firewood in for the cooking fire."

Before Ruby left the kitchen, she asked, "Aud, would you have accepted another wife?"

Aud's eyes twinkled as she looked directly at Ruby. "Never! I would have lopped off Dar's male part afore I would have allowed him to take another wife."

Ruby stifled a giggle at Aud's brazen statement. Then they both burst out laughing at the inconsistency of her logic.

"Ruby, the differences 'atween us are vast," Aud said in a more serious tone. "You jump right in and make huge waves, agitating people with your demands and assertions. 'Tis better to wait for the right moment. Patience truly can be a virtue. Heed my words."

But Ruby didn't have time for patience. In little more than a week, the Althing would assemble and Thork would leave Jorvik.

Exiting the kitchen, Ruby headed determinedly for the fields outside the bailey where at least a hundred Viking men of varying ages, but equal in their supreme physical fitness, engaged in serious military maneuvers.

"Where did they all come from?" Ruby asked Vigi, her ever-present guard.

"Some are from Dar's or Thork's *hirds,* their permanent troops. Others are freedmen who work Dar's lands, and still others were hired to protect the manor when Thork leaves."

"Mercenaries?" Ruby began to realize the extent of the danger lurking on the horizon.

When Thork finally saw her, his nostrils flared with anger. He stomped off the field in a rage, hurling vicious swear words at her. "Why do you bedevil me? Did I not warn you about approaching me again? Get thee inside the bloody keep and find some women's work to do, else I swear on Odin's head I will have you trussed and locked in your chamber."

Ruby could only gape at him dumbly, her words and intentions lost in the marvelous spectacle he posed before her. Holding his helmet in his right hand, Thork impatiently wiped the sweat off his forehead with a jerky swipe of his left forearm. He breathed heavily from the hard physical labor, and his chest rose and fell, delineating finely honed muscles under the close-fitting chain-mail shirt he wore. Corded muscles in his thighs rippled as he shifted restlessly from foot to foot, waiting for her to leave. His wet, braided hair framed fine cheekbones, drawing attention to blue, blue eyes which impaled her angrily.

"I just . . . I just needed to talk to you about something," Ruby stuttered, realizing she was being scrutinized by many of the males, including Eirik.

Eirik! For heaven's sake! Ten years old and wearing miniature armor similar to his father's. He carried a sword in one hand and a shield in the other! Ruby jumped on that as a warm-up topic before hitting Thork with her other ideas.

227

"It's about Eirik," she said indignantly. "You've got to do something—"

Ruby heard Eirik protest loudly, calling her a vile name. Thork gasped at her effrontery and picked her up, throwing her over his shoulder so quickly she could only grunt in reaction. When they reached the manor, Thork grabbed her bruisingly by the waist and lowered her to the ground, pinning her to the closed door with his palms against her shoulders.

"Heed me well, wench. Stay out of my way. In fact, stay out of my life."

To Vigi he snarled, "Last warning, halfwit! Keep her from my sight, or you are on the next slave ship to dock in Jorvik."

When she shuffled peevishly into the keep, Ruby saw Dar standing just inside the door near an open window. He'd witnessed the whole scene. Instead of lashing out at her angrily, like Thork and Eirik, he smiled slyly, as if he shared a secret with her.

The almost feral look on Thork's face at the evening meal halted any thoughts Ruby might have had about accosting him again so soon. He doggedly avoided looking in her direction, but then he disdained the fair Linette, as well, to Ruby's supreme satisfaction. Eating little, Thork drank one goblet of ale after another.

Once, for barely a second, Thork's sapphire eyes collided with hers inadvertently, and Ruby felt scorched by the blaze. Was it anger or passion?

Ruby knew that Thork was as attracted to her as she was to him, but he did a damn good job of fighting it. And he had good reason to do so, she admitted. After all, she couldn't promise him that she wouldn't leave Northumbria. Still, she needed to convince him that she came from the future, and it was destined that they be together for however long her sojourn in this land and time period lasted, perhaps even until death.

When Linette had finally had enough of Thork's neglect, she leaned over, hanging on his arm seductively, and whispered something in his ear. Probably X-rated. Ruby couldn't hear the sharp words Thork snarled back, shrugging off her hands in distaste, but she could see the hurt surprise that flashed across Linette's red face before she burst into tears and ran from the room. Ruby almost felt sorry for Linette.

"Didst thou hear the news about the bitch, Linette?" Ella asked, sidling up to Ruby.

"Ella, you shouldn't use such language, especially when you might be overheard. What news?"

Ella sniffed dramatically, prolonging the suspense as only a true gossip like her twin Rhoda could have done, then revealed, "Linette is to be wed."

Ruby's heart dropped and tears smarted her eyes.

"Tsk! Tsk! 'Tis the fool you are, girl. 'Twill not be Thork for her. At the mistress Aud's prodding, Dar has arranged a marriage for her with some Viking hesir in Denmark—Askold, by name. To be sure, he must not have heard of her many lovers, or else he may be ugly as the backside of a boar. 'Twill be a good match, think you not?"

Ruby could have wrung Ella's neck for scaring her, but she was so thankful to find her initial fears unfounded that she gave the thrall a quick hug.

Ella shrugged out of her arms uncomfortably, looking around to see if anyone had witnessed Ruby's unbecoming gesture to a lowly servant. When she saw that no one noticed, she smiled at Ruby.

"Askold comes to the Althing where they will wed and return to his farm in Denmark." Ella slapped her knee in glee. "Can you just picture Linette milking a cow?"

Aud walked up to them and inquired coolly of Ella, "Have you naught better to do than spread your tales?"

"Yea . . . I mean nay, mistress," Ella answered sheepishly and scurried away to the kitchen.

Aud turned her attention to Ruby. "We would have you entertain us with some songs tonight, Ruby. Much have I heard of your sagas and music."

Maybe because she'd been exiled to the lower end of the hall, Ruby thought. And because she was two steps away from the executioner's axe—or blood-eagling knife.

"Oh, not tonight, Aud."

"Dar has asked for you," Aud told her in a tone which brooked no argument. "Tomorrow the *skalds* will arrive with the first of our guests. They come from afar to travel with us to the Althing next week. We may never have another chance to hear your wondrous tales."

"Guests?" Ruby asked weakly. So the sand had finally sifted through her hourglass, and the Althing was almost at hand. Aud's pessimism about her not having another chance after this week did not bode well for the outcome of her "trial."

The family group had moved from the dais to the fireplace area. Dar sat sipping his ale, studiously avoiding Ruby's eyes as they approached.

What was the old goat up to now?

Occasionally he spoke to Thork, who seemed to answer only in monosyllables. Thork continued to down ale in alarming amounts. When Thork saw her, Ruby thought he would get up and leave. Instead, he glowered at her hatefully, with his upper lip curled, as if she were a vile toad.

After being handed a lute, Ruby sang the same songs she'd performed at Sigtrygg's castle—"Ruby," "Lucille," "Friends in Low Places," "Lord, It's Hard to Be Humble" and "All My Rowdy Friends Are Coming Over Tonight." The more she sang, the more Thork frowned. He looked tired, as well. Faint circles under his eyes and tension lines around his stubborn mouth spoke of sleepless nights. Was it simply because he'd made love all night long with the insatiable Linette? Or could it be that this building pressure between Ruby and her Viking "husband" troubled him through the endless nights, as it did her?

When she hit a shrill note, Thork snickered aloud, and Aud chastised him, "Thork, don't be a jerk."

All eyes widened and turned to Aud, who shrugged, "Well, he *was* acting the jerk." Then Dar and Thork riveted their eyes accusingly on Ruby, who smiled innocently.

Noticing Tykir and Tyra at the edge of the family gathering, Ruby sang "Jingle Bells," delighting them with the raucous carol, as well as her explanation of Christmas in her country. She'd been unable to think of any children's songs on the trip to Dar's home, but now she remembered the words to one folk song she thought they'd like, "Puff, the Magic Dragon." Did Vikings have sagas dealing with dragons? Ruby wondered. Somehow, the image fit.

Thork continued to glower like an old bear.

So Ruby told the story of "The Three Bears." Then she couldn't resist, probably some innate death wish, and told "Thork and the Beanstalk," to Thork's consternation. He probably restrained himself from violence because of the two dozen enthralled family members and hesirs gathered around Ruby. Even an uncharacteristically subdued Linette had come up to stand behind Thork's chair, unable to resist the charm of Ruby's stories and songs.

When Eddie and David had been small, she and Jack had sat like this with them in front of the fireplace, telling stories and singing songs. She'd forgotten the joy of those simple family evenings together, long before Jack stayed later and later at his office, way before she began bringing work home at night. They hadn't had much then—materially, that is—but, oh, how much richer their lives had been!

231

Tears of sweet memory—and regret—filled Ruby's eyes and she told her rapt audience huskily, "This was my husband Jack's favorite song."

Strumming the lute in her hands lightly, Ruby began the song, "Help Me Make It Through the Night." When she got to the stanza where the man asks the woman to lay her head down by his side, Thork stood rudely and walked away. Linette ran after him.

Everyone stared after Thork in surprise, but Ruby continued with her song, even though tears turned her voice raspy. At the end, she happened to glance at Dar. He beamed like a bloody moon.

The next morning, guests began arriving early. The benches built into the side walls of the great hall would serve as pallets for most of the men. Servants would be bumped to the floor or to the stables and outbuildings.

Everyone squeezed together to make room for extra people. Even Olaf's and Gyda's girls had to move in with them, and the girls' chamber was given over to a visiting jarl and his wife from beyond Northumbria. Luckily, Ruby's small tower chamber was too small to accommodate anyone else.

In the hustle and bustle that overtook the keep that day, everyone ignored Ruby, even at the evening meal where she sat so low at the tables she was practically out the doors. Not that she minded. Her safety lay in being inconspicuous.

Aud served a simple meal that night to the tired guests. Afterward, a *skald* told poignant sagas of noble Viking deeds. Ruby knew that these oral traditions would be the vehicles to carry the history of these fanciful people to modern times and that some would be lost forever, never being committed to paper. She vowed to search the next day for the *skald* to have him repeat for her one epic poem she found particularly moving. It involved two hostile half-brothers, Hloth and Angantyr, who both claimed their dead father's kingship. In the end, Angantyr searched the battlefield for his dead brother, saying:

> " . . . *Untold arm rings I offered thee, brother,*
> *a wealth of gold and what most thou didst wish.*
>
> *As guerdon for strife now hast gotten neither,*
> *nor lands nor lieges nor lustrous rings.*
>
> *A baleful fate wrought it that, brother I slew*
> *thee! Will that aye be told . . ."*

In listening to the poem, Ruby marveled that these primitive people could express themselves so sensitively. And she thought of Thork and his brother Eric, realizing that, like Hloth and Angantyr, they would never have the warm sibling relationship two brothers should have.

Aud was in her element the next morning as she directed the bustling activities in the kitchen. Gyda worked busily at her side, arranging meals for the day, including a sumptuous banquet for the evening.

A steady stream of servants, including a grumbling Ella, marched to the various chambers with linens and bowls of fresh water for the guests. The men had left before first light on a short hunting expedition to kill fresh game to supplement the usual fish and poultry fare. Some of the male thralls already returned with the first of the kill—a brace of rabbits, two deer and several wild grouse.

"Ruby, would you go with Vigi and collect some fresh mushrooms for dinner?" Aud asked.

"Of course." Ruby was glad to be of help and to keep busy. "Shall we pick some blueberries, too? They would be good with fresh cream or baked in a pastry." Aud's eyes lit up at that suggestion, and they exchanged ideas on how best to make a flaky crust for the dessert.

Before she left, Ruby invited Tykir and Tyra to join her, taking linens and soap with her, figuring they may as well combine her errand and a bath. Ruby saw several of Dar's and Aud's distinguished guests eye her T-shirt and jeans with cool curiosity.

When their baskets were full, Tykir and Tyra waded merrily near the edge of the pond. Later, Ruby told the children to go play near Vigi at the edge of the clearing so she could bathe in private. Before they left, she asked Vigi if she could borrow the eating knife he always carried at his waist.

"Why?" he asked suspiciously.

"Oh, really! It's not as if I could disarm you. You still have your sword. I just want to shave my legs, for heaven's sake! I'm beginning to feel like a porcupine."

Vigi's eyes widened in surprise. Ruby knew he already considered her half-crazy. He handed the knife to her, though, admonishing her to give it right back. He probably already rehearsed in his mind the fun he'd have back at the keep telling of this weird stranger's latest antics.

Tykir and Tyra thought it a great joke that Ruby had whiskers on her legs just like their fathers had on their faces. They asked her to lift her pant leg so they could touch them.

" 'Tis like the bristles on a hog's skin afore the butchering," Tykir declared in amazement. Tyra fell over in exaggerated glee at his words.

When she finished bathing and shaving her legs with soap lather and Vigi's razor-sharp knife, nicking herself only a few times, the children asked to touch her legs again. Their mouths formed little "o's" of surprise at the smoothness.

After she'd helped Aud and Gyda prepare the blueberry pastries, Ruby went to her room where Ella was laying out a lovely dress.

" 'Tis a gift from the master and mistress for yer story-telling yestereve," Ella explained.

Heavy gold braiding edged the hem, wrists and neckline of the simple burgundy silk dress, whose soft fabric molded her breasts and outlined her narrow waist, held in tightly by a gold braided belt. When she walked, the dress followed the lines of her narrow hips and long legs. Other than her lingerie, Ruby wore only a thin chemise, loving the feel of the sensuous cloth against her skin.

But Ruby went unnoticed, or so she thought, in the noise and bustle of the banquet room. Still exiled to the end of the room, Ruby was pleased to see that Linette had been bumped from the dais for the many visiting high-born Vikings. Many would go on to Jorvik and Sigtrygg's castle the next day, while others would wait until next week to travel with Dar and his family to the Althing. Everywhere the crowd buzzed with news of Sigtrygg's upcoming wedding.

Ruby's heart lurched, though, when she saw the young woman sitting next to Thork at the head table. Her long chestnut hair hung past her shoulders, held in place by a gold circlet around her forehead. No more than fifteen years old, she seemed to answer Thork's questions shyly, averting her eyes from his direct stare, then darting interested glances at him when she thought he wasn't looking.

It had to be the Saxon-Viking maid Elise that Dar wanted for Thork. Elise's father, whose lands adjoined Dar's, sat on one side of Dar, his wife on the other.

In disgust, Ruby took a hefty swig of the hearty Viking ale and choked. It was odious.

"Tastes like horse piss, does it not?" a young pimply-faced hesir whined next to her. "The best wine and mead go to the upper tables."

Ruby put her elbow on the table, holding up her chin, and wondered what else could go wrong. First Linette, now this beautiful young girl. Ruby watched painfully as Thork cut a prime piece of meat off the platter he shared with the girl and handed it to her considerately. She smiled sweetly at him in thanks.

Ruby thought she would puke.

Ella walked by with a tray of bannock, and Ruby stopped her. "Do you think you could bring me some wine?"

"Needin' ta drown yer sorrows, are ya?" she said, cocking her head toward the dais, but she returned shortly with a small jug which she'd hidden in her skirts.

"Do not let anyone see this," Ella said, sliding it under the bench at Ruby's feet. "'Tis from Dar's private Frisian stock."

Surreptitiously Ruby reached under the table, dumped her ale in the rushes and filled her cup with the red wine. Her hesir companion looked at her oddly, wondering aloud what she did down in the rushes, but she glared him into silence.

The first cup went straight to Ruby's head, out to her fingertips and down to her toes. She sipped her second cup more slowly, only gulping larger mouthfuls when she saw Thork doing something particularly distasteful, like touching the girl's sleeve gently when he asked a question or whispering in her ear when the noise level in the room got too loud. He ignored Ruby totally.

It was a futile battle, trying to get Thork to marry her, Ruby told herself in self-pity as she finished her second cup, touching her lips in wonder. How did her lips get numb? And her eyelashes felt as if they weighed ten pounds each. But, Lord, she couldn't remember the last time she'd felt this good.

As the tables were dismantled and people milled about in groups, waiting for the entertainment, she poured her third drink, feeling a drunken rush of self-confidence. Maybe it wasn't hopeless, after all. Maybe she should go right up there and demand that Thork marry her. Better yet, maybe she should get a sword and kidnap Thork. Lock him in her room with her for a week, and, guar-an-teed, she'd get a proposal from him or he'd be dead from sexual depletion. She giggled at the thought, getting the attention of her young hesir, who also stood alone.

"Why, you had wine the whole time!" he complained, noticing the jug at her feet. "What a pig to keep it all to yourself!"

"Not a pig. A hog. I have legs like a hog's skin, don't you know? Before the butchering." She giggled again, then hiccuped. After handing the young man the almost empty container, she weaved her way through the crowd toward the head of the hall, her half-empty cup of wine held shakily in front of her.

Dar and all his noble visitors had moved off the dais and were sitting or standing, listening to two young women with harp and lute who sang a soft melody. Ruby got her first close-up look at Thork and choked back her laughter. He wore a burgundy velvet tunic with gold braiding, almost identical to her dress—Dar's idea of a practical joke, she presumed. Wide gold bracelets gleamed on his tanned upper arms, and a gold pendant on a heavy chain lay against his chest. The hair on one side of his head had been braided and hung off the side of his head and down his back, highlighting the one thunderbolt earring.

He looks like a bloody Norse god, Ruby thought, and gulped.

Thork blinked with surprise at their matching clothing, then curled his lips with disgust. He shot an accusing glance at his grandfather who feigned innocence with a shrug. Then Thork stared pointedly at the wine Ruby still sipped as she leaned tipsily against the back of someone's chair. Anger flashed in his eyes as she raised defiant eyes to his. Thork stood and started to walk purposefully toward her, but Ruby slipped into the crowd and moved to the other side of the room.

When a visiting jarl rose from his chair to go to the garderobe, Ruby sank wearily into it, holding her chin in her hand. Dar gave her a disapproving look, but Ruby ignored the unspoken message that she was not high enough in their stupid class system to be sitting where she was.

Thork stood directly across the circle from her, glaring. Having had enough of his anger and rebuffs and orders, Ruby stuck her tongue out at him and thought his eyes would bug out. It felt so good she did it again and tried to look cross-eyed at him, but for some reason her coordination was bogged down, and her eyes just kind of rolled. But she'd succeeded in turning Thork's face almost purple by now. He would have vaulted the circle of guests if the *skald* hadn't started a long lyric poem.

Under normal circumstances, Ruby might have been interested, but she felt as if she were floating now—a glorious feeling! She let her empty wine cup slip from her fingers to the rushes.

The *skaldic* poem ended with a story about some Viking and his precious knife called Fealty and how it had saved him in some battle. "Good Lord! Only a Viking would name a knife, like a pet," Ruby muttered, and the Viking seated next to her shot her an annoyed frown.

Everyone congratulated the *skald* after he finished, asking him questions. In the short lull that followed, one woman guest talked cattily to Aud in a voice loud enough for many around her to hear.

"I understand your guest from Ivar—the one of the mannish clothing—has a most unusual manner of using a knife."

Everyone looked at Ruby. Aud and Dar raised questioning eyes to her. Thork looked as if he would have an apoplectic fit. Well, at least she'd finally piqued his interest.

Ruby blinked and then hiccuped loudly. She heard Dar guffaw.

The woman went on with relish, "She shaved her legs today with a knife."

Again, everybody looked at Ruby in astonishment.

" 'Tis true, Ruby?" Aud gasped.

"Where did the thrall get a knife?" Dar wanted to know.

"I will kill you," Thork mouthed silently.

With as much dignity as she could maintain in her inebriated condition, Ruby explained, "It's no big deal. Really. Women in my country shave their legs all the time. And their underarms. It's considered unfeminine not to do so."

They all gawked at her in disbelief. Several elderly matrons seemed about to have a stroke over the scandalous conversation.

Oh, hell! She was in deep trouble as it was. She might as well enjoy herself. Besides, she still wanted to get back at Thork for abandoning her the other night to be with Linette.

"Thork," she said sweetly, staring him straight in the eyes.

He refused to answer, incensed at the spectacle she'd created once again.

"Thork," she called out louder now. "Do you remember the time you shaved my legs for me?"

His mouth dropped open.

Dead silence reigned.

"It was our tenth wedding anniversary, and we were high on white wine and . . . and love. You remember, don't you? It was *your* idea, so don't glare at me. You made me stand perfectly still, like this."

Ruby stood with her legs slightly parted and almost fell

over. She straightened herself by holding on to the back of the chair.

Aud clamped her hand over her mouth at Ruby's outrageous conduct. Gyda seemed to be praying. Olaf smiled in appreciation of her daring. And Dar smirked from ear to ear with self-satisfaction, as if he'd planned the whole damned event. The young girl, Elise, was nowhere to be seen. It was probably past her bedtime.

"You lathered both my legs with cream and then you shaved them, ever so slowly," Ruby went on with gusto, "all the way up to here." She drew a line with her hand at the tops of both thighs.

Ruby felt fuzzy and disoriented, beginning to realize just how scandalous her behavior was, noticing the strained silence surrounding her. She started to back away as she saw Thork beginning to approach her around the circle of people, his eyes piercing her, his lips a pale line of white-hot anger.

Thork's continual anger was really starting to annoy Ruby. Criminey! she decided, I might as well put the icing on the cake. Her eyes narrowed and held his in unspoken challenge.

"Oh, and did I mention, Thork?" she said ever-so-sweetly. "We were both stark naked."

Thork gurgled with words that would not come out as all eyes turned on him, but not for long. "Damn you!" he bellowed and lurched across the remaining people separating them. "Warned you were, wench. Over and over you were told what would happen if you pushed me." Without another word, he vaulted over a chair, picked Ruby up and carried her from the hall and up the steps.

Ruby was oblivious to the cheering laughter and loud speculation on her fate that followed them out of the hall. She snuggled in Thork's arms, burrowing her face in his neck, which smelled so sweetly of her own Jack and yet somehow marvelously different. Tomorrow Ruby would worry about her fate. Tonight she was back in Jack's, no, Thork's arms, where she belonged, and that was all that mattered.

"Jack, honey," Ruby whispered and felt the muscled arms holding her stiffen, "I've missed you so much." Then she hiccuped softly in Thork's ear.

Chapter Thirteen

"Your tongue ever outruns your good judgement, woman!" Thork raged, pacing back and forth across his sleeping chamber. He raked his fingers through his hair in agitation as he shot icy glances her way.

Ruby watched him woozily on raised elbows from the cushiony softness of his massive bed where he'd thrown her in disgust after leaving the great hall. She wished he'd stand still. Her fuzzy tongue got in the way as she tried to speak in her own defense. She pushed the tip of her tongue between her lips to test their numbness, then giggled.

"You find mirth in this situation?"

"No . . . yes." Ruby tried to sit up, but the bed tilted crazily from side to side. Finally, feeling steadier, she sat upright. "I mean . . . it's funny because I feel as if I've just been to the dentist. My lips and tongue are numb, and—"

"Nay! Speak no more mysterious words and allusions to a future life that never was. More than enough have

242

I had of your hints of a life we shared together. It *never* happened."

Thork grabbed Ruby by the forearms, pulled her off the bed and shook her, trying to convince her of his seriousness.

It sobered Ruby a bit.

"Okay. Let's discuss this," she said, backing away a few steps. "You're upset because I said you shaved my legs."

"Arghh!" Thork threw his arms up in the air. "You do it again. Why can you not be biddable like other women?"

"Like the gentle little Saxon-Viking girl with the big cow eyes? Isn't Linette enough for you? Are you robbing the cradle now, too?"

Thork blinked at Ruby's fast-changing train of thought, but before he could respond, Ruby continued, "I shouldn't have said what I did in front of all your guests. I apologize for that. I'm not used to drinking so much wine."

Thork rolled his eyes as if that were the understatement of the year.

"But I didn't lie. I never lie. You *did* shave my legs on our tenth wedding anniversary. See," she said, pulling her gown up to the edge of her panties, displaying the full length of her smooth legs. "You shaved them so they looked just like this."

Thork stared at Ruby's exposed limbs, then sucked in his breath sharply. He seemed unable to speak for several long moments.

Sensing an advantage, Ruby braced her left hand on the wall and raised her right leg boldly so the toe of her leather shoe rested on his belt brooch. "Touch the skin," she invited outrageously. "See for yourself what I mean."

Ruby saw Thork's reluctance and knew he feared that if he took this one step he might take others. But he touched her leg lightly, nonetheless, with the fingertips of his left hand, then ran the callused palm from her ankle to the satin sleekness of her thigh and back again.

He smiled widely.

"I see why women—and men—of your country might like this practice. The smoothness creates images in a man's mind of other . . . practices." He looked up questioningly. "This dehairing . . . 'tis done in the eastern countries, as well, I hear." A crafty light flickered in Thork's pale eyes.

Geez! First Ivar, then Athelstan, now the Orient. But before Ruby could complain, Thork yanked up on her wobbly left leg with lightning swiftness and caught the back of her waist with his other hand. Quickly she grabbed his shoulders for ballast. In that split second, Thork somehow maneuvered her so that he held her with legs wrapped around his waist, hands anchored at his neck. Then he backed her up against the wall.

Dazed by the quickness of Thork's movements and the carnal position she found herself in, Ruby could only blink at Thork questioningly. No longer angry with her, Thork held her eyes in a glittering, promising glance, more intimate than a caress. She could not look away.

"For a month and more you have teased and taunted me with promises of delights we have shared in the past. What say you now?" he asked in a tightly controlled, low voice.

Holding her eyes, Thork began to undo the shoulder clasps of her outer gown. Ruby wanted to ask if he would marry her again or if he'd accepted the fact that she might have to leave, but, instead, she decided to follow Aud's advice for patience.

Ruby licked her lips nervously. She had to have made love with this man a thousand times in the past twenty years, but it seemed all new now. He was her husband and yet a stranger at the same time.

"Do you still insist we share a past?" he asked hoarsely.

Ruby scrutinized Thork closely, trying to see the differences, not the similarities, between him and Jack. It was hard. "I think you and I may very well make our own history tonight," she evaded.

Thork traced her jaw with a forefinger questioningly. "What is it about you, sweetling, that draws me so? Truly, in another time we could have been heartmates."

Ruby's heart melted at his softly spoken words of love. Yes, love, because this was probably as close to a declaration of love she could ever expect from this man.

"Thork, I love you," Ruby whispered.

"Shush," he said, putting his fingers over her mouth. "No lies. No promises betwixt us. Just let us enjoy what we can give each other now and let it be enough."

Still holding Ruby with her legs wrapped around his waist, Thork undid the brooches of Ruby's gown and pulled the tunic and the underchemise off her shoulders and arms until they bunched at her waistline.

Thork studied her wispy, black lace bra and smiled appreciatively. Leaning down, he flicked the tip of his tongue across the peaks of each scantily covered breast, creating the hardened peaks he wanted. Then he took one lacy peak in his mouth and suckled.

A swift, hot rush of blood lodged in the center of Ruby's femininity. She moaned and heard Thork chuckle in satisfaction while continuing his sweet torture.

"Ah, Ruby, 'tis as sweet as I remembered. Their taste has lingered in my mouth for days. Truly, you bewitch me."

Ruby could not speak as Thork leaned back, not waiting for an answer, and looked at the breast he'd been working on, admiring it through the wet transparency of the fabric, visible even in the flickering candlelight. Then he moved to her other breast. At the first sharp tug of his lips, Ruby jolted and bucked against him.

"Thork, wait. Let me down," Ruby begged. She didn't like the helplessness of her position. She wanted to participate, not be served in this manner.

"Nay. Not yet," he rasped out, trying to figure out how to undo the back clasp of her bra. Without his hands holding her upright, Ruby was forced to hold on to him tighter with her arm and thigh muscles. Finally the flimsy undergarment loosened in his hand, and he pulled it off her arms.

"Put me down," Ruby pleaded again, watching while he examined her sensitized breasts with his eyes and fingertips. His beautiful eyes glazed over with passion, and Ruby yearned to show her love for this man—whoever he was.

"Nay, I will not release you. This night I have a plan. Nay, a *master* plan." He grinned mischievously.

Master plan? Ruby would kill Ella. The gossip addict must have told someone about her plan to trap Thork.

"Wouldst thou like to hear my master plan?" He jiggled his eyebrows suggestively.

Ruby nodded hesitantly, pleased with this playful side of Thork.

"Tonight you will have many ... *many* ... of those orgasms you spoke of so eloquently to Brynhil and her women."

Ruby gulped.

"The first will come here in my arms. I will not let you down until it happens," he promised seductively.

Ruby's thighs spasmed at his words and she felt a gush of dampness at the apex of her legs. Thork's lips turned up at the corners and he looked down as if sensing what had happened, surely having felt the tremors in her legs at his waist.

Still holding her with legs wrapped around his waist, Thork adjusted their bodies so that he could undo her belt. Reaching to her ankles, he raised first her gown, then her underchemise all the way up and over her head. She now wore only Brynhil's emerald, her panties and a pair of soft leather shoes. Leaning back, Thork positioned her so that her shoulders were still braced against the wall and her arms extended to his shoulders. With his large left hand holding her buttocks for balance, he put the back of his right middle finger against the dampness of her silk panties, then looked up in pleased astonishment.

"For me, sweetling?" he asked in a raw, low voice.

Something moved in Ruby *there* and she felt her face flame. She could only nod mutely.

Thork smiled, well satisfied with her answer, and laid the back of his finger along her cleft. Up and down he rubbed in the groove he created. "Look down," he urged her huskily. "See how you swell for me, just as my manhood grows for you."

Ruby glanced down. He was right. Even through the cloth, she could see that her nether lips were engorged and that special bud of sensitivity rose slightly in waiting for his eventual touch. She closed her eyes in delicious anticipation of the pleasure to come.

"Nay, look at me. I want to watch your face when it happens," he whispered as his forefinger circled the nub, testing its shape and readiness. He flicked the tip of his finger up and down quickly, fascinated as it spasmed against him. Then, in earnest, he strummed it back and forth in ever-increasing rapidity until she groaned and arched her back away from him.

The spasms started small and short in duration. The faster he flicked her, moving the bud from side to side, the harder and longer they got.

"Look at me," he demanded softly.

When she did, Thork pressed her cleft against his rigid manhood. He bucked against her, and Ruby's spasms became convulsions of pleasure that spiraled into tiny explosions, shaking her so intensely she cried out his name.

Through the misty glaze of her passion, Ruby watched Thork's face as he continued to thrust against her. Finally

247

he held her against him tightly, with a hand on each of her buttocks, arched his head back over corded neck muscles and came against her on a drawn-out moan deep in his throat.

Weakly, Ruby lay her head against his chest, trying to get her breathing back to normal. She was too embarrassed to look up and see if her violent reaction amused him, but finally Thork put a finger under her chin and raised her face. She needn't have been self-conscious. Thork's flushed face and passion-hazy eyes proved he was just as out-of-control.

"And you say we have done this afore, sweetling? Nay, I do not believe I would ever forget such. Not even in another lifetime." He nibbled at her ear as he spoke.

"Perhaps not in quite the same way, but, yes, we made love so many times I couldn't count." She liked the feel of his hot, whispery kisses on her neck. "Can I get down now?"

"Yea, I would say you earned that boon and more."

He smiled tenderly. As he lowered her shaky legs to the rush-covered floor, Ruby raised flirting eyes to his. "Maybe by morning we will have awakened some of those memories." Ruby looked at Thork warmly, knowing without a doubt that she loved him, as completely as she'd ever loved Jack. The self-admission filled her, not with guilt, but an overwhelming feeling of incredible rightness. This was where she was meant to be.

Thork laughed warmly at her last words. " 'Tis more likely we will have created new memories to keep me awake during the long winter nights in Jomsborg."

Ruby's heart sank at his words. He still intended to leave her behind, even after they'd made love. Well, almost made love. She apparently had a lot more work to do in convincing him to take her with him. Ruby grinned with anticipation at that pleasurable task.

Thork undressed then, while Ruby watched. Something

tightened inside Ruby at the sight of his naked body. Broad shoulders, slim waist and hips, and a marble-hard stomach outlined his warrior's six-foot-three frame. His smile mirrored Jack's right down to the slightly crooked incisor, but innumerable scars and bruises covered much of his finely honed skin. And his body frame was different from Jack's. To get this kind of muscular development in the twentieth century would require steroids or hours of daily, concentrated workouts.

Thork winked at her, pleased with her perusal. "Do you like what you see?"

"Sweetheart, you are drop-dead gorgeous."

"Drop-dead gorgeous? What kind of compliment is that?" he asked with mock indignation.

"Believe me, honey, drop-dead gorgeous is good."

He chuckled and held out his hand invitingly. Ruby stepped into his arms and wrapped her arms loosely around his neck, arching her neck slightly to accommodate the height difference.

"Will you explain step two of your master plan now?" she asked sweetly, nuzzling the warm skin of his collarbone.

"Nay, I will show you, instead," he laughed. "Will you divulge the next step of *your* master plan, as well?"

"Never. The advantage is in your being surprised by my next move." Ruby jiggled her eyebrows suggestively.

"Hah! You have astonished me at every step since first we met. And what benefits have you reaped—exile by Sigtrygg, face slaps from Dar, threat of execution? In truth, you have fared poorly in our society, sweetling."

"Despite all those things, I am where I want to be at the moment, though I must admit I got here through no part of my master plan. My blurting out that stuff in the hall about you shaving my legs was totally unplanned."

A thoughtul smile played at the edges of his mouth. "Did your husband truly shave your legs?"

Sandra Hill

Ruby nodded her head, still having trouble reconciling the fact that Thork and Jack might not be the same person. She couldn't be doing these things with Thork if she didn't think he was, in some way, her husband. "What I didn't say was that by the time he was done I had lots of nicks on my upper thighs from his shaky hands."

Thork hooted with laughter and swung her around in his arms. "Since you've been so truthful with me, I will give you fair exchange. The next step of my master plan is to play the Kevin Costner for you—to kiss you till you are mindless with the wanting of me, till your toes curl, till you moan for me to stop, till you drip with nectar, till . . ."

And he did all those things and more.

Later, during a brief respite, Ruby lay on her side in his arms on the bed, his erection pressing against her leg. Ruby touched his kiss-swollen lips lovingly with her fingertips. He caressed her body gently with callused hands, waiting for her to regroup before his next assault. His heavy breathing told her it wouldn't be long.

"Are we on schedule with your master plan?" she teased, rubbing her breasts across the soft blond hair that covered his chest, then doing the same with a leg thrown over the curly blond hairs on his thighs.

"Yea, minx, that we are! By my accounts, you have come three times to my one thus far, and we have not yet really begun."

"Oh ho! Now you keep score. What is your final goal?"

"You know well and good what my final goal is," Thork whispered as he examined the interior channels of her ear with the tip of his tongue and placed a warm hand between her legs.

There was no more talking then, except for his sensuous whispers of what he liked, answered by her soft moans and writhing body.

"Enough!" she finally begged. "Please . . . now."

250

Thork slowly inserted a finger inside her to further test her readiness and groaned, "For the love of Freya! You are tighter than an untried virgin."

"Hardly that." But Ruby was glad she pleased him and could wait no more. She opened her legs wider and pulled Thork up and over her body.

"Now," she demanded, unable to stand the delicious assault any longer.

He bent her knees and placed himself at her portal. Then he raised himself on his elbows and arched his back, perspiration beading his forehead and upper lips at the control he exerted to hold back. With eyes locked with hers, Thork slowly began his sweet entry. Ruby felt herself relax and stretch to accommodate his size. Then he stopped.

He stopped.

Thork's eyes widened, then blinked unbelievingly, before he withdrew and rolled over on his side away from her, cursing her with coarse words.

"What? What is it? Did I do something wrong?" she asked, putting her hand on his shoulder.

"Do not touch me!" Thork snarled and shrugged away from her, sitting on the edge of the bed. His shoulders trembled as he tried to bring his aroused body under control. Finally he walked stonily over to the water pitcher and dumped its entire contents on his engorged staff. He pulled on his pants angrily before walking to the edge of the bed.

Ruby sat up in the bed, confused. Thork grabbed her forearms with pincerlike fingers and pulled her roughly toward him. He shook her so hard she fell back on the bed.

"You lying, stinking bitch!"

"What? What did I do now?"

"You are a virgin," he spit out reproachfully. "All those stories you told of a husband and sons were lies. All lies!

Who are you, and what do you here? Who sent you?"

"A virgin! Are you crazy? I've made love hundreds of times."

Thork leaned over her threateningly, pinioning her shoulders to the bed with the palms of his hands. "I know a maidenhead, madam, and you have one. The lies end here."

Tears streamed down Ruby's face, blurring her vision. There was nothing—nothing at all—she could tell him that would convince him of the truth.

Sweet Lord! A virgin! Ruby thought. Who would have ever thought it?

"You know you can work your wiles on me. You know how much I want the bedding of you, but know this, too— it will *never* happen now. Never! And if you lie about your virginity, what other duplicity do you practice? I would sooner bed with a snake than a deceitful woman."

Ruby sobbed aloud, but Thork seemed immune to her pain. In truth, Ruby knew he was in as much pain himself.

"Stay away from me if you value your life. I get no joy in my strength over the weaker sex, but you push me too far. I cannot promise I will not hurt you if you approach me again." Then he got up and stormed out of the room, barefoot and bare-chested. The door slammed after him, shaking the wood door frame.

Ruby cried for hours, alternately sobbing, then racking her brain for answers to the dilemma she was in. When dawn light streamed through the window, Ruby still hadn't slept, and she knew she needed help. Would it be Dar or Aud? She decided to try Aud first.

Ruby opened the door and saw Vigi sleeping across the entryway, barring her exit. "I'd like to go to the pond to bathe. Will you accompany me?"

"Thor's blood, woman! 'Tis scarce daylight. Besides, you bathed yestermorn." He stood and rubbed sleepily at his eyes, then glared at her.

"I need to bathe," she asserted. "Shall we wake your master Dar to get his permission?"

"Nay," he muttered grumpily. "I am awake now."

Ruby went first to her tower room to get a change of clothes and noticed the gift she'd brought for Aud and forgotten to give to her. She put it on the pile of clothing, linen towels and soap she would carry with her. She awakened Ella to come with her to guard against Vigi's roving eyes when she bathed.

"Are those bruise marks on your arms?"

"Yes."

"Because you told that barmy tale in the hall yestereve about shaving legs?"

"No." Ruby didn't want to tell her the whole story. Besides, she had a bone to pick with Ella. "Did you tell someone about my master plan to get Thork to marry me?"

"Who sez I did?" Ella's querulous voice rose indignantly.

"Thork knows about it."

"Well, mayhap I might have mentioned it to Vigi."

"Vigi! He's as much a scandalmonger as you are."

"Well, I never!"

"I don't mean to argue with you," Ruby sighed. "I just have to be careful with you, Ella, if you're going to repeat everything I say."

"Well, you never said *not* to say anything."

"Let's consider this a blanket statement for the future. From now on, I don't want you to tell anyone *anything* I say. Is that clear?"

"Yea, that it is." Ella shuffled along beside her, having been properly chastised, but it wasn't long before she asked, "So, why did he bruise you?"

Ruby couldn't help laughing at Ella's effrontery.

"Because he discovered I'm a virgin."

Ella's mouth dropped open, and Ruby could see a good

portion of her discolored teeth. "Nay, it cannot be so!" she exclaimed incredulously.

"That's what I thought," Ruby said with a laugh. "Apparently, it can."

Ella chuckled, then burst into a full-blown guffaw. "A virgin . . . a virgin . . . oh, 'tis too much . . . and I can jist imagine how 'twas when the young master found out. Was it before or after he dug his spade in the soil?"

"Ella!"

"That troublemaker Loki must surely love you. He made you a thorn in Thork's side apurpose, I wager, to punish him for some slight. Prob'ly cuz he has lopped off too many heads. Or broke too many maidenheads." Ella erupted with a deep belly laugh. At first Ruby glared at her. Then she, too, saw the humor in the situation. By the time they got to the pond, tears of humor streamed down both their faces.

"By the by," Ella confided later, with a jiggle of her eyebrows, "rumors flew the keep last night of a strange practice being performed in many of the sleeping chambers. Seems maids and matrons alike asked their lovers to send for bowls of water, soft soap and sharp knives."

"Ella! You're making that up," Ruby said with a disbelieving laugh.

"I swear on me eyeballs, 'tis true. Betcha there be lots of knicked legs under ladylike chemises this day."

"And you'll be the one to spread gossip about them."

Not knowing enough to be affronted, Ella concluded, "I tell you this true, my girl, I have not laughed so much in all me life as I have since I met you. I hope they do not chop off yer head."

Yeah, me, too.

As they walked through the bailey on their return to the castle after her bath, Ruby saw Aud going into the wool shed. She told Ella to go on into the manor, that she needed to talk to her mistress.

Aud looked up from where she was sorting bolts of fabric and took in Ruby's appearance in a glance, dwelling momentarily on the dark finger marks on her arms and her tear-ridden, sleepless eyes. "It did not go well, I take it."

Ruby nodded.

Aud touched the purpling bruise of one arm gently. "I have never known Thork to deliberately hurt a woman afore. He must have been sore angry at the words you spoke yestereve before our guests."

"No, it was something else."

"Do not tell me," Aud said with feigned sternness, "though I am dying to know. I have grown fond of you, and 'tis best I do not get involved and be forced to choose sides."

"You're a very wise woman, and I like you, as well. Here," Ruby said, handing her a linen-wrapped package.

Aud took it and raised her eyes questioningly at Ruby.

"It's a gift for you. I haven't had a chance to give it to you before this."

When she opened the package, Aud gasped, then put her hand over her mouth to muffle a giggle. It was a set of blue silk and white lace lingerie.

"Much have I heard about your undergarments," Aud said, running her fingers over the material admiringly and examining the fine needlework critically. "Do you think I dare to wear such at my age?"

"Of course. My grandmother wore similar lingerie, and she was much older than you. Besides, Dar told me to bring you a set."

"He did?" Aud's eyebrows arched in surprise. At Ruby's nod, she accepted the gift graciously. "Well, then, thank you very much." She held the panties up against herself shyly. "And you say my husband asked for such frivolous apparel? Hmmm. Tell me, did your grandmother shave her legs, as well?"

255

"Yes, she did." Ruby laughed at the Viking woman's shy curiosity. "But listen, Aud, I need to ask a favor."

Aud looked at her dubiously, wondering if she'd been hasty in accepting the gift.

"It's nothing bad." Ruby pulled the gold chain and emerald pendant over her head and handed it to Aud. "I have no money but I think this is valuable. Could I purchase some things from you with this?"

Aud examined the necklace with appreciation, then asked suspiciously, "What would you want to buy?"

"Fabrics . . . some silk, laces, whalebone if you have it, a needle, thread, and a few other items. Oh, I also want to prepare some food in the kitchen."

"Tsk tsk! You have not given up yet, have you, child?" Aud chastised her in a soft-spoken voice.

"How can I? I have everything to gain and nothing to lose." Ruby shrugged.

"You may have whatever fabrics you need, but this gem is worth much more than the few trifles you mentioned." She handed it back to Ruby. "Make another set of your lingerie for me. That will be payment enough."

Ruby agreed, thankful for Aud's generosity.

"What do you want to cook in my kitchen?"

Ruby grinned impishly. "I'm going to make Thork a cheeseburger for his dinner with baklava for dessert."

"After he treated you so, you would cook a meal for him?" Aud chided Ruby, indicating the marks on her arms.

"I intend to wear him down with all his favorite things. I'll conquer him with kindness." Ruby pressed her lips together in determination.

"Afeard I am to ask why you need the fabrics."

"I'm going to try to duplicate a gift my husband gave to me once. He bought it from Frederick's of Hollywood before I started my own lingerie company." Ruby rolled her eyes meaningfully. "The garment was a fitted black silk and lace teddy with a strapless, push-up bustier top and sides cut up practically to the hip bone."

Aud stared at her in open-mouthed amazement as she began to understand exactly what Ruby planned.

Chapter Fourteen

Dar's storage room was a treasure trove of exquisite fabrics, jewelry, tapestries, carpets, sterling and gold objects. Ruby controlled her impulses and selected only those items she really needed.

First she chose black silk and lace for her own teddy, along with thread and one precious needle. Then she cut lengths of blue, yellow, red and white silk to be made into lingerie for Aud and for the bartering required in subsequent steps of her plan.

She found a piece of flexible whalebone buried in the back of the room beneath two ivory tusks, probably intended for a craftsman. She needed the whalebone for support under the cups of her bustier and to tuck in and accentuate her waist.

Before they left the room, Ruby noticed a bolt of the finest midnight blue wool she'd ever seen. She touched it lovingly, knowing it would match Thork's eyes perfectly. She pictured in her mind a full-length cloak with embroidery along the edges, perhaps in a thunderbolt design like his earring.

She dropped the soft fabric regretfully. Her arms were already loaded with the items she'd selected. This would be asking too much of Aud's generosity.

Aud smiled knowingly. "For Thork?"

Ruby nodded.

"Why stop now?" Aud handed her the fabric, with a sardonically raised eyebrow.

Ruby gave her a quick hug as they left the room. She didn't get a chance to make the meal that afternoon as she'd planned because she spent so much time in the village bartering with a woodworker and a leather worker for some items she needed made. Both had young wives who practically drooled over the sample lingerie set she'd brought, urging their reluctant husbands to do the required work in an almost impossibly short time so they could have their own custom-made underwear. Ruby's task was made more difficult because she had no paper to explain her ideas and had to draw with a stick in the dirt.

On the way back, she made Vigi stop with her in a small orchard where she saw ripe peaches hanging from a number of trees. She picked a dozen of the biggest, most succulent ones. When she got back to the keep, she washed them at the well, found a round basket in the kitchen and asked Ella to take the gift up to Thork's bedchamber and put it on the table near his bed.

Ella grumbled at her task. "Seems to me 'twould have more meaning if you sent him a basket of cherries. Sour ones, no doubt!"

Ruby asked Aud if she could use the table in her weaving shed to cut her patterns since her own tower room was so small and poorly lit. She worked for hours until the light dwindled, then went into the keep to prepare for dinner. Vigi was livid at having to follow her around on her woman's work.

259

She hadn't seen Thork all day and was almost reluctant to run into him now. His anger when he'd left her the night before didn't bode well for how he'd treat her today.

Thork was madder than hell, and everyone around him that day knew it. He almost bit off his grandfather's head when he merely asked how things had gone with Ruby the night before. He nicked Selik's forearm with his sword during maneuvers. His spear broke during target practice because he'd thrust too hard. He noticed wryly that no one walked back to the keep with him before dinner that afternoon. When he got to the bailey, he called out to Tykir to get some soap and linens and meet him at the pond. "Let us see about that swimming lesson I promised you."

Tykir's face lit up like a candle. If he had been a dog, he would probably have wagged his tail, Thork thought guiltily. All because he had shown him a tiny speck of attention. *Thor's blood! I cannot allow myself to start feeling guilty over my sons, or I will never be able to leave them behind.*

Before he left the courtyard, he called Eirik to him. The boy almost jumped out of his skin at having his father address him in front of his hesirs. "Eirik, I understand you boast of your swimming abilities. Come with us. We shall see what a fish you are."

Eirik smiled from ear to ear like a dimwit.

Thork's heart lurched. *I better get the hell out of here and back to Jomsborg while I still can.* But he was so damned tired of the pretense. Let people think what they would of his taking two orphan boys for a swim.

Thork spent a pleasurable hour with his sons at the pond, for which he was sure he would be sorry later. Dar had many strange knights in his keep these days, any one of which could report back to his half-brother or Ivar or the Saxons.

He turned his back on the boys before entering the water to hide his male parts. He had been in a state of near erection the entire day, thanks to the enticing wench who occupied his mind constantly.

A virgin! By the love of Freya, who would have ever imagined it? Not him! She had the mouth of a seasoned whore and the sexual allure of an experienced woman in the bedding. And all those stories of a husband and two sons had been nothing but lies. He stiffened angrily, to think that he had been so taken in by her guile, that he had thought she might be different from all the other deceitful women he had known. Well, it would not matter much longer. He would be gone from Northumbria soon.

"Is it true that you want to foster at the Saxon court?" Thork asked Eirik on the way back.

His son's face flushed. "She had no right to tell you."

" 'Tis true?"

Eirik hesitated, then admitted, "Yea, 'tis. 'Twill be hard times coming for the Vikings in Northumbria. 'Tis logical that we must learn their ways in order to defeat them or to live with them, whichever comes."

Thork was amazed and proud that his ten-year-old son could express himself so well. Before he could tell him so, Tykir interrupted, "Nay, 'twould be better to fight them all to the bloody end. We must become better warriors." He blushed with embarrassment when his father and brother turned to him in surprise.

"So, Ruby was right. You would choose to be a Jomsviking."

The imp raised his chin defiantly. "Yea, and I will be, too."

When he got to his chamber, Thork was still towel-drying his hair when he noticed the basket of fresh peaches on the table. He ate one while he dropped his tunic and codpiece on the floor. He ate another as he dressed and combed his hair.

He shaved in front of a square of shiny metal. There were too many days on board ship and on the battle march when filth and fleas bred in a man's beard. He liked to be clean-shaven when on land.

He reached for a third peach, reminding himself to thank his grandmother for the thoughtful gesture, when he noticed a peach at the bottom of the basket that stood out because of its discoloration and odd bruising. Could it be poisoned? He looked closer. It had been deliberately marked to draw his attention. Then he saw the scrap of parchment under it. The message said, "I'm sorry. Ruby."

At first Thork picked up the basket, intending to throw the remaining peaches into the chamber pot, but then thought better of it. He shook his head from side to side. It was not such an awful thing she had done, leaving the fruit, but if she thought to make amends for all her lies with a basket of fruit, she would be sore disappointed.

He was biting into his third peach as he entered the great hall a short time later and caught Ruby watching him. She smiled tentatively at him. He turned away rudely, not about to give her any encouragement.

Throughout the meal, however, he could not help glancing her way down the long length of the tables which separated them. She wore the burgundy gown again, the one she had worn yestereve.

The wench had somehow become near gorgeous in his eyes, even with that silly short hair. What had she called him? Drop-dead gorgeous. Yea, that was what she was. He liked the phrasing and rolled it on his tongue silently. He knew his fellow hesirs did not share his appreciation for Ruby's beauty, that they found her too slim, too mannish, too coarse-tongued. To him, she seemed damned nigh perfect.

He felt his half-erection come full bloom and swore aloud, then apologized to the cow-eyed maid who gasped beside him at his vulgarity. Thor's blood! Elise was beautiful. Why had he thought of her as cow-eyed? Because Ruby had referred to her as such, that was why. Thork grimaced. He could not get the bloody wench out of his thoughts.

Thork considered taking Linette back into his bed to appease his raging lust but decided that would be unfair to Linette. She deserved the marriage his grandfather had arranged, and he would do nothing to jeopardize her future. Perhaps he would go to the pond again after the meal to cool his hot blood.

Thork sipped his wine thoughtfully throughout dinner and the endless entertainment that followed as his mind drifted, preoccupied with all he needed to do the next few days before the Althing. He was called jarringly back to the present when he heard Dar ask Ruby to sing a song for them.

"Oh, no, please, not tonight," Ruby begged off.

"I insist," his grandfather said, not unkindly.

Ruby balked, and Dar stared her down.

"Just one song then," she conceded.

She strummed the lute, bemused, apparently trying to pick an appropriate song for the crowd, which was still somewhat hostile after the scandalous show she had put on the night before.

She kept her eyes averted from his, probably thinking he would insult her in front of the guests. Mayhap he would. First he would wait and see if she pulled one of her usual stunts.

"I sang this song for you before and told you it was my husband's favorite . . ."

Thork stopped his cup in midair as he was raising it to his lips. She looked directly at him, then turned away quickly.

" . . . but tonight I dedicate it to another man who, when the winter nights seem long and lonely, will be able to think of this song and any special . . . memories he may have created with a woman he might have loved . . . and lost." Her voice wavered at the end. She sang "Help Me Make It Through the Night" in a husky voice that did not stray off key even once, as it usually did. The enthralled people leaned forward trying to hear all the whispery words. When she finished, Ruby bowed her head slightly in response to the congratulations the people showered on her, declined to sing another and walked stiffly out of the hall and up to her tower room—without once looking at Thork.

Thork's heart felt like the lead anchor on his ship. He closed his eyes wearily as the entertainment went on around him. How would he ever make it through the night, let alone the next week? Could he resist the overwhelming urge to make love with Ruby? And if he did take her to his bed, would that cure him of this raging fever in his blood? Somehow, he misdoubted it.

When he opened his eyes, he saw that Dar studied him speculatively. Then he nodded as if he had made some decision. Thork did not trust his grandfather one whit and wondered what he churned now in his devious head.

Ruby got up at dawn the next day, anxious to begin her sewing tasks. She worked the entire day and completed the sexy garment by midafternoon, having taken only one break to go to the garderobe and grab a bite to eat.

She called Aud up to her room to model her new design.

"What do you think?"

"Oh, my!"

"That good?"

"He will not stand a chance. My poor grandson!"

"I sincerely hope you're right."

She went down to the kitchen then and asked the cook for a sirloin roast and some baking supplies. The servant grumbled but did as asked when she saw Aud walk into the room behind Ruby. Ruby almost choked when the heavyset cook bent over, revealing numerous nicks on her hairless legs.

It took Ruby almost an hour to chop and pound the raw beef to the consistency of modern-day hamburger. It wasn't as finely textured as it should be, but Ruby was able to form it into round patties. Laying them aside with slices of hard cheese, Ruby cut four-inch circles out of bannock as a substitute for hamburger buns. She smiled, supremely pleased with her makeshift efforts thus far.

Then she made baklava—Jack's favorite ultasweet honey dessert. All the ingredients were available—walnuts, butter and honey—except for white flour. Ruby improvised with barley flour. She had difficulty rolling it to the required paper-thinness because of its gritty texture, but she worked at it diligently until she attained a reasonable facsimile.

While the baklava baked in the wood-fired oven, which Ruby watched closely, she started frying the hamburgers, making several extra for Aud and Dar to try. She made Thork's medium rare.

The baklava turned out a perfect golden brown, which Ruby cut into diamond shapes while still hot. She made up a platter for Thork with three cheeseburgers and a half-dozen pieces of baklava, then did the same for Dar and Aud. Placing both platters in a warming oven, she instructed Ella to place one before Thork after everyone was seated. "And make sure you don't put it in front of the young heifer next to him."

"Heifer?"

"You know, the cow-eyed girl."

Ella twittered, shaking her head. "What makes you think you can win the man through his stomach?"

Ruby shrugged. "They say you can trap more flies with honey than you can with vinegar."

265

"Huh?"

Ruby rushed back to her tower room and dressed hurriedly for dinner. She was one of the first seated in the hall after the tables were set up. Giant butterflies waltzed in her stomach as she watched Thork sit down beside "Cow-Eyes." He didn't even look toward Ruby.

The jerk!

The first course of dinner was already being served and still no Ella. Ruby pushed the food around her plate nervously.

"Been filching any more wine?" her pimply-faced hesir said snidely.

"Drop dead."

The young man blushed and turned away from her.

Finally Ella stepped up to the dais, carrying two platters. She placed the first in front of Aud and the other in front of Thork.

At first, Thork just stared at the odd items on his trencher, as if they might jump up at him. He picked up a cheeseburger gingerly between two fingers, examined it carefully, then took a hesitant bite. Ruby watched him chew slowly, break into a smile of appreciation, then wolf the three cheeseburgers down hungrily.

He was not so hesitant about sampling the baklava. One bite and he closed his eyes in ecstasy over the sublime sweetness. It was just what Jack did when she baked this dessert for him, although, she must admit, she hadn't made it in years. Ruby frowned at the thought.

Thork was eating his fourth piece of baklava when he glanced around and noticed that his dining companions weren't sharing the same fine fare. He chewed the piece thoughtfully. Ruby knew the exact moment he realized that she'd made these favorite foods for him. He looked at her suddenly, pinning her with his gaze. Studying her over the rim of his ale horn, he seemed to be trying to figure out her game.

Having accomplished her goal, Ruby nodded at him, much as a chess player might do when he'd checkmated a foe. She rose from her seat and went to her room, exhausted by her day's work, but extremely satisfied. She fell into a deep sleep, knowing she had a full day ahead of her tomorrow.

The minute she woke up, Ruby began rolling string into a tight ball and didn't stop until she had a three-and-a-half-inch ball. Next she covered it with soft leather she'd bartered from the cobbler, using fine stitches to hold the seams together.

It was the sorriest looking baseball she'd ever seen.

After breaking her fast in the empty hall and using the garderobe, she went to the pond with Ella and Vigi to bathe. Afterward, they walked to the village, where they first stopped at the woodworker's home.

Ruby examined the smoothness of the baseball bat the craftsman had made for her from a piece of solid hickory. It looked perfect to her, but she really knew little about the correct dimensions of a baseball bat.

Next, she asked for the jump rope. The woodworker had carved wood handles and attached them to a length of rope. Ruby took all the items outside.

First she tried out the jump rope on the hard-packed dirt. It was perfect. She thought Vigi and Ella would die laughing.

Then she instructed Vigi to step about twenty feet away from her and throw the baseball at her. At first he refused. "Nay, I will not throw a hard object at a woman."

"Oh, don't be silly. I'm going to hit it with this bat."

"Nay, you never are!" Ella exclaimed.

Ruby did, much to her delight.

They drew quite a crowd of scandalized villagers by then. Ruby decided it was time to move on to the cobbler. She gave the wooden high heels to the cobbler that the woodworker had just made for her, instructing him on how they would fit onto the leather soles of the high-heeled slippers.

" 'Tis half-witted you are to want such," he told her.

"Probably. I'll be back tomorrow to pick them up."

When they got back to the keep, Ruby sought out Eirik and Tykir to give them her gifts. She got a smile from both of them when she demonstrated the jump rope.

Tykir hugged her spontaneously in thanks. "Why do you give me me a gift?"

"I wanted you to have something to remember me by if I have to leave Jorvik after the Althing." She didn't want to scare him by mentioning the fact that she might be dead. He probably knew that anyway.

Next she showed Eirik how to use the bat and baseball, drawing a picture of a baseball diamond in the dust with her finger. She threw a few practice throws at him, and he was surprisely good right from the start.

No hugs from Eirik, though he did thank her begrudgingly. She told herself not to be disappointed, that the delight on his face should be thanks enough. Before Ruby left them to go into the manor, Eirik called after her, " 'Tis a fine gift." Ruby turned and saw him blush at this retreat from his innate hostility.

Oh, hell! What do I have to lose? Ruby walked back and hugged the boy tightly. Despite the stiffness of his body, he did not turn away from her embrace, and Ruby felt she'd finally accomplished something in her travel through time.

Thork stomped back to the manor at midday, looking for a dozen young hesirs who were missing from the practice field, not to mention Eirik. He stopped abruptly when he reached the field just outside the bailey.

A diamond shape had been marked in the grass with what seemed to be barley flour, and small sacks were laid at each of the points. Selik was throwing a round leather object to Eirik, who attempted to hit it with a stick of wood. When the wood finally connected with the ball, Eirik shrieked with laughter and ran toward one of the sacks while the boys and young men in the field scrambled to catch the ball.

It was the first time in a long, long time Thork had heard the boy laugh. How could that be? He was only ten years old. He frowned thoughtfully. Why hadn't he realized before what a solemn child Eirik was?

Thork's attention was diverted to the bailey where Tykir was jumping up and down over a rope that he swung over his head, counting all the time. Each time he missed he started over again, laughing delightedly in a way Thork had never heard.

Thor's blood! Not Tykir, too!

His eyes narrowed. It was Ruby's doing, he was sure. She was turning his family and his life upside down. "Selik, get the hell back to the practice field and take the rest of these milksops with you," Thork yelled.

Selik jumped guiltily.

Then Thork smiled and complimented Tykir, "Very good," as he passed him before going to the well for a drink of water.

Thork stifled an impulse to seek Ruby out and demand to know what she was up to, but that was probably just what she wanted. In fact, she probably stood at one of the windows now watching him. He stuck out his tongue at the nearest window, just in case, then sheepishly ducked his head when he recognized his grandfather's gray hair.

"Testing for rain?" Dar asked, sticking his head through the window.

Thork shook his head from side to side. The wily wench would make him as strange-headed as she was by the time he finally departed. And, Lord, he was beginning to realize just how much he was going to miss her. He could not imagine a time when he had not known her. He hated to

269

think of how empty his life would be without her. When he finally arrived back at the practice field, he roared at his men, "You men have become bloody weaklings. Perchance I have not worked you hard enough. Today, I swear, we will work *all* the kinks out or die in the trying." He ignored the grumbles of complaint and those men he heard griping, " 'Tis all the fault of the wench from hell."

Ruby wasn't watching Thork. She was in her room, working frantically to complete his cloak. In two days, they would all leave for Jorvik and the Althing.

She'd always been a fine seamstress and enjoyed working with her hands, especially when the material was as fine as this wool. Ruby had made her career based on a sewing talent, so making a cloak for Thork was an easy task. She cut and sewed the voluminous garment in half a day, including the finely stitched hem. The embroidery took much longer. Ruby decided to alternate the thunderbolts worked in silver thread with Thor's gold hammer called Mjollnir, or lightning. The cloak would be stunning. Ruby expected to complete it by tomorrow night.

At dinner that evening, Thork made no pretense of his interest in Ruby and disinterest in the shy maid beside him. Ruby squirmed uncomfortably under his constant gaze from the head table but refused to kowtow to the warning messages he sent. She knew the baseball and jump rope had become an instant hit among young and old alike.

Thork probably interpreted her gifts as further goads aimed at him. That wasn't true. She had other things in mind to rattle the arrogant Viking.

Thork surprised her by approaching her end of the hall after the meal. "No more tricks tonight from your bag of sorcery? No peaches or toys? No special meals to tempt the mouth?"

"I decided to give you a rest for tonight," Ruby replied enigmatically.

"Were you not warned to stop pushing me?"

"I'm not afraid of you. The Althing and Sigtrygg and some of these other vicious Vikings—yes, I fear them—but not you."

Thork gritted his teeth, and his face turned stormy.

"Do you question my manhood?"

"Are you kidding? That's the last thing I would question, but I think you care for me, more than you realize. You wouldn't harm me."

"Wench, you are above yourself. If I thought for one moment you spied for Ivar or were a threat to my family, I would kill you in a trice."

"That's just it. I'm none of those things."

"But a liar you definitely are. That was proven when I discovered your virginity."

"Oh, Thork!" she sighed woefully. "Why won't you just give in and marry me?"

Thork laughed at her persistence. "Nay."

"Will you stand up for me at the Althing?"

"Why should I?"

"To save me from being killed."

"Save your breath, wench. I will not betray my fellow Vikings to save your skin. And think again if you consider yourself aught but an enticing piece of flesh to me. Never will you win this battle."

"Never say never, sweetheart," Ruby challenged cryptically and walked away from him haughtily, swaying her hips in exaggeration. She heard several hesirs laugh behind her, but realized too late what Thork planned. He reached out and tweaked her behind, ensuring he got the last laugh from the hooting hesirs.

Ruby turned back indignantly. "You are a vulgar, vulgar man."

"Nay, wench, you asked for that, swishing your arse

271

like a dockside tart," Thork defended himself with a laugh.

"I did not," Ruby declared lamely and left the hall, her prideful chin still held high.

Ruby finished the cloak the next day, then went to the village to pick up her leather, high-heeled sandals. They weren't quite what she'd planned. The woodworker had somehow made one of the heels slightly shorter than the other, causing her to hobble when she walked. There was no time to fix them since they left for Jorvik the next day.

"Do you try to get Thork's pity by making him think you are a cripple?" Ella inquired.

"No, men in my country like to see women in high heels. They think it makes a woman's legs look sexy."

Ella eyed her skeptically. "Even when they walk like a crone?"

"No." Ruby laughed. "Women can walk fine in them. In fact, it causes them to sway when they walk in sort of a sexy way."

Ella rolled her eyes.

"Perhaps I'll just pose in them. Now that I think about it, moving around in these primitive high heels probably isn't a great idea."

"Mayhap you have lost your mind completely."

The next night Thork decided to retire immediately after the meal. He had no intention of returning to his grandfather's estate after the Althing, so he had spent an exhausting day loading wagons with the last of the trading goods for his ships.

He noticed Ruby's absence from the evening meal.

"Mayhap her stomach ails and she could not sup," the thrall Ella said, shifting her eyes slyly when he asked about her whereabouts.

" 'Tis nervous she is about the Althing and wanted to rest," his grandmother offered and also averted her eyes from Thork's direct gaze.

"How should I know?" his grandfather snapped. "Think you I know her every move?"

"I will probably find a snake in my bed," Thork grumbled as he walked away, excusing Dar's abrupt manner as regret over his imminent leavetaking.

Thork yawned widely as he opened the door of his darkening chamber. He laid his sword and knife on a chest, lit two soapstone lamps, then yawned again. It would be a long day tomorrow with all the wagons and guests who would travel with them to Jorvik. He hoped to get an early start. He turned then and jumped.

"Thor's blood, woman, what do you here? Wouldst thou fright me to death to accomplish thy goals?"

Ruby stood at the far end of the room in a dim corner wearing a magnificent bright blue cloak with fine embroidery around the edges. 'Twas odd, though, because it dwarfed her with its massive folds, and its hem hugged the floor.

Thork narrowed his eyes suspiciously and started back toward the door, not wanting to tempt fate by being in the same room with the wanton wench—virgin though she may be. And where was that cursed Vigi? He was supposed to be guarding Ruby at all times, keeping her away from him.

"No, don't go," Ruby said and wobbled toward him, probably hampered by the oversized garment, Thork thought. "I just want to give you a going-away gift. This cloak. I made it for you and did all the handwork myself. Do you like it?" Her voice wavered nervously.

" 'Tis a fine cloak, but why wouldst thou make me a gift?" Truly, the garment was a work of art, as fine as any he had ever seen in his travels. Thork glanced at her suspiciously. "Do you bribe me now?"

"No. This gift has no strings attached. It's just a memento of our time together. I offer it as sort of an apology for all the trouble I've caused you."

273

Like all Vikings, Thork appreciated the giving and receiving of gifts. It would be rude to deny her offering. Thork nodded his acceptance. Besides, 'twas true she had caused him much trouble.

"Turn around so I can put it on your shoulders and see if it fits properly."

Thork turned away from her and felt her reach up and place the cape on his shoulders. Actually, he was glad she was taking their parting so well. 'Twas best to part with a woman amicably, no bad feelings left to ferment. He was a man slow to forgive his enemies, but Thork was in a magnanimous mood on the eve of his departure for Jorvik, and, after all, the wench had not really done anything that evil. True, she had lied about her virginity and more, but 'twas no different from any other self-serving female he had encountered. 'Twas the nature of the species. He turned to tell her that and gasped in astonishment, "Holy blood!"

Ruby had stepped away from him and stood next to the bed holding on to the bed post as if for support. She wore this . . . this thing that pushed her breasts up and out at the top and exposed her legs from the hip bone all the way down to her . . . oh, my God!

"What the hell are those things on your feet?" The wench leaned precariously on wobbly legs. No wonder! Her feet were encased in leather slippers with wooden stilts.

"High heels. Do you like them?"

"What purpose do they serve? Can you walk?"

"Yes . . . no. Well, normally I could, but your village woodworker made one heel shorter than the other. Men in my country think it makes a woman's legs look sexy. Don't you?"

"I am not sure. Come near so I can see." Thork had trouble controlling the twitch in his lips.

Ruby moved closer, using the balls of her feet in a

sliding motion so she wouldn't limp. That gave him a better view of the garment she wore. For the love of Freya! The black silk and lace wisp barely covered her from the tips of her breasts to the vee at her legs, pushing in and out at strategic places. He could see the shadow of her nipples and the dark curly hair that covered her womanhood through the thin lace. Never in all his years of travel had he seen such a marvel—not even in the Eastern harems.

Thork gulped and looked again. It appeared as if she'd shaved part of herself *there* to accommodate the revealing lines of her garment. He was no longer in the mood for laughing.

"Turn," he directed through a suddenly dry throat.

The thought that Ruby would go to so much trouble to entice him touched Thork with the force of a rolling boulder. His heart constricted oddly in his chest. No one had ever shown so much caring for him afore.

When she turned, Thork felt the blood drain from his face at the sight of her nether cheeks half exposed by the slant of the outfit's bottom edge. A burgeoning arousal pulled sharply at his groin.

"Do you like it?" she asked uncertainly when she faced him again.

"I like it fine." Holy Thor! Was the wench blind? Could she not see just how much he liked it?

"Only fine?" Her lips turned down in disappointment.

"What do you want from me, wench?" Thork grated out between gritted teeth. He wasn't sure how much more of this he could take or even if he wanted to resist anymore.

"I think you know." She looked up at him hopefully through the shadows of her half-lowered lids.

"I cannot," he groaned.

"Why?" she asked softly, tears welling in her eyes.

"You would want more than I could give."

Ruby shook her head. "For tonight I call a truce. I will

ask no more than you are willing to give."

Thor's blood! The woman was a tempting negotiator. "And tomorrow?"

She smiled and shrugged. "I can't make promises about what I'd do after today."

" 'Tis a trick."

"No, just a man and a woman . . . making memories."

Thork's heart lurched at her words. He moaned thickly in surrender and started to move toward her. He was stopped short by a loud pounding at the door.

"Thork! Come quickly," Olaf yelled.

"Go away," Thork shouted menacingly.

"Nay. 'Tis important. Someone set fire to one of the trade wagons. Men were seen on horseback riding away from the keep."

Thork cursed and opened the door slightly so Olaf could not see Ruby in her scanty attire. "Where were the guards when the fire started?"

"It happened so quickly. 'Twas little damage, but the attackers are long gone, probably back to Ivar. Only he would try these cowardly hit-and-run tactics."

"I will be right down. Do not bother sending men out searching tonight, but put a double guard around the keep."

When Thork closed the door and turned back to Ruby, he saw her sitting in a chair by the cold fireplace, weeping silently. The sight tore at his innards like a barbed arrow.

"Why do you cry, sweetling?" he asked, kneeling in front of her.

She sobbed loudly now. Between gasps, she told him, "I wanted us to be together before the Althing. Tonight was our last chance."

Ruby's tears touched him even deeper than her intense sexual magnetism. "Mayhap I can come back to my sleeping chamber later . . . if you would wait."

"No," she sniffled sadly, "once you leave this room you'll have second thoughts and convince yourself this is for the best. Probably decide I had something to do with the attack on your wagons." She dried her tears on the edge of the new cloak.

Thork nodded unhappily, acknowledging she was right. Still, he kissed away her tears, kneeling at her feet. He wanted to prolong this bittersweet moment with her as long as possible, endlessly, sensing there would never be another. Finally he tore himself away, but the image of her in the wispy garment stayed with him through the night as he stood guard, prisoner to his conflicting emotions. When he returned near dawn, he saw the blue cloak folded neatly on his chest.

Ruby was gone.

Chapter Fifteen

Several miles outside Jorvik, they arrived at the wide plain where the national open-air court would assemble. Aud had explained to Ruby on the day-long trip back to Jorvik that district *Things,* or courts, were held several times each year, though not as often as in the old days, while larger *Althings* were held only once a year.

Hundreds of bright tents—stripes, checks, solids, in all the colors of the rainbow—fluttered throughout the wide-ranging fields in the manner of a giant fairground. Instead of wild animals and hurdy-gurdy shows, these tents housed the fierce, law-loving Vikings who came from many miles around to socialize and participate in the primitive justice system.

As Dar's household began to erect their own tents, Olaf and Gyda said good-bye to Ruby. They would be staying at their home in Jorvik.

"'Twas a pleasure meeting you," Gyda said, hugging Ruby warmly. "We did not get to spend much time together at Dar's manor, but I bid you the best of luck at the Thing. I wanted you to know that I wish you no harm."

"Thank you. You've been so kind to me. I can never repay you." Ruby's voice choked on the last words.

"Think naught of it. Leastways, you more than repaid me with the yellow undergarments." Gyda rolled her eyes in Olaf's direction. "They were a huge success. Mayhap they will result in another son come spring."

When Gyda's words sunk in, Ruby grabbed the Viking woman and gave her a quick squeeze. "Congratulations! Another baby! How I envy you!"

Olaf stepped up next and shifted uncomfortably. "I will stand behind you at the Thing," he informed her in a blustery fashion. "A strange wench you surely are, but not a spy to my thinking. If thrall you are declared, I will offer to buy you."

Ruby accepted his oblique support with a nod, then turned to the girls. She embraced each of them in turn, including Tyra who couldn't wait to get home and see her ducks and kittens.

Later, after they'd eaten their hastily prepared meal outside the tents, Ruby walked with Thork, Eirik and Tykir around the campsite, stopping often to speak with their old friends. Since last night at Ravenshire when they had almost made love, Thork seemed to have softened toward her.

They were almost like a family.

Eirik had brought his bat and baseball and soon had a game going. Since it was still summer, the skies would not darken for another hour or two. Ruby sat on the grass watching Eirik explain the rules to each of the newcomers who approached.

Thork's casual stance as he watched his sons empha-sized the lines of his powerfully muscled body under a coal-black tunic. Through half-shuttered lashes, Ruby admired his long, sinewy legs—like bronze marble—beneath the thigh-high garment. She yearned to touch the silken blond hairs just barely revealed at the open laces of his neckline.

"You were always a good baseball player," Ruby recalled, tipping her face up to him as she lay back on the sun-warmed grassy slope. "Why don't you play?"

Thork's handsome face split into a quick, open grin at her words. "Me? Playing children's games? Never!" He dropped lithely down to the ground and lay on his side watching her, propped on one elbow. The sparkle of his lazy smile kindled a fire in her.

"Surely you played games as a child," she commented, increasingly distracted as Thork's long, skillful fingers traced invisible, sensuous circles on her arm, starting at the wrist and moving slowly upward.

"Hah! The only games I recall were hiding from my brother Eric, and that was more a deadly pursuit." His slowly stalking hand had reached her collarbone, which he tenderly brushed with featherlike strokes.

Ruby swallowed hard and tried to change the subject. "Men play baseball in my country, as well as children. In fact, the really good ones get paid a fortune for it."

"You make these tales up as you go, I think." He smiled wickedly as his fingertips crept under the loose collar of her gown and began making little spiraling circles on the ultrasensitive skin. The light caresses ignited delicious tingles wherever they touched.

"Stop it!" Ruby gasped and whisked his hand away. "I can't think when you do that."

"Do what?" Thork asked, his blue eyes wide with feigned innocence.

Ruby laughed at this playful side of Thork. "You know exactly what I mean, you tease. Anyhow, instead of trying to seduce me, why don't you get rid of some of your excess energy down there on the ballfield?" When he seemed reluctant to remove himself and his feathery fingers, Ruby challenged him, "Come on, big guy. I bet you can't even hit the ball."

"Excess energy!" Thork laughed. "Is that what they call it in your country?" He leaned closer, his hot breath tantalizing her parted lips. With a smug grin, Thork whispered, "And what do I get if I win the wager?" Dipping his head, he lowered his mouth and grazed her lips lightly in question. When he pulled away, Ruby's lips followed his instinctively. He chuckled gleefully at her open response.

"I have nothing of value that you would want," Ruby rasped out softly and sat up, hugging her knees. Thork followed suit and held her eyes steadily.

"Nay, never think it."

Ruby arched her eyes in doubt. "I offered more to you than any woman could, and you rejected it every time."

"Hah! Not because I did not want you, sweet witch. Nay, never that!"

Ruby smiled widely at his backhanded compliment.

Thork poked her in the ribs with a forefinger playfully and cautioned, "Do not think you have won any great battle with such a meager concession on my part."

"Oh, no, I would never think that, but a teensy little skirmish . . . couldn't I claim that?" she bantered. Actually, Ruby felt as if she'd won the whole bloody world with his admission. Was this a first step toward something more?

"Ah, sweetling, do not look at me like that."

"How?"

"Your smile is edged with sadness, but your eyes glisten still with hope. Can you not accept the fact that there will be no future betwixt us, Ruby?" He shook his head in emphasis, then added softly, "Even though 'tis pleasant to think of what might have been."

He stood abruptly then, obviously uncomfortable with the direction of their discussion. Gazing down at her, he asked with overbearing confidence, "So you think I could not hit a piddling-sized ball with a hunk of wood? We shall see." He strode off down the slope to the field where the boys played ball. Over his shoulder, he informed her with jiggling eyebrows, "I will decide on my forfeit later."

Thork talked to Eirik for a few moments before he picked up the bat. Like a true athlete, he held it in several positions to feel its weight, scrutinized the angle of the pitcher's position, seemed to smell the wind, then took the batter's position.

THWACK!

Ruby wasn't surprised when the ball whistled over the astonished heads of Eirik and the other players and continued in a flying arc way past the outfield. Eirik beamed with pride at his father's expertise. Thork declined to run the bases, only wanting to prove a point to her, and handed the bat to the next player. He flashed Ruby a huge smirk when he turned and strutted arrogantly toward her.

Good Lord! A Viking jock!

"Shall we negotiate my forfeit, wench?" Thork asked smoothly as he reached out a hand and hauled her to her feet. Ruby's heart skipped a beat when he twined his fingers in hers. Like a lifeline, she felt his pulse beat against hers in their joined palms as they walked back to the tents. "You did not wait for me yestereve," Thork complained softly.

"I didn't think you wanted me to." Ruby glanced sideways at him in surprise at his abrupt change of subject. Had he been disappointed to find her gone? "I thought the moment had passed, that your usual cool reason had doused your hot blood by the time you returned to the room."

"Hot blood, huh?" Thork grinned. "Didst you think I only wanted you when you had stoked my lust with that"— Thork stopped for loss of words and smiled with a shake of his head—"with that tiny wisp of a garb designed, no doubt, to make a man's tongue hang out. Not to mention other body parts. By the by, I found it under my bed this morn."

Ruby's heart soared with hope. What exactly did he mean? She studied his inscrutable face, seeing only the intensity of his expression. Thork seemed to deliberate for several moments the wisdom of disclosing his inner thoughts. With the knuckle of his right hand, he caressed her jaw from ear to chin and back.

Wistfully he finally whispered, "Sweetling, I want you in the morn when I waken and remember my night dreams of you boldly seducing me." His blue eyes locked with hers to seal his soul-wrenched message, and Ruby felt her world tilt. "I want you when I see you touch my sons with kindness. I want you when I hear you sing about making it through the night. I want you when you speak of kisses that last three days. God's blood, I want you when you make me laugh. Yea, I do. But one thing you must never misdoubt, sweetling—*I want you.*"

Ruby had trouble speaking over the lump in her throat. "But you resist me, Thork. Despite everything you say, you won't let me get close. Whether you believe what I say about the future or not, you obviously recognize this bond between us." She put her hand up to his face and stroked it lovingly. "I don't know if you're Jack or just a time reflection of him, but I love you. I know that now, and, dammit, I don't know what to do about it anymore." She raised tear-filled eyes to his, looking for answers. "I've tried every stupid trick in the book to seduce you, and—"

"Shush," Thork whispered, pulling her into his arms, his lips in her hair. "'Tis not our time, Rube. In truth, 'twill never be. Mayhap 'tis why your God gave me another chance in another lifetime, if your tales of the future be true." His voice was deep-timbered with regret for his heartfelt words.

Rube! He'd called her Rube. "Why did you call me that?"

"What?"

"Rube. You called me Rube."

Thork shrugged, puzzled at the importance she placed on a simple word. "It just came out that way. Do your people never shorten names?"

The fine hairs stood out on Ruby's arms. "Oh, Thork! Rube was Jack's pet name for me. Can't you see that your use of it is like an omen, as if God, or some higher being, were telling me everything will be all right?"

"Let us speak no more of it, sweetling. It can only cause us both needless anguish."

Choked with emotion, Ruby asked with a tearful laugh, trying to lighten Thork's mood, "What did you do with my teddy? Will you put it under your pillow on the long winter nights in Jomsborg to remind you of what you might have had?"

"You call that lacy man-teaser a teddy? How odd!" The corners of his lips lifted enticingly, even though his eyes remained dull with a resigned sadness.

Ruby wiped at the wetness rimming her eyes with the back of her hand, laughing despite her desolation. "Well, it's a special design of mine—a combination bustier and teddy." Her eyes narrowed and she asked menacingly, "You wouldn't think of giving it to another woman? If you do, I swear I'll put a curse on you—from wherever I am."

Thork laughed and swung her around in his arms with pure joy. When her feet touched the ground again, he answered, "Nay, you are the only woman 'twould suit. Leastways, I decided on my forfeit for our baseball wager. You must model the teddy for me again. One last time."

"You better make it soon . . . before the Thing," Ruby declared grimly. "The outfit goes better with a head, and you'd never be able to get the bloodstains out of silk."

"I find your humor ill-timed and inappropriate." His jaw tightened at her sick joke. Then he turned and walked away from her stiffly.

Ruby decided that Thork must care for her, more than he would acknowledge to himself, and the prospect of her death frightened him. That didn't speak well for Thork's optimism about her fate at the Althing. Ruby shivered apprehensively.

Just before she stepped inside the tent, Ruby saw Selik approach with shoulders drooping. "What's the matter?" she teased. "Did you strike out tonight?"

The uncommonly handsome man had a notorious reputation for attracting females. Ruby pitied Astrid if she hoped to keep this womanizer tied to a hearth fire.

"Strike out? I did not play baseball tonight." Selik arched his dark brows, a sharp contrast to his almost-white hair. He tilted his head quizzically as he looked Ruby over from head to foot, probably assessing whether she would be worth the trouble of his amorous advances.

"I wasn't referring to baseball," Ruby said, amused at his transparency. "I meant that you looked like a horny male who hadn't been lucky tonight."

"Lucky? What language do you speak?"

"Oh, Selik! It's just an expression. You know, if you found a woman to share your tent, you might say, 'I got lucky tonight.'"

His face lit up with understanding. "So to be unlucky is to strike out?"

"Right!"

"I like that," he said with a nod, "although I usually only hit home runs."

When she made a tsk-ing sound of disgust at his conceit, he smiled widely, exposing the whitest, evenest teeth Ruby had ever seen outside an orthodontist's office. Despite his devastating good looks, Ruby felt no attraction whatsoever toward him. She was deliberating over that sudden insight when Selik asked in a low, silky voice, "Did your husband really shave your legs?"

"Yes, he did," Ruby answered, laughing at his bluntness.

"Mayhap I would enjoy doing that for you . . . seeing as how you have no husband to—"

"Mayhap you would like to have your balls cut off."

Ruby and Selik both jumped at the voice behind them. It was Thork.

"Hardly," Selik answered dryly, crossing his legs comically to cover his genitals in pretended horror.

"Then get the hell to your own tent where you belong."

Ruby and Selik gaped at Thork, finding it hard to comprehend Thork's anger over a casual conversation.

"Methinks the man is testy because he was *unlucky* tonight," Selik bantered, glancing pointedly at Ruby, then inquired sweetly, "Didst thou perchance strike him out?"

Ruby bit her lip to stifle a giggle.

"Do not push me, Selik. You will not like the results."

"Methinks you play the dog in the manger," Selik said with a grin, apparently undaunted by Thork's dire warnings. "If you do not want the wench, Thork, there are others who do." Selik winked slyly at Ruby.

"Ruby is my responsibility, *boy*. Go find some dimwitted slut who knows not the difference between a man and a boy."

Instead of taking umbrage at the insult, Selik hooted with glee at the expression on Thork's face. "Smitten! Thor's blood! Ne'er did I think to see the day! The maid has skewered you good and fine."

After Selik left, Ruby and Thork continued to hear his fading laughter.

"So now you practice your wiles on boys."

"I did not."

"Best you be praying instead of flirting, wench," he lashed out, reminding her of her dire circumstances.

Before Ruby fell asleep that night, she decided she liked Thork's proprietary manner. It spoke of deeper feelings he would not admit.

When she awakened early the next day, she ate a cold meal and washed up in a stream, then went to the opening ceremonies for the Althing with Aud. Women didn't participate, except as occasional witnesses, but they were permitted to watch. A massive, open-sided tent screened a low platform from the summer sun. Sigtrygg sat in the place of honor, along with twenty well-dressed jarls, including Dar. At least five hundred freemen of Northumbria, who had the right to vote, surrounded them on the ground.

"With the law shall the kingdom be built up, and with lawlessness wasted away," a booming voice called out, officially declaring the opening of the Althing.

"That is the law speaker, Assen." Aud pointed to an imposing figure who had moved to the head of the jarls. "He will read one-third of all the laws contained in the Danelaw legal codes from memory, then one-third next year and one-third the following year. Listen, he explains the Viking law and specific crimes and punishments."

While some of the punishments were downright barbaric, such as chopping off a hand for thievery, or stoning a witch, or decapitating a traitor, most of the laws were based on a simple premise: an innocent man should not be unjustly accused, and the guilty should not be protected.

"Your case will not come before the Thing today," Thork said, coming up to Ruby where she sat on a slight hill to the side of the platform. She and Aud had a perfect view of the proceedings under Vigi's diligent guard.

Ruby breathed a sigh of relief at Thork's words.

"There are so many disputes to hear, it may be two days afore they get to you."

"Is that good or bad for me?"

"It could go either way." He shrugged. "Depends on

287

the mood of the jarls—or Sigtrygg. Need I warn you to behave yourself until then?"

Ruby shook her head. Thork looked as if he wanted to say more, then thought better of it before he turned and walked away to join his friends.

First the assembly discussed King Athelstan's proposal that King Sigtrygg marry his sister. Sigtrygg stood, an impressive sight in a jewel-studded purple tunic and a gold circlet around his forehead denoting his rank. "Good people, I would announce my betrothal to the Saxon sister of King Athelstan."

A murmur of protest arose in the crowd.

"Nay, think not that I wish this joining, but I have been convinced 'twould be in the best interest of all Vikings in Northumbria." Sigtrygg looked pointedly at Thork in the front row. He went on to discuss all the advantages that Thork had mentioned at the castle the first night Ruby had arrived in Jorvik.

The assembly decided that a representative of the king should attend Athelstan's coronation ceremony on the fourth of September at Kingston, where a date would be set with Athelstan for a fall meeting between the two kings and a January wedding at Tamworth.

Then the Thing moved on to the routine business of settling legal disputes—everything from disagreements over property lines to murder. Ruby sat fascinated for hours, even after Aud went back to the tent to rest.

Each time a new case came up, the law speaker outlined the charges or the dispute to the panel on the platform, loud enough so that all could hear. Each side brought their supporters or witnesses with them. They faced each other, with the law speaker acting as arbiter, fielding questions from the king and jarls, as well as freemen in the assembly. Questions were decided on a final vote, not by a ballot or voice vote, but by *vapnatak*, the rattle of weapons.

Most of the fines were paid in a complicated system of *wergild,* a person's worth measured in silver or wool or cows. If a slave had been murdered, the *wergild* to be paid would be less than for a hesir. For raiding a neighbor's lands, a Viking could be outlawed, which meant exile from the territory and forfeiture of lands and belongings. Anyone could kill that man with impunity if he stayed.

"Do you enjoy our Thing?" Byrnhil asked, sliding down onto the grass next to Ruby.

"Byrnhil! How wonderful to see you again!"

The king's mistress wore a spectacular red silk, full-length tunic, her attire more suited to a palace than an outdoor event. Gold bracelets and brooches studded with rubies and emeralds flashed in the sunlight, and she had a narrow gold circlet on her forehead, like a queen.

"This is fascinating," Ruby said. "I can't believe the Vikings have such an intricate justice system."

"We Vikings have always had a great respect for laws. Why would you think otherwise?"

Ruby smiled, ignoring her question, and put her arm around Byrnhil's shoulders. She hadn't realized how much she'd missed her friend. "Have you been jogging lately?"

"Yea, I have, and now travel twice as far each morning as we did afore."

"Four miles! Not bad!"

"'Tis strange. I get this wonderful feeling when I run, almost like the intoxication from fine wine. I cannot see why more people do not do this exercise."

"Endorphins," Ruby informed her on a giggle. "It's called a jogger's high."

Byrnhil smiled at Ruby's strange words and asked her to join her for the midday meal. Vigi, of course, followed them. As they walked, Ruby feasted her eyes on all the sights. Servants roasted whole pigs and deer over open fires. In one massive, wood-lined pit, thralls dropped chunks of meat, juniper berries, mustard seeds, garlic and other herbs into water kept boiling with hot stones—a primitive form of slow cooking. Men roped off areas for the evening's competitions—weightlifting, wrestling, stallion fighting, races and games of skill, like archery, spear throwing and swordplay.

Craftsmen and merchants set up tables in front of their tents to sell their wares. She and Byrnhil stopped repeatedly to look and touch—everything from carved ivory combs to silk scarves from the Orient to the much-valued amber beads.

"What do you think will happen to me at the Thing?" Ruby finally asked. She and Byrnhil sat on elaborately carved chairs inside a large tent set up for Sigtrygg near the edge of the clearing.

"I doubt the assembly would order your killing unless someone has come up with some evidence to prove you do spy." She scrutinized Ruby's face for hidden answers. "'Tis a most grievous offense, to be proven a spy. Then no one could save you."

Later, when Ruby and Vigi returned to their tent area, they saw that the men had already returned from the Thing. Thork, Dar, Selik, the two boys and a dozen hesirs were gathering linens, soap and changes of clothing to take to the stream where they would bathe before the evening meal and entertainment.

Selik started to walk toward Ruby, but Thork grabbed him by the neck and pulled him along with the men.

"Odin's spit, you will break my neck," Selik grumbled.

"Better that than another part of your body."

Selik looked back at Ruby over his shoulders and rolled his eyes dramatically.

"Act your age," Thork barked at him.

When they were gone, she and Aud exchanged glances.

"'Twould seem my grandson has a burr under his skin. He behaves like a jerk."

Ruby laughed. "You like that word, don't you?"

"Yea, almost as much as 'male chauvinist pig.' Dar mislikes my using the words, though. So I practice on the servants." Her eyes twinkled mischievously.

That evening, the family walked back to their tents from the king's section of the campsite where they'd spent hours listening to music and the skald's renditions of Viking sagas. Ruby held back to talk with Thork.

"What? Is Selik busy this eve?" Thork sneered.

"Don't be an ass," Ruby chastised, though secretly pleased with Thork's jealousy. "Do you honestly believe I would want to be just another notch on Selik's womanizing belt?"

Thork understood what she meant instantly and laughed, shaking his head from side to side. "You have a gift, wench, for pulling me from my bad humors. 'Tis your way with those silly words. What will you come out with next?"

"Well, I did think of something that might save me with the Thing?" She looked up at him hopefully.

"And what, pray tell, might that be? I hope it does not involve me in any way," Thork said with a wary smile, knowing she had a knack for surprising him.

"Don't be sarcastic. It just occurred to me that since there are Christian churches in Jorvik I could seek the protection of the church. I've read about that in historical novels."

"You would go into a nunnery," Thork hooted and began to laugh uproariously. Dar and Aud looked back to see what amused Thork, but he dismissed their interest with a wave of the hand. Still chuckling, he told Ruby, "I can just see you wearing the staid religious garb with that 'teddy' underneath. 'Twould be enough to make the saints turn over in their graves."

Thork burst into another fit of laughter and called Dar back to share in his mirth. When they began howling at the picture of Ruby in a nun's robe, she stomped away.

It wasn't *that* funny.

Ruby and Aud looked at each other in disgust and both said at the same time, "Jerks!" Then they erupted with their own peals of laughter.

It ended up being four days before Ruby's case was called. By then she shook with nervousness and broke out in tears at the least provocation, especially because of the brutal punishments she'd witnessed so far. Six thieves had had their right hands chopped off before the entire assembly. They'd stoned an adulteress. A thrall who had killed his master had been decapitated, a sight Ruby refused to watch. While Aud agreed the punishments were gruesome to witness, she couldn't understand Ruby's condemnation of the process since the victims had been given "fair" trials.

Finally it was her turn. Dressed in her best clothing, the burgundy tunic dress Dar had given her, with Byrnhil's emerald pendant, Ruby stood to the side while the law speaker called out her "crime."

"Ruby Jordan, you are accused of being a spy for Ivar. What say you?"

"I am not guilty."

"Are those your supporters behind you?"

"Huh?" Ruby turned in surprise. Lined up behind her were Dar, Aud, Olaf, Gyda, Selik, Byrnhil, and . . . Ruby's heart lurched . . . Thork. His solemn eyes held hers for a moment before he nodded slightly, and she turned back to her accusers. "Yes," Ruby replied meekly, tears filling her eyes. She wasn't sure what their support meant but she thanked God for it.

The law speaker read off the long list of complaints against Ruby: that she'd shown up in Jorvik mysteriously, had no logical explanation for her background, wore a shirt that appeared to be a message from Ivar, preached birth control to their women and, in essence, could be a spy for one of their enemies. When he held the T-shirt up for the assembly's inspection, a rumble of outrage rolled through the crowd at the words *Brass Balls.*

"What say you in your defense?"

"I come from America, a land beyond the Atlantic Ocean," Ruby explained, trying to avoid mention of the future, not even sure if they called it the Atlantic Ocean then. "I'm lost but I'm certainly not a spy for anyone. Other than the shirt, which has no meaning whatsoever except for childish humor, I don't think there's any evidence to prove I'm a spy."

"What say you to the charge that you want to kill off our young?"

"That's ridiculous!" Ruby exclaimed, then clenched her fists to calm herself and the increasing stridency of her voice. "I don't favor killing babies, either in or out of the womb. The only reason I mentioned birth control at all was the ladies in Jorvik were talking about a young woman who had ten children and who was in danger of dying in childbirth. I thought such a female could benefit from birth control information. I still do."

"And the only reason she told the women in the palace about birth control was because I ordered her to," Byrnhil inserted defiantly. "*Some* women would like to learn how to *prevent* conception."

Sigtrygg barreled forward in anger at Byrnhil's challenge, and hostile murmurings rippled through the crowd. "Remove thyself, woman," Sigtrygg ordered sternly.

Brynhil could see she wasn't helping Ruby, and she walked silently to the back of the tent.

Dar stepped up to the front and intervened, hoping to swing the crowd back to a more sympathetic mood. "The wench claims to be the granddaughter of Hrolf, The Marcher. Can we punish her on so little evidence without checking her claim first?"

Olaf, Aud and Gyda spoke then, telling of their associations with Ruby and convictions that she was just misguided in her words and actions, no real danger.

"I trust her with my daughters and would not do so if she were a spy," Gyda declared with fierce loyalty.

God bless her Viking soul, Ruby prayed.

Finally, Thork cleared his voice to speak. When he stepped to the center of the tent, the silence of the crowd bespoke the respect he garnered. His proud stance was that of an authority figure used to having his opinions valued.

"The wench has been *my* responsibility, thanks to your orders, Sigtrygg," Thork explained in a clear, articulate voice directed at the king, "and a bedeviling one, at that." He grinned ruefully at Ruby in memory of just how outrageous some of her actions had been, then went on, "Whilst her background is still a mystery to me, I believe she merely suffers an ague of the mind."

An ague of the mind! Give me a break!

Once again, Ruby had to clench her fists and press her nails painfully into her palms to restrain her temper, but her flashing eyes told Thork just what she thought of his *ague of the mind.*

"I disbelieve she spies. 'Twas proven when we captured and killed two true spies from Ivar," Thork continued, addressing his comments to the noble Viking jury in true lawyerly fashion. He breathed deeply and concluded, "I would ask that the assembly absolve Ruby of all charges."

"And do what with her?" Sigtrygg asked indignantly. "I want naught of her in Jorvik, spreading her tales, riling the women to trouble." He threw his last words at Byrnhil who stood stubbornly in the background.

Thork's face flushed at the question. Obviously, he didn't think that her future, beyond this trial, was his continuing responsibility, Ruby realized painfully. He seemed to deliberate his next words carefully before speaking. "Perchance, if she were released, she could make her way back to her own country or to Hrolf in Normandy on a trading vessel. I would be willing to pay her fare."

There was much questioning and discussion back and forth among the jarls on the platform. The free men on the grass clamored to offer their opinions, as well. Finally, the law speaker raised both arms in the air for silence.

"These are the issues to be decided here today: Is Ruby Jordan guilty of spying for our enemies? Is the spreading of birth control information a crime under our law codes? Should the accused's alleged kinship with Hrolf be at issue here?" Assen inhaled deeply and said loudly in a typical court crier voice, "Hear ye, good Norsemen all, what be your verdict?"

"Chop off 'er head," one man in the crowd yelled.

Ruby cringed. So quickly, they were back to that decapitation stuff.

"Cut out 'er tongue," another advised.

"Torture 'er till she confesses." On and on the vile suggestions went, to Ruby's dismay.

When everyone finished voicing an opinion, the speaker called for a vote. On the first charge of spying for Ivar, the assembly could not come to a majority opinion. They agreed to come back to that charge after discussing the others.

On the second question—whether her birth control lectures constituted a crime—Ruby was found innocent, though a fine was assessed for poor judgment and to discourage her from repeating the same mistake.

"I have no money to pay the fine," Ruby said. "All I have is this." She handed the law speaker her pendant.

"'Twould be sufficient," he concluded after examining it carefully for its value. He handed it to Sigtrygg, who turned bright red with rage.

"That belongs to me," Sigtrygg yelled at Ruby.

"No! You gave it to me and I gave it to Ruby." Byrnhil contradicted him, coming forward once again.

Sigtrygg looked as if he'd like to throttle Byrnhil. "Shut

Sandra Hill

your teeth, woman, lest I bring you afore this assembly for theft and aiding a spy. You overstep yourself mightily." Sigtrygg sat back down, seething as he glared alternately at his mistress and Ruby.

Uh oh! Things were not looking good.

On the next question, of Ruby's relationship to Hrolf, her supporters' arguments convinced the assembly that the possible blood ties were worth investigating.

Brynhil sidled up to the king and whispered something in his ear. Thork looked at Ruby suspiciously, as if she and Brynhil conspired together. Finally, seeming to be fed up with the proceedings, Sigtrygg pulled away from his mistress and announced dogmatically, "I suggest the woman Ruby Jordan be taken under guard to Hrolf's court in Normandy. If 'tis found she has lied, that will be taken as evidence that she had evil intents here in Jorvik—whether for Ivar or the Saxons or some other enemy—and she is to be beheaded on the spot. She is *not* to be brought back here for further trial."

"What say you to King Sigtrygg's suggestion?" the law speaker called out to the entire assembly, now restless after a long day of hearings and anxious to begin the evening's entertainment.

Ruby crossed her fingers and said a silent prayer of hope.

The assembly agreed overwhelmingly, by voice and the loud clanging of battle shields, to the king's solution, then stood to depart the Thing area. It happened so quickly that it took Ruby a few moments to realize that the Vikings had essentially found her innocent, at least for the time being. A thankful smile began to split her face, and she turned to share her happiness with Thork.

But Thork didn't look happy at all. A frown creased his forehead, and his perplexed gaze darted from Ruby to Brynhil to the king and back again. "Wait!" Thork raised his voice, calling to Sigtrygg's departing back, "I understand naught of your intent. What exactly happens to the wench now?"

King Sigtrygg stretched his massive frame and yawned hugely before turning to Thork and smiling craftily. "Why, 'tis simple. *You* will take her to Normandy, and *you* will behead her if she is not granddaughter to The Marcher."

Chapter Sixteen

"Nay, I cannot do such," Thork shouted, not caring if it was his king he addressed. "I go to Jomsborg." His eyes blazed furiously.

"You can take the wench on the way to Jomsborg," Sigtrygg advised unctuously, his face rigid at Thork's questioning of his orders.

"On the way . . . on the way . . . ," Thork sputtered. "Normandy is nowhere near the route to Jomsborg."

"I trust you, Thork, more than any other to undertake this task for me," the king cajoled.

"What makes you think I would behead the wench?" Thork asked, running his fingers through his hair. "I have already said I do not think her a spy." He flashed Ruby a quick look that said he would have plenty to say to her when he finished with the king.

"Yea, but that signifies naught. You cherish honor more than aught else. If Hrolf denies her, you would kill her if you had sworn me your pledge. Of that, I am certain."

Thork snorted rudely at the blatant trickery in Sigtrygg's oily words.

"Oh, and didst I mention," Sigtrygg added, coolly examining his fingernails, "you will represent me at Athelstan's coronation."

Thork turned dark red as he cursed wildly.

"Do not think to say me nay on this," Sigtrygg said in a steely voice that bespoke his rigid determination. "You know well and good you are the only Viking who knows his way round the Saxon court well enough to avoid a knife in the back."

Thork's eyes shot rebellious daggers at his king, but Sigtrygg faced him off stubbornly, with arms folded implacably over his mountainous chest. The retainer of royal bodyguards moved forward in a line behind Sigtrygg, daring Thork to defy the orders.

"I will find someone to do these duties for you," Thork offered. "Mayhap Olaf could—"

"*Nay! I cannot,*" Olaf asserted loudly, affronted that Thork would throw him this unwelcome task. "Wife and family have I who need me here in Jorvik."

"And I have a Jomsviking oath which I have ignored for two years."

"Do you refuse my *request?*" Sigtrygg asked Thork bluntly.

"Can we discuss it further?" Thork evaded.

"Were you not the man who convinced me of the importance of a marriage alliance with Athelstan?"

"Yea, but—"

"Can you name one man who could carry out my orders as well as you?"

Thork thought for a moment. Then his eyes narrowed as he turned with deliberation. "Yea, my scheming grandfather could do the job very well. He has met both King Athelstan and Hrolf afore."

Aud gasped and turned in outrage on her grandson. "For

shame, Thork! Ne'er did I think you would do such to us."

"You know I will be needed to protect my lands once the Saxons attack," Dar said icily.

"You are right," Thork said sheepishly. "I apologize. In my anger, I did not think."

Dar and Aud nodded, accepting his apology.

"Well? What say you?" Sigtrygg asked Thork once again. "Enough time have we all wasted on this wench, and I mislike your churlish attitude. Thor's blood! Surely one more month will not signify in your return to Jomsborg."

"So be it then," Thork conceded ungraciously. He started to storm away, then stopped abruptly in front of Ruby. Piercing her with icy blue eyes, he pointed a finger at her chest menacingly and stalked her as she backed away from him. "'Tis your fault. You will rue the day you ever met me, wench."

Things were not going as Ruby had hoped. She should be deliriously happy. She had at least another month with Thork. Why couldn't he share her good fortune? She tried to apologize. "I'm sorry, Thork. I never meant to be so much trouble to you."

He said a very, very foul word.

"Thork, I—"

"Nay, speak not your lies," Thork continued. "'Twas what you and Brynhil planned these four days past whilst you whispered and twittered like busy birds. You win, wench, but hold on to your tempting backside because you will pay well and good for each and every day you have delayed my departure." For emphasis, he whacked her sharply on the rear, laughing mirthlessly, then motioned for Dar to join him.

While he waited, Thork derisively mimicked her apology aloud in a falsely feminine voice, "I never meant to be so much trouble to you."

Ruby couldn't believe she'd escaped Sigtrygg's bloody temper once again, only to have her exultation over her death reprieve cut off by Thork's resentment.

Thork soon gave Ruby another reason to feel less than exultant. As she and Aud walked behind the men back to their tents, Thork told his grandfather with tired, but resolute, resignation, "If you think a marriage alliance with Elise would protect your holdings while I am gone, begin the betrothal negotiations." He ignored Ruby's gasp of hurt surprise.

"What?" Dar exclaimed. "I understand naught of your change of heart, boy. Why would you suddenly agree to marry when you have been so strongly opposed afore?"

"These past four days, as we have talked to our friends who live closer to the Wessex border, you and I have been given more than enough evidence that Athelstan plays a deadly game. He will attack at the first sign of weakness. We must do everything we can to protect ourselves."

"Even if it means your marrying?"

"Even *that*," he said, his lip curling with distaste.

"Well, the maid's father did promise arms and men to aid us if there were a marriage pact. Mayhap a betrothal contract would suffice for now. Could we have the signing afore you depart?"

Thork nodded grimly. "Her brothers are in camp. We can send word to her father today and perchance have the signing on the morrow." Thork pulled at his lower lip thoughtfully. "I will not give up Jomsviking. Think you the maid would accept that?"

"Hah! Little say she would have in the matter!"

"Even if they agree to a betrothal, it may be two years afore I could return for the wedding, but that should be no hindrance. Elise is only fifteen—a child."

"You always said you wanted no children or family to tempt your brother Eric's blade."

"And still do not. I swear by Thor's sword, there will

be no other child of my loins born into this world," Thork exclaimed vehemently. "But say naught of that to them for now. As for Elise, she has five brothers and a powerful father to protect her from Eric. My brother is no fool. He chooses his victims well. Leastways, he will know from my long absences how little affection I harbor for my wife. She will be safe, I warrant."

"'Tis a cold man you have become, Thork."

"'Tis a cold world in which I live, Grandfather."

Colder than both of you can ever imagine, Ruby thought, as tears streamed down her face on overhearing their chilling words. If Thork married another woman, there could be no future with her. It didn't matter if he loved Elise or not. She could not have a relationship with Thork, of any kind, when he was bound to another woman.

Oh, Lord! Ruby cried inwardly as her heart seemed to splinter into a million shards. Thork was truly lost to her now.

Ruby tried to approach Thork several times that evening, but he flatly refused to listen. Brynhil had already spoken with him after the Thing, and presumably he now directed his blame for his missions to Kingston and Normandy on the king, not a conspiracy between her and Brynhil. But he still raged over her interfering in his life and causing him unnecessary delays. His final words to her were, "You will pay good and true for every piddling prick of annoyance you have caused in my life, wench. I will have one month to enact vengeance, and I plan to use every bloody minute of it."

Ruby didn't ask what kind of punishment he had in mind. She really didn't need anything else to worry about right now.

Late that night, after bolstering her courage with a cup of red wine, Ruby crept into Thork's tent, needing to talk about the most important thing troubling her—his betrothal to Elise.

The Reluctant Viking

"*What?*" Thork jumped from a sound sleep when Ruby crept up to his sleeping furs. Pushing her aside, Thork stood and lit a candle. "Get the bloody hell out of my tent," he seethed. "I swear I will sell Vigi on the morrow for his continual lapses in guarding you."

"Thork, just give me one minute. Then I promise I'll leave quietly."

He turned, and Ruby inhaled sharply. The flickering light played shadow games on his almost nude, magnificent body as he confronted her, dressed in only a loincloth sort of garment.

"Spit it out, Ruby," he growled. "Elise and her family will be here in the morn to sign the betrothal contract. Wouldst you have her balk afore the deed is done because of the scandal you might cause in my bed furs?"

He thought she had come to seduce him again, Ruby realized. She felt her face flame, then quickly tried to correct his misconception. "Thork, that's just why I've come. You can't marry Elise, not after—"

In two long steps, Thork was in front of her, breathing heavily with frustrated anger. Ruby closed her eyes for a second at the heady intoxication of his body heat and his skin's healthy sleep scent.

"Yea, best you close your eyes and pray, wench," Thork gritted out as he grabbed her by the upper arms and lifted her off her feet so her face was level with his. "Mark my words well, the betrothal will take place on the morrow. Nothing you say can change that."

"But, Thork, I love you," she whimpered, her feet dangling above the ground. "I know you . . . care for me, too. How can you possibly marry someone else?"

"Woman, you overreach yourself," he replied icily. "When have I ever promised marriage to you? Never! In fact, over and over have I told you that it would never happen. And love? Hah! 'Tis the least of my concerns."

303

"What you said, Thork, was that you would never marry anyone, and I—"

"Argh!" he exclaimed, rolling his eyes upwards. "I am plagued. First, my grandfather. Now, this shrewish woman." He removed his hands from her arms abruptly and she dropped to the ground, stumbled, then fell to her knees. He didn't even bother to help her to her feet. Instead, he glared at her in stony silence.

"How could you promise to marry Elise?" Ruby asked tearfully. "How could you do that to me . . . to us?"

"How could I not?" He threw his hands up in despair. She could see the muscles tense in his clenched jaw.

"But you're married to me."

"Nay, that I am not . . . nor ever will be," he replied tiredly, as if he were sick of repeating his denial.

"Then it truly is over," Ruby said softly, with numb resignation.

Thork shook his head doggedly. "Nay, it has not yet begun, witch."

Ruby stared at him in disbelief. "There can be nothing between us now. Nothing."

"'Tis not for you to decide."

"What are you suggesting?"

Thork leaned his face close to hers, almost nose to nose, and smiled, but the warmth never reached his ice-blue eyes. "My meaning is abundantly clear. You have bedeviled me and delayed me. For that, I intend to exact payment . . . in full . . . and you know perfectly well how."

"No!"

"Oh, yea! Never doubt it."

The tent flap swung open suddenly and Vigi peeped his head in tremulously. "Master Thork, the wench be missing."

"Oh, really?" he said, stepping to the side so that Vigi could see Ruby still kneeling on the hard-packed earth.

Vigi's eyes almost popped out as she scrambled to her feet.

Tears welled and overflowed Ruby's eyes as Thork directed Vigi, "Take her back to her tent and guard her well this time. She is not to leave the tent the entire day. If I see her anywhere near the betrothal ceremony in the assembly tent, you will have not only your sale to a slave trader to contend with, but a lack of limb, as well."

Ruby looked back at Thork over her shoulder as Vigi led her out. His steely countenance barred any further exhortations on her part.

"I do not wish to speak to you again, wench, until you are on my ship two days hence, and then you will understand well and good how you will pay."

The next day, Ruby was, in fact, imprisoned in her tent. She could hear the bustle of festive activity outside, probably the betrothal feast. Vigi brought her meals in the morning and midday and removed her chamber pot, but he would say nothing to her many questions. Finally, when it was almost dark, Aud came to her. She took one look at Ruby's sleepless eyes and tear-ravaged face and opened her arms for comfort.

"Oh, child, why do you torture yourself so?" she crooned as she held Ruby kindly. When she pulled back finally and wiped her face with a square of linen, Aud asked, "Dost my grandson mean so much to you?"

Ruby nodded on a sob.

"But 'tis only a betrothal, and he has no fondness for the girl."

"Oh, Aud, can't you see? This means we can't ever be together. I thought . . . I thought because he looked just like Jack that Thork would love me, too. I wanted this to be my second chance to make things right with my husband."

"If 'tis any consolation, Thork looked as miserable the

305

entire day as you do now. He barks at any who comes near him."

"Even Elise?" Ruby whispered.

"Most of all, Elise," Aud replied with a sad grin. "The girl probably cries her eyes out as we speak."

"Do you mean . . . do you mean Thork isn't with her?" she choked out hopefully.

Aud laughed at Ruby's obviousness. "Girl, is that what you have been thinking, that the marriage is to be consummated this eve? Nay, some couples do such, but not in this case, especially because of Elise's age."

Ruby felt an odd consolation in knowing that Thork would not make love to his intended bride. And who knows where she would be in two years when Thork and Elise finally married?

"Be forewarned, Ruby, my grandson claims to have unfinished business with you. You may consider things well and over betwixt you. He does not."

The next day, Ruby watched dolefully as Thork bid his farewells to Elise and her family. She didn't see him again until the following day when she stood at the rail of one of his six dragonships, waving tearfully to Aud, Dar, Gyda, Olaf and Tykir, who watched stoically from the shore as the boats prepared to sail.

"May God, the Father, the Son and the Holy Spirit, bless you and keep you on this voyage," Archbishop Hrothweard, head of the Eoforwic diocese, intoned in a voice that carried clearly to the ship. "May he accept into his heavenly gates all those who will not return from their journey. May he lead you on the holy path of righteous military might, just trading and successful negotiations."

The high church leader stood at the quayside, blessing Thork's five ships and the kneeling sailors, tossing holy water into the air with a gold scepter he dipped repeatedly in a gem-encrusted bucket.

No sooner did the priest turn his back than the sailors exhorted their own Viking god, Thor, patron of the seas, as well, to guide them as they sailed through the waters of his domain. A massive roar echoed through the air then as the three hundred sailors raised their arms to the sky and yelled exuberantly, "A-Viking! A-Viking! A-Viking!"

Holy cow! They weren't going raiding now, Ruby thought. Maybe it was sort of like a rebel yell.

To Ruby's relief, Aud had convinced Thork to leave Tykir with her and Dar for the time being, promising they would guard him every minute. Heated arguments had flown back and forth for two full days, but finally Aud had won out, aided by Tykir's tearful pleadings. Eirik was traveling with them to Athelstan's court where Thork reluctantly had agreed to place him for fostering with his young uncle Haakon, but only on the condition that two of his servants remain with him as bodyguards.

Thork's decisions relating to the two boys represented a compromise in his long-standing refusal to present the boys openly as his sons. As much as she had encouraged Thork to do so, Ruby hoped their safety wouldn't be jeopardized.

Selik waved to her from one of Thork's other ships as they eased out of the harbor. They would head southward down the Ouse to the Humber, then eastward to the North Sea, and south to their first stop, Kingston, just southwest of London.

As the crews raised heavy masts that must have weighed more than five hundred pounds and hoisted colorful red and black checkered sails, Ruby watched Thork in fascination. Expertly, he directed the giant men who moved like lightweight ballerinas as they maneuvered the ropes attached to the yardarms and square sails, hoping to catch the late-August winds.

The serpentine ships, with their richly carved wood prows, sliced gracefully through the water like the fierce dragons they represented. In shallow waters, the men lifted the lightweight boats out of the water and carried them on their shoulders while Ruby walked the shoreline.

Ruby hadn't had much chance to talk to Thork since they set sail, although he'd smiled enigmatically at her whenever their eyes happened to meet. His expression spoke volumes of the unfinished business between them. But he did not seem angry with her, just determined to exact some revenge.

At another time, Ruby might have thrilled to think what that might be. She'd won a victory of sorts at the Althing, but it had been at Thork's expense. There was no question that a reckoning would come eventually. But all she could think about was Thork's decision to marry Elise. She glanced miserably at him now and saw the heavy betrothal ring gleam in the bright sun as he worked the sails.

A heaviness of spirit weighed her down at what she considered his betrayal. Ruby knew all the reasons why Thork felt it was necessary to secure an alliance with Elise's family. She told herself she was being irrational and selfish. After all, she might return to the future at any moment.

Ruby's mind accepted the logic. Her heart was a different story. Despite everything, she wanted Thork for herself.

Ruby shook her head free of the sad thoughts and turned back to the activity surrounding her. Thork acted the helmsman to his crew, moving the tiller on the steering oar to change direction, guiding them around treacherous rocks. The sixteen sailors on each side of the ship sat on large wooden chests, which held all their personal belongings, as they strained mightily, rowing the long wooden oars. Another thirty-two men stood ready to spell them or to assist, two men to an oar, during times of danger. Heavy battle shields gleamed in the sunlight from where they hung compactly along the outside of the boats.

Thork loved this sea life. Ruby could see that as he threw his head back often, inhaling deeply of the tangy air, and smiling. How could women, or children, compete with the exhilaration this life-style gave the Vikings? Ruby wondered.

"You should stay under the canopy," Thork advised, coming up behind her. He pointed to a canvas shelter that had been erected for her in the center of the ship near the mast pole. "By midday the sun will bake your fair skin."

"I'm too excited to sit down right now, but I promise I won't get in anyone's way," Ruby said woodenly, knowing she needed to avoid contact with Thork as much as possible.

"Best you do not," Thork advised gruffly. "'Tis easy to fall overboard, especially when we hit the open seas."

"When will that be?"

Thork shrugged. "We camp tonight along the Humber. The next day, winds willing, we will reach the North Sea and camp on its shoreline."

Thork stood with feet widespread to counteract the rocking motion of the ship. His sun-bleached hair, like that of his sailors, had been braided to keep it off his face in the wind.

A reluctant smile tugged at the corners of Ruby's mouth.

"My appearance amuses you in some way?"

"No, I was just marveling that I could be attracted to a man who wears braids."

"You are attracted to me?" Thork asked in a low voice, leaning closer to her as they both rested their arms on the rail.

Ruby slanted her eyes sideways at him. So now he chose to talk to her—when it was too late.

"What do you think I've been trying to tell you since

we first met?" she replied wearily. "As much as I hate the dark side of your nature, the one that could possibly blood-eagle a man, as much as I disapprove of your militant life-style, I recognize that you're the other half of me."

Thork inhaled sharply.

Ruby wanted Thork to understand why she was so hurt and why his actions had sealed her future—a future without him in it. "We are soulmates, Thork. Whether you accept that we knew each other in another life or not, I believe you and I were meant to be together just as much today as we were in the future. At least, I did before you announced your wedding plans."

Thork ignored her reference to Elise. "Feeling like a *soulmate*, you let your husband leave. Nay, you drove him away." His forehead creased in puzzlement.

Ruby felt her face flush with heat. She brushed a wisp of hair off her face distractedly. "I didn't realize my mistakes then. I would change things if I could go back."

"And so, even as you proclaim I am some vital part of your life, you yearn for your husband." Thork's eyes searched her face intensely.

"You don't understand. To me, you and Jack are the same man."

He shook his head despairingly at her refusal to face the facts.

"Hah! What I understand, and you do not, is that there never was a husband. Ruby, you have been caught in lie upon lie. You are a virgin, unwedded and unbedded. But know this, sweetling, the latter will soon be remedied the first private moment we have."

"No, it won't. Your engagement to Elise changes all that."

"I am not wed yet," he countered, moving closer.

"But you will be," Ruby pointed out and put more distance between them.

"What difference does the betrothal make to you?"

"A lot! Oh, Thork, how can you even ask such a question? I can't . . . I won't be a one-night stand for you."

"Hah! More like a one-month stand! Besides, why all the scruples when a week ago you came to my sleeping chamber more than willing?"

"That was different."

Thork arched an eyebrow. "How so?"

Ruby turned to face him directly, her eyes pleading with him for understanding. "A woman needs to think a man makes love with her because he cares for her, that there is at least the possibility of commitment. When the man is promised to another woman, they don't make love. They make lust."

Thork laughed. "Lust sounds pretty good to me. Yea, methinks I will settle for that."

"I won't."

"'Tis out of your hands now, *soulmate,*" Thork declared with a low laugh, turning to walk back to his shipmates. "Best you accept that here and now. The course has been set and cannot be changed."

Ruby suddenly realized that she had a rapt audience. The men snickered and looked to Thork to catch his reaction to her shrewish behavior. Clearly, many of them could not understand Thork's attraction to her, especially when she behaved in such an unfeminine way.

"Thork, if you cannot handle a simple wench, I would be glad to take her on this ship," a grinning Selik called out from the rail of his ship, which rode close beside theirs in the wide river. He goaded Thork with further taunts, egged on by the cheers of his shipmates.

At first Thork frowned, but then he laughed and directed his friend to do something very vulgar to himself. Then he asked Selik, "Why do you not pick up an oar and work off some of that misplaced mirth?"

"'Tis much more fun watching you be snaggled by a mere wench."

311

"You are one to talk of being made the fool by a woman! The wenches lead you around by that tail between your legs."

The sailors laughed lustily at the ribald exchange.

"Oh ho! Now I learn the truth," Selik hooted. "You are envious of my male prowess."

"You witless whelp! We shall see who has what when the ships are pulled ashore tonight."

Late that afternoon, when they entered the mouth of the Humber River and the five boats pulled toward shore for the evening's campsite, Thork deftly jumped from the rail of his ship to that of Selik's. In the blink of an eye, having the advantage of surprise, he picked up Selik, who equaled him in size, and dumped him in the shallow water. The men in all five ships laughed at the spectacle of Selik coming up sputtering out of the water, shaking his hair like a shaggy dog.

Thork jumped back to his own ship and bragged loudly to Selik, "'Tis a cool head you need to match wits with a man, my boy." Then he turned and flashed a dazzling smile Ruby's way and teased, "'Twould be a pleasure to feed you to the fishes, as well, if you cannot curb your waspish tongue."

"You and twenty other men!" Ruby challenged, disgusted with his childish behavior and this whole time-travel experience. She walked back to the canopy area for her personal belongings to be taken ashore.

In a flash, Thork scooped her in his arms and jumped up on the rail, weaving back and forth precariously. Smiling from ear to ear, enjoying the spectacle he made of her, Thork asked his shipmates loudly, "What say you, men? Wouldst she not make good fish bait?"

"Put me down! Stop being so immature," Ruby demanded. She wasn't afraid of the water, but heights had always alarmed her. When he refused to release her and continued to rock forward and backward on the rail, Ruby did the only thing a woman in peril could do. Keeping her left arm wrapped tightly around Thork's neck, she reached down between their bodies with her right hand and pinched his groin area as hard as she could, hoping he would put her back on the deck.

"Arghh! For the love of Freya!" Thork shouted in pain. He lost his balance on the rail, and they both spilled over into the river, lucky to land on their feet.

The water was shallow enough to wade thigh-deep to shore. Hampered by her wet garments, she was still able to walk proudly out of the water, throwing her shoulders back. When Thork came up out of the water with a whoosh, he glared at Ruby's back. The laughing men stopped all activity to watch the hilarious spectacle.

Outraged, Ruby said a very vulgar word, one she'd never used in all her life.

Thork was laughing when he finally emerged from the water and directed his smirking men to get back to work. He couldn't believe Ruby had actually said that obscene word. The impudent wench!

"I deserved the soaking for teasing you so," he admitted, walking up to her, "but did you have to try to emasculate me in the process?"

Ruby turned to face him angrily, and Thork got his first look at the sodden clothing which outlined her body. He swallowed hard before grabbing her arm and pulling her into the trees. "Have you no shame, woman? You look like a wanton, flaunting yourself in front of three hundred men."

Actually, she looked damned nigh irresistible to Thork with her tunic plastered to her slim form. Her nipples, puckered from the cold water, stood out like sentinels, begging for his touch. Even her short, wet hair hugged her face in an attractive manner, accentuating the sharp lines of her cheekbones, the greenish hue of her eyes, the creaminess of her complexion.

313

Thork groaned, hoping his men didn't notice his half-arousal. Lord, the woman would be the death of him yet.

He had seen the hurt in her eyes the past few days. He knew that his decision to marry Elise offended her, but 'twas beyond his comprehension why that should be so. *Bloody hell!*

"What would you suggest I wear?" she asked, hands on hips in an exasperated pose. "All my dry clothes are on the ship."

"Stay here," he directed and went off to get her garments. He saw Selik look at him curiously, glance down, then bleat with laughter like a bloody sheep.

When she'd changed, Thork told her to stay out of the men's way while they set up camp. The one ship holding their horses was brought as close to shore as possible. Then all the men moved to one side so the boat tipped over on its side in the shallow water, and the animals walked off.

Fires already blazed with caldrons of meat and vegetables in boiling water. Tents were erected, with oil lamps on metal posts in front of some of them. Vats of cheese and butter were opened to be eaten with the bread baked early that morning in Jorvik.

"Do you think our Jomsviking comrades will return to Northumbria with us next year to prepare for the Saxon onslaught?" Selik asked worriedly while they set up camp.

"I know not. 'Tis why I did not tell my grandfather of our hopes. I did not want to raise the old man's hopes needlessly. As you well know, the Jomsvikings may already be committed to other obligations."

Selik nodded. "The hesirs you hired will help."

"Yea, but I fear they will not be enough. That is why in the end I consented to the hated marriage." He slammed his fist against a tree in frustration.

Ruby raised questioning eyebrows from where she sat

314

some distance away in front of her tent, combing her short hair.

"You do know, my friend, that she will never have you now that you are honor-bound to another?" Selik commented, tilting his head in Ruby's direction.

"She will have me. Make no mistake about that. And it better be soon."

Selik snickered, understanding Thork's meaning well. "And after you take her, then what? Will you leave her in Normandy with Hrolf?"

"Mayhap . . . if he will have her. If not, providing she pleases as much as I expect, I may offer to set her up for a time in Jomsborg as my mistress, even though I would have to live at the fortress."

Selik looked incredulous, then laughed uproariously. Bent over at the waist, slapping a hand on his knee, he exclaimed, "My friend, I would love to be a fly on the wall when you make *that* suggestion to the winsome wench. I wager she may tear your eyeballs out. Nay, better yet, she may yank out your balls and cast them in bronze like the picture on that fetching shirt she wears."

"Why would you think such?" Thork frowned. "'Tis no dishonor in being a man's bedmate. I treat my women generously. None have complained afore."

"I cannot believe you think this woman is of the same mold as any other. Never, *never,* will she agree to be aught but wife to you."

Inside, Thork secretly wondered if Selik might not be right. After all, he'd been down this route with Ruby afore. Seduction, pursuit, withdrawal. First she would. Then she wouldn't. Of course, he had changed his own mind a few times, as well, he reminded himself ruefully.

Ruby watched the two men through narrowed eyes, sensing they were up to some mischief, probably involving her since they kept looking over at her slyly.

They were outrageously handsome men in their knee-length tunics, worn belted at the waist over slim trousers. Selik was slightly taller with platinum hair, which contrasted sharply with his bronze, sun-baked skin, but, to Ruby, Thork was much more attractive. His impressively toned body and finely chiseled facial features were definite assets, not to mention his drop-dead gorgeous smile, but what appealed to Ruby most in this roguish clone of her husband Jack was his unselfish love for his sons and family. Then, too, his quick wit always caught her off-guard, and the boyish hurt he sometimes failed to hide in shuttered eyes drew Ruby strongly. She wanted to help wipe out the years of childhood abuse, to smother him with so much love he would forget he'd never been given much of that precious emotion.

That was *before* his betrothal to Elise. Ruby knew she would have a hard time resisting Thork now. After all these weeks of attempting to lure him into her bed, she could understand his confusion over her change of heart, but it was the only way.

Ruby loved Thork, and she wanted what was best for his future, even if it wasn't her. Obviously, it couldn't be her. If she and Thork made love, Ruby knew from past experience that a full-blown passion would develop between them. It would not end in a few days or even a month, as Thork predicted.

And it would be wrong. Thork belonged to another woman. She belonged to another man.

Oh, Lord!

Then there was the fact that, since she'd probably been sent back in time for a purpose, it would seem that she'd already accomplished those goals. Tykir was in the loving hands of his grandparents. Eirik would be at the Saxon court where he wanted to be—at least safe, if not loved. And Thork—well, he would marry and possibly grow to love his gentle wife *if* Ruby did not fall into his bed and bind him with invisible ties of love.

Knowing that all these events had been set in motion, Ruby almost feared she might return at any minute to the future, abandoning Thork in the past. And that's exactly how he'd feel if she let him fall in love with her. Could she hurt him like that? No! This was the only way.

But it hurt *so* bad.

And the pain grew worse and worse during the trip to Kingston as he teased and tantalized her with sweet smiles, fleeting caresses, promising glances, and whispered words of sensual fantasies he conjured of her each night in his lonely tent.

"Soon," he kept telling her; "soon we will be together."

"No, we won't. We can't," she continually countered, but he ignored her protests with a beguiling, confident smile as they drew closer and closer to the Saxon court.

Chapter Seventeen

They finally arrived in Kingston at dawn on the day of King Athelstan's coronation. She, Thork, Selik and Eirik went directly to the cathedral, leaving Thork's men camped along the river, guarding the five ships.

Athelstan's coronation ceremony turned out to be everything and more than Ruby had ever imagined. Like a page straight out of the Dark Ages court of King Arthur and Camelot, the gentle Saxon prince—the golden dragon of Wessex—was crowned.

Ruby wore the burgundy dress Dar had given her with Thork's dragon brooches. Thork thrilled her by wearing the blue cloak she'd made for him over a magnificent black tunic and matching trousers, or braies, offset by the now familiar thunderbolt earring, and jewel-encrusted arm rings, brooch, pendant, belt and sword, all suited to a representative of an important Viking king.

Selik turned the eyes of every female they passed, wearing a turquoise short-sleeved tunic which showed off the wicked gleam of his gray eyes and the muscles of his well-developed chest and arms outlined in chunky silver arm bands and neck chains. As they sat down in the church, Selik winked at her, obviously noticing her complimentary appraisal. He blatantly ignored Thork's frown of disapproval.

Both men looked like barbarian Viking princes and carried themselves accordingly with arrogant self-confidence.

When Ruby smiled at Selik, Thork reached discreetly in the folds of her garment and pinched her behind, whispering, "Behave thyself, wench, or I will carry you off now. Sore tired I am anyway of this waiting for a private place to bed together."

Ruby started to tell him once again that she would not make love with him, but he placed a forefinger over her lips and said in a low, silky voice, "Nay, you protest too much, sweetling. 'Tis going to happen, and soon. Do not resist the fates that Odin—or mayhap your God—have set in motion. In truth, sometimes I wonder if they are not one and the same—"

"Shush! 'Tis a church, not a marketplace for gossip," a woman in the pew behind them chastised.

Thork and Ruby sheepishly turned back to the coronation ceremony at the altar, not realizing they'd been speaking so loudly. Athelstan stood godlike for his consecration by the highest archbishops of the church. The churchmen handed him the royal regalia, finger rings, crown and sceptre. "We anoint you, Athelstan, son of Edward, grandson of Alfred, to be the King of the English and ruler of all Britain. May you rule in peace under God's holy wisdom . . ."

The slender, flaxen-haired man of medium height, no more than thirty years old, stood solemnly under the bishop's ministrations. Thork had explained to her earlier that the church's approval was essential politically to Athelstan's acceptance as ruler of all the kingdoms he hoped to unite. King Athelstan glanced occasionally to the hundreds of ealdormen, thegns and royal emissaries of many nationalities who came to pledge their loyalty to him at the beginning of his reign. At the end of the ceremony, the charismatic nobleman performed a number of symbolic acts.

"In the name of my favorite saint and ancestor, St. Cuthbert, I restore to the Cathedral Church of Canterbury an estate in Thanet for the help given to me in gaining the English throne." Before he left the high altar, the new king also freed a slave, Eadhelm, and his children, a public act intended to show his generosity and humility.

When he moved to the second-floor chapel with its outdoor balcony overlooking the vast complex consisting of the royal and episcopal palaces and all their accessory buildings, the young king told the thousands of people gathered outside, "I make three pledges to you, my people: First, I will keep you and those you love in peace."

A roar of approval went through the crowd, most of whom were sick to death of warfare and the toll it had taken on them and their families.

"Next, I forbid robbery and wrongdoing by all men, regardless of their place in society. All men shall be treated equally under the law."

At first the stunned people exchanged glances among themselves over this novel idea of justice, wondering whether the king was serious. A cheer began as a ripple, then echoed thunderously as the lowly subjects realized the import of his words.

Ruby, too, began to look at the Saxon king in a new light. These were very democratic ideas for such a primitive society. Why hadn't she ever heard of this farsighted visionary?

"Finally, I promise a kingdom where the rule of law shall be just and merciful, spelled out clearly in law codes for all to understand and obey. Above all, with your help, we will unite this kingdom, making it the most peaceable, law-abiding land in all the world."

The king had said the exact words the people wanted to hear, and they cheered wildly as he moved with his royal retainers and guests to the palace where the celebration would begin in earnest. More glamorous and opulent than anything Ruby had seen thus far in these primitive times, King Athelstan's massive great hall teemed with dignitaries from around the world, each straining to get closer to the new king and ingratiate themselves in his favor. The room was so crowded that Ruby could barely see the walls adorned with priceless tapestries and works of art.

At least five hundred men and women, dressed in the finest garments and jewels, tried to find their places at the tables, arguing with servants about why they were not closer to the dais where the king sat with his highest nobles and visiting heads of countries.

Ruby held tightly to Thork's and Selik's arms, not wanting to get lost in the mob. Eirik had been sent off with two servants to find his young uncle Haakon.

There were no wood trenchers at this banquet. Instead, matching ivory-handled gold and silver spoons and knives lay at each place setting, flanking intricately wrought sterling platters shared by each couple.

Enormous *subleties,* towers of pastries in the shape of castles, complete with battlements and arrow-slitted windows, garnished with nuts and almond paste and topped with sugar knights, were placed on the high table and several lower ones, as well. Who would ever dare to eat them and mar the magnificent culinary works of art? As if reading her mind, Thork reached over and popped a whole knight in his mouth, then winked at her.

Ruby shook her head in disgust and turned to Selik at her other side, but he was engrossed in the daughter of a Saxon ealdorman beside him. When he finally turned to Ruby, he raised his wine cup in toast and said in a low voice, "I think I may get *lucky* tonight. What think you?"

He jiggled his eyebrows for emphasis.

Ruby laughed and looked around the huge hall with its many beautiful women, a large number of whom had already noticed the handsome Viking with the dancing eyes. "The odds are in your favor," she remarked.

Then Selik leaned in front of her to address Thork. "Think you, friend, that you will get *lucky* tonight?"

"I think you will be lucky if I do not slit your loose tongue," Thork said as he sipped his wine.

"Ah!" Selik persisted. "The man dost refuse to answer my question. Methinks he will not be lucky."

Thork laughed good-naturedly at his friend's baiting. "Methinks there is naught of luck in it at all, but expertise, which you must lack, or you would not make such an issue of it."

Selik pretended mock offense. "You wound me with your words." Then he turned once again to the maid on his other side.

Thork and Ruby laughed at Selik's humor. Then Ruby jumped when Thork squeezed her thigh under the table.

"Stop that."

"Why?"

"Because I said so."

"Oh! If you wish," he said too quickly, then twined the fingers of her right hand with his left and proceeded to torture her by making slow, sensuous circles in her palm with his thumb, all the time looking toward the dais as if he didn't know damned well what effect he had on her.

Ruby tried to pull her hand away, but Thork held her firm and whispered in her ear, "Nay, do not pull away from me or I swear I will draw circles on a part of your body that will draw gasps from the women around us and cheers of encouragement from all the men, even the virgin king.

Ruby blushed at his risqué comment and slapped his hand away. Then she asked, "A virgin king?"

" 'Tis rumored Athelstan has taken a vow of celibacy and will groom his young atheling half-brothers for the throne. Since he is illegitimate and they are marriage-born, he wants to preserve the royal blood lines."

"Do you believe that?" Ruby was skeptical that such a handsome, virile man would remain celibate.

"Who knows?" Thork shrugged, then grinned. "Mayhap he would be interested in some of your birth control information. He could achieve his goals without the gelding—so to speak."

Ruby and Thork shared the same platter and cup of wine throughout the sumptuous feast, far grander than any Viking fare. The food and drink flowed endlessly.

"So, how many multiple orgasms did you have in one night with that fantasy husband of yours?" Thork asked suddenly in one of the conversation's lulls, showing Ruby exactly where his mind was. She coughed on the wine she'd been drinking, and he clapped her on the back jovially.

"That many, huh?"

"How could you ask such a thing?" she whispered, profoundly embarrassed that someone might have overheard.

"What? You are the one who bragged—"

"I never bragged. I merely told Byrnhil—"

Ruby never got a chance to finish as the king and all his party on the dais stood, announcing he was about to receive the gifts and messages from all the royal emissaries present, after which the entertainment would begin.

As an indication of the new king's standing, several royal princes sent fine gifts, hoping for one of Athelstan's sisters in marriage. His cousin Adelolf, Count of Boulogne, who represented the Capetian ruler Hugh, a Frankish duke, sought his sister Eadhild. Henry the Fowler, Saxon king of the Germans, wanted Athelstan's sister Edith for his son Otto. Conrad the Peaceable, King of Burgundy, would take any sister he could get. Athelstan's sister Eadgifu had already married Charles the Simple, the Frankish king, six years before.

Among the priceless gifts they brought were the Holy Lance of Charlemagne, allegedly the one used by the Roman centurion to pierce the side of Christ. Also, the sword of Constantine the Great with a nail from the True Cross in its hilt, and a crown of thorns set in crystal, not to mention precious gems the size of hen's eggs, magnificent horses, and rare perfumes.

"It seems Sigtrygg should be honored by Athelstan's proposal to marry his sister if such distinguished men clamor for his family ties," Ruby whispered to Thork.

" 'Tis nothing of honor to it. The king will do what is to his best advantage, like any other."

It was Thork's turn to go forward on behalf of King Sigtrygg.

"Thork! Back so soon!" the king exclaimed and embraced him like an old friend. "Do you check on your brother Haakon? I thought you were not fond of court life."

"I come on behalf of King Sigtrygg of Northumbria who pays homage to you as ruler of the English. Also, I bring you his formal acceptance of the betrothal contract for your sister." He placed in the king's hand a magnificent Viking sword with a twisted metal blade and a solid gold hilt embedded with rubies.

There were disgruntled rumblings behind them from some of the nobles about Athelstan's giving his sister to what they considered a heathen barbarian while they waited in line like lowly beggars. Athelstan stopped them with a cold look.

"When will he wed my sister?"

"Would the thirtieth of January suit?"

"It would. Will you come to my solar tomorrow afternoon to discuss further details?" When Thork nodded, the

The Reluctant Viking

king asked who accompanied him, and Thork introduced Ruby and Selik.

"Ah, the godly handsome Norseman who breaks the hearts of sweet maids from here to the Holy Land and beyond!"

Selik tilted his head in arrogant acknowledgment of his dubious reputation and bowed to the king.

Then the king turned to Ruby.

"Surely not the woman who claims to come from the future?" he asked Thork, who nodded, then frowned, probably wondering what spy network reported to the Saxons so well on events in Jorvik.

"Wonderful!" He clapped his hands together and demanded, "Bring her with you on the morrow. I want to hear all her stories. I understand I could learn much from her."

They were about to be dismissed in favor of the long line of people waiting to be presented to the king when Athelstan asked, "Where do you stay?"

Thork shrugged uncertainly. "We just arrived this morn. With all the crowds here in Kingston, we will no doubt go back to my men who camp in tents near my ships."

"Nay, you will not." The king directed a servant to find a room for Thork and "his woman."

His woman! Where did he get that idea? Ruby wondered as her face flushed hotly.

"And one for Selik, as well. 'Tis certain he will find his own woman afore the night is over."

Thork smiled so smugly as they walked away from the dais that Ruby had to elbow him in the ribs.

"A private room at last," Thork whispered, putting his arm around her shoulders intimately, uncaring of the people's stares. "Your time of sweet reckoning has come, dearling."

"I'm not going to sleep with you," Ruby whispered to Thork as they walked up winding stone steps to the

325

second and then the third floor of the massive palace. They followed a grumbling servant who complained incessantly of the demands put upon him by a king who thought there were endless rooms to be had.

Selik was shown his broom-closet-sized room at the top of the third-floor steps. When Ruby started to enlist his aid in escaping Thork's inevitable amorous advances, Thork clamped a palm over her mouth and laughingly informed his friend, "Overcome with emotion she is over the night to come." She tried to bite Thork's palm, but he held her too tightly. The overworked servant just stared at them in tired boredom, as if people behaved in this manner all the time.

The small tower room he showed them was spartan, but clean. Thork indicated with a satisfied grin that its biggest asset was the full-sized bed, rather than the expected pallet.

Ruby thought the servant would have a heart attack when Thork asked him what the chances were of having a bath.

"On the third floor?" the old man choked out. But he quickly overcame his exhaustion when Thork offered him a coin which would be matched by another if he brought the tub and water in record time.

"Master, 'twill be here afore you have your clothes off," he promised, adding solicitously, "Wouldst ya be wantin' perfumed soap fer yer lady?" He flashed Thork a lascivious, toothless grin.

Oh, great! A conspiracy of like minds.

"We have to talk while that servant is gone," Ruby asserted quickly, while Thork rummaged through the large leather bag that held their belongings. So studiously was he searching for something and ignoring her words that finally Ruby asked, *"What* are you looking for?"

"This!" Thork held up her homemade teddy-bustier and grinned. "After you bathe, I want you to put this on. I have dreamed the picture for days," he explained huskily.

"No!" Ruby exclaimed, despite the wild hammering of her heart.

"Oh? Methinks you will." His blue eyes, warm with promise, locked with hers.

"I want to talk," Ruby groaned.

"I want to make love," Thork argued.

His words moved Ruby, despite all her good intentions. The glaze of passion in his misty eyes compelled Ruby to surrender, but still she started to turn away, trying desperately to resist. "Why are you doing this?" she moaned.

"Are you serious?" He looked meaningfully down to his already burgeoning arousal.

Ruby closed her eyes for a moment, hoping to regain some semblance of control, then admonished, "Don't be crude. I meant, why now? When I tried to seduce you, you thought our making love would be a bad idea. It *is* a bad idea. I realize that now. Think about it."

A slight grin tugged at the corners of Thork's lips as he listened, disbelieving, to her words. "Sweetling, that is *all* I can think about." He laid the teddy on the embroidered bed cover and removed his sword and belt and tunic. He sat down to take off his soft leather shoes.

Panicked, Ruby realized she didn't have much time to convince him. With a shaky voice, she urged, "Thork, let me tell you why we are *not* going to make love."

Thork's lips twitched infuriatingly. "I am listening."

Hah! His mind was about as open to her arguments right now as a teenager with a bad case of raging hormones. And she wasn't doing so great herself.

Still, she had to try. But, before she could speak, he walked barefooted to her where she still stood frozen by the door. He gave her a quick, light kiss on the lips and said huskily, "You are beautiful."

"I am not. You're beautiful. I'm attractive, at best."

"You think I am beautiful?" He seemed inordinately

pleased at that idea. "Can you imagine the beautiful children we might have made together?" he asked wistfully, then shook his head as if it were a wasted thought. "Not that I want any more children or ever intend to have more, but 'tis a tantalizing idea, is it not?"

"Oh, Thork, even your words prove why this can't work."

"How so?" he said, cocking his head quizzically. Meanwhile, he peeled off his slim black pants and stood before her immodestly in only a codpiece that resembled a modern-day jock strap.

Ruby groaned.

The candlelight flickered on the smooth planes and battle scars of his bronzed skin, highlighting the golden strands in his hair, making his eyes appear a darker shade of blue. When he leaned to pick up his clothing and jewelry and place them in a neat pile in the corner, corded muscles in his back and buttocks rippled with his graceful movements.

He looks like a damn golden god, for heaven's sake!

The servant brought in the tub, followed by four other men carrying two buckets of hot water each. He left with the other coin in his pocket and a big smile on his face, telling Thork to push the tub outside to the hall when he finished.

"Do you want to go first?" Thork asked after he filled the large oval tub, similar in size to a Colonial copper wash boiler. When Ruby shook her head, he dropped his last garment and lowered himself into the steaming water with a shudder and then a sigh. It barely held Thork's massive frame. He had to draw up his knees to fit.

Ruby swallowed hard and tried to continue her explanation of why they couldn't do that which she wanted to do so damn bad her teeth ached. While Thork soaped his body and washed his hair, Ruby chattered uneasily. "In the beginning, there were two main reasons why I pursued

328

you, Thork. I was concerned about my safety here in a strange land, and I wanted us to be together to provide a home for Eirik and Tykir."

"And?"

"Well, I'm safe now, at least until we get to Normandy."

"And the boys?"

"Tykir lives with your family now and won't be as lonely as he was in Jorvik, and Eirik, well, the fostering isn't an ideal situation, but he's where he wants to be. I'm sure he and Haakon will be good for each other. What I'm saying is that, if I suddenly had to . . . go away, I wouldn't worry about them. Well, not too much, anyway."

"Go away?" Thork snapped. "Do you still harbor plans to escape?" He stood abruptly in the tub and water sloshed over the sides. Reaching for a towel, he dried himself briskly while he glared at her, awaiting an answer.

Ruby chose her words carefully. "It's not something I'm planning deliberately, but I could be returned to my home suddenly. I wouldn't have a choice. That's why I didn't want to leave loose ends with the children, who are just like my own boys—"

"Nay, do not start that future-life nonsense again. You are an untried virgin. You have no husband, and you most definitely have never borne any children."

Ruby tried not to look at Thork's nude body as she continued, "Still . . . if I suddenly, mysteriously, have to leave, that's another reason why our making love would be a mistake. You have to know I love you. I have for twenty years. You love me, too. You just don't know it yet, but—"

"You love me?" Thork asked, choosing selectively which of her words to hear. He moved toward her with open arms and a wide smile.

She ducked under his arms and moved to the other side of the room. "—I also know how much it hurt when

329

you . . . when Jack left, and I wouldn't put you through that pain, Thork."

Thork threw the wet towel down and looked at her with growing impatience. "We will part eventually, anyway, either at Normandy or at Jomsborg, if I decide to take you there. So, what does it matter if we make love?"

"Jomsborg?" Ruby's forehead furrowed. What did he mean?

Thork hesitated, obviously not wanting to get into this particular discussion right now. "It is of no import now. Just a thought I had." He picked up an ivory comb and pulled it through his wet hair absently. "If you decide not to stay in Normandy and if you please me in bed, mayhap I would consider taking you to Jomsborg with me."

Please him in bed! Little alarm bells went off in Ruby's head. Ruby looked at him suspiciously. "As your wife?"

"Nay!" Thork exclaimed, then tried to soften his tone. "Why do you persist in this talk of weddings?"

"Then what?" An icy chill ran up her spine.

"Selik warned me that you would react thus," Thork muttered in disgust.

"Selik! You discussed this with Selik? Exactly what are we talking about here?"

"A bedmate, pure and simple," Thork blurted out. He saw the outrage on her face and quickly added, " 'Tis no disgrace in that, Ruby. I would treat you well, purchase you a home, fine clothing, jewelry, and you would be free to go when . . . when . . ." His words trailed off.

"When what?" she asked through anger-gritted teeth. "When you tire of me?"

The noncommittal expression on his face told her everything.

"You pond scum!" Ruby cried out miserably. "You egotistical, self-centered, male chauvinist pig!" Tears that she hadn't realized were welling in her eyes streamed down her face. She turned jerkily and opened the door, wanting to escape Thork's presence.

He followed her into the hallway, completely naked, the towel around his waist having come loose. A drunken ealdorman asked with a slur, "Need any help, young man? I have a whip in my room if the maid be too much for you."

Thork ignored him and pulled Ruby back into the room. "Take off your clothes and get in the tub," he demanded angrily. "More than enough have I had with words. I have coddled you for weeks and put up with more foolery than any man should. Enough! Promises aplenty you have made, and my reckoning time is more than due."

"No!" She pulled herself out of his grasp.

"Then I will do it for you."

Ruby backed away from him, and he stalked her around the tub toward the other side of the room. The bed separated them but not for long. Thork leapt over it and pinned her against the wall with her arms above her head, his hips against her stomach.

Laughing, enjoying the lusty pursuit, he informed her, "You can take the dress off yourself, or I will rip it off in shreds." When she stubbornly refused, he transferred both her wrists to his right hand and placed his left hand in the neckline of the silk dress. With one swift movement, he tore it from neck to hem. Then he did the same with the underchemise.

Spreading both garments apart, he feasted his eyes on her small, firm breasts which strained the thin fabric of her black lace bra, then on the triangle of her femininity which hid behind her black silk panties. Easing the straps off both shoulders of her struggling body, he picked her up and threw her facedown on the bed, almost smothering her in the deep coverlet. He cursed as he struggled to unsnap her bra in back, finally succeeding. Then he flipped her over roughly and slipped off her panties and leather shoes.

Sitting on her waist, holding her hands pinioned above her head on the bed, he inquired smoothly, "Now will you take a bath, or must I wash every inch of your body for you?"

The tears streaming down her face didn't move him at all. Ruby nodded her acquiescence.

Thork dumped four bucketfuls of bath water out of the glassless window, uncaring of who might be walking below, and added four clean buckets to the tub. Allowing her no modesty whatsoever, Thork watched her with smoldering eyes as she walked sullenly to the tub and slid into it up to her neck.

"Make haste. I will not wait all night," Thork warned in a low, primitive voice.

Ruby pursed her mouth sulkily but did as he asked.

Sitting in a chair which he pulled closer to the tub, Thork sat watching her languidly, heavy-lidded, like a large cat anticipating a tasty meal. His naked body stretched out immodestly.

"Your hair grows longer," he commented. "How long would it take to reach your shoulder blades?"

Ruby shrugged. "A year." Then she added snidely, "Do you think you will have tired of me by then?"

Thork smiled, refusing to rise to her bait. "Mayhap."

When she was done, Ruby asked for a towel. Thork brought one over, but before he gave it to her, he pulled her to a standing position, then soaped a washcloth lying at the edge of the tub. The tub water reached only as far as her knees.

Ruby gazed at him questioningly, her face flaming with embarrassment to be standing exposed before him.

"You did not wash there," he said hoarsely, pointing to the vee at her thighs. "Move your legs apart and do it whilst I watch. Slowly."

"No," Ruby choked out and tried to get out of the tub.

"Yea," he demanded softly and forced her to stand in

place. He spread her upper thighs several inches apart, then handed her the soapy cloth with an implacable expression on his face. "Do it, sweetling."

She did. And would have died of mortification if she hadn't soon realized that her actions had cracked the composure of Thork's self-control. A pulse-beat in his straining neck told her how hard he tried to appear unaffected by her actions. His shaft attested to his rock-hard readiness.

"Now can I dry off?" she rasped out finally.

"Nay. Stay where you are."

Thork took a bucket and emptied the tub's water out the window until Ruby stood in water barely up to her ankles. What was he up to now?

Ruby got her answer soon enough as Thork knelt before the tub and gripped her ankles in his hands, then moved them two feet apart. He lathered her legs from her ankles to the top of her thighs. Then he smiled wickedly at her, took a sharp knife in his hands and began to shave her legs.

"Do not look at me so, sweetling. This was your idea, not mine," he growled, "but I must admit I have been picturing the shaving in my dreams for weeks." When she did not speak, Thork chuckled softly and went on, "Sometimes I shaved you as you lay, arms and creamed legs widespread, on that flat boulder by Dar's pond. Then, too, I visualized you lying on the masthead of my ship with each lathered thigh on a rail of the prow opening. My favorite, though, was me sitting naked on a chair and you likewise nude, but astraddle the arms of the chair, with my hardened staff just barely touching the dew of your woman's opening, and then I soaped you . . ."

Ruby was speechless under the onslaught of his softly spoken fantasies. Her blood felt thick. Her skin, all over, seemed to expand.

Thork rambled on seductively with his sexual images

as he slowly, methodically, shaved her legs with all the concentration of a veteran barber. If occasionally the hair of his bent head brushed the nipples of her breasts or her pubic hair, Ruby couldn't tell whether it was deliberate or not. All she knew was that his actions had ignited a fire in her which seared her skin and centered in a tiny pleasure point of her body which seemed to swell and ache for touch. Ruby bit her lip to keep from moaning.

"Why do you tremble, sweetling?" Thork asked with smug delight as he wielded his razor-sharp blade on the inside of her upper thigh. "Do you not trust me to be careful?"

Ruby said nothing, unable to utter a word. Suddenly the fingertips of one hand which had been encircling her thigh to hold it steady inadvertently touched her feminine inner folds.

Ruby gasped.

Thork's passion-hungry eyes shot up in surprise, then delved deeper for confirmation. He moaned hoarsely and dropped the knife on the floor.

"You are wet," he declared with a groan.

"From my bath," she choked out.

Thork laughed. "Nay! 'Tis for me, dearling. For me!"

He turned and picked up the teddy. "Put it on for me," he said huskily. His face was flushed and his lips parted slightly in anticipation. Ruby didn't need to look down to see how much he wanted her.

"No," she refused recklessly, fighting with all her fast-fading willpower the fire that flamed between her legs.

"I will not force you, but you *will* put it on—one way or another," Thork promised tautly.

When Ruby still balked, Thork picked her up and carried her to the bed. Throwing her on her back, he followed quickly after her, not allowing her to squirm away. Pushed beyond the limits of his control, Thork was not the gentle lover a virgin would want for her first time. But then, Ruby did not feel like a virgin.

He kissed her possessively, hungrily, plunging his tongue deep into her mouth, meanwhile holding both breasts in his palms and flicking the tips with his thumbs, then rubbing the soft curls of his calves and thighs over her legs, obviously enjoying the feel of her smooth-shaven legs. His hands were everywhere at once, learning all her intimate secrets, discovering her special spots of sensitivity. Each time Ruby tried to push a hand or leg away from one place, he found another, equally tantalizing place to torture her with sweet pleasure.

When his hot mouth closed over her breast, Ruby couldn't help but arch in sheer pleasure. "More," she moaned, then, "Lord, please don't stop."

"Like this?" Thork whispered against her wet nipple and circled it with the tip of his tongue.

"O-o-h!"

"And this?" he asked in a passion-strained voice as he suckled deeply.

Ruby could not speak. Little sparks of pleasure ignited at each rhythmic indrawn movement of his mouth and lit the fuses to all the erotic points on her body. When he finally flicked the rigid edge of his tongue rapidly over the hardened nubs, the fire blossomed full-force. Ruby bucked and then pressed her hips up against his lower body as the first explosive flames licked her into climax.

Thork was panting for breath. Beads of frustration pearled on his forehead. "Will you don the garment now?" he gasped finally, looking down at her from where he lay over her on straightened arms, gasping for breath. His hard arousal pinned her to the bed.

Ruby wanted to, but some tiny bit of logic in that perverse part of her brain which was not yet turned to molten lava intruded, and she shook her head.

Thork looked at her disbelievingly for just one moment

before he laughed at the challenge of her resistance. A resolute determination washed over his expression. Holding her arms firmly at her sides, he slid down her body and knelt between her knees, spreading her thighs wide. Then he slid even lower and began an assault with his tongue that caused Ruby to arch her hips high off the bed and scream . . . and scream . . . and scream with pure, satiated, ravaging pleasure.

Thork was panting heavily. "Do you concede?" he asked hopefully, sitting back on his knees.

Ruby nodded and could not move when he rolled over for her to get up and put on the lingerie he handed to her. She slid to the edge of the bed and tried to stand. Her knees buckled ignominiously, and Thork caught her, laughing appreciatively at the havoc he'd wreaked on her body.

With a grim smile, he helped her dress—a ludicrous operation, considering they both were in a whirling dervish of sexual frenzy. Veins stood out on Thork's engorged erection, threatening to burst their sensitized nerve endings. Ruby knew that only one touch from her would put him over the edge.

When he finally got the teddy on with clumsy fingers, Thork lay back on the pillows of the bed languidly, with arms folded behind his head. He asked her to walk across the room. She did.

"Now, take it off," he whispered.

Slowly, sensuously, Ruby removed the teddy in the way Jack had shown her pleased him most, peeking back at him over her shoulder, brushing her own breasts "accidentally" with her fingertips when she pulled the garment down. Standing with her legs slightly spread, she inserted both hands in the waistline and pulled it down, then bent and pulled it lower over one leg and then another.

"For the love of Freya!" Thork exclaimed finally, unable to stand any more. He pulled her to the bed with him.

Holding her tightly in his arms, gasping for air, he tried to regain some semblance of control. Finally he laid her back gently on the pillows and brushed the damp tendrils of her hair off her face.

"What shall we do now?" he rasped out with a wry grin. "I must admit you have taken me beyond the bounds of everything I ever thought to experience with a woman and not yet consummated the act."

Ruby could no longer fight her attraction to this devastating male. She smiled her surrender and put both hands on either side of his face, pulling him closer. The time for resistance had passed.

Chapter Eighteen

"I want you inside me," Ruby admitted huskily. "More than anything else, I want . . . oh—"

"Here?"

"Please."

"Like this?"

"Oh, my goodness!"

Whispering softly, Thork moved over her, spread her thighs and bent her knees. With sweet gentleness, he placed himself at the door of her womanhood and slowly tried to breach the lock that should not be there. A gush of wetness seeped from Ruby, and Thork groaned, easing in the tip of his hardness. Ruby's body spasmed and welcomed him in an orgasmic clasp. She turned her face away in embarrassment over her body's premature, raging reaction to such a small touch.

Thork took her chin in his hand and forced her to look at him. He gazed at her in wonder as the little aftershocks inside her body clutched at him still. Then, while his eyes were still locked with hers, he moved slightly. Her body stretched to accommodate him until he finally gave one last lunge, causing only a pinch of pain.

"Oh, sweet Freya!" he gasped and closed his eyes momentarily to savor the intense pleasure.

Ruby's inner body grasped him in a welcome caress as his velvet width swelled and filled her so tightly she couldn't ever remember such an exquisite sensation.

"Do . . . not . . . dare . . . move!" Thork warned. His eyes were shut tight and his mouth formed a thin, white line of tension. Still imbedded in her, Thork finally opened his eyes and held hers intensely, waiting for her readiness to accept his strokes. He brushed her eyes, her ears, the edges of her mouth with feathery kisses.

Ruby felt her center of pleasure begin to swell and throb. She took his finger and placed it there, even as they were still joined. Nodding his understanding, he stroked her there, then spread her folds so her swollen bud would abrade his crisp hairs as he rocked from side to side.

Whispering hoarsely, Thork told her in disjointed, soul-wrenched phrases what she did that pleased him. He asked seductively if this or that intimate touch was to her taste until she could not speak, only moan. Relentlessly, he continued his ministrations until the bud grew and ached, until the inner muscles of Ruby's body convulsed wildly around his shaft in a paroxysm of splintering, exploding little orgasms.

Only then did Thork arch his body over her, arms straight, head thrown back. He began with long, slow strokes that caused her bottom to rise off the bed. She thrashed from side to side in sweet torment.

"Nay, sweetling, lie still. Let me set the rhythm."

Wrapping her legs around his waist, he rode her slowly, tortuously, at first, with exceedingly long strokes that took him almost outside her body. By the time he drove her hard and fast, he'd pushed her to the other side of the bed and almost over the side.

When he almost reached his peak, Thork spread her legs even wider so that each time he pounded into her he'd hit her nub of pleasure. Ruby was a keening, convulsing spasm of nerve endings before he finally arched hard, then pulled out of her body and came heaving onto her stomach as wave after wave of pleasure shook him.

They lay that way for a long time, gasping breathlessly as their bodies slowly eased back to normal. Then Thork moved off her and up to the pillows where he lay back, with Ruby in the crook of his arms. Gently, he wiped his seed off her skin with the edge of the bed linen. Kissing the top of her head, he whispered tenderly, "We are well-matched, heartling. Do you not agree?"

"Heartling. I like that."

She rubbed her cheek catlike against his chest and fell fast asleep. But Thork did not let her sleep much that night. He awakened her sleep-warm body soon after, whispering words of ideas he had for testing how well they matched. At one point, he teased, " 'Tis good you keep your body fit with that jogging exercise of yours for you are well able to keep up with me."

"No. You've got it all wrong," Ruby countered with a laugh. "It's good that you engage in all those military exercises so that you are able to keep up with *me.*"

That time Thork fell asleep, and it was Ruby who awakened him later with a jolt of surprise. She sat astride his half-erect shaft.

"A sad specimen of a man you are, Thork, that needs a woman to prod your . . . interest."

He deftly flipped her over, laughing appreciatively, and showed what a specimen he actually was. In the end, he pounded against her relentlessly until she admitted his superior talents.

In the predawn light, Ruby awakened not to Thork's

lovemaking but to a slight humming noise. Thork was leaning on one elbow, watching her sleep, a slight smile turning up the edges of his relaxed mouth. He sang softly.

"What?" Ruby asked, disconcerted. "Why are you watching me? And what's that you're singing?" Ruby had never heard him sing, even when all the other Vikings in Sigtrygg's hall burst into song.

"I've got friends in lo-o-o-ow places," he broke out in a beautiful, husky baritone voice and showed her with his hands and a jiggle of his eyebrows just what low places he had in mind. Garth Brooks never did it so well. He sang the whole song through, to Ruby's delight and surprise. She'd never realized he even listened to her songs.

"Now that I know you can sing so well, we'll have to do a duet the next time I'm asked to entertain in one of the great halls."

"The only duet I plan with you is right here under the bed linens," Thork growled, and the song they made then was, indeed, sweet.

They slept late the next morning and did not awaken until an embarrassed Eirik entered their room at midday to inform them that King Athelstan had asked for them. Thork had forgotten the ruler's request to meet him in his solar.

"See if you can find a servant with balding hair and a big mole on his cheek," Thork told Eirik. "Tell him to send another tub of bath water up here."

"A bath! On the third floor?" Eirik balked.

"Go, or I will make you carry it yourself."

Eirik shot a disgusted look at them both and left in a grumbling snit.

Thork turned to Ruby who had the coverlet pulled up to her chin. "Do you think we shocked him?"

"More like revulsion," Ruby said wryly as she got out of bed to search through Thork's leather bag for some decent clothing now that he'd ruined her burgundy dress.

"I'm not his favorite person, you know."

When she dropped the coverlet, Thork inhaled sharply. "Did I do that to you?"

"What?"

"You have bruises and finger marks all over your body. I did not realize I was so rough." He came up behind her and feather-kissed the finger bruises on her upper arms, the brush burns on her throat. "Sweet, sweet Ruby," he murmured.

"You don't look so great yourself," Ruby noted as she turned in his arms and linked her arms around his neck. His lips were swollen from her kisses, and, good Lord, was that really a bite mark on his shoulder?

Thork smiled warmly at her, and Ruby's heart lurched with the intensity of her emotion. "I love you," she breathed against his parted lips. "No, don't say anything," she added, putting a finger over his mouth. "Whatever else happens with us, I want you to know that everything that I did with you last night was done for love, not because you forced me, or seduced me, or for any gain I might want."

Thork swallowed hard, holding her eyes with his, but any words he might have said were forestalled by the arrival of the greedy servant.

Happily the sly man pulled in the tub, while Ruby leaped under the bed linens once again. A troop of young pages followed him with buckets of water, towels, soap and even a tray of food. "Thought ye might want to break yer fast with yer young lady after a night of hard work," the ingratiating servant said. Thork rewarded him with two coins. "My pleasure, master," he called out as he went back downstairs whistling a happy tune.

When they finally entered the king's solar, fingers entwined, Selik already waited there for them. "I will not ask if you two got *lucky* last night," he commented sarcastically. "Freya's tit! You both look like you have rubbed each other raw. If you do not stop that smiling, King Athelstan will think you lackwitted."

Thork glared at him, but Ruby just smiled.

At first Ruby and Selik stood in the background while Thork discussed the details of Sigtrygg's marriage with Athelstan's sister. Ruby was dying to see what the sister looked like, but she was nowhere in sight.

While they talked, Ruby looked around the opulent room, filled with the priceless books the young king collected. He had his scribes and clerics copying manuscripts from around the world. Fine Persian rugs warmed the stone floors, coordinated with the bright-colored tapestries and a few paintings on the walls. In fact, an artist stood in one corner painting a portrait of the king, even as he conducted his royal business.

Ruby walked over and looked. The painting showed King Athelstan presenting his favorite St. Cuthbert with a book. The young painter looked up and told Ruby, " 'Twill be the first painting of an English monarch ever done. 'Tis important to King Athelstan that he be viewed as the new Charlemagne."

He turned back to his work, and Ruby returned to Selik's side just as Thork told the king, "My son Eirik wishes to foster here at your court along with his uncle Haakon. Wouldst you permit such?"

"Of course! Highly respected are you here, Thork, as a fighter, as well as a tradesman. I consider you a friend. Well, as much a friend as a Saxon and Viking can be," the king said with a wry smile that lit up his handsome face. Ruby knew that Thork didn't trust the Saxon king, and that Thork's guards had orders to remove Eirik at the first hint of any mistreatment. It was hard to imagine cruelty in so seemingly gentle a man as Athelstan. Also, Ruby wondered if it could be true that this handsome man was celibate.

"I did not know you had children," Athelstan continued.

"Why did you not tell me afore? Are there others? And a wife?"

"I have two children but have denied they are my sons for years because of the—"

"—danger," the king finished for him. "How well I understand the danger posed by greedy men, especially brothers."

Thork and Athelstan exchanged knowing looks before Thork continued, " 'Tis Eirik who would like to be your fosterling. He has seen ten winters. And, nay, there is no wife . . . yet, though I just betrothed myself." He went on to describe Elise's family and the reason for the alliance.

Ruby's heart sank at his cold words about the children and the reminder of his upcoming marriage. With all she'd shared with Thork the night before, she'd forgotten he was promised to another.

The king nodded. " 'Twould be a good match. I know the family and the location of their lands well."

Thork's eyes connected with Ruby's in gentle apology. He seemed to know that words of his marriage hurt her.

Then the king turned to Ruby, asking her many questions about her claims to be from the future. He scoffed at her words of time-travel but said he suspected she might be one of those talented seeresses who can see into the future. Surprisingly, he wasn't so much interested in his own personal fate as what would be happening in the future with art and literature and education.

"Every child is entitled to a free education up through twelve years of school?" the king exclaimed after listening to Ruby for a short time. "How extraordinary! But how can it be so? Are they not needed as fighters in times of war and farmers in times of peace? And what could they possibly be taught for twelve whole years?"

Ruby smiled at his enthusiasm. She looked at Thork and Selik who sat in big carved chairs with legs outstretched, shaking their heads in wonderment at the things she conjured up.

"In my country there is no longer a military draft. The army draws from a volunteer force. Farming is only a small part of the economy. And the school curriculum," she said, trying to use words he would understand, "well, it includes history, working with numbers, studying plants and animals, music, art, exercise, reading, writing . . ."

"*Everyone* is taught to read and write?" the king asked in amazement.

"Yes, of course."

Ruby could see this was more than all three of them could comprehend.

"I will tell you one thing about the future that would interest you, since you seem to love books so much. A product will be invented called paper. It's like parchment but much thinner and very cheap to make. Everyone has books in their homes in my land, not just the wealthy."

"I think I would love to visit your land someday," the king said on a sigh, then asked if she would tell him some of the stories for which she'd gained much fame, as well as sing her celebrated songs.

Ruby related her entire repertoire of children's stories, and the king bemoaned the fact that his best scribe was ill and wouldn't be able to transcribe them for him. He suggested she visit his scriptorium the next day.

Then she sang "Ruby" and "Lucille" for him and added the title song from the Broadway show *Camelot,* which she thought would especially appeal to King Athelstan since his court seemed to embody many of the same ideals. He was overjoyed with them all, even though the Welsh King Arthur was noted for his valor in fighting *against* the Saxons many years earlier. He asked if she would entertain his guests that night.

"I must decline for Ruby," Thork interrupted. "We

leave first thing in the morn for Normandy."

"Normandy! Why?" he asked, his eyes narrowing.

Ruby suspected that the king did not like her powerful Viking ancestor Hrolf. Certainly, she suddenly realized, it wouldn't bode well for Saxon England if a coalition were formed between Northumbria and Normandy.

"Ruby claims kinship with Hrolf," Thork said. "King Sigtrygg has directed me to take her to him."

God bless Thork for not revealing any more details to the king, Ruby prayed silently. She looked thankfully to him, but he ignored her, giving his full attention to Athelstan, who still scrutinized them suspiciously.

"How interesting," the king said, looking at Ruby with new eyes. Then he turned back to Thork. "Since you do not depart until the morn, why not go now to your ships to make final preparations and come back for the evening's festivities?" Athelstan suggested. "Leave Ruby here to talk with me."

Thork didn't seem to like that idea at all, but said nothing, drawing his lips together in a thin line. Selik was clearly amused by Thork's jealousy and irritation.

The moment they left, Athelstan pulled his chair closer to Ruby and told the nobles and retainers who stood behind him to leave. "When I was a child, my grandfather Alfred placed a scarlet robe around my shoulders and fastened a wondrous sword sheathed in gold at my side," he confided to her as soon as they were alone. "Some people think that means he intended me to be king, that I was 'born to the purple,' but 'tis not so. My mother was a beautiful woman, but only a shepherdess, and my father Edward never wed her."

"I don't understand. Why are you telling me this?"

The king held up his hand as if he was getting to that. "My father married twice and acknowledged both women as queens. I am a mere caretaker king. 'Tis important to me to preserve the Alfredian succession for the young atheling princes, my half-brothers. To do that, I must remain—"

"—celibate," Ruby finished for him, finally realizing the point of Athelstan's discussion.

"I have heard that you—"

"—opened my big mouth in Jorvik and told the women about birth control."

The charismatic young king smiled, pleased that she understood him so well. "This celibacy is not an easy virtue," he said with a twinkle in his eye.

Ruby leaned forward and told him all she knew, which wasn't all that much, but he was extremely interested in all of it.

That evening Ruby was already in the great hall, wearing the green silk tunic Astrid had given her with Thork's dragon brooches and belt, when Thork and Selik finally returned. She sat at the high table at King Athelstan's invitation, while Thork and Selik were placed several tables down below the salt.

She tried to listen attentively to all the king said to her, but her gaze kept turning to Thork who pierced her with his angry stare as he drank cup after cup of wine. Selik smiled, enjoying Thork's discomfort immensely, clapping him on the shoulder in a comradely manner, which Thork shrugged off disgustedly.

An observant man, King Athelstan finally whispered to her, "Thork turns green with envy, my dear. He must love you very much."

Actually, Thork's face was red with rage at the king whispering so intimately in her ear, and Ruby feared he might do something to provoke a fight. "I must go now," she told Athelstan.

"Oh, not afore you sing for us," he demanded, and raised his hand for the dinner to end and the tables to be dismantled.

Ruby sang all her songs once again, even "Help Me

347

Make It Through the Night," and looked right at Thork, hoping he knew she sang it for him. The minute Ruby told the king she could sing no more, Thork was at her side, pulling her furiously from the hall.

"Never, never do that to me again," he said through gritted teeth.

"What?"

"Flaunting yourself in invitation afore the king. Has he given up his vow of celibacy yet?"

Ruby would have laughed if Thork hadn't looked deadly serious, and if she hadn't sensed hurt beneath the angry words. She thought about telling Thork of her birth control discussion with the king but decided he wasn't in a mood to appreciate the humor of it now. Maybe later.

"I did not flirt, or tease the king," she told him patiently. "I just talked to him."

"Thor's blood! He fawned all over you."

They were on the third floor, almost to their tower room, when Ruby broached a subject that had been bothering her all day. "Thork, we have to talk about what happened between us last night. It was wonderful, but it was a mistake. I was reminded of that when you told the king about Elise. We have to be strong. We can't let it happen again."

Thork opened the door, pulled her in, then pinioned her against the wall with his body and kissed her hungrily. Not satisfied with that, he lifted her off the floor by the waist so her feet dangled free and the vee of her legs met his raging arousal.

He groaned and rasped out, "God, Rube, I missed you so much today. Didst you even think of me?" He lifted her even higher, wrapped her legs around his waist and made a few deft adjustments of their clothing. Within seconds, he was driving into her with her back against the stone wall.

Ruby forgot about being strong. She forgot that this

wasn't supposed to happen again. She forgot everything except the moment, this man and the love she felt for him.

A few minutes later, Selik knocked on the door, saying that he needed to tell Thork something about their departure in the morning.

"Go away," Thork grumbled, but when the knocking persisted, he finally opened the door with a loud curse.

Selik's mouth dropped open. He gawked at their rumpled clothing and labored breathing.

"Good Lord, Thork, dare you to ever criticize me again I will remind you of this night. Forsooth! You have only been gone from the hall a few minutes, Thork. Canst you not control yourself better than this? Tsk tsk!"

Thork slammed the door in his smiling face.

The next morning, they arose at dawn, and after gathering their personal belongings in Thork's bag, they went to look for Eirik. They found him in the great hall where he slept on a pallet next to his uncle Haakon. Eirik rubbed his eyes groggily, then looked sadly up at his father.

"You go now, so early?"

"Yea, we must make the tides by midday. Are you sure you want to stay, son? You can still change your mind."

"Yea," Eirik replied with a hesitant nod.

"So be it. I have left enough coins to cover your expenses for two years if I am not able to return afore then. If there is aught you need, or if you suspect danger of any kind, or if you no longer choose to foster here, you can send a message to your great-grandfather Dar through Vigi or one of the guards who stay with you. Do you understand?"

Once again, Eirik nodded, but tears welled in his eyes, the imminence of his father's departure finally hitting him.

Thork quickly scanned the hall to see if anyone watched them. Feeling it was safe, he brusquely pulled Eirik into his arms, and they embraced each other tightly for a long time.

It was the first time Ruby had ever seen the father and son show physical affection for each other. Ruby closed her eyes briefly, painfully, at the sheer intensity of the moment. How many such moments had there been in the past?

Next it was her turn. "Eirik, take care of yourself. Always know that there are people in this world who love you very much—myself included," Ruby choked out. "I think you can learn a lot from this Saxon king about what is important in life, besides military might. Take advantage of everything he can teach you." Then, uncaring of whether he would resist her or not, Ruby hugged him warmly and kissed his cheek repeatedly, wetting his face with her tears.

Ruby wept silently as she and Thork and Selik walked across the bailey in stony silence toward the stables and the horses that would take them to the Thames River and Thork's ships. Only once did she speak: "Thork, how can you bear to leave a ten-year-old boy like that?"

The hard, desolate eyes he turned on her almost broke Ruby's heart. She wilted under Thork's silent condemnation of her hasty words. Then he strode ahead, leaving her behind with Selik.

Even Selik was not his usual joking self. "Best leave him alone for a while. 'Tis how he always acts when he must leave his sons."

With all the river traffic from King Athelstan's coronation, it took Thork's five ships a day to maneuver through the Thames to the open seas. The smells, congestion and frustrating delays managed to transform bad moods into even worse ones by the time they camped for the evening.

That night in their tent, which was pitched on the periphery of the campsite, Ruby took the initiative in their lovemaking, trying to make up to Thork with gentle caresses and sweet words for the loss she knew he must feel over leaving his son. How he had done it all these years was beyond her comprehension.

When she'd first met Thork, Ruby had thought of him as cruel and unloving to abandon his two sons. Now she wondered if he wasn't, in fact, an incredibly brave man who was bleeding inside with loneliness.

Over and over during the night, Ruby whispered, "I love you." He never returned the words to her, and that tore at her heart, but Ruby said them nonetheless because she was increasingly convinced that no one, not a father or mother, not a child, not even a loved one—*no one*—had ever said the words to him before. How could any person—man or woman, child or adult—live without ever feeling loved? It was a chilling thought.

They didn't depart for Normandy the next day. Instead, all the goods on the five ships were unloaded and rearranged around their campsite. Apparently, while they relaxed at Athelstan's coronation, Thork's men had been busy trading in London and had sold what amounted to two shiploads of goods.

Thork decided that two empty ships would return to Jorvik where Olaf would reload them with trading products and then meet Thork and Selik in Hedeby, a trading town on the southern tip of the Jutland peninsula. After Thork finished his business in Normandy, he and Selik would go on to Hedeby, then Jomsborg, where the ships would be transformed into military vessels.

During the day, the men snickered at the soft glances Thork and Ruby exchanged constantly. At night, through whispered words and feathery caresses, Ruby and Thork spun webs of love, unspoken on his part, that drew them closer and closer together. Limited by the close proximity of Thork's shipmates in their nearby tents, their love-making was gentler and quieter than their wild, frenzied coming together in King Athelstan's palace, but equally satisfying.

Ruby no longer fought their lovemaking as an unwise decision. Instead, she treated it as fate—an inevitable progression in her strange travel through time, something that was preordained for some reason she was yet to understand.

Thork still intended to marry Elise. Ruby accepted that fatalistically, even though they never spoke of it or their own future together. Thork probably expected that she would go with him to Jomsborg as his mistress—at least for a time. Ruby's emotions were crystal-fragile at the moment, and she avoided a confrontation with Thork over the issue. In truth, she feared she might break into a million pieces if she pressed for a commitment and Thork told her that's all she meant to him—a "bedmate."

So they made love and pretended all was well, each avoiding discussion of the festering canker between them. One day at a time, that was all Ruby could handle right now. But she did pray a lot.

Finally the three ships crossed the English Channel for Normandy, while the other two went back north to Jorvik. No sooner had their ships dropped anchor in Normandy than a contingent of armed men lined the shore. Having recognized the ships' colors, the Norman Vikings escorted them back to Hrolf's keep. They treated Thork with distrust because he was, after all, son of Harald, high-king of Norway, a hated enemy of Hrolf.

Surrounded by guards with menacing weapons, they entered the great hall of Hrolf's fortified palace in Rouen. A huge man, at least six-foot-five and built like a tree, stood to greet them. Ruby could see how he'd earned the nickname The Marcher. Truly, not many horses could hold a man his size.

"I bid you welcome to Normandy, Thork," Hrolf said in a polite but cool voice. "Come forward and share some ale with me." Meanwhile, his eyes pierced him with icy mistrust.

Hrolf drew them to a roaring fire, which offset the damp chill of the misty day. Several well-dressed men and women sat there, including one lady whom he introduced warmly with a pat on her arm as Poppa. Ruby wasn't sure if she was his wife or mistress.

Thork shifted uneasily and came right to the point. "I come from King Sigtrygg and then go from here to Hedeby, then to Jomsborg where I resume my Jomsviking duties."

Hrolf's intelligent eyes examined Thork keenly. "What does that wily old bear want from me now?"

Thork cast an inscrutable gaze at Ruby, seeming to weigh his thoughts carefully before he drew her forward with a hand at her elbow. "He sent me here with this woman—Ruby Jordan. She claims to be a kin of yours."

"Mine? How could that be?" Hrolf demanded with consternation, glancing apologetically to Poppa. "Some get on a village maid? What claim you, girl?"

All eyes turned on Ruby, and there was a collective gasp as the group then turned to look at a middle-aged woman seated at the edge of the seated circle. Ruby looked exactly like the woman must have at a younger age. Ruby soon learned that Eddha was Hrolf's oldest sister. Thork and Selik stared disbelievingly at Ruby, realizing she must have spoken the truth all along. Relief softened Thork's tense features as the implications of the resemblance became clear.

"Now you won't have to chop off my head," Ruby whispered morbidly and jabbed him in the ribs with her elbow while Hrolf and his family agitatedly discussed the situation among themselves.

"Nay, but I may smack your rump," Thork responded with dry humor. "What else do you hide from me?"

Ruby was about to remind him that she'd been telling him the truth all along when Hrolf called Ruby closer and asked her to sit in the chair next to him, which he freed by shooing a young hesir away. Thork and Selik dropped into heavy armchairs brought forth by scurrying servants and sipped at the cups of wine placed in their hands.

"Now tell me true. Who are you?" Hrolf demanded.

Ruby looked at Thork, wondering if she dared tell the real story. He rolled his eyes up to the heavens, which was no help at all. She decided to give it a try. "I come from the future, the year 1994," she began slowly, and immediately saw the entire group stare at her in stunned disbelief, wondering if this was a trick or she was crazy.

Hrolf glanced angrily at Thork, who shrugged in mock despair, laughing. "You can see why Sigtrygg sent her here. He was convinced she spied for Ivar and wanted to behead her—"

"That whoreson would execute someone who claims to be my kin?" Hrolf interrupted with narrowed eyes.

"Nay. 'Tis why he sent me here, to make sure of the blood tie. He did not want to offend you."

"And if I deny her?" Hrolf drew his lips in thoughtfully, calculating Sigtrygg's game.

Thork clenched his jaw, and his lips straightened in a rigid line. He took a long time before he answered, a betraying nerve twitching near his stern lips. "He ordered me to behead her."

Hrolf looked back and forth between the two of them, then burst into laughter so loud the rafters seemed to shake.

"By the blood of Odin, that rascally king of yours does enjoy putting you in the tight spot, Thork, does he not?"

Thork didn't answer, clearly unamused by Hrolf's poking fun at him.

Hrolf turned back to Ruby, demanding with a smirk that bespoke his disbelief of her time-travel, "Tell me more of yourself."

Ruby stiffened her back at his mocking tone, but inhaled deeply to control her temper. "Well, I did a family tree years ago, tracing the history of my father's side of the family back more than a thousand years. I was able to do that easily because there were a number of famous people along the way, like James, Duke of Ormond." Ruby hesitated, sensing the twitters of laughter among the whispering people. Oh, heck! she thought. She may as well lay it all on the line. "I figure you are my grandfather about fifty times removed."

Hrolf stared at her blankly, and total silence blanketed the hall, except for the crackling of the fire.

"I don't remember all of it," Ruby went on doggedly, "but I do know that your great-great-great-grandson will be William the Conqueror."

"William the what?"

"William the Conqueror, one of the greatest military leaders of all time. The Norman conqueror who becomes the king of all England."

Fascinated, ignoring the snorts of disbelief around him, Hrolf asked excitedly, "You say one of my descendants will vanquish all England and become its king?"

Ruby nodded, and a pleased smile split Hrolf's craggy face.

"Also, although you are not called a duke now, the history books will refer to you as the first Duke of Normandy."

"Do you give similar compliments to Sigtrygg, hoping to get on his good side?" Hrolf scoffed suspiciously, probably thinking she made up these false prophecies to bolster his ego.

"Hah! I think Sigtrygg is a pig who has this fascination with decapitation," Ruby exclaimed inmpulsively, then clamped a hand over her mouth, realizing how inappropriate her comment must sound. But the men laughed heartily and the women giggled in appreciation of her vehemence against a man they did not admire.

"Tell me more predictions of my family," Hrolf

demanded, while a servant handed Ruby a cup of sweet wine. Ruby realized that Hrolf, like King Athelstan, thought she was a seeress, a person with talents to foresee the future.

"I don't remember much about all the children and grandchildren," she ventured carefully, deciding not to force the issue of time-travel, "but I do know about the direct line. You have a son, William Longsword, who will expand your duchy a great deal by adding Cotentin, or Cherbourg—"

Everyone pivoted to glance at the young man who stood behind Poppa's chair, then back to Ruby. The teenager's eyes widened at her mentioning his name.

"—and William will have a son, Richard I, called The Fearless, who will have a son, Richard II, called The Good, and he will have a son Robert, alternately called The Magnificent or The Devil. Robert's only child will be William the Conqueror."

The charged silence that followed her words told Ruby nothing. She didn't know if she'd said the right or wrong thing, if she'd gone too far, or not far enough.

Finally Hrolf exhaled loudly. "Well, well, well! What a fine mess we have here. Clearly, girl, you do not come from the future. 'Tis impossible, but 'tis equally clear you are of my blood. The resemblance to my sister cannot be mistaken, despite that short haircut." He examined her hair closer. "Are you perchance diseased? Is that why it has been chopped so?"

Thork choked on his wine and Selik bit his lip to hide a grin.

"No, it's the style in my country," Ruby said, raising her chin proudly.

"Where might that be? No, do not tell me," Hrolf laughed, holding up a hand to halt her response. "No more am I in the humor for fantasies of the future this day."

He turned on Thork and asked stiffly, "What relation-ship do you share with my *granddaughter?*" His emphasis on the word of kinship seemed to give official stamp to Ruby's acceptance at his court, if the sharp looks exchanged by his family were any indication.

For a long moment, Thork's eyes held hers as if trying to come up with answers he hadn't yet resolved himself. Then he looked Hrolf directly in the eye. "She is my woman."

Ruby's heart leapt joyfully in hope.

"Are you married?" Hrolf persisted.

"Nay. I pledged my troth to another afore I left Northumbria," Thork admitted, and then explained the circumstances leading up to his reluctant betrothal.

Hrolf nodded. "And would you marry Ruby, too?"

Thork glanced at Ruby again, obviously not wanting to speak publicly of private matters, but he finally acknowl-edged, "Nay, I have taken on too many Christian ways to have more than one wife. In truth, I would prefer none. I will not forsake Jomsviking."

Ruby could feel the color drain from her face at the familiar words he spoke—cruelly cutting words, despite her having heard them before.

Seeing the pain on Ruby's face, Poppa spoke for the first time. "And what of Ruby? Do you have no feelings for her? Do you love her?"

Thork's jaw clenched tight. He clearly didn't want to answer Poppa's questions but knew his silence would be considered rude by Hrolf.

"What has love to do with it?" he evaded.

Surprised, Poppa pursued the subject. " 'Tis obvious to me you care for the girl. Wouldst you abandon her here when you go on to Jomsborg?"

Once again, Thork's jaw tensed at the personal questions. His troubled eyes locked with Ruby's, trying to communi-cate his apology for this public airing of their problems.

She saw him flex his fingers tensely before answering, "I would prefer to take her with me to Jomsborg when I leave, but it will be her choice to come with me, or to stay here . . . if she is welcome."

Ruby sensed how hard those words were for Thork to speak, and loved him for his honesty of emotion.

But Poppa spoiled the moment by pressing him angrily, "As bedmate? You would ask her to accompany you with a status little higher than a thrall?"

Thork looked at Ruby bleakly before asserting defiantly, " 'Tis for Ruby and me to discuss, in private. 'Tis our concern and no one else's."

Hrolf took exception to Thork's words. "Nay, that is where you err. When you brought her to my court for my acceptance as family, she became my business. A good marriage I would have for her, not a loveless arrangement with a man who could leave her in a thrice, if he so chose."

Seeing the angry rebellion in Thork's eyes and his clenched fists as he rose from his chair, Hrolf declared unequivocally, "No more for today, my friend. We will discuss it again later."

Ruby stood in horrified silence, listening while they discussed her as if she were a piece of meat with no rights to determine her own destiny. Did Hrolf mean she would have no choice in the decision to go with Thork or to stay? Had she jumped from one frying pan into another?

"Take Ruby to a chamber near ours, Poppa, so that she may rest and prepare for dinner," Hrolf ordered, then told Thork in a tone of voice that brooked no argument, "You and Selik may share a chamber in the wing where my hesirs sleep."

Ruby looked helplessly at Thork, whose eyes held hers accusingly for a few long moments. Did he think she had planned this? After all they'd shared on their trip from Jorvik, how could he doubt her love, or that she wanted to be with him? Despite her tear-filled eyes, he turned his back on her with icy disdain.

An inexplicable feeling of emptiness overcame Ruby, followed by a foreboding that her future with Thork was in true peril.

Chapter Nineteen

Ruby was treated like a newfound pet during the following week—given special tours of the castle and a newly built cathedral, dressed in the finest clothing, adorned with jewels, accepted as a long-lost loved one come home. At night, she sat at the high table with Hrolf's family and favored guests. Afterwards, they cajoled her into story-telling and singing until she pleaded exhaustion, then couldn't sleep for want of Thork.

She was miserable.

Hrolf and his court conspired to keep her apart from Thork. They were given no opportunity to speak in private, let alone touch or kiss or share a bed. Ruby ached for him across the distance of the hall, unable to bear the accusing, wounded looks with which he seared her. He seemed to think the separation pleased her, that she'd used him to achieve her ultimate end—the safety of Hrolf's protection.

Three nights before, Thork had pushed his way through

the retainers who surrounded the Norman ruler, demanding, "By your leave, Hrolf, I would speak to Ruby in private." Ruby could see how the polite words grated on Thork when he really wanted to bellow at Hrolf for his underhanded tactics.

"Later. Later," Hrolf had coolly evaded, asking, "What think you of King Athelstan's buildup of fortified *burhs?*"

Then last night, Thork had tried again, but Hrolf had deflected him by urging, "Come, tell me of the goods you carry on your ships. Mayhap you have some items I need for my troops, or trinkets Poppa would cherish."

Finally, tonight, Thork didn't even try. He drank heavily, watching Ruby with hawklike eyes, surely taking in the fact that she'd lost weight and had dark circles under her eyes from lack of sleep. Ruby yearned to go to Thork, to assure him of her love, but two guards posted near her at all times thwarted such efforts.

Observing Thork's excessive drinking and the insolent glares he cast toward him, his host, Hrolf, slammed his goblet on the table and directed a servant icily, "Tell Harald's fleabitten get that I wish to speak with him— if he is not too besotted with my ale."

Despite the large amount of alcohol he must have consumed, Thork carried himself with rigid dignity to the dais, pointedly ignoring Ruby who sat nearby. His bloodshot eyes spoke of sleepless nights and unspoken hurts. Ruby stood to go to him, but a guard placed a firm, forbidding hand on her shoulder, pressing her back to her seat. Thork's impassive face showed no emotion, but Ruby noticed his fists clenching and unclenching where he held them behind his back in a seemingly casual pose. The movement sent ripples up the corded muscles of his bare arms.

"Didst the misbegotten whelp of Rognvald wish to address the misbegotten whelp of Harald?" Thork snarled at Hrolf, throwing the insult in the Norman ruler's message back in his face.

Thork's arrogant stance, as well as the foolhardy words, infuriated Hrolf. He stood angrily, dwarfing everyone around him with his size and temper. Only Poppa's hand on his arm kept him from attacking Thork with his bare hands. Instead, he sat back down and scrutinized Thork with flashing eyes. "When dost thou leave for Jomsborg, Thork?" Hrolf inquired through tense white lips, his tone making it rudely apparent that Thork had worn his welcome thin. "Surely thou dost not worry over Ruby's safety still?" His lips curled with contempt before he added, "I thought Jomsvikings were not permitted to leave their fortified palaces for more than three days at a time."

Thork curled his lips, as well, mimicking Hrolf, and answered in a surly voice, "I had permission to conduct my grandfather's business and to handle my own trading concerns, but, yea, I will depart soon. But first, I *will* speak to Ruby."

"To ask her to accompany you to Jomsborg?"

"Yea."

"I will not permit it."

"*You* will not permit it!" Ruby gasped aloud. "Since when did I hand over control of my life?"

"Hold thy tongue, wench, or leave the hall," Hrolf told her.

"She has a say in this," Thork contended. The warm look he gave her showed his obvious pleasure in her having stood up to her imposing relative.

"Nay, she does not. As my granddaughter, I would have her wed, secure in the bonds of matrimony."

"You talk from both sides of your face, Hrolf. For many years Poppa·sat at your side without the marriage ties."

Hrolf stood to his full height, livid with rage, and his retainers drew their weapons. "No man speaks disparagingly of Poppa. In the eyes of the Christian rites I took at the Treaty of St. Clair-sur-Epte, the king's daughter Gisela became my wife. Even then, I considered Poppa my true wife, and I married her as soon as Gisela died."

Sincere regret immediately flushed Thork's face, and he hastened to assure Hrolf, "I apolgize for my inept words, Hrolf. There are many things for which I would heartily insult you, but ne'er would I slander Poppa. I merely meant to say that the *more danico* and the taking of mistresses is practiced widely by you and others without impunity."

Hrolf gave a grudging nod of acceptance to Thork's backhanded apology. He sat back down and tapped his fingers thoughtfully on the table.

"You may have my granddaughter *only* on the marriage bed," he finally said, "and that is my final word. One last bit of advice—I would suggest you depart on the morrow afore bad deeds, as well as words, pass betwixt us."

Thork held Ruby's eyes questioningly. She was stunned by the finality of Hrolf's command, and her shoulders slumped in defeat. Before she could say anything, Thork turned and stormed from the hall, with Selik following after him.

"Please let me speak to him," Ruby pleaded with Hrolf. "Just talk. That's all."

"Nay!" Hrolf growled, still angered by Thork's words. " 'Tis best to end it thus."

Ruby ran from the hall in tears. What if Thork left Normandy without seeing her again? She had so much to say to him. Would she go with him if she could? Probably. No, actually, Ruby wasn't sure. She needed first to know Thork's feelings and what their relationship would be if she went to Jomsborg with him.

Ruby never would have been able to accept the role of "other woman" in her future life with Jack. Could she now? *Oh, Lord!* Ruby cried inwardly as the questions hammered away inside her head.

Poppa followed Ruby into her bedchamber and comforted her, " 'Tis really for the best, my child. Believe me, I know well the pain of living with a man you love without the sanction of the church."

"Would you have rather lived without him?"

Poppa smiled. "I did not love Hrolf at the start. He killed my father, Count Berengar of Bayeau, and took me captive. 'Twas later I grew to love him."

"How could you?" Ruby asked, but, at the same time, she remembered Thork's cruelty in imprisoning her in Olaf's barn for five days and yet she still loved him.

"Hrolf is a hard man. Ne'er doubt it," Poppa explained patiently, "but he is a just one, as well, and an outstanding leader. When we came to Normandy, Hrolf instilled the old Norse laws, especially those relating to the respect for a man's property. So much did he want a peaceable land that he ordered his people to leave their valuable farm tools out at night, tempting thievery. If anything was stolen, he said he would be responsible."

"Oh, Poppa, what has this to do with me and Thork?"

Poppa smiled indulgently and went on, "There was this farmer's wife at Lonpaon who hid her husband's plow, then asked for compensation for thievery. When Hrolf discovered the truth, he hung her, but, more important, he killed her husband, as well, for not controlling his mate better."

"Are you warning me that Hrolf means what he says about me and Thork?"

"Yea, but I also ask that you remember he does what he considers fair." Poppa shrugged and smiled enigmatically. "Mayhap it will all work out for the best."

Ruby didn't see how that could be. For hours she wrestled with all the questions swirling in her brain, unable to come up with answers that would satisfy her heart, as well as her morality. Finally she cried herself to sleep but tossed restlessly, not knowing if Thork would be gone when she awakened in the morning. In the middle of the night, she dreamt of him.

His feather-soft caresses swept her from neck to toe. Her breasts swelled and ached under the soft, circular caresses of his callused palms. The wet tip of his tongue traced the crevices of her ear and plunged inside, then repeated its sensuous path again and again. Soft, wet lips suckled her breasts, and practiced fingers teased her nether folds until they opened and swelled for him.

So lifelike was the dream that Ruby could smell the masculine scent of his warm skin, and his lips tasted of raging passion and virile man. Was it Jack or Thork? Whoever! To Ruby, he was the consummate dream lover.

When the firm lips played their sweet music on Ruby's mouth, entreating her to open for his more sensual assault, she tried to moan, but the sound was caught by hungry kisses that alternated between gentle coaxing and deep, ravaging plunges.

"I love you, heartling."

The softly whispered, precious words drifted on the air and penetrated Ruby's dreams. She awakened immediately.

Ruby found Thork lying over her, naked. She leaned into his long fingers which gently stroked wisps of hairs back off her forehead. Her first reaction, though, was fear for his safety. "Thork, are you crazy? Hrolf will kill you if he finds you here."

"Where?" He grinned and buried himself in her dream-readied sheath with one long stroke. "Here?"

Ruby gasped. The exquisite pleasure of the hot melding of their two bodies caused shudders to ripple across her skin like the fluttering of a million birds' wings. Purring, she pulled Thork closer by wrapping her thighs around his waist.

Braced on his elbows with head reared back over tautly stretched neck muscles, Thork held himself immobile inside her body's tight clasp, unable to move. Through gritted teeth, he finally asked with a devilish laugh, "Shall I leave?"

"Don't . . . you . . . dare!" Ruby warned hoarsely and arched her hips, welcoming him with all the love and unsatisfied yearning she'd built up during the past week of separation. Threading her fingers through his long hair, she pulled his face down to hers and moved her lips back and forth until she'd shaped his mouth for her gentle kiss.

"I love you, Thork. Always. I've missed you so."

With her soft words, Thork lost control and plummeted her with his deeply felt, unspoken emotions. "Rube . . . oh, sweet . . . oh, Lord, oh, Lord . . . let me . . . please . . . aaargh!" he murmured disjointedly until he reached his soul-shattering climax, taking Ruby over the edge of eternity with him on a flight of pure bliss.

When they lay spent and gasping for breath in each other's arms, Ruby traced the silky hairs on his chest with a forefinger and whispered against his lips, "I thought I was dreaming of you at first, Thork. I thought you said you loved me, and it was the most wonderful feeling in the world. That's what awakened me." Questioningly, she raised her eyes to his face, now relaxed in the afterglow of their sweet loving. She saw conflicting emotions battle in his tense facial muscles, even as he drew her closer in the crook of his arm.

For several long moments, Thork said nothing. Ruby could feel a nervous pulse in his neck beat erratically. His heart thundered under her palm, still racing from the excitement of their lovemaking.

He inhaled deeply and began to speak, running his palm caressingly over her shoulder as he spoke, "I am not sure I believe in love or that I am capable of such an emotion anymore." He stopped and turned her face so that he could see her eyes. He continued in a thickened voice,

"Yea, I said the words, but they just slipped out. I do not even know if I meant them." He grinned sheepishly and admitted, "The words did feel good in the saying, though."

Tears of joy filled Ruby's eyes and misted her vision. "Oh, Thork, I love you, too." She rolled over on top of him then, bracing her arms on either side of his face so she could see his face more clearly. With a quick brush of her lips, she urged, "Will you say the words again? Oh, please, honey, I need to hear you say them."

Holding her eyes, Thork lifted her above him and lowered her onto his manhood, which had hardened again on their soft caresses and sweet words. When she straddled him, forging their bodies as one with her heat, Thork rasped out, "I love you, sweetling."

"Again," Ruby demanded as she moved on him.

"I love you, sweetling."

"Again," she gasped as Thork took hold of her hips and set his own rhythm.

"I . . . love . . . you . . . ah! . . . no, do not stop . . . yes, there . . . I . . . love . . . ," he jerked out brokenly.

To the tune of those whispered words and others, said over and over between them, Ruby and Thork pledged a love for each other that they swore would never end.

"I will love you till I die," Thork swore on one long, slow endless stroke that ended with her keening wail and his low, prolonged, throat-wrenched growl.

"Thork, wait a minute. I need to . . . I . . . oh oh oh! . . . I can't stand any more . . . please," Ruby said brokenly as each of his deep thrusts took her to a new plane of mounting tension.

"Rube!" Thork exclaimed softly when he reached his shuddering peak. "We can make it work!"

Jack's words! Ruby blinked dazedly, not sure if it was Thork or Jack who spoke the familiar words to her. Truly, she no longer knew or cared. Fate had put her in this time and place. Surely, this man was her destiny. On that hazy thought, Ruby snuggled closer in Thork's embrace and fell into a deep sleep.

They awoke at dawn to a loud pounding, followed by the harsh noise of wood splintering as Hrolf's massive frame broke through the locked door. Three armed retainers and Poppa followed him into the room.

Their naked bodies told a story that inflamed Hrolf. He spit out a string of expletives, then snarled, "You bloody bastard! You are Harald's son through and through. Stand so I can put a knife through your traitorous heart."

"No!" Ruby screamed, and stood with a fur wrapped around her nakedness. "Don't hurt him. He came because I wanted him here."

"Do you stand behind maids now in cowardice?" Hrolf taunted Thork.

"Nay, I do not!" Thork stood, uncaring of his nudity. The three guards grabbed his arms and held his struggling body in place with his arms pinioned behind his back. Hrolf drew a long-handled knife.

Poppa pulled at Hrolf's arm, trying to intercede. "They love each other. Do not do this thing. For my sake, if not for your new granddaughter's, spare him."

The muscles in Hrolf's face were rigid with the self-control he could barely exert. Ruby knew he would just as well kill Thork, but in deference to Poppa he offered grudgingly, "Will you marry my granddaughter if we bring the priest now?"

Thork's eyes turned bleak. "I cannot. Honor-bound am I to Elise." He looked at Ruby sadly and implored, "Please understand. I would if I could."

Poppa pleaded with Hrolf once again, "Do not let your temper rule. Wait till the bloodlust settles."

Hrolf's angry eyes impaled Thork, but he finally turned to Poppa. "For your sake, I will delay my rage." He told his retainers, "Take him to the guardroom and secure him well until I decide his fate. And someone find that whoreson Selik and bring him to my chamber. The lusty rogue is probably plowing one of my daughters."

Ruby wept and pleaded for Thork's release after they took him away, but Hrolf shrugged her off coldly. "You shame me, wench. Heed me well, if there is a babe bred on you already, you *will* have a husband—be it Thork or a stableboy."

Ruby had no idea what Hrolf said to Selik in his chamber, but the angry shouts could be heard throughout the keep. Selik left the castle soon after under armed guard, and no one would tell Ruby where he went. Hrolf refused to speak with Ruby and banished her to her rooms, under double guard. He suspected, rightly so, that she would try to release Thork. Ruby didn't know if they tortured Thork, or if he was even alive. She feared that Hrolf looked at Thork as a means of finally avenging himself on King Harald.

Thankfully, Thork escaped two days later, slitting his captors' throats and slipping off into the darkness on one of his ships, which Hrolf had commandeered and which still lay in the harbor. For days Hrolf and his retainers followed Thork in their own ships, but to no avail. They returned to the castle in a rage.

"The bastard returns to Northumbria, not to Jomsborg," Hrolf announced that night. He looked Ruby coldly in the eye and said, " 'Tis sure he goes to wed the Saxon wench Elise. Why else would he go back there?"

"Maybe he went back to get troops to return here to fight you," Ruby offered defiantly, trying to keep her eyes wide open so the tears would not spill over and embarrass her.

"Thor's toenails, girl! Are you so besotted you cannot see in front of your face? Jomsborg is closer than Northumbria. If Thork intended to fight me, he would have sought his Jomsviking comrades."

Seeing how distraught Ruby was, Poppa interceded for her, "Leave off, Hrolf. Canst you not see how your words wound?"

"Thor's blood! Would you have me lie to her? The man refused to marry her. 'Tis a fact. The sooner she accepts that, the better."

Ruby bent her head and let the tears slide silently down her face.

Softening, Hrolf said gruffly, "If you do not carry the scoundrel's babe, I will find a good husband for you."

"I'm not pregnant," Ruby snapped, shrugging off the comforting hand he'd put on her shoulder, "and I don't want you to find me a husband."

"Oh, I will find you a mate, of that you can be sure," he warned on a harder note, displeased with her shrewish attitude, "and it will not be an easy task, with you not having a maidenhead."

Ruby threw up her hands in disgust. "I haven't had a maidenhead for twenty years."

Hrolf's eyes hardened at her vulgar, illogical words. "Best you clean your tongue afore I introduce you to any man, or I may cut it out for you."

The two glared at each other, each refusing to back off. Finally Poppa asked the skald to tell them a good, long saga.

Despite the turmoil over Thork's escape, the castle returned to normal activities. The slaughter of cattle, hogs and other game was held on Michaelmas Day at the end of September. Everyone in the castle and surrounding region was kept busy with the butchering, salting and dividing of the provender for winter. The women cleaned the intestines for sausage making, which caused Ruby to remember with a sad smile the condom controversy in Jorvik, but she was too depressed to even joke about it with Poppa.

As unhappy as she was, Ruby couldn't be sorry that

Thork had escaped Hrolf's wrath. She would rather have him married to Elise than tortured or dead in Normandy, especially since she'd heard the servants talk furtively of the harsh treatment Hrolf doled out to his enemies. To Hrolf, Thork now deserved the worst punishment, not only for his treatment of Ruby, but for killing the guards on his escape.

Poppa and her women watched Ruby closely for several weeks, waiting for her monthly flow to come, which it did, of course, as Ruby knew it would, thanks to Thork's persistent caution. She felt curiously saddened when the blood showed. A baby with Thork would have been like the one she and Jack had planned and never had.

Hrolf treated Ruby with cool politeness, feeling she'd betrayed him by her actions and lack of remorse. Ruby walked the halls of the great manor for the next month like a zombie. She ate, slept, helped Poppa with the household chores and went to chapel every day for Mass and prayer, but she never laughed, and she refused to sing or tell her stories. She knew Poppa worried about her, but she felt helpless, smothered by the dark mood that settled over her in a weighty cloud.

Was this how she would live out the rest of her life—a living limbo, never returning to the future and never finding love in the past? Ruby realized that she had somehow subconsciously come up with a reason for her time-travel. She'd rationalized to herself that if she could have brought love to Thork and enhanced his life, it would have made up for what she'd failed to do with Jack. It now looked as if she'd screwed up all over again.

"Aren't you hungry?" Poppa asked gently, jarring Ruby's thoughts back to the present and the food she pushed around her plate with a small knife.

"No." Ruby tried not to be rude to Poppa. The dear lady tried so hard to ride the fence between her and Hrolf. She reminded her a lot of Aud.

Aud! She hadn't thought of her and Dar in ages. Ruby wondered how Tykir was getting on in Aud's household. And Eirik? Would Thork and Elise visit Eirik at Athelstan's palace? On their honeymoon? Would they have a baby together, despite Thork's intentions to the contrary? Were they making love at that very moment?

Oh, God! Ruby closed her eyes on a silent moan of anguish.

"Ruby, why do you weep? You must put Thork behind you. 'Tis time to—"

Poppa's words broke off as a young hesir burst into the hall and ran toward the high table, gasping for breath. Without waiting for permission to speak, he burst out, "Hundreds of armed men come in ships bearing the colors of Thork and his grandfather Dar."

Pandemonium broke out.

Hrolf and all the men in the great hall jumped up, grabbed whatever weapons were at hand and ran outside to join their own troops. Hrolf directed some men to the walls, others to follow him to the gate.

Distraught, Ruby rushed to the tower with Poppa and her ladies to watch. In a field outside the keep, Thork and Hrolf stood arguing, arms gesticulating. Dar held back at least four hundred men, and an equal number of fierce warriors lined up behind Hrolf.

Finally Thork, Selik, Dar and a handful of other leaders headed toward the manor with Hrolf, while the troops set up a campsite in the distance.

"What's happening?" Ruby asked Poppa.

"I have no idea, but at least they do not fight. 'Tis a good sign."

Hrolf sent a message ordering Ruby and Poppa to stay out of sight, but before they went back to the solar, Ruby got a quick look at Thork's stormy face. He was probably furious over his ill-treatment by Hrolf and had returned for revenge. Still, it was wonderful to see him again.

For hours Ruby and Poppa fidgeted nervously, trying futilely to work on a tapestry. Finally Poppa sent a servant to see if she could overhear anything in the hall.

"They negotiate a marriage contract fer her," the wide-eyed thrall reported when she returned, pointing to Ruby.

"For *me?* With whom?" Ruby gasped. She turned to Poppa. "Hrolf threatened to find a husband for me, but why would he discuss it with Dar and Thork?"

"Nay, you mistake my meaning. 'Tis the master Thork fer you," the maid interrupted.

Ruby and Poppa inhaled sharply and looked at each other in mutual incredulity. Poppa urged the maid to go on.

" 'Twould seem the Saxon maid Elise cried off onct she learnt that her betrothed traveled here to Normandy with Ruby. Elise bade her father make other marriage arrangements fer her. Sore mad, Dar sez she was. Thork should have wed the maid afore setting sail, the girl's father said."

Ruby smiled widely and hugged Poppa. "And now Thork wants to marry me?"

"Well, not quite," the servant said. " 'Tis more like he wants the master, Hrolf, ter send men ter protect his grandfather's lands in payment fer jailin' him. And he blames you fer losin' the Saxon maid and the protection of Dar's neighbors."

"*What?*"

"Now, Ruby, a few hours ago you would have given anything to have Thork back," Poppa chided. "Do not be waspish over the details. And best you pray Hrolf will agree. Sore mad he is at being bested by Thork."

But Hrolf did agree, to Ruby's immense satisfaction, although no one seemed happy with the marriage pact. Hrolf begrudged the fighting men he would have to pledge to Dar and the son of his hated enemy, Harald. Thork balked at a forced marriage and the vast number of gifts

373

Sandra Hill

Hrolf demanded for Ruby's dower. And Ruby wasn't so happy that all these plans were being made without her being present.

Regardless, Thork was a glorious sight to Ruby when she walked uncertainly into the hall. Wearing the blue cloak she'd made for him, Thork sat talking in a leisurely fashion with Hrolf, Selik and his grandfather. He stood immediately when he saw her approach and held out his left hand. She took it gladly and twined her fingers intimately with his, then looked up shyly for some message in his stern face.

Without speaking, he pulled her off to the side where they could talk in private, but not so far away she couldn't see Hrolf's sullen glare and Dar's self-satisfied wink. Thork leaned one shoulder against the stone wall of the keep, but still held her hand firmly, absently rubbing the inside of her wrist with his thumb. His eyes held hers for a long moment, their unfathomable blue heightened by the deep color of the cloak.

"Do you know why I am here?"

"Yes, I think so." Ruby's heart beat wildly in fear at Thork's aloof countenance. He could surely feel it through the rapid pulse at her wrist.

"We will marry on the morrow," he declared. No asking. Just a flat statement of fact.

Ruby really was beginning to worry now. This was not the way she'd imagined their reunion would be. She nodded, unable to speak over the lump in her throat. Lord, she wished Thork would smile or say something to disclose his feelings about the event.

"I never wanted to wed."

Ruby's heart dropped and she lowered her eyes to hide the pain. "I know," she said softly. "You told me so often enough." A sense of foreboding enveloped Ruby.

"Marriage is a trap that ensnares a man in deadly emotions."

374

"It doesn't have to be," Ruby said shakily, raising her tear-filled eyes.

Thork quirked an eyebrow and wiped an errant tear that hung on the edge of her eye with the pad of his thumb.

"Marriage could be the melding together of two people destined to be together. It could be a sharing—a partnership of a man and a woman with a common goal. It could be a touch of paradise on earth." Ruby couldn't believe she was spouting such flowery words, or that she actually meant them. She closed her eyes bleakly.

"Is that how you envision our marriage?" Ruby's eyes shot open. For the first time, Ruby noticed the raspiness of Thork's voice, the odd glow in his eyes.

"Yes," she whispered hopefully and restrained herself from reaching out to brush a strand of hair that fell over his forehead.

"Even if I wanted that kind of marriage, what do you think my brother Eric would do?" Thork said huskily. "Think you that he would let me plant my feet in one spot for long? That he would not harm those I cherish?"

Cherish! Ruby's hopes soared. Hesitating several moments to select just the right words, Ruby finally said, "Life is so short. It seems to me such a waste to spend those precious days looking over your shoulder, worrying about what might happen. We *have* to grasp the moment." She inhaled deeply and scrutinized his face to see if he understood what she was trying to say. "Oh, Thork, wouldn't you rather have a day of happiness than a lifetime of 'what might have beens'?"

A gentle smile turned up the corners of Thork's lips. " 'Tis odd that you should say that."

"Why?"

" 'Tis the selfsame reason I returned for you."

Ruby studied his handsome face, which just now seemed to relax from some rigid tension that had held him in its grasp. She frowned in puzzlement, not sure what he meant.

375

"When Hrolf and his men bound me and I lay two days with no food or drink in his prison, I had to face the prospect of dying. Oh, 'twas not a new threat. I flaunt death at every turn as a Jomsviking. But the idea of dying and never seeing you again—that, I discovered, I could not bear."

"Thork, what are you saying?"

"Nay, let me continue. I asked myself this question as I lay contemplating death: What would you do today if you knew there would be no tomorrow? The answer was simple: I would marry Ruby and cherish each moment, no matter how few they may be."

Ruby hesitated for only a second, then threw herself into his arms, despite the dozens of people who watched from the other side of the hall. He caught her and lifted her so her toes barely touched the floor. Ruby buried her face in his neck, sobbing out the weeks of desolation she'd suffered in his absence.

"Shush, sweetling. 'Tis over now."

"You beast," she accused tearfully, "standing here like a statue, letting me think you didn't care."

"You deserve a little torture for all you have put me through," Thork teased as he nuzzled her neck. When he pulled away slightly and looked down, he exclaimed with feigned horror, "Good Lord, woman, you are sopping my entire cloak with your tears." Lowering her to the ground but keeping an arm looped over her shoulder, he said in an aside to Hrolf and Dar, who had moved closer, "Is this what I will have to put up with for the rest of my life— a weeping, slobbering woman?"

Hrolf gave his grudging congratulations, and Dar bear-hugged her, stating gruffly, " 'Tis all as I had planned." Poppa joined them, and they discussed the ceremony to be held the next day.

Thork winked mischievously at Ruby and ordered with mock sternness, "I would like to have cheeseburgers and baklava for my marriage feast tomorrow, woman. Dost think thou could manage that betwixt your bouts of blubbering?" Then he followed with his now familiar, annoying pattern of tweaking her behind.

Ruby didn't care. He'd said *"for the rest of my life."* That was a promise she liked.

The hastily arranged wedding in the Rouen cathedral went off surprisingly well the next day, considering the small amount of time they'd had for planning.

Ruby did, in fact, supervise the making of cheeseburgers and baklava to supplement all the sumptuous foods Poppa ordered for the nuptial feast. It turned out to be a monumental task. The Vikings, known for their voracious appetites, consumed two hundred cheeseburgers and fourteen platters of baklava.

"Can you move?" Ruby teased, patting Thork's flat but stuffed stomach.

"Yea, I can, and will show you just how well in a short time. Ne'er doubt it." The heat in his eyes showed how much he wanted to do just that. Hrolf had infuriatingly refused to allow them to sleep together on the eve of their wedding.

"Well, I don't know. You are an over-the-hill married man now, and—"

Thork gave her a quick kiss on the mouth to stop her devilry. That caused their guests to bang their goblets on the tables, calling for a more serious effort. He laughed, pulling Ruby onto his lap, and kissed her thoroughly.

Later, as he spoke to his grandfather on his other side, Ruby marveled at the contrasts between this wedding and her previous one, and the similarities. She still couldn't separate the two men in her mind. In a way, she felt as if she'd married Jack all over again—an earlier, more primitive version, but her husband just the same.

And the biggest constant of all was her all-consuming

happiness. Jack had been her perfect first love. He'd brought her everything new and hopeful in the world, and together they'd forged a life based on the youthful belief that anything is possible in the gift of life if the package is tied with the strings of love. Thork was the other side of the same coin. Not so young. Certainly jaded, seemingly without hope. Definitely not perfect. But he loved her, and that's what real, mature love was all about, Ruby realized. When a man and woman love each other despite their flaws, despite the stumbling blocks life throws their way, that is true love.

"Why so pensive, sweetling?" Thork asked, running a rough palm caressingly up and down the sleeve of her silk dress.

"I was just thinking how happy I am," she answered, pleased to see the joyous leap in his eyes at her words. "You know, I had a professor in college who was discussing the poet John Milton and his principle of 'cloistered virtue.' Milton contended that the truly virtuous person is not the one who hides from the world in a monklike fashion, but who lives in the midst of life's muck and still manages to be moral—"

"Oh, Ruby," Thork said with a laugh, pulling her onto his lap once again. "You make my mind fuzzy with all your confusing words. What have monks to do with love?"

Ruby slapped his arm playfully. "Let me finish, you rogue. I just meant that Milton's philosophy could be extended to include 'cloistered love.' Don't you think the stronger love is the one which has been tested and forged by adversity, rather than one which has been sheltered and based on unrealistic expectations?"

"What makes you think, dearling, that I do not have high expectations for our love?" Thork said in a soft, serious tone. "But, yea, I agree that our love will be stronger for having overcome some . . . obstacles." He grinned then and blew teasingly in her ear. "There are some obstacles

I expect you to overcome for me . . . and soon. I have missed you sorely, sweetling."

Ruby sighed and forced herself to turn back to the banquet. Fidgeting in Thork's lap, she tried to take in all the events—jugglers on one side, skalds on another and a musical group composed of a lutist, two harpists and a singer.

Thork cradled Ruby in his arms as she turned constantly to view all the activity in Hrolf's hall. Truly, Ruby's grandfather had been gracious in providing such a lavish wedding feast, especially while harboring such ill will toward him. But, damn the merrymaking. He wanted to be alone with Ruby. It had been more than six weeks since he had left her bed. Six long, celibate weeks!

"Are you truly happy, sweetling?" Thork whispered, remembering with a smile her words of, what was it, "cloistered love." *Holy Thor!* The woman was a fount of high-flown, foreign words.

Ruby beamed at him, and Thork's heart slammed against his chest. He closed his eyes for an instant on the almost painful intensity of emotion the sweet witch stirred in him. The deep green pools of her eyes were so open in their love. Even if she tried to hide it with the lush length of her auburn lashes, as she did now, he could still see how much she cared. No one had ever loved him so unconditionally afore. He truly did not deserve it.

"Happier than you can ever know," Ruby answered, turning misty eyes on him which glistened with the tears of her joy. The muted green silk gown that Poppa had given her as a wedding gift swished enticingly as she twisted once again in his arms. Suddenly her movement struck Thork as odd, pain-ridden.

Thork put his hand gently on her arm and asked, "What ails you, wife? You are as jittery as a cat on hot coals." *Wife!* Lord, that word had a sound to it he liked. He rolled it silently on his tongue. He touched Ruby's hair gently, no longer repulsed by the short style, and moved his hand smoothly down her back, then stopped abruptly below her shoulder blades where a rough object protruded slightly. "What in the name of Freya is *that?*"

"Whalebone."

"Whalebone! You never cease to amaze me. Is it a talisman or such that you wear?"

"You could call it that." Ruby smiled enigmatically at him through half-veiled lashes.

In an instant, Thork understood and burst out laughing, hugging her to him. Dar and Hrolf turned to see what amused them so.

"Oh, sweetling, have you been wearing that teddy all day? For me?"

"Yes, and you better appreciate it, you brute. I can hardly breathe."

"Mayhap we best go to our chamber and remove it at once afore you expire of suffocation," he said with a devilish grin.

"My thought exactly."

But Hrolf and his guests would not allow them to leave so hastily, demanding that Ruby sing at least one song for them. Ruby balked, but Hrolf insisted it was the least she could do after saddling him with Harald's get for a grandson-in-law. Thork pinched her to comply.

The sly vixen challenged ominously, "I'll show you." She darted a meaningful glance at Thork as she stood and picked up a lute. "Since this is my wedding night, I think it would be appropriate if I sing a song for my new husband, just in case he doesn't know quite what to do," Ruby said with mock sweetness as an introduction to her ballad.

The men in the hall roared with laughter at her jest and called out ribald remarks to Thork about a woman having to teach him such. But then Ruby poked fun at the masculinity of all the other men, as well, by saying,

"Actually, from what I've heard from the Viking women, a lot of you men out there could use a lesson from this song. So listen well. You, too, Selik," she called out and actually caused the rascal to blush.

She announced a Pointer Sisters song, then looked directly at Thork as she began in a low, husky voice to tell of her need for a lover with a slow hand. Several stanzas later, he began to understand the graphic message of the song.

Slow hand! Easy touch! Heated rush!

The entire hall twittered, then burst into full-blown laughter by the time she ended the song. A few of the women turned red with embarrassment, but most of them nodded their heads in agreement with her sentiments.

Ruby grinned impishly at him.

"Perchance, are those Pointer Sisters acquainted with that Kevin Costner person?" Thork asked dryly.

Ruby laughed. "I doubt it."

"So, I do not satisfy you in bed?" Thork had trouble holding back the twitch of amusement in his lips.

"I didn't say that."

"Oh ho! Now you back down. 'Tis a slow hand you asked for, and that is precisely what you shall get," he warned seductively.

The impertinent wench surprised him by winking and countering saucily, "I will hold you to that promise."

Slow hand! By the faith, where did the woman come up with these ideas? Already that day, he had overheard Poppa and her women discussing lingerie and the shaving of legs. Hrolf told him in no uncertain terms that he was to make sure his wife did not discuss birth control in Normandy. As if he could direct her actions!

Then Ruby demanded that Thork reciprocate by singing a ballad for her. "Not on this side of Valhalla!" he refused, but he finally agreed to recite a few lines from a skaldic poem he remembered—"Rigspula," or "The Song of Rig."

381

Oddly, although the poem dealt with the humorous, certainly unromantic, notion of the Viking social order, a few of the lines reminded him of Ruby and himself:

" . . . *Her brows were bright, her breast was*
   shining,
Whiter her neck than new-fallen snow . . .

Blond was his hair, and bright his cheeks,
Grim as a snake's were his glowing eyes . . ."

The tears that sparkled in his wife's eyes when he finished were compensation enough for any discomfort he may have felt in reciting poetry in front of his fighting men. When they finally escaped the great hall and were alone in their sleeping chamber, Thork quickly removed his clothes and lay naked on the bed with arms folded behind his head, inquiring, "Shall you entertain me now, wife, by modeling your undergarment for me?" He yawned loudly and stretched languorously, adding, "Or do you think there will be a dullness to our lovemaking now that we are wed?"

Ruby's eyes lit up at his challenge. "Hah! Not if I can help it."

"And this slow hand business—does that go both ways? Or is it only women who are permitted to seek such lovers in your country?"

"No, it goes both ways." Ruby grinned. "Shall I show you?"

And she did. Oh, Lord, she did!

Chapter Twenty

Ruby shed her clothing slowly, teasingly, drawing out the process an exceedingly long time. When she was down to the teddy, she posed and dawdled, removing the wispy garment one bloody inch at a time until Thork was sorry he had ever voiced a liking for the foolish item.

"Come to bed now, Ruby," Thork urged raspily when she was naked. But, nay, the contrary miss had other plans. He ground his teeth and waited, refusing to grovel for her favors, especially on his wedding night.

"Not yet," Ruby evaded with a teasing lilt in her voice. "First I want to ask you something," she said, coming closer to the bed, but not so close he could grab her, which Thork was sorely tempted to do as Ruby leaned forward provocatively. Her firm, upthrust breasts swayed slightly, enticing him to do anything but engage in a conversation.

And her hips! Holy Freya! The wench's slender waist flared out just so to the cradle of hips he'd hoped would be under his by now, then on to the down-covered delta

Sandra Hill

he planned to explore endlessly this night.

If she ever got into bed!

"Thork, you're not listening to me."

"Huh?"

Ruby smiled knowingly and asked a totally irrelevant question, to his frustration. "Do you remember that first day I arrived in Jorvik?"

Thork nodded his head suspiciously. What was she up to now? Lord, she would have to be blind not to see his raging need. Hah! If she would only come a little closer, he would teach her a few memory games. He forced himself to remain calm, to wait for just the right moment to pounce.

"Remember when we were walking to Olaf's house, and you said you could never be attracted to a woman like me, that Viking men liked women who were softer and less waspish?"

"I remember it well. Surely, you do not hold that over my head now, of all times! Come to bed, sweetling."

"In a minute." The mischievous maid turned slightly, giving him a wicked view of her rounded buttocks. Thork felt his arousal swell practically to bursting. He gritted his teeth as she looked back at him over her shoulder and asked in a low, seductive voice, "I was just wondering . . . don't you think I'm sweet at all?"

"Sweet! 'Tis the last word I would use to describe you. Maddening, alluring, yea. Sweet, never!"

Ruby's lips twitched. "That's just what I thought you'd say." She turned and picked up a small crock with a spoon in it from a table near the bed.

Thork sat up and stared at her. It was a pot of honey. Did she intend to feed him? Now? Holy Thor! That was not the raging hunger he needed to appease, but he did not want to hurt her feelings.

"I wouldn't want you to be married to a woman who wasn't sweet," she said coyly and dipped her fingertip in the thick syrup and coated her lips with it. Then she took the spoon and . . . oh, my God! . . . drizzled the honey over her breasts, onto her stomach, down the inside of her thighs, then . . . for the love of Freya! . . . between her legs.

Thork lurched from the bed and tried to haul her back with him, but she eluded him by ducking under his arm with a low, sensual laugh.

"Don't be so anxious, husband. I want this to be a wedding present you'll never forget."

A wedding present! She will put me in my grave, instead.

With the palm of her hand pressed against his chest, Ruby moved him back to the bed, teasing, "I thought you were going to have a slow hand."

"Slow hand! Hah! You will not even let me touch you."

"Lie down, sweetheart," she ordered gently.

"Why?" he asked suspiciously. "Come with me."

"I will. Just relax."

Relax? Was she bloody, out-of-this-world touched in the head?

When Thork was on his back once again, Ruby stood at the edge of the bed and streamed a thick dollop of honey in a steady stream from his neck to his burgeoning manhood. He almost shot off the bed at the intensity of pleasure caused by the warm syrup oozing around his rock-hard staff. With a smile, she laid the crock down and crawled onto the bed.

"It's just as important that men be sweet as women."

"Woman, this bed is going to be sticky as a beehive by morn," Thork growled appreciatively, pulling her into his arms.

"Oh, really, I don't think so. I always lick my plate clean. How about you?"

Thork almost lost his control then. *Almost.*

Ruby moved over him, rubbing her honey-slick breasts

across the hairs on his chest. At first they both just laughed at the mess they made, but their laughter soon died and turned into breathless pants as the slickness of their rubbing skin created tingles of aching sensation wherever they rubbed.

"Thork, do you think I'm silly trying all these outrageous things to please you in bed?" Ruby asked shyly in a low, aroused whisper, her eyes downcast.

Thork put his forefinger under her chin and raised her face. Her eagerness to please him touched Thork deeply, almost as much as her uninhibited ability to share in sexual gratification.

"Oh, Rube, I love you so. Do you not know that everything you do pleases me?"

Tears welled in her eyes, and she seemed to have trouble speaking. "I love you, too, husband." She put her hand up to his face and stroked it softly. "Let's promise each other, Thork, that this night, our wedding night, will be the first of an eternity of nights for us."

Thork nodded, then teased, "All of them filled with loving?"

"Of course!" she said with a weak laugh.

"Don't you think we should get started then, wench?" he said with a low growl, rolling her onto her back. "We have a quantity of honey to consume." He put both hands on either side of her face, holding her in place for his hungry kiss. First he licked the honey from the edges of her lips with the tip of his tongue, then outlined the seam. When she parted her lips on a sigh, Thork smiled with satisfaction and laved her entire mouth with wide sweeps of his tongue.

"Mmmm! You taste so good," he murmured.

"Let me taste," she urged softly against his lips.

He inserted only the tip of his tongue. She circled it with her own, then drew deeply on the honeyed moisture. "So sweet," she whispered appreciatively. "Give me more."

Smiling against her lips, Thork sheathed his tongue in the warm cavern of her mouth, then slowly slid it in and out. Ruby wouldn't stand for that. She drew on it tightly, then suckled him. Thork felt a spasm of pleasure start in his tongue and travel that invisible line straight to his male organ which jerked against her belly.

He pulled away slightly, panting, and Ruby leaned up, following his lips, wanting to continue the deep kisses.

"Nay," he said firmly, putting both hands on her shoulders and pressing her down. "As of now, I take over control of these wedding night maneuvers," he proclaimed in a voice so raw and low he barely recognized it.

He slid down her body, literally, until his mouth was level with her breasts. With a forefinger, he circled the aureole of first one, then the other, then put the finger in his mouth to taste. "So good," he murmured. Ruby just gazed at him, mesmerized, with parted lips. He repeated his actions, but this time offered the finger to her. She leaned up and licked the tip with her pink tongue, then the slick sides in wide sweeps. Finally she took the whole finger into her mouth, sucked it tightly, then, using both hands, moved it in and out of her mouth in long strokes, simulating the sexual act. Holy Freya! How would it feel if she did that to—

He pulled his finger away abruptly, fearing he would embarrass himself by ending this game prematurely. He moved back to her breasts and consumed every speck of honey with his licking tongue. When he leaned away to inspect his work, Ruby moaned, arching her breasts up off the bed.

"Please, don't stop," she begged.

"Show me," he choked out.

She put a hand on one breast and the other around the nape of his neck, pulling him down, but he refused to put his mouth to the nipple until she told him exactly what she wanted. Finally she obliged with husky explicitness.

Thork groaned against the hard peak and drew on her again and again, alternating deep pulls with fast flicks of his tongue, until she was keening aloud with urgency, bucking her hips against his in raging need. Then he moved to the other breast, giving it equal, tortuous attention.

When Ruby flailed from side to side and tried to rub herself against his staff, Thork rolled over to his back and refused to allow her to follow him. When he'd got his breathing under control, he moved back, leaning over her.

"Lie still," he ordered hoarsely, holding her shoulders down with the palm of one hand and moving the other to the honeyed vee between her legs. Groaning at the abundant wetness, most of it made by her own hive, he spread her legs and knelt between them. With sticky fingers, he examined all her intimates recesses, giving particular attention to the bud that swelled and bloomed for him. Spreading her legs wider, he bent her knees so he could see better. Dipping his fingers in the honey pot on the nearby table, he coated the pouting flower framed by engorged pink petals. He circled it, stroked it, then moved it back and forth rapidly until he saw it spasm. Ruby raised her hips off the bed and stiffened on a long moan, "Oh . . . oh . . . ooooh!"

But still he was not done with her. When she panted breathlessly and tried to close her legs to hide the oversensitized bud, Thork inserted a long, callused finger inside her body, then two. Her eyes widened with the shock of his entry, so quickly after the other orgasm. He didn't give her time to protest. By the time his abrasive fingers had thrust in her three times, he could see by her glazed eyes and panting breaths that she was starting on another erotic journey. He held the fingers in place, letting her ride him, setting her own pace, meanwhile using his other hand to finger-flutter her bud once again. She bucked. She wailed. She begged him for satisfaction until her inner body convulsed over and over around his plummeting fingers.

She lay flat across the bed, arms and legs outspread, totally sated. "Oh, Thork," was all she said in a softly wondrous voice.

Ruby's uninhibited response to his touch inflamed Thork to the breaking point. "Oh, no, you do not rest yet," he warned softly, pulling her back up with a laugh. " 'Tis your turn, cat, to clean my plate."

By the time she did just that, with greedy relish, Thork was the one moaning for release, especially when she ended with his rigid, honey-coated manhood. When he could stand no more, he pulled her under him. With one long, hard stroke, he entered her, filling her with his flesh. Her slick folds grasped him spasmodically. He closed his eyes on the pure perfection of the moment. Lord, her woman's heat enveloped him like a warm glove.

He reared back and gazed at his wife. *Wife!* Thork marveled at the oddly wonderful-sounding word. Ruby's face was dazed with mindless passion. Unfocused, her eyes begged him for release from this monumental, searing buildup of sexual arousal that had them both in its clutch. Never had he experienced anything like this fever of building tension.

"Ruby," he entreated in a savage whisper.

"Now," she answered shakily, trying to move her hips against his, but he was still buried deep, immobile in her.

"Come with me now, sweetling. Together," he urged.

She nodded. The time for gentle loving had passed, and Thork pummeled her with long, hard strokes that caused explosions of red lights behind his eyes. Ruby was keening loudly, or was it him? On and on, he thrust into her until wild eruptions of exquisite pleasure rocked him, careening into Ruby's body, then ricocheting back through his manhood.

They lay panting, side by side, for a long time afterward. Thork felt as if he had died and come back to life. He hugged her close, unable to speak, not sure he could explain what had just happened if he tried. When he finally felt he could utter a word without sounding like a eunuch, Thork rubbed her shoulder in the crook of his arm and chuckled softly.

"Do you know what I love most about you, wife?"

"What?" she whispered, nibbling his neck.

"You make me laugh."

Ruby punched him in the stomach. "That's not a compliment."

"Yea, 'tis, sweetling," Thork said, holding his stomach in feigned injury. " 'Tis a gift you give every time you make me smile."

By the time morning arrived, Thork swore to himself, he would make her smile a time or two, as well. And he did.

The serving women who brought a tub and fresh water the next morning were aghast when they saw the bed linens.

"I spilled a pot of honey on the bed," Ruby explained with a blood-red face.

One elderly thrall darted a wry glance her way. "Oh? And what bee spilled it in yer hair and on yer toenails?"

Thork laughed heartily from the chair in the corner where he sat with legs outstretched, wearing only a pair of braies, waiting for his bath.

The woman cast a disgusted look his way. "And you, young master, I suppose those red marks all over yer body are bee stings."

It was Ruby's turn to laugh.

When they were both dressed, much later, Thork handed Ruby his two dragon brooches. "I did not have time to purchase you a *morgen-gifu*. Will you accept these for your morning gift?"

Ruby arched a brow in question.

" 'Tis a custom for a husband to gift his bride with some

special token the morning after the first bedding to show his pleasure. In fact, the marriage is not considered valid in some places until the *morgen-gifu* is given."

"Really?" Ruby asked, looping her arms around his neck and giving him a quick kiss of thanks. "And were you pleased?"

"How can you doubt it?" he growled into her ear.

By the time they arrived down in the hall, the servant grapevine had carried the story. Hrolf and Dar laughed rudely in their faces, and all day he and Ruby were subjected to wide speculation on exactly what they did with the honey. Some said it was even on the floor and walls, which was, of course, ridiculous.

For two days, they basked in their newfound love, spending long hours in bed, walking or riding through Hrolf's lands, planning their future together.

On the afternoon of the second day, Thork told her, "I must return to Jomsborg for a while. I have a commitment to fulfill." Ruby turned sad eyes on him, and for the first time ever Thork wished he was not pledged to the Jomsvikings.

"Will you quit then?" she asked hopefully.

"Yea, I will, but not until my duty is completed."

"How long?"

He shrugged uncertainly. "I know not. I promise it will be as soon as possible."

"Then where will we live? What will you do?"

"Trading is what I do best," he said tentatively, "but where we settle will be determined by safety." Thork's first choice would be to stay on his grandfather's lands, but chances were Eric would hound him there. In truth, to him it really did not matter where he lived, as long as Ruby and the boys were with him.

Thork hugged Ruby closely to his side as they sat down under a tree on a carpet of new-fallen leaves, and Ruby told him of the first time she and Jack had made love in such a crisp bed. Thork nuzzled her neck, trying to halt her words, not wanting to hear of her love for another man, even if he only existed in her mind.

"Then we shall make love here, sweetling. I will erase the old memories for you."

Ruby said nothing, but he could see the pain in her eyes. She would never forget this Jack, the imaginary husband. Before she surrendered to his imploring hands, Ruby asked sweetly, "Do you think I could start up a small lingerie business? You could sell the sets on your trading voyages."

Lord, the witch had a habit of asking irrelevant questions at the most inopportune times. Thork's chest shook with suppressed laughter.

"What? Why are you laughing at me?" Ruby asked, shoving him in the chest.

"I cannot believe you want me to become a trader in women's undergarments. Next it will be condoms."

Affronted, Ruby asked, "Don't you think there would be a market for lingerie? And, no, I wouldn't sell condoms."

"You are serious, are you not?"

"Sewing and making lingerie is what I do best," Ruby explained. "You have already said you don't want more children. What would I do all day? Besides, if you're too embarrassed to sell women's underthings, I could come with you and do the trading."

Now that was a thought to boggle the mind. Ruby on his trading voyages! Thor's balls! He would accomplish naught but making love until his staff wore itself out from overuse. He smiled down at his enticing wife. Ruby's tunic and chemise hung off one shoulder from his persistent efforts. He reached out a hand and touched the creamy skin.

"Well?" Ruby persisted.

Huskily, he agreed, "If 'tis what you want, wench, I

will let you put some women's lingerie among my trading goods." Lord, he probably would have agreed to lace his boots at that point.

Then the crunch of autumn leaves under their nude bodies and whispered love words wiped out all thought of business.

Later, back in their chamber where they laughingly picked crumbled leaves from some very intimate places on each other's bodies, Thork began to have second thoughts. Ruby talked excitedly about plans for her lingerie business. And she wasn't talking about a few sets of undergarments sewn together in her spare time. She spoke of a separate building for cutting and producing the lingerie, hiring a half dozen women to help her, then expanding later. Thor's blood! She would fill a ship with her lingerie alone.

"Ruby, this is not what I had in mind when I agreed to trade some of your lingerie products," Thork said.

"What do you mean?"

"Well, I enjoy being married to you. It pleases me immensely to imagine you waiting for me in our own home each night when I return from my business dealings or when I arrive home after a voyage. I picture Eirik and Tykir at your side. My heart fills at the thought. How would you have time for all those things if you were busy running your own business affairs?"

Thork expected Ruby to be pleased with the soft words he had taken such pains to form. Instead, she lashed out, "You male chauvinist pig! I can't believe this! It's Jack all over again!"

"Jack, Jack, Jack! I am sick of the man's name."

Ruby glared at him and ran from the room.

Thork did not understand. Most women would be pleased that a man cherished them so well that they would not have to drudge. He decided to seek his grandfather's advice, but that was not necessary. Dar rushed toward him, telling him, "Come quickly." He pulled Thork into a private chamber.

Dar was extremely agitated, and he clutched a small parcel in his hand tightly. His fingers shook.

"What is it?" Thork asked, worried by the intensity of his grandfather's fear.

"'Tis Ivar!" he choked out. "He kidnapped Eirik and asks for ransom." He handed Thork the linen-wrapped package. "Oh, Thork, I would spare you this pain if I could."

Thork's heart hammered loudly as he unrolled the cloth. A small finger fell out. A thousand explosions went off in his head, and he had to hold on to a chair for support. Closing his eyes tightly on the pain, he whispered, "Do not tell Ruby. It would kill her. Whatever you do, she must not know."

Ruby was in an absolute rage. It wasn't so much the lingerie business. Even though she'd stormed away from Thork, she was sure they could work all that out somehow, but now Thork came to their chamber and told her coldly that he was going to Jomsborg immediately, that he'd been summoned for some mission. Worst of all, he wouldn't take her with him. She must go back to Northumbria with Dar.

"No! I want to go with you," she cried, while Thork hastily threw his clothing and personal belongings in his leather bag. "Please," she begged, seeing the unbending look on Thork's face. "I'm sorry I argued about the lingerie company. Don't leave me, not now. I can't bear it again."

Thork turned and took her by both shoulders, forcing her to look him in the eyes. They were a cold, desolate blue which frightened Ruby.

"I love you, sweetling. Remember that. Always."

He kissed her with an odd desperation and held her

tightly for a long moment. When he pulled back, he scrutinized her face, as if memorizing its features. And Ruby could swear she saw tears in his harsh, warrior's eyes. What was happening here? And why so quickly?

"Go with Dar back to Northumbria," he told her implacably. "Wait for me there with Tykir." He choked on the last words.

Then he really frightened her when he added, "And, Ruby, something else. Pray for . . . me."

On those ominous words, he left her standing openmouthed in their chamber. Once she realized he was actually going, Ruby ran after him, down the steps and out to the bailey. He and several dozen men sat on horses talking to Hrolf while half of the armed men they'd brought with them were heading toward the ships.

"I will dispatch two hundred men as soon as you send word of your whereabouts," Hrolf promised. "May God and Odin go with you."

Thork turned to Dar. "You will return to Northumbria immediately?" At his nod, Thork went on, " 'Tis unwise to leave your lands so unprotected. I will send word as soon as possible. Godspeed, Grandfather."

Thork saw her then, standing in the background with tears streaming down her face, reeling under the shock of disbelief that he was abandoning her. A muscle flickered beside the thin line of his tight lips as he maneuvered his horse through the people toward her. He leaned down and lithely pulled her up in front of him on the saddle.

"We will meet again, sweetling. I love you."

I love you, too, Thork, Ruby thought, but the words clogged in her throat as he kissed her briefly, then set her down and rode off.

Hrolf and Poppa looked on her with pity, but would disclose nothing when she hugged them tightly before boarding one of Dar's three ships the next day. They told her she would always be welcome in Normandy.

The two-week trip back to Jorvik was horrible. Ruby lay on her back most of the time, racked with seasickness in the troubled waters. Despite her protests and wild weeping, Dar's hard face turned away from her when she demanded explanations for Thork's hasty actions. Back in Northumbria finally, she fell into Aud's welcoming arms on a sob and kissed Tykir until he pulled away in childlike embarrassment.

For weeks, Ruby alternately pitied herself and raged at Thork for his actions, meanwhile waiting desolately for word from him. When it finally came, the message was for Dar, not her. Dar closeted himself in a chamber with Olaf, who'd delivered the missive. When Olaf left, he took one hundred men with him, leaving Dar with only a hundred to guard his keep. Still, Dar wouldn't answer her questions about Thork's whereabouts.

"He will let you know when the time is right."

Finally Ruby buried herself in work. She talked Dar into giving her one of the wool sheds for her lingerie business. Enlisting the help of six village women, Ruby was aided by Ella, who turned out to be a born administrator, bullying the women into extra work, making them laugh while they did it. They cut the bolts of silk and laces brought to them by Aud, who insisted on being a partner in the enterprise.

Within weeks, the business was a resounding success. Making the lingerie in all sizes, Ruby sent her first fifty sets into Jorvik one day with Dar. He delivered them to a merchant who agreed to sell them on consignment. They sold out in two days, thus launching Ruby's lingerie company.

Ruby purchased extra materials with the profits, hired six more women, and built a large hearth so they could work during the winter months.

Ella turned into a blooming entrepreneur, planning how

much money she could save over what period of time, how she could buy her freedom and perhaps get a small house in the village. Her dreams transformed her into a new person.

" 'Tis amazing!" Aud said as they sat down to dinner one night. "At first, I only gave you the fabrics and encouraged your work to ease your mind over Thork. Now it appears I will be a wealthy merchant. What think you of that, Dar?"

"Huh? Oh, yea," he answered distractedly. There had been no word from Thork since that first message, and he worried constantly.

Ruby was torn between anger over Dar and Aud cutting her off from their great mystery and concern for whatever was troubling them. She thought she had a way to make them feel better. "Dar, Aud, I have some news that should make you happy."

They both looked at her as if nothing could cheer them up, and Ruby wondered once again what they hid from her.

She smiled at them both and disclosed softly, "I'm pregnant!"

A stunned silence greeted her words.

Their failure to respond hurt Ruby. "What? You're not pleased to have a new baby here?"

"Oh, nay, 'tis not so!" Aud declared and jumped up belatedly. She hugged Ruby warmly.

"Yea, 'twill be wonderful to have . . . another great-grandchild," Dar choked out and left the hall abruptly.

Puzzled, Ruby turned to Aud.

"Do not mind him. He has much to think on these days. But what about Thork? I thought he did not want more children."

"He doesn't. I'm not sure how it happened. He was always so cautious," Ruby said, trying to think when he might have been careless. Was it their wedding night, with the honey, or was it the day in the autumn leaves? She hoped it was the latter. Then it would seem almost like Jack's child, too.

"I'm sure Thork will be pleased once he gets used to the idea," Ruby went on. "I hope it's a girl, with blond hair and blue eyes."

Despite Ruby's happiness over her pregnancy, she worried about Dar, who was growing increasingly morose. Several days later, Ruby went looking for him to force an explanation. He wasn't in the chamber where he worked on manor business. She was about to leave and look in the stables when she noticed a small, linen-wrapped package lying on a piece of parchment.

Ruby had seen Thork clutching such a parcel the day he left her in Normandy. Ruby's ears began to buzz and her pulse raced wildly as she walked woodenly toward it, sensing somehow that all her questions were about to be answered. Slowly she unwrapped the layers.

Gagging, Ruby stared at the small finger, its skin dried up and beginning to deteriorate. She rocked from side to side in shock, a keening wail beginning low in her throat.

Why would anyone save such a morbid thing? Could it be Thork's finger that his brother Eric had cut off years ago? No, that would be bare bone by now. This was more recent.

Ruby's keening grew louder and the ringing in her ears reached deafening proportions as she continued to rock back and forth. She reached shakily for the stiff parchment and read the horrifying words:

Grandfather,
Ivar still holds Eirik. He will not release him, even for the ransom demanded, even in exchange for me. Damn his evil soul! He wants Sigtrygg's head. We go to battle tomorrow. Pray for us.

Thork

Ruby screamed over and over and over, then fell unconscious to the floor. She awakened hours later in her bed, surrounded by Dar, Aud and Ella.

"Why didn't you tell me?" she asked Dar accusingly.

"Thork did not want you to know. He said you would blame yourself."

"It *is* my fault. He warned me over and over about the danger to his family, but I wouldn't let things stand. I insisted he leave Tykir with you, and Eirik at Athelstan's court. It's all my fault."

"Then we are just as much to blame for wanting Tykir here with us," Aud asserted. "Nay, 'twas the right decision. Thork could not live his entire life looking over his shoulder. These are dangerous times. All Vikings live with the possibility of death every day. We cannot stop living because we fear dying."

"Haven't you had any news from Thork since that note?" Ruby questioned fearfully.

Dar shifted his eyes, and Aud exclaimed, "Dar! Have you heard something and not told me?"

He shrugged forlornly. "I did not want to worry you. Two days past, 'twas word in Jorvik of a fierce battle that took place weeks ago." He inhaled sharply before continuing, "'Tis said that Ivar won and many Jomsvikings died, along with hundreds of other fighting men. Fifty Jomsvikings were captured and are to be executed."

Oh my God oh my God oh my God! Ruby clamped a hand over her mouth in horror, not wanting to hear more, yet needing to know the truth.

"I know naught of Thork or Eirik. Nor Selik and Olaf," Dar choked out.

"Sweet Jesus!" Aud wailed and fell into Dar arms.

Ruby watched in shocked silence, tears streaming down her face, with both hands over her stomach as if to protect her baby from the shock of these latest events.

399

Chapter Twenty-one

The battle had been a bloody nightmare and a resounding defeat for the Jomsvikings, thanks to Ivar's devious tactics. He'd lured them into a vulnerable position with promises to exchange Eirik for a king's fortune in gold. Thork had been prepared to pay it.

Thork slumped his head in weary remembrance of the carnage. So many men dead! So many friends gone on to Valhalla, or the Christian heaven. In truth, he did not know if he believed in the existence of either after what he had witnessed the past few weeks.

Worst of all, Olaf was dead, slain by Ivar's own sword. Damn his evil soul! Thork would gladly have exchanged his own life for his good friend's. He would probably die anyway. The hole in his chest, just below the heart, festered and continued to bleed. And Ivar, the vicious bastard, refused treatment for any of his prisoners, especially the Jomsvikings.

Today, Ivar promised, the real torture would begin. Hah!

As if they hadn't been tortured enough. Thork looked down at the three additional fingers that had been chopped off his left hand and grimaced. His lone, swollen thumb stood out grotesquely.

"Good thing you can still swing a sword with your right hand," Selik said dryly from his position next to him on the ground. All fifty of the Jomsvikings were tied together with one long length of rope. "Think you that you can still please your wife with all those fingers missing?" Selik teased morbidly.

Thork closed his eyes on the painful thought of Ruby and the fact that he would never see her again. When he got his emotions under control, Thork tried to grin at Selik over the intense pain in his chest.

"Is that all you can think of? Ivar starts the executions today and you have a woman's parts on your mind! Thor's balls! What woman will look at you with that ugly scar on your face now?"

"Do you think it ugly?" Selik countered arrogantly. "Methinks it makes me look the rogue. Methinks the women will love me more."

"Mayhap you are right," Thork conceded, examining the unhealed scar which ran from Selik's right eye to his chin.

"Well, at least Eirik is all right. Ivar does not seem to plan any more harm to him."

"Yea. Pray he will not," Thork sighed. Lord, 'twas all he lived for now, to see Eirik safe. He no longer hoped to save his own skin. "Selik, if we should not make it through this day, please know that you have been a good and true friend." He had trouble swallowing over the lump in his throat before he continued, "Perchance we will meet again in heaven—or Valhalla—whichever it may be."

Selik appeared to choke up but then gathered his usual wits about him. "'Tis sure you are we are headed in that direction? Mayhap you have been more the saint than I have."

Despite his excruciating pain, Thork smiled, but he knew they might not have another opportunity to speak and he had much to say yet. "Selik, if you should survive, promise that you will look out for my children . . . and Ruby." *Oh, God! Ruby! We had so little time together. So little time!*

Ivar's soldiers came and led the Jomsvikings, roped together in a long line like beads on a string, to the bailey outside the fortress. Hundreds of his followers gathered to witness the downfall of the famous Jomsvikings, wanting to see how their renowned valor would withstand death.

Thork saw Eirik off to the side with a group of other prisoners. He lifted his chin deliberately with a jerk to signal his son to be brave. Eirik, God bless his soul, raised his head proudly, his tearless eyes meeting his father's in youthful courage. Holy Thor! He was too young to have to display such valor.

Ivar's men released the first three Jomsvikings from their bonds and led them to the executioner, who twisted sticks in their long hair to bare their necks for his sharp blade.

Ivar stepped forward, preening before the crowd. If he only knew what a bloody replica he was of his hated enemy Sigtrygg! Having the same mountainous size, both bore the scars of numerous battles. Both carried themselves with an arrogant, vicious countenance. Both were ugly as sin.

"For years I have been told how brave you Jomsvikings are," Ivar said loudly to the assembled group. "'Twill be interesting to see if Jomsvikings die different from other mortal men," he sneered, then turned to the first Jomsviking brought forth. "What dost thou think about dying now?"

Ingolf, a veteran Jomsviking of at least twenty years,

curled his lip contemptuously at Ivar. "Jomsvikings do not fear death, just cowardice." He lowered his head to the block, and it was chopped off neatly in one stroke.

The next Jomsviking, Gaut, spit at Ivar's feet and snarled, "I die with a good reputation. You, Ivar, shall live with shame." Gaut, too, was decapitated.

"*Ram!*" shouted Hedin, the third Jomsviking, then "B-a-a, b-a-a, b-a-a." Ivar stopped the upraised hand of the executioner, a puzzled frown making his face even more ugly. "What is your meaning?" he bellowed.

Hedin lifted his chin a fraction from the block and stared out at Ivar's troops, "Are those not ewes who follow you?"

"You bastard!" Ivar yelled, spittle foaming at the edges of his mouth, and motioned for the executioner to continue.

When Ulf, a drinking companion of Selik's, was brought forward, he commented bravely, "I am well content to die as are all my comrades. But I will not let myself be slaughtered like a cow. I would rather face the blow."

The executioner hewed him in the face with his bloody sword.

By the time the tenth Jomsviking stepped up to the executioner, Ivar was clearly agitated because the executions were not going as he had planned. Undoubtedly, he wanted to see the elite Vikings grovel for mercy, to cry for salvation. The crowd was turning against him, murmuring with admiration for the brave warriors. Even his own soldiers no longer cheered over the deaths.

But Ivar doggedly repeated his question to the next man, Jogeir. "What dost thou think of dying?"

"I would like to piss first."

Thork shook his head at Jogeir's defiant vulgarity. Ivar's face turned almost purple with outraged disbelief but nodded his permission to do so. When Jogeir finished relieving himself boldly in front of the masses, he commented casually, "Life certainly turns out differently than expected. I had thought to skewer your wife afore returning to Jomsborg." At that, he shook his staff arrogantly, to the crowd's laughter, then pulled up his braies. His head was gone afore the pants were tied.

Thork closed his eyes painfully as Selik stepped forward. A few women in the crowd sighed loudly at his beauty. Apparently, Selik was right. The scar did not mar his handsomeness, after all.

"I have had a good life," Selik boasted, playing the crowd expertly, throwing his magnificent hair back over his shoulders. "I do not wish to live any longer than those brave comrades who have fallen afore me, but please give me the dignity of being led to my death by a warrior, not a mere thrall." He contemptuously scrutinized the executioner, who looked as if he might like to decapitate Selik with his bare hands. "Also, spare me that vile stick in my fine hair." He raked his fingers through the silver strands, and Thork saw several women in the crowd stare at him open-mouthed. "Instead, hold my hair away from my head and pull the head sharply so my hair does not become blood-stained. I wouldst enter Valhalla in all my beauty."

The crowd sighed in admiration at his beauty and bravado. The foolish lackwit! He joked even on the way to death. Thork blinked away the tears in his eyes.

Selik's daring words and godly appearance pleased the crowd so much that they cheered loudly and banged their shields, urging Ivar to grant the wish. He agreed reluctantly, calling a nearby hesir to assist. In a kneeling position, Selik bent his neck so his forehead touched the block. The soldier grabbed the thick strands of hair and twisted them into a queue, pulling painfully up and over his head. The executioner raised his blade, but at the last moment, Selik deliberately jerked and the hesir's arm was lopped off at the elbow.

The wounded man screamed as he clutched his bleeding stump. Enraged, Ivar grabbed the executioner's sword and was about to behead Selik himself. But the crowd loved Selik's audacity and moved forward in a wave of support.

"What is your name?" Ivar asked through gritted teeth, cautiously keeping an eye on the mutinous mob.

"Selik."

"How old are you?"

"Eighteen."

"Wouldst you join the ranks of my troops?" Ivar's eyes shifted uneasily to the mob which was quickly turning against him.

"Nay, I could not, but . . . ," Selik hesitated, seeming to assess the crowd's mood before continuing more boldly, "but if you would release me and my Jomsviking comrades, along with the boy, Eirik, I would swear an oath that we will leave your lands and never return."

Ivar judiciously turned to the angry people, asking, "Should the Jomsviking Selik be spared?" With shouted cheers and clanging shields, they voted to stay his execution.

Thork blinked disbelievingly. Selik would not die. In truth, they were all spared who lay here still on the ground awaiting execution. He started to smile, but then saw Ivar approaching. The hate on his face contorted his features into an ugly, monstrous mass of puffy flesh. He walked directly up to Thork and snarled, "Give this message to Sigtrygg: I will see him dead yet." For emphasis, he kicked Thork in the chest with his heavy boot.

Thork's wound opened again, and he fell into blessed unconsciousness.

For weeks, Ruby and Aud only went through the motions with their lingerie business. Orders continued to come in, and they filled them, thanks to Ella's amazing transformation into a businesswoman.

The next time Ruby was paid with a bag of coins for her lingerie sales, she asked Dar if she could buy Ella's freedom. He shooed away her offers of money and told her Ella was a gift to do with as she willed.

"I cannot belief you wud do this fer me," Ella blubbered when Ruby told her she was no longer a thrall. "There be naught in the whole wurld I wud not do fer you."

"There is something, Ella. If something should happen to Thork . . . ," Ruby choked out, "and if I should disappear suddenly, promise you'll always be here to help Tykir . . . and Eirik. Dar and Aud are old. They may need your help."

In fact, it was Ruby who needed Aud's help in assisting her to her room two days later when the message came:

Thork received grievous chest wound. Eirik and I make haste to bring him home. Have healing potions ready. Does not look good. Olaf is dead.

Selik

They traveled the next day to Jorvik to be with Gyda and her family in their mourning and to await Thork's ship. A red-eyed Gyda told Ruby that night after they'd tucked the frightened girls into bed, "Twould seem that conversation we had long ago is about to come true for me."

"What do you mean?"

"Remember when you asked if I craved equality, to be partners with Olaf in heading our family? I said that I am more than capable of running all our affairs when forced to do so, but I preferred to defer to my husband."

"Yes, I remember now. We were talking about a woman's identity."

"Yea, that was it." Gyda raked her fingers distractedly through her unkempt hair which had come loose from its usual braid. "No choice do I have now in defining myself.

I am Gyda. I am no longer Olaf's wife."

Gyda wept, letting loose all the pent-up sorrow she'd been unable to release in front of the children. As much as she tried to comfort Gyda, Ruby wondered if she wouldn't be in the same position on Thork's return. Until that happened, Ruby tried to help Tykir as much as she could.

"I wish I wuz older," the fierce, frightened little boy exclaimed, trying hard not to cry. "I wud be a Jomsviking and go to save my father. I wud chop off Ivar's head just like that." He made a slash with his arm to demonstrate.

Aud came in then, and they both comforted the boy.

"Whatever happens, Tykir and Ruby, you will have a home with us in Northumbria. We are family, and we must stay together. Family. That is everything."

A distraught Dar brought the first news a week later. "Thork's ship entered the Humber at dawn and will not stop to camp. He will be here by nightfall, God willing."

Ruby and Aud went to the Church of St. Mary's and knelt in hopeful prayer for hours. The entire family walked solemnly to the harbor as evening approached. In fact, little by little, hundreds of people arrived, standing silently, come to pay tribute to the fallen warriors. Even Sigtrygg and Byrnhil stood respectfully at the front with the royal retainers, awaiting the ship.

Stone silence greeted the dragonship as it slid into its berth. Gyda's keening wail grew increasingly loud at the sight of the first cloak-wrapped body carried off the ship on a litter. Olaf's trusty sword lay on top. Gyda and her sobbing daughters followed the body to a waiting wagon.

Ruby held tightly to Tykir's hand as dozens of men came next, some missing limbs, all wounded in some horrible way. Their bleak eyes stared straight ahead.

Finally Thork emerged, supported by Eirik and Selik. He was barely conscious, and blood seeped from a white linen bandage wrapped around his chest. His long, blond hair lay dirty and matted with blood—the same beautiful hair that Ruby had admired, especially when braided off to one side, highlighted by the scandalous earring.

His dazed eyes scanned the crowd anxiously. When he found Ruby, he smiled. At least he tried to smile. It seemed to hurt him to do even that.

Ruby bled inside at the pain in Thork's bleak eyes, the unhealed scars on his forehead, chin and arms, the bleeding chest wound. Then she saw his fingerless hand, with only a thumb left. She gasped and closed her eyes briefly for strength.

Oh, God, just let him live. That's all I ask. Just let him live.

Tykir ran to his father and wrapped his arms around his waist, sobbing pitifully. Thork patted his shoulder with painful effort.

Ruby walked up then and put both hands on either side of Thork's head. She kissed his cracked lips gently, tears streaming down her cheeks. She tenderly stroked the cuts on his face.

"Seems to me you are blubbering every time I see you, wench," Thork teased in a shaky voice. There were tears in his eyes, too. "I told you I would come back. Did you doubt me?" Then he pulled her brusquely into his arms, burying his face in her neck.

Her body shook with sobs. She could not speak.

Thork pulled away and examined her face, alarmed at how haggard she looked. His eyes sparkled sadly as he tried to joke, "You look a sight, woman. Mayhap you have had no one to tweak your sweet arse whilst I was gone and that has turned you weepish."

"Oh, Thork!" Ruby smiled weakly. "Come with me. Let me take you home."

Several men, including Selik who now had a horrendous scar down the side of his face, helped Thork to the straw-filled wagon which would carry him to Sigtrygg's palace, there being no room for invalid care in Gyda's home. Thork's wounds would never withstand the trip to Dar's home.

By the time they got to the palace, fever racked Thork's body. In the days that followed, he alternated between delirious fever and weak consciousness. When he was lucid, he insisted on talking to Ruby, who stayed by his side.

"Thork, we're going to have a baby," she told him the first chance she could. "I know you didn't want any more children, but—"

"Oh, Rube," he said incredulously, twining her fingers in his good hand, "we made a baby together."

"You're not angry?"

"Nay, sweetling," he said, a gentle smile tilting his lips upward. "'Twas inevitable that some of my seed slip in your womb. I visited so often." He squeezed her hand to show he jested. "Truly, 'tis wondrous that you and I made a child together. The babe will be magnificent, I wager."

Even those few words strained his strength, and he fell back on the bed, closing his eyes. But a slight smile relaxed his lips as he slept. Ruby hoped it was dreams of their child that pleased him so.

The next day he told her, "If I die, my brother Eric should relent. No, Ruby, you must listen. Eric would have no reason to pursue my sons if I am gone."

The next time he awakened, he exclaimed feverishly, "I love you, sweetling. I did not realize how much till I left you. If I had it to do over, I would take your advice and cherish the moment. We had so little time together, Ruby. So little time. There should have been more."

King Athelstan arrived on the third day, totally unannounced. He and his resplendently clad guard strode through the palace with Sigtrygg to Thork's chamber. Luckily, it was one of Thork's lucid periods.

Athelstan sat in a chair next to the bed, nodding first

at Ruby, then taking Thork's fingerless hand in his. "My friend, I am so sorry. 'Tis my fault the boy was taken whilst in my care. Whether you live or die—and God willing, 'twill be the former—Eirik is welcome back in my court, and this I promise, I will guard him with my own life this time."

"'Tis the boy's decision." Thork's words trailed off, and he slipped back into his fever.

Eirik had been a remote, solitary boy before he left for Athelstan's court. Now he stood vigil silently at his father's bedside, a ten-year-old boy but no longer a child. God knows what he'd been through while held captive by Ivar.

"I will pray to St. Cuthbert for his intercession on Thork's behalf," Athelstan told Ruby sympathetically before going off with Eirik and Sigtrygg. He came back several times during the next two days to talk with Thork, but there was nothing he could do for Thork and he finally departed.

Despite Ruby's prayers and the powerful healing herbs he was given, Thork grew weaker by the day. Dar and Aud were practically catatonic with grief. Tykir was kept away from his father's chamber because of his outbursts of fear which upset Thork and everyone else. Eirik was stoic in hiding the turmoil which must have been rocking his soul. Ruby lived one day at a time, trying to survive, hoping for the best.

One week after Thork's return to Jorvik, a great uproar took place outside the palace. Ruby was too disheartened to make the effort to go to a window and see what was happening. Soon the loud voices entered the palace, accompanied by a booming voice and much running.

"Where is my son?" someone bellowed imperiously.

Ruby looked up to see an enormous bear of a man filling the doorway, blocking out all of the people behind him.

Outraged, Ruby hissed, "Get out of here! Can't you see we have a sick man here?"

The giant didn't budge. "Who are you, wench?" he demanded with supreme arrogance.

"I'm Thork's wife. Who the hell are you?"

"I am Thork's father." He glowered down at her as he scrutinized her through pale blue eyes—eyes that mirrored Thork's.

Stunned, Ruby examined the old man more thoroughly. Dressed in a black velvet cloak, embroidered with gold thread and studded with precious jewels, he towered over her, about the same height as Thork but bulkier. His pure white hair hung exceedingly well-groomed all the way to his shoulder blades, held in place by a gold circlet around his forehead.

Ruby saw through the open doorway that a number of splendidly dressed noble Vikings filled the hallway, probably companions or family to this King Harald of Norway. Even Sigtrygg stood in the background in deference to the mighty ruler. But Ruby wasn't impressed. This was the same father who'd neglected his son for years, who'd failed to protect him from his vicious brother, who'd never showed an ounce of affection.

Without being invited in, Harald walked regally to the bed and sat down in a chair. You would have thought it was a bloody throne. Placing a hand on Thork's chest, he said in a surprisingly gentle voice, "Thork, 'tis your father come to see you."

Thork opened his eyes slowly and blinked in astonishment. "Father! What brings you here? Have I died already and gone to hell?"

Harald smiled wanly. "Nay, alive you are, and if I can help it, you will remain so. I have brought my own healer with me. I came as soon as I heard."

Thork arched his eyebrows disbelievingly at his father. "Didst your brother Eric have aught to do with this?"

411

Harald's mouth formed a thin line of displeasure and his eyes narrowed dangerously.

"Nay, not this time," Thork answered with a short laugh at his father's belated concern over Eric's deadly games. "'Twas Ivar."

"This I promise you, son, Ivar will be dead within the month, a blood-eagle on his back and your name carved in his chest."

Thork tried to shake his head as his strength faded again. "'Tis no longer important—the killing. 'Tis all a waste."

"No man harms my son and lives to boast of it," the Norse king avowed with a steely voice.

"It all comes back to you, as always, does it not, Father?" Thork accused tiredly. "Why then didst you let my brother pursue me so?"

King Harald's face grew hard and his lips trembled with indignation at his son's harsh words. Finally he said, "I let him loose on you to make you strong, and it succeeded. You are the strongest of all my sons—the best of the litter."

"The litter!" Thork choked on the exclamation. Ruby glared at Harald, trying to tell him silently that he was not helping his son. Thork muttered weakly, "'Twas all I ever was—one of your vast get, no more important than a dog."

Harald inhaled sharply at Thork's insult, then said softly, almost apologetically, "'Tis not true, Thork. I did care, and I promise you this, if you should die, Eric will never harm your sons."

Thork grew agitated then and tried to sit up. "Do not think of taking either of my sons back with you. Stay out of their lives. I will not allow you to ruin their lives as you did mine."

Harald stood, leaning angrily over his son, and appeared about to argue with him, then stopped suddenly. "So be it.

You have my word. I will also let it be known throughout the Viking world that any who harm the boys will answer to me and my armies."

Thork's eyes turned to Ruby as he sank back down to the bed. He held out his hand to her. Ruby sat down on the mattress next to him and caressed the back of his hand.

"The boys will be safe now, sweetling. I can rest now. Whatever else he does, my father honors his word."

Unfortunately, King Harald's personal healer was unable to help Thork. Most of the time now, he lay in delirious fever, his lips cracked and bleeding, his eyes closed. At dusk on the twentieth day, Ruby stood near the window, staring ahead sightlessly. She looked down at the dragon brooch she held in her hand, caressing the pin fondly. Absently she stuck it in the pocket of her jeans, which she'd taken to wearing again while King Harald was in residence, just to infuriate him.

Thork suddenly sat up in bed with a shout and opened his eyes wide, looking straight at Ruby. "I saw us, Rube. I saw it all," he exclaimed. "There was a long tunnel and at the end nothing but beautiful brightness. Then I saw you . . . and me. At least it looked like me . . . but somehow different."

Perspiration beaded on his furrowed forehead, and Ruby tried to get him to lie back. He refused, having somehow regained his strength.

"Thork, lie down. It was just a dream," Ruby soothed, trying to push him gently back.

"Nay, listen to me, Rube. 'Tis important," he rasped out, as if it hurt him to speak. He clutched her hand in an iron grasp. "The images I saw at the end of the passageway . . . you and that other me . . . together. 'Twas so precious. It made my heart swell with happiness. Do not lose it, Rube. Whatever you do, do . . . not . . . lose . . ."

He fell back then, heavily, his hand still clutching hers

413

tightly. Ruby didn't have to touch his chest to know the truth.

Thork was dead.

Ruby screamed and threw herself over Thork, shaking him, trying desperately to get him to awaken. Then, as if rising outside her own body, Ruby saw Aud, Dar, Tykir and Eirik staring at her and Thork from the other side of the bed—pitifully—with tears streaming down all their faces.

Ruby heard a high-pitched, wailing scream somewhere. It got louder and louder, closer and closer, seemed to move inside her head, swirling, swirling. Then it exploded.

Utter, eternal silence billowed over her like a soft, comforting cloud.

Chapter Twenty-two

"Click! Click! Click!"

Ruby opened her eyes slowly, reluctantly, and looked down. She blinked disbelievingly.

A cassette player lay in her lap, clicking away. The motivational tape had run its course. Ruby pressed the off-button with a dull robotlike movement.

Not sure if she was still dreaming, or finally awake, Ruby put a palm to her chest as if to calm her wildly thudding heart. Goosebumps swept her skin like slow-moving dominoes as awareness crept into her consciousness degree by infinitesimal degree.

She had returned to the twentieth century.

Or had she ever left?

Ruby could no longer separate the dream from reality. Sitting up straight, she put the tape player aside and held a hand to her forehead, trying desperately to understand what had happened to her.

Jack had left her, Ruby remembered with a groan of

despair. She'd come into his library and put one of his motivational tapes in the machine, hoping pathetically to come up with some answers to the mess she'd made of her life. The speaker on the tape had promised that anything in life was possible if a person willed it strongly enough, and Ruby had foolishly wished she were twenty years younger and could live her life over knowing what she did today.

Oh, Lord!

Had she really traveled back in time? No, it wasn't possible.

Searching her brain for other alternatives, she wondered if she might be having a nervous breakdown. It was a definite possibility, but people having nervous breakdowns flipped out totally, didn't they? Oh, well, if there was such a thing as "walking pneumonia," maybe she was having a "walking nervous breakdown."

Disoriented, Ruby frantically searched Jack's study for clues. Everything remained the same, just as it always was. The clock on the shelf above the desk ticked away. Five o'clock. *Oh, my God!* Only two hours since Jack had left! How was that possible?

Suddenly, memory rolled over Ruby like a tidal wave, and she cried aloud with the pain of it.

"Thork! Oh, please, God, don't let Thork be dead." She frowned. What was she saying? Thork didn't exist. Jack did.

Ruby raked the splayed fingers of both hands through her hair and held them there. Rocking back and forth, she wailed sorrowfully in desolation over the death of her Viking husband. An inner, nagging voice viewed her mourning as irrational, and yet, at the same time, Ruby could not stop herself.

Her head pounding with the beginnings of a killer migraine, she stood and walked woodenly to the downstairs bathroom for an aspirin. As she filled a cup with water, about to put the pill in her mouth, Ruby looked into the mirror above the sink. The cup and aspirin fell from her shaking hands.

A tear-streaked, thirty-eight-year-old face stared back at her with its chic Sassoon hairstyle. It was an attractive face, but with the first stages of those hated tiny laugh lines flanking her eyes and mouth.

Thirty-eight! Hell!

Ruby looked down at her son's Brass Balls T-shirt and her jeans. She hesitated, sensing what she'd find, then undid the waistband of her jeans and peeked below.

Yup! Stretch marks!

"Shit!" Ruby said aloud.

She could almost guarantee that if she pulled the jeans down farther she'd find the beginnings of cellulite on her thighs. *Well, just a little!* Ruby told herself with near-hysterical irrelevance. A slight grin tugged at the corners of her mouth. Criminey! She was having a nervous breakdown and making jokes with herself.

The hall phone rang, jarring Ruby's senses. She picked it up on the second ring. Maybe it was Jack.

It wasn't.

"Mom, can I go to Greg's house after football practice? His mom said I could sleep over. We're gonna rent videos."

"I guess it would be all right, Eddie, as long as his parents will be there," Ruby said, the normalcy of her voice striking her as odd. Actually, she was thankful to put off her painful discussion with her sons about their father's leaving. "Make sure you behave yourself, and don't forget to thank Mrs. Summers for having you."

Ruby realized then, with a rueful giggle, that maternal instincts must kick in automatically. They didn't require sanity at all.

"Oh, yeah, I'll behave," Eddie promised with sick teenage humor. "I promise not to puke all over their carpet during the beer party."

"Eddie, that's *not* funny."

"Lighten up, Mom. It was just a joke."

Ruby realized then that David should have been home from school. "Do you have any idea where your brother is?"

"Are you losin' it, Mom? You told him this morning that Grandma was pickin' him up after school and that he could spend the weekend with her."

"Oh, that's right. I remember now."

"Mom, are you all right?" Eddie asked worriedly.

No, I am definitely not all right, Ruby thought, but she told her son, "Sure, hon, I just woke up from a nap and I'm a little groggy."

"I'll see you tomorrow afternoon then."

"Bye-bye, hon."

Ruby walked into the kitchen and made herself a cup of instant coffee. Sitting at the kitchen table, she drummed her fingers distractedly. Thoughts twirled at random in her head.

Okay, these were the facts. Something had happened to her today, Ruby was convinced of that. It didn't matter that only two hours had passed. She could never have dreamt all those characters and events—Jorvik, Gyda, Olaf, all their daughters, including lovable Tyra, Dar and Aud, Eirik and Tykir, gossipy Ella. Ruby grinned at that last thought. Imagine dreaming of a Viking version of her cleaning lady! Not to mention all those other people—Sigtrygg, Byrnhil, Selik, King Athelstan, King Harald.

And Thork! Most of all, *Thork!*

Ruby's heart ached for her Norse husband who was Jack but not really Jack. Her sweet, ferocious Viking who had suffered so and then died. They'd had such a short time together.

It was all so confusing.

Suddenly inspired, Ruby went back to Jack's library where she pulled several encyclopedias off the shelf. With each enlightening paragraph she read, Ruby's heart beat faster and her head spun. Good Lord! York, England, had indeed been called Jorvik during the Viking period. A Norse king, Sigtrygg One-Eye, did marry a sister of the Saxon King Athelstan, and the vain Harald, high-king of Norway, did have many wives and children who fought bloodily among themselves for his crown.

"How could I have known all those things?" Ruby wondered aloud.

Reading more, she found that eventually Eric Bloodaxe, Thork's half-brother, became the king of Jorvik, and, in fact, was the last of the Norse kings to reign in Northumbria. Young Haakon, Thork's other half-brother, later called Haakon the Good, ruled Norway. Perhaps Athelstan's scholarly court had influenced Haakon in the right direction.

The revealing information stunned Ruby. Unable to absorb any more for now, she put the books down.

"Mizzus Jordan, I'm leavin' now."

Ruby jumped in alarm at the voice and went out to the hall. "Rhoda, what are you doing here so late?"

"I was jus' finishin' up the ironin'. Do ya want me to come two days next week soz I kin start on the windows?"

Ruby nodded, then smiled, seeing the *National Enquirer* rolled up under Rhoda's arm.

"Ya okay? Ya look awful funny." Rhoda scrutinized her myopically through her bifocals.

Oh, yeah! I'm just bloody wonderful. Did you happen to see a longship in the backyard? Ruby quipped silently, but kept her thoughts to herself. She didn't need ditzy Rhoda involved in this nightmare. Calmly she answered, "I'm fine. Just tired."

" 'Member what I toldja 'bout that bug that's goin' 'round. Read about it in my papers. Came all the way from China. Only thing that kin cure it is garlic pills."

419

Ruby paid her, with a grin, and shooed her out the door before Rhoda launched into retelling one of her tabloid stories. She'd probably explain Ruby's whole time-travel experience as something involving aliens from outer space.

What now? Ruby wondered as her nerves unraveled one strand at a time. Perhaps a shower would help. After that, she would try to resolve the mess she'd made of her life, try to understand what was happening to her.

Standing in the bathroom, about to remove her clothes, Ruby happened to glance in the full-length mirror on the door and saw something sticking out of her jeans pocket. She gasped on recognizing it, then sank to the floor. All the tension she'd been holding inside exploded with loud, shuddering sobs that racked her body.

Ruby cried for Thork and his death. She cried for the short time they'd had together and the love they'd shared too briefly. She cried for the two "sons" she'd left behind and mourned the primitive life-style and brave, fierce people she had come to love and would miss dearly. And she wept for the mess she'd made of her life with Jack.

And all the time she clutched in her hand one of the priceless dragon brooches Thork had given her. She really had traveled back in time—whether in a dream or actuality, she didn't know. It didn't matter. All Ruby knew was that somehow she'd visited there. The experience had been real, not imagined. What she had to figure out now was why.

When the tears dried up and Ruby could cry no more, she stepped into the shower and let the hot spray soothe her. Afterward, like a puppet being led by someone else's strings, Ruby rummaged through her closet until she found just the item she wanted—a black teddy Jack had given her years ago before she formed her own company. She always wore it on special occasions. After she dressed, she went down to the kitchen and made another cup of coffee.

It was only seven p.m. She felt caught in a time warp.

Ruby opened the freezer door and searched for the box of phyllo dough in the back, hoping it wasn't freezer-burned after all this time. She took the paper-thin dough out, along with the other ingredients, and began to make a tray of baklava.

"You're going over the edge, girl," Ruby told herself later with a shrill laugh as she removed the tray from the oven. "Do you really think you can lure a husband back with a plate of pastry?"

Ruby stopped suddenly in the midst of cutting the diamond shapes. Was that what she wanted? To get Jack back?

Yes!

Ruby wrapped her arms around herself and closed her eyes on a warm rush of relief. Finally she was beginning to see a light in this jumble of questions. For some reason, God only knew what, she'd been handed this time-travel experience to learn something. Ruby had sensed in her "dream" that she'd been given an opportunity to understand her problems with Jack by being with Thork, his Viking-age equivalent.

Could it be that God, or whoever, had played this massive joke on her and was really offering her a second chance with her husband—if only she could learn a lesson from the past?

Ruby smiled widely and steeled herself for the ordeal ahead. Now that she knew her mission, Ruby hurriedly wrapped the plate of baklava in plastic, grabbed her purse and locked the house. Within minutes, she was on the highway that led to the lake house. During the one-hour trip, she pondered her strange time adventure and tried to fathom the lessons to be learned.

When the bright lights of a small shopping mall caught her attention, Ruby pulled over, having a sudden flash of inspiration. She made her few purchases and walked out of the department store with a mischievous grin on her face.

If her scheme didn't work, at least she'd give Jack a good laugh. Ruby grimaced at the thought.

A cloud of darkness blanketed the sky when Ruby pulled up to the modern A-frame she and Jack had purchased ten years ago on the lake. Jack had parked his BMW at the side.

She shivered when she got out of the car with her shopping bag and baklava. She hadn't realized how chilly it was when she'd left the house without a coat. Or maybe it was nerves.

Ruby knocked lightly on the door, then walked in without waiting for Jack to answer. If he was entertaining "company," then so be it.

Jack lay on the sofa before the fireplace with a glass of Scotch in one hand, still wearing his suit pants and white shirt. He'd removed the jacket and opened the first two buttons of the shirt, but other than that, he looked much the same as he had earlier that day. The television screen was dark, but soft music played on the stereo.

Jack stood when he heard the door shut and confronted her with a questioning tilt of his head. Sparks of a strong, indecipherable emotion flashed briefly in his pale blue eyes, a sharp contrast against the remnants of his summer tan. A tense muscle jerked in his cheek.

After all the turmoil she'd been through that day, Ruby yearned to throw herself into the comfort of Jack's arms, but she knew they had too many issues to resolve first. Instead, she feasted her eyes on him, as if seeing him for the first time. She took in his wide shoulders which strained the fabric of his cotton shirt, tapering down to an athletically slim waist and hips, and a flat, well-conditioned stomach. He put both hands in the pockets of his pants with deliberate casualness, thus pulling the fabric taut across his strong thighs and hard buttocks.

Ruby's throat tightened and she forced her eyes back up to his face. He needed a haircut, she noticed irrelevantly. His dark blond hair hung to the edge of his collar. She tried to picture it even longer, braided on one side, and his ear lobe sporting a thunderbolt earring. She couldn't help but smile at the image. Jack frowned, probably thinking she was amused at his expense.

Good Lord! Jack looked just like Thork when he glared like that. A little older, a few gray hairs, a little less muscle, but what a remarkable resemblance!

"What the hell are you doing here, Ruby?"

He gazed at her with burning concentration, but there was no warm welcome in his voice. Ruby's heart sank. This was going to be much harder than she'd thought.

"Where is she?" she asked weakly, grasping at the first words that entered her head.

"Who?"

"Dolly Parton. I thought you would've found her by now." Ruby's voice wobbled with nervousness.

Jack stared at her quizzically, shifting impatiently from foot to foot. Suddenly he remembered and a grin curved his lips slightly, but did not reach his eyes. He shook his head incredulously.

"I wasn't up to Dolly Parton tonight. Jack Daniels suits my mood better."

His discerning eyes impaled her, not giving an inch.

"Are you up to *me?*" Ruby asked shakily, hating the vulnerability of her question.

Disbelief swept Jack's features before he forced them back to impassivity. "Go home, Rube," he ordered flatly. "You've already pushed me to the edge. I can't guarantee what I'll do—"

"Jack, I'm sorry. Please, let's talk about—"

"No!" he declared icily, grabbing her arm and turning her forcibly toward the door. "I told you this afternoon that the time for talking was over. Dammit, can't you see that I've had enough?"

Ruby's heart ached at the sad hopelessness in Jack's eyes. Lord, she must have been blind not to have seen how much she'd hurt him these past months. She had to convince him that their marriage was still salvageable.

"Jack, please listen to me. Something important happened to me today after you left," Ruby injected quickly as she pulled out of his grip and ducked around him and back into the living room. "I need to tell you about it."

"What?"

"Well, I had a really weird experience," Ruby began, licking her dry lips, "This thing that happened . . . well, it made me do a lot of thinking, and anyhow, I made some baklava for you, and I wondered if I could make some coffee to go with it and we could talk." Ruby knew she was rambling senselessly, but how could she possibly explain her time-travel to Jack with him hovering over her, so resistant, practically pushing her out the door?

"What the hell is going on with you?" His eyes narrowed suspiciously as they raked over her. "You look different."

"I *am* different. That's what I've been trying to tell you." Choking back tears, she turned to the kitchen, needing a minute to get her emotions under control. She kept swallowing hard to prevent herself from crying. Pity was not part of her plan.

Plan! Ruby remembered another plan, in another time, and how that had turned out. She closed her eyes on the painful thought.

"Are you crying?" Jack asked, exhaling sharply with exasperation as he followed her into the kitchen.

"No," she lied on a broken sob.

"Please, Ruby, you know I can't stand it when you cry." He put a hand on her shoulder and turned her, only to

424

exclaim, "Where did you get that pin?"

"Huh?" Ruby looked down and saw the dragon brooch on the lapel of her blouse. She smiled and touched it gently. "From you," she answered without thinking.

"Cut the crap, Ruby. I never gave you that pin, and whoever did must have spent a fortune. It looks *very* valuable." His bleak eyes accused her angrily before he pivoted away.

He was jealous. Oddly pleased, Ruby put a hand on Jack's arm, running her fingers tenderly over the crisp fabric before she could stop herself, and told him softly, "Jack, I didn't get it from another man. And I've never been with anybody but you." Well, that was sort of the truth, Ruby rationalized.

He jerked his arm away from her, but when he turned back, Ruby saw that the anger and jealousy had disappeared, replaced with a weary desolation. Adultery was not the problem between them, and never had been.

"Where are the boys?"

Ruby told him, and he seemed satisfied. She was glad he didn't ask if she'd told them yet about his leaving. While she prepared the coffee, he sipped his drink and watched her every move with wary suspicion.

"Will you pour me a brandy until the coffee is ready?" she asked. As she sipped the potent liquor, hoping it would give her courage, she prepared a tray to take into the living room. Finally she set the tray on a table near the couch while Jack put more wood on the fire.

"This room and that fireplace bring back so many memories of happy times here," she said wistfully.

"Give me a break, Ruby. You haven't been here in more than a year," Jack reminded her. "The boys and I are the only ones who come anymore—for fishing."

Jack finished his drink in one long swallow, then sat down and ate one of her pastries, sipping the black coffee. Then he ate another, and another. Ruby realized that he probably hadn't eaten all day. The kitchen showed no evidence of use.

Ruby stared at him miserably as he sat eating in cold silence. How could she get through that shield he'd erected around himself?

"I remember when you bought this place," Ruby mused, running her fingertip absently around the rim of her empty coffee cup. "It was our tenth wedding anniversary. Your business was booming and you wanted to celebrate in a big way."

Jack stared at his hands, listening but saying nothing. Suddenly Ruby remembered something else. "Do you remember how we christened the house? Right here in front of the fireplace?"

Jack jumped up off the sofa and stood hovering over her.

"Stop it, Ruby. Just stop it." He picked up his suit jacket and jerked out, "If you won't leave, I will."

Desperation overwhelmed Ruby. She had to stop him.

"Jack, what would you do today if you knew there would be no tomorrows?" The foolish, desperate question was tossed at his departing back.

Jack swiveled and his eyes shot up in surprise. His lips curled downward with annoyance. "Rube, I'm not in the mood for silly games. Give me a break and—"

Ruby halted his words with a raised palm. "No, I'm serious. It's an important question. Please, Jack, indulge me."

Jack stared at her for a long moment, then dropped his jacket on a chair and sat back down, staring forlornly into the fire. Finally his eyes lifted and stabbed hers demandingly.

"You tell me, Rube."

"Well, actually, I did ask myself that question today after this weird experience that I'll tell you about later," Ruby began hesitantly. "I didn't even have to think twice.

I realized I would beg you to come home and give me a second chance. This love you and I had . . . have . . . is too precious to lose."

Precious! That was the word Thork had used just before he died.

A muscle twitched beside Jack's lips. "I love you, Rube. I probably always will, but love isn't enough for me anymore."

"What do you want me to do? I'll do anything if you'll just—"

"Don't beg, and don't make promises you can't keep," Jack said.

Ruby blinked rapidly to keep the tears welling in her eyes from overflowing. Swallowing the lump in her throat, she continued to plead her case. "You probably don't remember this, but I was thinking today about that time when we were eighteen and you asked me to marry you. You said, 'We can make it work. I'll love you forever.' And then—"

"I remember," Jack interrupted coldly. "I remember *all* of it, but that was a long time ago."

"—and then I thought of all the good times we've had," Ruby persisted. "I can't just let it go without a fight."

"Why are you doing this? And why now?" he groaned and put his hands over his eyes. Lifting his head, his gaze met hers again, full of pain. "Nothing, absolutely nothing, is any different. I told you this afternoon that the time for words was over. I want out. I'm going to miss you like hell, Ruby," and his voice cracked before he went on, "but I'm sick of the arguments and pain. Our marriage sucks."

"That's not true," Ruby choked out.

"Ruby, let it go. You're breaking my heart. We're breaking each other's hearts."

"Maybe we needed to do that to start healing. Mayhap we can glue each other's hearts back together again, and be even stronger."

"Mayhap?" Jack asked with an arched eyebrow.

Ruby grinned at her slip into the Viking speech pattern and continued to plead, "Things *are* different now. I'll show you. I'll make it up to you. Just let me try."

"How?" Jack demanded as he stood over her with hands on hips. "Are you going to give up your business? Are you suddenly going to become Supermom? Will you make my breakfast in the morning and be waiting for me at the door at night?"

Ruby gulped at his harsh words. "Is that what you want?"

Jack ran his fingers through his hair in agitation.

"Hell, no! I want a woman to love, who will love me in return. I want to be the most important thing in her life, not a G-string."

"You are."

"I'm not and haven't been for a long time."

"You *are!* I just haven't told you or shown you enough, I guess."

"Damn right, you haven't. When was the last time we made love, Rube?"

"I . . . I don't know," Ruby admitted feebly, trying hard to remember. How could she forget something so important?

"Well, I do. It was six weeks ago, and you were so tired I may as well have been screwing a light bulb."

Ruby gasped at his condemnation of her lovemaking. Her stomach churned at the deterioration she saw in her plans for tonight and for their future. Suddenly the implacable expression on his face sunk in.

Their marriage was over.

"I feel sick. I have to go to the bathroom."

Jack looked incredulous that she'd interrupt their conversation so abruptly, then threw out his hands. "What's the use! I feel like puking my guts out, too."

Ruby saw her shopping bag as she dashed for the

The Reluctant Viking

bathroom and picked it up. The last thing she wanted was for Jack to look inside and discover the extent of her foolishness.

Locking the bathroom door, she sank down to the floor and bit her fist to keep Jack from hearing the sobs that racked her body.

It was too late for them. Jack had made that clear. She'd waited too long.

It appeared that all her lessons had gained her nothing—Gyda's words of family and making the man feel important, the head of the household; Thork's telling her to cherish the moment and relish the gift of love; her realization when his death appeared imminent that family and the love of a good man constituted the most important things in the world, not business success.

She remembered, too, with a sad grin how Thork had told her on their wedding night that he loved her most because she made him smile. Well, dammit, that was one thing she could still make Jack do—smile. If nothing else, this marriage would not end with a whimper. It would end her way—with a bang of laughter.

Ruby took off her clothes with angry determination, right down to the stupid black silk teddy which she'd donned earlier to please Jack.

"Are you all right in there?" Jack asked through the closed door.

Now he worried! "Go away!"

"Let me in."

"Leave me alone. I'll be out in a minute."

Ruby swiped at her eyes and pulled her purchases out of the shopping bag. She smiled with wicked delight. She'd show her stubborn husband. He'd see just what he would be missing. Then he'd be sorry.

At least, she hoped that was the way it would turn out. She sighed woefully, then lifted her chin resolutely.

First she twisted and contorted her body to fit into the

siren-red, skin-tight, spandex body suit, then slid her feet into a pair of matching high heels. Next she pulled the long blond wig out of the bag and put it on. She looked in the small mirror over the sink, and almost fainted.

Giggles bubbled on her lips. Good heavens! In trying to look like the blond chippie in spandex that she'd told Jack about earlier today, the one he would probably be looking for once he left her, she'd turned herself into an aging Madonna. If she struck out with Jack, she quipped to herself ruefully, she could always stop at a bikers' bar on the way home.

But, even as she made mental jokes with herself, Ruby wept inside at the thought of losing Jack forever.

Jack was leaning his head against one forearm on the fireplace mantel when Ruby returned. His other hand held a second glass of Scotch.

Ruby faltered at the look of abject desolation on his face. She had brought him so low. But then, she figured she had nothing else to lose, and neither did he.

Ruby posed provocatively against the door jamb, fearing she looked more silly than sexy.

"Hey, buddy, could you give a girl a ride in your new Corvette?"

Jack turned and his glass fell to the floor, shattering and splashing liquor on the carpet.

"Holy shit!" He swallowed hard and gaped at her, then burst out laughing. Not a little laugh. This was side-splitting, deep-from-the-stomach mirth.

Ruby frowned in annoyance, but went on weakly, "I told you earlier today that you would probably be wanting to find a young chippie in spandex." Ruby wilted, beginning to feel extremely foolish while Jack laughed his stupid, bloody head off. "I just figured maybe I . . . maybe I could be that chippie," she faltered.

"Chippie? Chippie? Oh, my God! Are you out of your mind?" Jack choked out, holding his side as if in pain.

"Some chippie you make with mascara running down your face." He burst out laughing again.

Ruby touched her hot cheeks. Her fingertips came away black.

When Jack's laughter died down and he'd wiped his still-twinkling eyes, he asked in surprise, "Why are you crying anyhow?"

"I am *not* crying," Ruby denied, even as tears streamed down her cheeks. She turned blindly to run back to the bathroom, mortified to have made such a fool of herself.

Jack caught up with her in the hall and pulled her back to the living room, struggling all the way. Finally he picked her up and held her in his steely arms to prevent her escape. She kicked him with her high heels, and he said a foul word, but would not release her. They both fell back, half on, half off the couch.

She continued to fight, and Jack forced both her arms over her head and held them down with his hands. He pinned her lower body to the edge of the sofa with his hips, his face buried against her neck. Ruby smelled his cologne and the sweet scent of honey from the baklava. She closed her eyes and ceased struggling for a moment, wanting to surrender to Jack's glorious embrace.

But it wasn't really an embrace, Ruby soon realized as Jack smiled against her neck, whispering, "Oh, Rube, you haven't done anything this outrageous since the time you talked me into shaving your legs."

"*What?* I did no such thing," Ruby asserted indignantly, trying unsuccessfully to buck him off. "*You* are the one who seduced *me* with *that* idea."

She felt his heart hammering against her breasts, and it felt so good. No, darn him, it wasn't his heart; his chest was shaking with laughter again.

"Let me go," she demanded on a sob.

Jack pulled away, just a little. His knowing look and gleaming eyes told her he'd been teasing. He'd known

431

exactly who had seduced whom, could probably remember every damned enticing word he'd spoken to her that long, passion-filled night. A dazzling smile split Jack's face as he looked down at her with amusement and . . . what? Ruby couldn't quite figure it out.

"Your wig is all crooked," Jack observed with a tilted grin, shaking his head in wonderment at the ridiculous sight she must be.

Ruby grabbed the wig off her head and threw it toward the fireplace angrily. Jack caught it deftly in one hand.

"I think I'll save this. To remind me of this night," he said dryly.

"Keep it. I don't think I'll want to remember anything about this day *or* night."

Suddenly she felt so tired, exhausted to the bone. Lord, she just wanted to get out of this house, away from Jack and her embarrassment and pain, so she could lick her wounds in private.

Jack put his hands on her hips and expertly maneuvered her so she lay fully on the couch, and he followed her quickly, not allowing her to escape. He pinioned her struggling body down with his own, then held her wrists above her head with his left hand while he reached for a cocktail napkin with the other.

Gently, almost lovingly, he wiped the smeared mascara from her face with the napkin—a losing battle, because she began to cry in earnest.

Jack released her hands and rolled to his side, taking her with him. He put one hand on the nape of her neck and held her face in the crook of his neck. His other hand made wide, caressing circles on her back.

"Shush, Rube, don't cry. I'm sorry. Please, honey, don't cry." He fell silent and rocked her gently for a few moments, then offered tentatively, "Maybe we can make it work. Please, honey, don't cry. Next you'll have me crying, too."

"You never cry," she sobbed.

"Don't count on it."

But the more he spoke, the more Ruby sobbed. She'd been through so much that day—Jack leaving her, the dream, Thork and his death, coming to the lake house and being rebuffed by Jack. She just couldn't take any more.

Finally Jack tried to silence her sobs with a kiss. At first he just brushed his lips against her lips, then her eyes, her forehead, her cheeks, her lips again, all the time whispering disjointed words, "Rube . . . honey . . . please . . . don't cry . . . so sorry . . ."

Then he seemed to lose himself in the process and gripped her head in both hands, holding her firm while he shaped her tear-wet lips to fit his. When his tongue entreated her lips to part, Ruby whimpered and complied. With an answering moan, Jack filled her mouth, and the gentle kiss changed dramatically from sweet and comforting to red hot and demanding.

With his mouth and husky love words, Jack conveyed all the pent-up hunger of the past lonely weeks. Openmouthed and wet, his lips clung to hers, moving rapaciously, deepening. Ruby forgot her sorrow for the moment and answered his kisses with all the love and passion she felt for this husband of twenty years.

Between searing kisses and hoarse whispers, Jack eased the spandex off her, laughing softly when he realized it wasn't going to be an easy task. He smiled and held her eyes intimately when he saw the black teddy, recognizing it immediately.

"You fight dirty," he growled.

When she lay naked, Jack knelt on the floor next to the sofa and examined her reclining body with passion-glazed eyes and tender brush stokes of his fingers. "You're so beautiful," he said thickly, touching the peaks of her breasts with a fingertip, then sweeping down over her

Sandra Hill

flat belly, laying a large palm possessively over the down-covered vee.

"No, I'm not," Ruby protested. "I'm thirty-eight years old, and I have stretch marks and laugh lines and—"

He put a loving hand gently over her mouth to stop her words, holding her eyes warmly. "Yes, you are beautiful, sweetheart. Our children put those stretch marks there. I love them. And the laugh lines," he said, his lips twitching with a grin, "well, I don't really see them, but if they're there, I like to think I caused them by making you happy a time or two."

He stood then and, for just a second, Ruby panicked, thinking he intended to leave. But he added another log to the fire and began to take off his clothes, slowly, his eyes locked with hers the entire time in a smoldering gaze filled with regret, passion and promise.

The firelight played shadow games on his muscular shoulders and the ridges of his abdomen. He opened his belt buckle and began to unzip his pants, giving Ruby a seductive glimpse of the soft blond hairs that arrowed down over the hard planes of his stomach and beyond.

When he stepped out of his pants and then his briefs, he stood proudly in his savage nakedness, like a Viking god. His hard arousal proclaimed his physical want of her; his pleading eyes told of his emotional need.

"Oh, Jack, we've been married twenty years, and you still take my breath away."

"Ruby! What a thing to say!" he exclaimed softly.

"It's true." And she started to cry again.

"Come here," Jack demanded in a passion-raw voice from where he still stood in front of the fireplace. He held out a hand in entreaty.

Ruby closed her eyes for just a second, wondering if they were doing the right thing—making love before they'd had a chance to resolve their problems. On one last weak note, she said, "You told me earlier today that we could go upstairs and screw our brains out and it wouldn't solve our problems."

Jack laughed in a low, seductive voice.

"I changed my mind. Let's screw each other's brains out anyway and see what happens next."

"I'd rather we made love."

He shrugged and grinned wickedly. "Let's do both." His voice rasped with the intensity of his desire.

Ruby got up and walked into his embrace. At first they just stood in each other's arms, enjoying the feel of familiar skin and body scent.

"Oh, Rube," was all Jack said as he groaned and pulled her down to the rug with him. She tried to put her arms around his neck, but Jack told her with soft words and hoarse whispers to lie back, he wanted to enjoy her first.

With his mouth and tongue and teeth and inventive fingers, Jack paid homage to her body, strumming those points he knew to be especially sensitive, discovering new erotic zones to be examined and tested and heightened to the point of spiraling, intensifying pleasure. He kissed her forever until her lips swelled and grew slick with wetness.

He spent endless moments adoring her breasts, teasing the tips with flicks of his moist tongue, pulling lightly on the hardened nubs between his teeth and only suckling her deeply when she begged and flailed with loud moans.

When his fingers moved lower to her cleft, Jack's eyes shot up to hers in surprise at the wetness.

"Oh, Rube," he groaned. "Do you want me so much?"

She nodded, unable to speak.

Moving between her legs, he gripped her ankles, then pushed up and out. He gazed at her exposed body for a long time with glazed eyes and passion-slack lips, murmuring soft love words. Then he lowered himself and used his tongue in rhythmic strokes against the flowering bud until she shook with mindless want before exploding into an earth-rocking climax. He adjusted himself and was about to enter her when Ruby protested, "No, wait."

She got up and huskily instructed Jack to kneel so they faced each other. Then Ruby used all the love and uninhibited skill she possessed to pay homage to his magnificent body, from his drugging lips, to his muscular chest, to his deliciously flat stomach, and lower to the marble hardness of his manhood. Love, tested and true, guided Ruby to all the familiar places on her husband's body.

Finally Jack broke away from her and choked out, "No more!"

He placed her back on the floor and positioned her body for his entry. With a long thrust, he filled her, and Ruby held on tightly, wanting to savor the wonderful rightness of being melded with the man she adored.

Before he began to move, Ruby held his head between her two hands, and whispered, "I love you, Jack."

"I love you, too, babe. I never stopped."

Then the time for words was gone as he began the sweet rhythm they both knew so well. With each hard stroke, Ruby keened louder and louder.

She couldn't be sure in the flickering firelight if Jack's blond hair was collar-length or down to his shoulder blades, if that sparkle near his ear was a reflection from the fire or an earring. Both men—Thork and Jack—merged into one. Perhaps for all eternity.

Ruby and Jack both moaned and spoke softly of the intense pleasurable sensations spiraling through their bodies.

"Slower," she pleaded.

"Like this?"

"Yes . . . oh, yes!"

Sweat beaded on Jack's forehead as he tried to slow his pace to meet her needs.

"Now harder," she demanded.

"No . . . lie still . . . don't you dare move . . . damn, you're killing me."

"No, you're killing me," Ruby groaned, accompanied by a little mewling sound of pleasure. She spread her legs wider and wrapped them around Jack's waist.

Then neither could speak as a frenzy of passion took over, and Jack drove her hard, seeming to thrust out the anger and loneliness, frustration and regret that had ruled his life so much of late, but mostly he assaulted her with love and sheer, raw need. When her body stiffened on a cataclysm of progressively increasing spasms, ending with a mind-shattering splintering of all her nerve ends, Jack reared back and shouted, "Aaah, Rube . . . Rube!" then pressed into her deeply, exploding into climax.

Much later, they lay depleted in each other's arms, murmuring softly, touching each other gently.

"I love you so much, Jack. I'm so sorry for hurting you."

"Shush, I love you, too." Then he chuckled. "Rube, we haven't made love like that in years," Jack said in awe. "I felt like we were eighteen again."

Ruby smiled against his chest, not wanting to tell him just yet of her time-travel experience, but deciding to reveal a little. "I had this really strange dream this afternoon, and in it we made love five times in one night."

"Five times!" Jack exclaimed with a laugh. "And just what did you do to bring that about?"

Ruby tantalized him with a few descriptions of some of the sexual antics she had tried with her Viking husband.

"Honey? Now that's an interesting possibility," he said with a laugh.

When he finally stopped grinning at her dream reminiscences, Ruby turned serious. "Jack, I want you to know that I'm cutting back my hours at Sweet Nothings at least half-time beginning immediately."

She felt Jack stiffen beside her.

437

"I think it would be best if I work three full days and take off the rest of the week, rather than part-time for five or six days. What do you think?"

"Rube, you don't have to do this."

"Yes, I do."

"Well, if you're serious," he said, pulling her closer, "I was thinking that maybe we could merge our two companies. Real estate is doing better, and my profits are up since I expanded into commercial development. I know our businesses are completely different, but I still think we could form a partnership. Then we could both begin to delegate more responsibility and spend much more time at home. What do you think?"

Ruby thought she should take Gyda's advice. "Whatever you say. You decide."

"Maybe we could even buy a large sailboat and travel with the boys next summer."

"A boat?" Ruby asked incredulously and stared at Jack. *"A boat?"*

"What? You don't think a boat is a good idea?" Jack's puzzled eyes held hers.

Ruby laughed at the irony. "A boat is a great idea."

She rolled over to face the fire, and Jack pulled her close against him, spoon-fashion, one arm under her head, the other over her stomach.

"What was that? Are you hungry?"

"What?"

"Your stomach lurched."

Ruby put her hand over her stomach. Sure enough, there was a quickening movement.

Oh, my God!

She couldn't believe it. Ruby realized with sudden amazement that she was still pregnant. She turned around to face Jack, tears pooling in her eyes, and whispered, "How would you feel about doing something else next summer?"

"Like?" he asked suspiciously, alert to the emotion in her voice.

"Like having a baby."

She placed his palm over her stomach while she spoke, and saw the moment when Jack felt the baby move again. When he finally understood, Jack turned solemn and stood up abruptly. Puzzled, Ruby got up, as well.

"Is that why you came back?" he accused. "Is that what this whole love scene was about?"

"No, it's not. I didn't really know I was pregnant until just now." She started to tell him that she'd really known before, in another time, but decided to save that explanation for later.

Jack smiled then and pulled her into his arms. "A baby? After all these years! I always wanted to have another child," he confessed, his voice cracking with emotion.

"I know," Ruby said, caressing his face lovingly. "I know."

"A baby!" Jack repeated with awe. "Are you happy about this?"

"Ecstatic!"

Jack hugged her tightly to his chest. "We can make this work, Rube."

"I know."

Then Ruby jumped and squealed. "Ja-a-ack! Why did you do that?"

"What?"

"Pinch my behind."

"I did no such thing. I will if you want me to, though," he offered with a twinkle in his eye.

Ruby just smiled.

Then Jack asked with seeming nonchalance, "Do we have any honey in the house?"

Windmills In Time

Victoria Bruce

New Yorker Dierdre Brown is an independent modern-day woman. She doesn't need a man for anything; not love, not money—*not anything*. So when a twist of fate casts her back in time to the wild Nebraska plains, she is sure that with the fierce determination she learned on the city streets, she'll find her way back home. But when handsome cowboy Jesse Colburn takes her in his arms on the wide-open grassy plain, she feels an intensity in his embrace that she has not known in the men of her own time. And she begins to wonder if this is where she belongs: close to the earth, close to Jesse.

___52280-2 $5.50 US/$6.50 CAN

Lady of the Night — Cordia Byers

Manacled to a stone wall is not the way Katharina Fergersen planned to spend her vacation. But a wrong turn in the right place and the haunted English castle she is touring is suddenly full of life—and so is the man who is bathing before her. As the frosty winter days melt into hot passionate nights, she realizes that there is more to Kane than just a well-filled pair of breeches. Katharina is determined not to let this man who has touched her soul escape her, even if it means giving up all to remain Sedgewick's lady of the night.

___4404-8 $5.99 US/$6.99 CAN

BELIEVE
Victoria Alexander

Tessa thinks as little of love as she does of the Arthurian legend—it is just a myth. But when an enchanted tome falls into the lovely teacher's hands, she learns that the legend is nothing like she remembers. Galahad the Chaste is everything but—the powerful knight is an expert lover—and not only wizards can weave powerful spells. Still, even in Galahad's muscled embrace, she feels unsure of this man who seemed a myth. But soon the beautiful skeptic is on a quest as real as her heart, and the grail—and Galahad's love—is within reach. All she has to do is believe.

___52267-5 $5.99 US/$6.99 CAN

VICTORIA CHANCELLOR

Bestselling Author Of *Forever & A Day*

In the Wyoming Territory—a land both breathtaking and brutal—bitterroots grow every summer for a brief time. Therapist Rebecca Hartford has never seen such a plant—until she is swept back to the days of Indian medicine men, feuding ranchers, and her pioneer forebears. Nor has she ever known a man as dark, menacing, and devastatingly handsome as Sloan Travers. Sloan hides a tormented past, and Rebecca vows to use her professional skills to help the former Union soldier, even though she longs to succumb to personal desire. But when a mysterious shaman warns Rebecca that her sojourn in the Old West will last only as long as the bitterroot blooms, she can only pray that her love for Sloan is strong enough to span the ages....

_52087-7 $5.50 US/$7.50 CAN

REFLECTIONS IN TIME

ELIZABETH CRANE

Bestselling Author Of *Time Remembered*

When practical-minded Renata O'Neal submits to hypnosis to cure her insomnia, she never expects to wake up in 1880s Louisiana—or in love with fiery Nathan Blue. But vicious secrets and Victorian sensibilities threaten to keep Renata and Nathan apart...until Renata vows that nothing will separate her from the most deliciously alluring man of any century.

__52089-3 $4.99 US/$6.99 CAN

Flames of Rapture

Lark Eden

"Great reading!"—*Romantic Times*

When Lyric Solei flees the bustling city for her summer
retreat in Salem, Massachusetts, it is a chance for the lovely
young psychic to escape the pain so often associated with
her special sight. Investigating a mysterious seaside house
whose ancient secrets have long beckoned to her, Lyric
stumbles upon David Langston, the house's virile new owner,
whose strong arms offer her an irresistible temptation. And
it is there that Lyric discovers a dusty red coat, which from
the time she first lays her gifted hands on it unravels to her
its tragic history—and lets her relive the timeless passion that
brought it into being.

_52078-8 $4.99 US/$6.99 CAN

Dorchester Publishing Co., Inc.
P.O. Box 6640
Wayne, PA 19087-8640